D0064833

BURNING GARBO
A NINA ZERO NOVEL

ROBERT EVERSZ

SIMON & SCHUSTER
New York   London   Toronto   Sydney   Singapore

SIMON & SCHUSTER
Rockefeller Center
1230 Avenue of the Americas
New York, NY 10020

SIMON & SCHUSTER and colophon are registered trademarks
of Simon & Schuster, Inc.

For information about special discounts for bulk purchases,
please contact Simon & Schuster Special Sales at
1-800-456-6798 or business@simonandschuster.com

Designed by Jan Pisciotta

Manufactured in the United States of America

1   3   5   7   9   10   8   6   4   2

Library of Congress Cataloging-in-Publication Data
Eversz, Robert.
Burning Garbo : a Nina Zero novel / Robert Eversz.
p.   cm.
1. Zero, Nina (Fictitious character)—Fiction. 2. Los Angeles (Calif.)—Fiction. 3. Women
photographers—Fiction. I. Title.
PS3555.V39B87 2003
813'.54—dc21   2003052807
ISBN 0-7432-5013-3

For Al Hart,
in appreciation of his faithful,
wise, and literate counsel

We began to congregate on street corners
at night, Santa Monica and La Brea,
to erect searchlights
and marquees announcing premieres
for which there were no films.
We looked upward

as if what had been taken from us
were somehow etched in starlight above
their sacred city. We began
to chant, demanding their return—
to learn, for once, the meaning
of their desperate, flagrant love.

—GERALD COSTANZO,
from "Dinosaurs of the Hollywood Delta"

BURNING GARBO

ONE

On the morning of my thirtieth birthday I scaled the hills above the
Malibu estate of a movie star who hadn't been seen in public for
the last decade. I hiked in jeans and a T-shirt, my camera equipment
packed into a bag on my back. The late-October sun burned over my
shoulder and the resinous perfume of coastal sage plumed into the air
as I kicked through the brush. I had been trying to get a tabloid-
worthy photograph of Angela Doubleday for three days, commissioned by the editor of *Scandal Times* to coincide with the tenth
anniversary of the death of a stalker killed in her arms.

Midway up the hill I paused to plot a course to an outcrop of rock
above the estate. The rock, worn sandstone jutting from the chaparral, would serve as the paparazza's equivalent of a duck blind, con-
cealing me while I waited out the shot. Doubleday was not an easy
woman to photograph. Years of self-imposed exile had honed her
skills at seclusion. She may have left the house once during the three
days I tracked her, ferried to Beverly Hills in the back of a stretch
Cadillac driven by a liveried chauffeur. The passenger windows were
smoked and the limousine cruised the streets of Beverly Hills without
once pulling to the curb. The chauffeur could have been transporting
a flock of parrots and I wouldn't have known the difference.

I hiked to the rock briskly enough to work up a sweat, aware that I'd be sitting for the remainder of the afternoon. Celebrity stake-outs demand hours of idleness and solitude, valuable job skills I acquired at California Institute for Women. I've learned to take my exercise when I can. I unpacked the Nikon and glanced through the viewfinder. Cypress trees had been grown at the back of the estate to screen the pool and house from the view of jackrabbits, coyotes, lost hikers, and the occasional enterprising paparazza with a telephoto lens. I crouched beside the rock and attached the longest lens I owned, a five-hundred-millimeter beast the size of a rhinoceros horn. The cypress trees spired yellow-brown against the blue horizon, struck by a drought or blight that had stripped the needles near the trunk. I lined up my shot through a gap in the branches, focusing on a set of French doors that opened to the pool. I waited, a dry Santa Ana wind whipping at the tendrils of my hair. Though I sometimes had moral qualms about shooting people who didn't want to be shot, I was happy in my work. Six months earlier, the California Department of Corrections had paroled me four years into a seven-year fall for manslaughter. Nobody in my family spoke to me. I had associates, but no one I'd call up just to say hello. I was good at my job, and in the absence of any sustaining human relationships, that was good enough.

I pulled from my camera bag the Leonard Maltin biography of the woman I'd been hired to shoot and passed the time reading, my eye routinely flicking up to glance through the lens. Angela Doubleday made her first film appearance in a 1970s James Bond movie, playing a Las Vegas showgirl. The role was not coincidental. She had strutted the Vegas stage since the age of eighteen, wearing an elaborately stitched headdress of the Eiffel Tower and little else. A casting director noticed that her figure stuck out a little more here, tucked in a little more there. The two million men who bought the issue of *Playboy* featuring her that year noticed it, too. In the early 1960s, she might have been molded into a Marilyn Monroe–style sex icon, but by the '70s women whose figures seemed pumped by an air hose were looked up to only in automobile garages, truck stops, and other shrines to the pneumatic female. She was young enough to pattern herself with the changing times and did. She grew her hair long and straight, dispensed with bra and cosmetics, and rather than emulate the bleached-blond bimbos of the past, she portrayed a spaced-out hippie chick, which in retrospect was still a bimbo, just one redefined by the tastes of a different era.

An hour after I began my vigil an unfamiliar figure breached the French doors behind the pool. The man's zinc-colored hair marked him on the far side of fifty—or so I thought until I focused on his face. It wasn't a bad-looking face, the lips full and the nose prominent, like the nose on the bust of a Roman senator, but the skin at his cheekbones pulled with the tautness of youth, and a single, manly crease marked his brow. Save for that crease, his face looked as smooth as a swept sidewalk. That alone was not proof of anything, not since L.A.'s seekers of eternal youth discovered Botox, a neurotoxin that when injected into the face paralyzes the muscles and as a side effect erases nearly every wrinkle from the skin. You can't accurately judge anyone's age in L.A. anymore, not from the neck up, not unless you put a gun to their head, tell them to wrinkle their brow. Those on Botox can't.

I dipped the lens to check out his moccasin-style loafers, Gap khakis, and striped polo. He glanced over his shoulder, perhaps at somebody in the house, then stared intently up the hill. I fought the impulse to duck behind the brush. The point of his gaze struck above me, near the crest. I'd staked out enough celebrities to know that movement attracts the eye. I knew enough to sit perfectly still, except for the twitch of my finger on the shutter release. Maybe I was looking at Doubleday's lover. Maybe he was the pool man. Maybe he'd turn out to be both. Only the collective imagination of *Scandal Times* would know for sure. The reflection of the pool in the glass shimmered when he slammed the French doors. I waited a few minutes for him to return. He didn't. I propped the Maltin biography on my knee and turned to the next chapter.

Had Angela Doubleday continued to play a spaced-out hippie she would have finished in a one-bedroom apartment far from the studios and not on a two-acre estate in Malibu. The defining moment in her career came when the director Sidney Lumet cast her in the role of

Anna, the voracious young wife in Eugene O'Neill's *Desire Under the Elms*. Doubleday played Anna like a cornered lioness. The Academy of Motion Picture Arts and Sciences likes nothing more than a surprise turn by one of its stars and gave her the nod for the first of four Academy Award nominations, the last for a low-budget independent production in which she portrayed an aging Las Vegas showgirl battling drug and alcohol addiction.

The stalker attacked on the night she celebrated her nomination. He broke through a security barrier outside Spago in Beverly Hills and slashed a guard with his penknife. The stalker had been following her for two months. Something glinted in his raised hand as he charged forward. Everybody swore it was the knife. An off-duty cop shot him. The stalker grabbed the bodice of Doubleday's dress as he fell. He weighed no more than 130 pounds and was mortally wounded but gripped her so fiercely they sprawled together to the ground. The bullet had clipped his aorta. He bled to death in seconds. When the guards peeled him away they found a doll in the hand where the knife should have been. The doll was dressed and painted to look like Angela Doubleday. In the note pinned to the doll's dress he wrote that he intended to give it to her.

I put my eye to the viewfinder again and panned from the house to the sea, where the stiff offshore breeze whipped a flotilla of catamarans and windsurfers beyond the wave break. For a moment the real world vanished. Only the image existed, bright and beautifully distant, the four corners of the viewfinder framing the world into a coherency I found lacking to the naked eye. A crack of brush behind me pulled my face from the camera. A man crashed through the chaparral on the opposite side of the rock, charging down the hill at such speed that when he glimpsed me in passing and tried to stop he skidded ten yards into a clump of sage. I yanked the five-hundred and inserted a fifty-millimeter lens, not thinking much about him at the moment except that he was too close for the telephoto. The man had a wild and winded look, one hand grabbing the sage for balance and the other hidden behind his back as he stared at me, wide-eyed and panting. I didn't confuse him for a day hiker, not after glancing at his corduroy pants and slick-soled loafers. I lifted the viewfinder and focused on his face. He didn't look too happy about the camera. A four-day growth stubbled his jaw, which was the style of the moment, combined with black hair gelled back in thick grooves. His eyes were a bright, psychopathic blue. I figured him for a body-guard, someone hired to keep creeps like me away from Angela Doubleday.

I took the shot.

He released his hold on the sage to climb up to me but the soles of his loafers wouldn't hold on the hardpan and he slipped to one knee.

I took that shot, too.

He pushed off the ground, slung a pistol from behind his belt, and told me to give him the camera. He didn't bother to point the pistol at me, as though I'd drop dead at the mere sight of one. I lowered the Nikon, let him see my face. I have a nice face. Some men find me at-tractive, particularly ones who don't expect a woman to look like a Barbie doll, unless it's one who dresses in black, wears a nose stud, and can do a hundred push-ups in less than three minutes. I've done time, and when someone tells me to do something I don't want to do, I've learned how to make my face a hard place to look at. I moved my lips carefully, in case he was slow to understand things. I said, "No."

He took two nervous steps uphill, afraid of falling. "Look, I don't have time to fuck around."

"Then leave," I said.

He inched up the hill again, dug the heel of his downhill foot into the dirt, and pointed the pistol at me street-punk style, one-handed, the grip parallel to the ground. Instinctively, I raised the viewfinder to my eye, as though the magic prism of the lens would shield me from a bullet. Aggressive bodyguards are one of the hazards of my job. I asked, "What are you going to do, shoot me?"

I watched his finger tighten around the trigger, a movement simul-taneous to my own finger pressing against the shutter release. A thought rimmed my mind as we waited for each other to shoot. If he actually did pull the trigger and I caught the flash of the muzzle as the bullet fired I'd rate a Pulitzer Prize in photography, if a posthu-mous one.

I took the shot.

Fired upslope, the bullet struck the camera at the join between lens and body. The viewfinder slammed into my eye like a good left cross.

I don't remember going down.

Two

Some time later, smoke burned my nostrils like a dose of salts. I wedged a hand into the crevice of a sandstone boulder and pulled myself vertical. The taste of copper clung to the back of my throat, and memory throbbed with the dull perception that the strand of time had been cut and spliced together with a scene missing. I'd been concussed often enough to know that balance and nausea would be more of a problem than pain. The skin above my right eye felt numb, and an exploratory finger returned wet with blood. A yard down-slope, the Nikon stared blindly at the sky, its back ripped open. The bullet had shattered the optics inside the lens, cracked the mounting ring, and gouged the frame before ricocheting farther up the hill. I tossed what was left of the camera into my bag. The roll of film I'd shot was gone.

A second waft of smoke bit into my nostrils. I groped inside the bag for my water bottle and pushed against the rock, thinking if the bullet had sparked the brush, I could douse the fire while it still smol-dered. I waited for the vertigo of standing to subside and turned uphill, the wind on my face, a hot, desert wind, a Santa Ana wind. Whatever damage the bullet had done to me, I couldn't hold it responsible for the source of the smoke. Less than a hundred yards distant, flames swarmed down the chaparral-packed hillside. I steadied myself against the rock, fearing I hallucinated. Embers soared and dipped on gusts of wind, bright spots of yellow and red against the sky, like kites set afire and loosed from their strings. They descended to the brush in puffs of smoke, jumping the fire with the speed of the wind.

I shouldered my camera bag and strode toward a ridge that sloped down to the Pacific Coast Highway. The fire swept down the adjacent ravine and leapt amid plumes of resinous smoke to ignite the brush along the opposite ridge. Shrieks pierced the roar of fire, first one and then four, five, six in a row, lancing up from the ravine, where spheres of flame shot from the smoldering brush, then sputtered and writhed, igniting the chaparral where they fell. Another two streaked from the flames—jackrabbits bolting too late from their thickets. I climbed a spur of rock to the ridge and ran downhill, each jolting step a hammer blow to my head. The air inside Doubleday's mansion expanded to blow out the windows with a bright popping sound that turned my head as I ran. The tinder-dry cypresses at the rear of the estate ignited like torches. The average acre of Malibu hillside contains forty tons of chaparral and burns at temperatures up to 2,000 degrees Fahrenheit. Drapes, rugs, and wood combusted like cardboard tossed in a kiln. The house burst into flame before the fire reached its walls.

The ridge abruptly steepened. I hurtled down the hill too fast for my legs to keep pace and kicked out hard to avoid going down face first. I tucked my arms around the camera bag and tobogganed down the slope on my back, lashed by chaparral and coastal sage. The ridge ahead dropped sharply away. I braked my heels into the dirt too late and launched off the side of the cliff. The air whooshed beneath my back, and I thought I'd die where I hit, fire or rock. The ground rose quickly. I struck it a glancing blow, bounced into the air, and came down again in a blistering slide. My boots struck a thick clump of sage and the impact catapulted me into the sky like a hapless cartoon character, Wile E. Coyote or Sylvester the cat, a befuddled look on my face the moment before I swan dived into waist-high grass at the base of the hill.

I pushed myself to one knee, amazed that nothing had broken

except the seat of my pants. Smoke billowed from the base of the ravine and rolled over me like a wave. I pulled the neck of my T-shirt over my nose and stumbled forward. The cotton proved as effective at clearing the smoke as the filter of a cigarette. My eyes burned and I suppressed the terrible urge to cough. A black-and-white sheriff cruiser pulled to the shoulder of the highway a hundred yards ahead of me. I dropped to the ground where the smoke thinned enough to draw breath and staggered forward again. A squadron of fire engines sped past, sirens in full howl. The head of a female deputy popped above the cruiser roof to mark my progress. The fire trucks and sheriff cruiser were the only vehicles in sight, the highway closed to through traffic. The air cleared near the shoulder. I let the collar fall from my mouth, took a tentative sip of air, and coughed my lungs out.

"You mind telling me what you were doing up the hill?" The sheriff uniform didn't do much for her figure. The big gun belt flattens the hip curve and makes most female officers look as blocky as the front of a freight truck. This one was a strapping California blonde a good six inches above the minimum height requirement, and like all law she scared the hell out of me. I unbuckled the flap of my camera bag, and when I noticed gun wariness flicker in her eyes, I croaked, "ID."

She took her time examining the press credential from *Scandal Times* and parsed the information on my California driver license with the caution of a remedial-reading student. When I thought she was ready to hear it, I described the man on the hill and showed her the damage his bullet had done to my camera. She poked at the lens with the blunt end of her pen, went to the trunk of her patrol car, and returned with an evidence bag and fingerprint kit. She bagged the camera as evidence and took my prints for comparison against the prints that might be found on the lens or body.

"Everybody's needed for fire control right now but somebody from LASD arson will want to talk to you." LASD was the Los Angeles Sheriff's Department abbreviated, the law in Malibu and in more than half of Los Angeles County. "Paramedics'll be here in a minute, so you stick around, get them to check you out, and after that someone will come talk to you."

She stepped into her cruiser, flashed the lights, and jetted down the highway. I sat on the ocean side of the road for a while, happy that

I could breathe again. The paramedics didn't show, not immediately, and neither did anyone from arson. It was good to breathe again but I'm a restless person by nature. I walked away. My head and back hurt and my lungs ached but unless I did something else really stupid the odds were good I'd live out the day. On the beach below, sunbathers and stranded motorists stood and cheered the fire. Out past the wave break, figures black as seals bobbed in the water. The weather report had predicted a six-foot swell. A wave rippled across the surface of the sea like the tail of an immense beast. A half dozen surfers paddled frantically to catch it, and as the wave rose up, one figure leapt to his feet and raced the curl beneath an ashen sky, surfing the apocalypse.

I walked on.

A black dog the size of a baby bull emerged from a thicket of coastal sage as I approached El Matador State Beach, where I'd parked my car. The dog sniffed at my hand and fell in beside me. When I was young my dad would try to keep a dog around the house. He liked to beat them, and like my brothers and sisters they cowered until they ran away. I wasn't afraid of dogs, not even a big Rottweiler like this one.

"Pretty big fire, you think?"

He looked up at me when I spoke, his tongue rolling out of his mouth from thirst. I pulled the water bottle from my bag, knelt by the side of the highway, and let him drink from my cupped hand. I was thirsty too, dehydrated by the heat and smoke. Together we finished off the bottle. I patted his head, told him he was a good boy but it was time to go.

I jogged the final hundred yards to my car, a 1976 Cadillac convertible with 130,000 miles under it. The dog trotted at my heels. I told him to go home. He sat. I didn't know if he was dumb, confusing the command for "home" with "sit," or just patient. I got behind the wheel, thinking he'd figure it out when I drove away, but before the door closed he leapt over the frame and into the backseat.

I said, "No, uh-uh, I'm not taking you with me."

I give him credit, he didn't try the sad-eye treatment, just a lolling tongue and a level gaze that announced he didn't plan to move.

I stepped out of the car and pitched my voice to a tone of high excitement. "C'mon boy! Let's go! Here we go now! Out of the car!"

He lay out flat.

I reached for his collar and pulled. He was eighty pounds of stubborn muscle and didn't want to go. I tugged, he dug in, and all I succeeded in getting out of the car was his collar. I looked at the tag. It said his name was Dog, didn't list an address. I slipped the collar back over his ears, wondering who would name their dog Dog, and it was then that I noticed the Rott had no teeth.

THREE

I lived then in a third-floor walk-up a block from the boardwalk in Venice Beach, paying an inflated rent for the glamour of living in a high-crime neighborhood where half my neighbors were homeless. Free and legal parking spots near the beach were rare in any season, and I considered myself lucky to find a space at the corner, where the Caddy's rear fender extended less than a foot into the red zone. I knew I couldn't count on a blind eye from the parking patrols. Applicants for jobs with the city of Los Angeles are screened for compassion and pity, and those found most completely lacking are employed as meter maids. But the alternative, parking a mile inland, meant walking a strange dog through heavy traffic, and I didn't think he'd appreciate escaping the fire just long enough to get hit by a car. I shut off the engine. The Rott jumped from the backseat as though he'd known all along where we were going and followed me up the stairs. I believe in being honest with all creatures. I didn't want to give him false hopes. "You can stay tonight," I said. "But this is only temporary, understand me? Tomorrow I'm taking you to the dog pound."

The Rott looked up, worried by my tone of voice.

"Yes, I know what happens to dogs at the dog pound and I'm sorry that you run the risk of getting gassed a month down the line but you're not my dog and the world is a cruel place."

When the door keyed open he nudged me aside and trotted into the living room. The living room is also the family room, master bedroom, guest quarters, and library. Not counting the bathroom and closet, it's the only room in the apartment.

"You can see for yourself the place is barely big enough for one, no way you'd be happy here."

The Rott's truncated tail wagged so hard he spun in circles.

The answering machine's message light blinked red on the upended fruit crate that served as my bed table. I pressed the play button. I didn't expect my mother to call, birthday or not. We hadn't talked much since I got into trouble with the law. The voice on the machine belonged to the editor at *Scandal Times* who'd commissioned me to photograph Angela Doubleday. He wanted to know when he could expect photographs of the fire. His was the only message. I switched on my mobile phone just long enough to tap out a succinct SMS: *no pics.*

The sound of lapping water echoed from the bathroom. The Rott stood with his head in the toilet bowl, drinking his fill. "Good," I said, "I don't have to worry about getting you a water bowl." I opened the refrigerator door, intending to cook a hamburger. The Rott poked his head around my leg and sniffed the shelves. I was accustomed to shopping for one. The package of hamburger meat weighed less than a pound. I broke the meat onto a plate. He wolfed it with a toss of his head, then backed away from the plate, eyes quick with expectation. I knew what he was thinking. If he stared at the plate hard enough, maybe barked once or twice, more food would appear. I cracked a half dozen eggs into a bowl. When he finished the eggs, I washed down four tablets of ibuprofen and took a bath. I took the bath fully clothed. When the water soaked loose the grip of dried blood, I cut the jeans free with kitchen scissors. The water stung but three fingers of whiskey took care of that. I stood and tossed the jeans into the corner. A glance at my backside in the bathroom mirror suggested I shouldn't try wearing a bikini for the next few weeks. Not that I ever did. I should also avoid having sex in situations where I had to remove my clothes. Not that I ever did that either. I dried off, dressed, and took the Rott for a walk on the Venice Beach boardwalk.

Picket sat a seventh row bench in the bleachers above the outdoor basketball courts, identifiable at a distance by his Air Jordans and thigh-length black leather jacket. Ten players streaked from basket to basket below us, five of them shirtless. I asked, "Who's up?"

"Skins by five." Picket was a broken-down gym rat with a bum knee and connections to every housebreaker and sneak thief west of the San Diego Freeway. "That your dog?"

"Just for the night."

"Don't like dogs. Thirty-five Nikon, right? Any lenses?"

A camera was only good for a couple of months in my profession. Surly actors and bodyguards took their toll. "Just the fifty."

"Enjoy the sunset," he said. "Looks like a good one today."

That was my exit line. He didn't like customers hanging around watching the way he conducted his business. I glanced back once, when the Chicano point guard playing shirts, the shortest guy on the court by six inches, skied at the end of a fast break and dunked the ball. Picket nodded once at the play, talking to somebody on his mobile phone.

I bought a couple of sausages at a beachside stand and took them to the last ridge of dry sand before the beach sloped into the sea. The Rott watched me eat, the expression of sorrow in his eyes deepening with each bite, as though I intentionally starved him. "You're just a big baby, you know that?" I cut the second sausage into coins with the blade of my Swiss Army knife and fed it to him. The sun plunged through a hellish sky, crimson from the smoke in Malibu. When I returned to the basketball courts, Picket had the Nikon waiting for me in a plastic bag.

The Rott woke me before dawn. His bark resonated, deep and ferocious, like the bite of a power saw on hardwood. I woke reluctantly, angry at the dog for disturbing me, until I heard the tramp of feet up the stairs. I knew the law stood at the door from the knock, an aggressive pounding meant to scare me senseless. I counted three officers by the sound of their steps, more than a courtesy call but short of a full raid. A booming voice announced the presence of the Los Angeles Sheriff's Department and ordered me to open the door.

Nothing in the parole release agreement demanded that I answer the door naked. I opened the closet and pulled a baggy pair of black jeans and a matching T-shirt from the stack. The fist pounded at the door again. The Rott continued to bark as though his jaws were ripping through the floorboards. I dragged him by his collar into the bathroom and shut the door. Maybe he didn't have any teeth but I didn't need a strange dog gumming a cop in my living room.

The three faces on the other side of the door were among the least friendly I'd seen since leaving California Institute for Women. The detective who pushed to the front stuck me with a glare meant to make women weep and small children tremble. His hairstyle scared me more than the scowl. Combed straight up and greased back, it looked like a boomerang stuck to his head. His partner stood respectfully behind, a freckled young woman more beige than black, with a gap between her two front teeth. She looked new at this kind of thing. My parole officer hung at the rear of the landing, examining the polish on her short-heeled black pumps.

The guy with the bad hair said, "You're Nina Zero?"

"My parole officer is standing right behind you. Why don't you ask her?"

"Because I'm asking you."

"You weren't smart enough to ask her first?"

The detective thrust his jaw forward. I thought he was going to bite me. "You want to have this conversation in the back of a patrol car?"

"If it means keeping you out of my apartment, sure."

My parole officer glanced up from the inspection of her shoes with a look that brooked no argument. "You know the rule, Ms. Zero. Please stand away from the door. We need to talk to you."

"Anything you say, Ms. Graves."

I retreated behind the kitchenette counter and kept my hands in clear view. The rule: a parole officer has the right to enter the parolee's home or place of work unannounced and at any hour of her choosing. I may have been released from prison, but I wasn't free. Parole Officer Terry Graves was a 140-pound ball at the end of a very long chain. The detective ordered her to search the apartment. That was another rule: a parole officer is empowered to search the premises of a parolee on demand. The Los Angeles Sheriff's Department needed probable cause. Graves opened the closet door without much enthusiasm. She was a midthirties morality junkie who always played me tough but fair. I knew by her deference to the cop in my apartment that he carried the juice to make trouble. I asked to see his ID. He flipped open his badge wallet. His name was Ted Claymore. He was a detective on the LASD arson squad.

I asked, "How can I help you, sir?"

He snapped the badge wallet shut and wandered about the room, looking at everything and touching nothing. "What were you doing in the hills above Matador State Beach yesterday?"

"Trying to get a photograph of Angela Doubleday."

"Why would you want to do that?"

"It's my job. I'm a paparazza."

"What would that pay you, a photo of Doubleday?"

I walked right into it.

"*Scandal Times* paid me two-fifty up front, plus I get reprint rights on the back end. My agent handles reprint rights. A good photo of Doubleday, one clear enough to make out it's her, might gross more than twenty grand."

"Twenty grand." Claymore unwrapped a stick of peppermint gum, one tinfoil leaf at a time, until the stick lay exposed on the white inner wrapper, then folded the stick in half and popped it into his mouth. The moment he had the gum between his teeth he chewed furiously, as though killing it. "Enough to set a match, isn't it?" He walked toward me, the sound of his chewing like cracking glass, and when he didn't slow at a distance of half an arm's length I backed into the kitchen cabinet. Still, he didn't stop, not until his face came within three inches of mine. His eyes were shot with blood. When he spoke his breath reeked of mint and venom. "You set the fire and waited for Miss Doubleday. You planned to ambush her with your camera when she ran out of the house. Reclusive film star flees fire. Front-page photo. Twenty grand. Bingo."

"Not twenty grand," I corrected. "*Scandal Times* gets a cut, then my agent takes half of what remains."

He stepped back, glanced down at the fruit-crate end table and the futon beside it, then up to my brick-and-board bookcase. "Doesn't look like you've spent a lot on home decor," he said. "Having money problems?"

"I pay my rent on time," I said.

"Sure you do. But you like a little spending money too, don't you? I've seen people kill for a nickel. No reason you wouldn't torch a dozen acres in Malibu for ten, twenty grand."

"I volunteered a statement to the deputy yesterday. I have nothing to add to it."

"Volunteered? A deputy challenged you. You were told to wait. You fled the scene of a crime."

"I waited. You didn't show. I left."

"Fleeing the scene of a crime, isn't that a parole violation?"

My parole officer glanced over her shoulder, shut the closet doors, and moved to the bookshelf. No comment.

I said, "You doubt my word, look at the camera your deputy bagged. No way I could take pictures with it."

He picked the new Nikon from the breakfast table and pointed the lens at my face. "You carry this as your backup yesterday?"

I was stuck. I couldn't admit that I'd bought it after the fire. The camera was hot. Buying a hot camera was a parole violation.

"Bingo again. You hammered a dent in an old camera, gave yourself a little cut above the eye, claimed you were shot by a mysterious gunman, then planned to take your photos with the backup."

"Didn't happen that way."

"I have your word as a murderer on that?"

"Manslaughterer." I put the emphasis on the first syllable. The court didn't convict me of murder. Just manslaughter. The so-called victim ran an organization that shot a friend of mine in the head. They shot him because they were looking for me. Two of the men who hunted me were shot to death—no reliable witnesses—and the third drove his car 60 miles an hour into a gas pump. He lost control of the car because I was chasing him with a Harley and a .38-caliber handgun. The jury decided that was manslaughter. "Tell you what, if the tabloids publish photos of Angela Doubleday fleeing the fire and you see my name on the photo credit, you can come back and arrest me. But that won't happen."

"There are no photos of Angela Doubleday."

"Not by me."

"There are no photos of Angela Doubleday because you underestimated the speed of the fire. You set it at the top of the hill and ran down. People always underestimate brushfires around here when the Santa Anas blow. You probably didn't think the fire would get that big and move that fast. But it did, and if you're lucky and smart enough to cut a deal, you'll fall a second time for manslaughter. If you're not smart enough to cooperate, you'll go down for murder."

Graves pretended to search my books for contraband while she obliquely watched the interrogation. I didn't believe anything Claymore said. I turned to her. She crouched to lift the corner of my futon, showing her back to me.

"Somebody burned to death in the fire," I guessed.

"Bingo."

"Doubleday?"

"Her house. Shake you up a little?"

"Every woman's death diminishes me."

"We'll see how a life sentence diminishes you," Claymore countered. "Or maybe you'll get the death penalty. We execute murderers by lethal injection here. She burns, you get the hot shot. Poetic justice."

FOUR

The news bullpen at *Scandal Times* occupied the second floor of a two-story former sewage-works warehouse converted to office use near the crossroads of the Ronald Reagan and Golden State freeways in Pacoima. The only walls were those screening the bathrooms. Even on a slow news day, the noise cranked just short of deafening. The paper defined scandal broadly enough to allow the usual tabloid fare—freaks of nature and alien abductions, usually depicted as evidence of government conspiracy—but excelled most in its coverage of celebrity scandals, where it was the most authoritative source of rumor, if not fact.

Frank Adams sat sprawled against the back of his chair as I approached, ragged high-tops propped on the corner of the desk while his fingers banged at the desktop computer keyboard nestled in his lap. Nobody ever accused *Scandal Times*'s lead investigative reporter of handsomeness, not even his mother, and long ago Frank had learned to turn his appearance to advantage. His eyes were razor-blue slits of light in a haplessly round face. He was fifty pounds overweight and didn't care. He carried the weight as a disguise, excess flesh puffing from his jowls like a mask. His hair hung over his ears in a lank gesture of antistyle, and his preferred dress, day or night, featured windbreakers and torn-neck T-shirts depicting one Chicago-area team or another, worn over faded blue jeans two sizes too large, all signaling the great care he took in caring little about his appearance. When he interviewed a subject, his head down as he jotted quotes into a reporter's notepad, he looked like just another fat-boy loser. The subject might say a little more than prudence dictated, and think nothing of it, until the next issue roasted his liver on page 1.

"Tell me you brought photos of the fire," he said loud as a jack-hammer.

I stared at him over the top of my thrift-special shades. I didn't say yes. I didn't say no. I didn't nod or shake my head. I just stared. It took him some time, but his keen, journalistic eye finally picked out the change in my appearance. He said I looked like somebody tagged me with a left hook. I told him how it happened. He dropped his feet and if he didn't exactly sit up straight, his habitual slouch grew less pronounced. When I told him the fire cop considered me his chief suspect, he commented, "That's great," without apparent irony. "We still got another six hours to deadline, should be able to wrap it up in time for this week's issue. You driving?"

He speared the corner of his mouth with a cigarette and fingered his silver Zippo like a strand of rosary beads as he led the way out the office and down the stairs to the street. The moment his face broke into fresh air the Zippo flamed and he sucked a good quarter inch of ash onto the tip of the cigarette.

I coughed, lungs still aching from the fire.

"I hope that isn't a political statement," he said, trailing smoke. "They haven't outlawed smoking on the street, not yet anyway."

"I smoked half of Malibu yesterday. I think I can handle the secondhand smoke from your cig."

"If it bothers you," he suggested, "walk upwind."

Along Pacific Coast Highway the waves crashed to shore like rolling sheets of glass. Frank balanced a laptop computer on his knees and tapped out paragraph after paragraph of my eyewitness account, an unlit cigarette dangling like a pacifier from his lips. The Rott hung his head out the window behind me and snapped at the air, certain anything that slapped him in the face could be bit. He began to whine at the first scent of burn, just north of Trancas Canyon. I didn't know whether he was traumatized by memories of the fire or by the fear that I was going to abandon him. He was a good animal, but I reminded myself that he wasn't mine. He'd need to go the following day to the animal shelter over the hills from Malibu. I parked in the lot above El Matador State Beach and left the Rott in the car, ragtop up but windows rolled down a crack for air, while I led Frank across the highway. We hiked slowly up the ridge I'd come down the day before. Frank wasn't in good enough shape to catch the bus. That morning, neither was I. Halfway up the hill I stopped to rest, covering my discomfort with a question. "The piece you're going to write, what's the headline?" The air rasped in my lungs like aspirated alcohol.

"'Burn, Stars, Burn!'"

"Catchy."

Frank's smiles were rare things of beauty, a sudden bloom of lips that softened the edge of his glance. He took advantage of the pause to light another cigarette, then puffed merrily up the hill. "I'm going for the Pulitzer on this one."

It hurt so much when I laughed that I coughed up soot from the day before.

"What, you think the Pulitzer review committee is prejudiced?"

"Not at all. When they get around to tabloid journalists, sometime after they honor greeting-card scribes and graffiti artists, your name is certain to be at the top of the list."

"You can make all the fun you want but this is going to be a major story. Granted, nothing new about Malibu brushfires, and celebrities have been burned out of their homes before. But this is the first one to result in a celebrity fatality. That's what makes it so special."

"You're twisted."

"Thanks."

"I take it then Angela Doubleday was killed in the fire?"

"We can only hope."

I skirted Frank on the ridge and headed toward the outcrop of rock where I had concealed myself to photograph the Doubleday estate. "No positive ID then?"

"The body was burned beyond recognition, my sources say, but nobody's seen her since the fire and her accountant is panicking." Frank studied the crest of the hill, then swept his gaze down the ridge to the estate. He slipped a long, narrow notebook from his back pocket and a cheap ballpoint from the neck of his T-shirt. "The gunman, you figure him for the arsonist?"

"I thought he was the bodyguard at the time."

"Why run down the hill? He was no nature boy, the way you describe him. Why not set the fire near a road and drive away?"

"Maybe he was stupid, lit the fire from the downhill side."

"And suddenly found himself separated from his car by the same fire he'd set?" A staccato sound, more bark than laugh, boomed down the hillside. Frank didn't laugh often, but when he did he put his lungs into it. "Anybody that stupid would have gotten himself killed in puberty, but we'll let that go for now. There was somebody in the house, you said?"

"Not the chauffeur. Somebody I'd never seen before. He came out once to look up the hill."

"Think he spotted you?"

"I didn't think so at the time, but how else does the gunman know I'm there, unless he stumbles over me by mistake?"

"Okay, the guy lights the match, runs down the hill rather than up it for one reason or another, sees you hanging around the bushes with a camera. You photographed him, didn't you?"

"I didn't ask him for a date."

"What kind of gun?"

I closed my eyes, saw the picture I'd taken the moment before his bullet slammed the viewfinder into my eye. It would have been a great photograph too, the bastard. "Blue steel automatic, black grips. Not a popgun, a 9 millimeter, Beretta or one of the knockoffs. And the guy had hairy knuckles."

"What do I care the guy had hairy knuckles?"

"I thought you wanted to win the Pulitzer. That kind of detail's important, you want to win the big prizes."

"Right." He back-pocketed the notebook and lifted the Nikon from my bag. "Take a few steps down the hill and point toward the ruins so I can get both in one shot."

"I don't want my picture in the paper."

"C'mon, everybody wants to be a star."

"Not me." I'd been in the paper too many times. Bad times.

"What else is gonna convince this fire cop to back off? The story has to be about you and it has to show your beautiful, innocent face. Don't laugh. You look like a choir girl."

"Right. One with a nose stud and a cut above her eye."

"He won't be able to frame you for this, not with your story on the front page. Are you afraid of the arsonist? Is that why the hesitation?"

"I just don't like to see my picture in the paper."

"This arsonist, he already shot you once. Did it kill you?"

"No."

"Did it even put you in the hospital?"

"No."

"That clinches it. You're bulletproof. But if the past is any indication of your future, you're not jail proof."

I posed for the shot.

FIVE

An hour before dawn the approaching wail of a siren stirred an ancient memory in the Rott's blood, and he answered with a low, mournful howl. He lay just off the edge of the futon, ears pricked and head raised from the pillow he'd made of crossed paws. I like to sleep. I don't like being woken at 5:00 A.M. two days running. I told him to shut up. He tipped his nose to the ceiling and sang. No matter how he tried, he couldn't hit the high notes, and he couldn't harmonize either. To add to all his other problems, the poor animal was tone-deaf. I said, "It's not another dog, you idiot, it's a siren. We live in a high-crime area. Sirens blow by here every night. If you howl at every one, you'll lose your voice. No teeth and no voice, then what kind of a dog will you be? You won't have a bite or a bark."

The siren receded and abruptly clipped to silence some blocks to the south. The Rott listened intently, as though divining whether the other canine had successfully mated or killed, and coming to some unfathomable animal conclusion, he turned two circles to his left, four to his right, dropped to the floor, and fell asleep again.

I wasn't so lucky. I kicked around the sheets while the sky turned gunmetal gray. The Rott slept like a hibernating bear. I gave up all hope of sleep and put on my running clothes. A month after my release from prison I took up jogging because every morning I liked to remind myself there were no walls to stop me. I kicked the Rott in the butt to wake him and tied a length of rope to his collar. When he realized we were going for a walk he pranced like he was happy I'd awakened him. It usually took me a good hour to go from sleep to my first smile of the day, but the Rott could do it in less than ten seconds. Maybe he could teach me something.

I'd never run with a dog before and within fifty yards of the front door it was pretty clear the Rott had never run with a human either. Our ideas about what constituted a morning run were completely different. My routine was to set a slow but constant pace at the start, then to accelerate when the endorphins kicked in. The Rott preferred to race ahead until a scent distracted him, then stop to sniff or lift his leg, sometimes both, depending on what it was. I tried to pull him along on the end of the rope, but my shoulder gave out before his neck did. I'm not even sure he was aware I pulled on him. A fifteen-minute mile into the run I gave up and untied the rope. What did I care if he ran off? I was taking him to the pound that day. If he disappeared I'd have one less thing to do.

Freed of the rope, the Rott raced ahead, then fell behind, then raced ahead again, rarely straying more than a five-second sprint from my side. My endorphins kicked in and I ran, lungs still raw from the smoke, until I spotted a newsprint photograph of a familiar face behind the plastic shield of a boardwalk news vending machine. I pulled up, fed a couple of quarters into the slot, slipped a new copy of *Scandal Times* from behind the shield. The Rott loped to my side and sniffed at the paper, probably wondering if he could eat it. I rolled the paper into a tube and continued the run.

The face on the front page was mine.

The moment I shut the Rott on the opposite side of the bathroom door, intending to shower in privacy, the animal began to whine, as though he feared something terrible was about to happen to one of us. I turned on the shower, thinking I wouldn't hear him under the stream of water, but knew that wasn't the right thing to do and leaned back to turn the knob. The Rott bulled open the door the moment the latch clicked and dropped heavily to the floor. I said, "All this anxiety, it's about the pound, isn't it?"

The Rott glanced up at the sound of my voice, a wounded look in his eyes, then laid his head on crossed paws and sighed.

"You're a good dog, don't get me wrong. I mean, okay, the howling-at-five-in-the-morning thing, that's got to stop, but otherwise I don't have a problem with you. The thing is you're not my dog, you're big as a horse and I live in a place barely big enough for me. Besides, you probably have owners out looking for you, and the place they're going to look? Right, the pound. It's not so bad there, really. Lots of other dogs like yourself. It's not like prison at all. Think of it as more like summer camp."

The Rott closed his eyes. I stepped into the shower. The water stung like hell, the scrapes on my skin still raw. I don't think the Rott believed me. I didn't believe myself. I'd be taking him to a place where half his cell mates would be gassed within the week. He'd probably survive. A big and handsome pure breed, someone would be sure to want him. But then they'd see his mouth, think it over, decide to wait for one with teeth to come along. Still, it was none of my business. You can't save every lost cat, dog, or boy who crosses your path. Most of the time, you can't even save yourself.

The Agoura office of the Los Angeles County Department of Animal Care and Control serves a hundred square miles of mostly rural communities on the western fringes of the county, including Malibu. There were two ways to get there from Venice Beach: muscling through thirty-five miles of freeway traffic or taking the coast road and snaking inland through the canyons. It was another beautiful day, 70 degrees Fahrenheit and 180 degrees of sky cupping the earth and sea like a blue bowl. I took the coast road. The route took longer to travel, but I thought I'd enjoy the drive. I did, until a Chevy sedan the color of a paper bag locked its sights onto my rear bumper southeast of the Doubleday ruins and gave me a three-second burst of siren. I dropped my eyes to the speedometer. The Cadillac was rolling five miles per hour below the limit. I pulled to a stop in a legal zone by the side of the road. When I saw the mirrored reflection of the fire cop launch out of the unmarked Chevy I understood that I hadn't been pulled over for a traffic violation. His left hand hung freely in sight and his right hand seemed to tug at the back of his jacket, as though he carried a backup piece under his belt. The Rott whined in the passenger seat. I turned my glance from the rearview mirror to reassure him, but I didn't take my hands from the wheel. The fire cop coughed sharply behind my ear. The Rott turned his big black head toward the backseat.

"Afternoon, Officer. Can I help you with something?"

I wanted to be polite to him, no matter how much trouble he was intent on making for me. He asked for my license and registration. It was a formality.

"Are you aware you were driving erratically?"

"You're not a traffic cop. What do you care?"

I smiled, to show I meant no offense.

"Have you consumed any alcoholic drinks in the past eight hours?"

"No."

"Then can you explain the pint bottle of Wild Turkey in the back-seat?"

I glanced over my shoulder. The neck and shoulders of the bottle poked from a brown paper bag. The seal had been broken and the glass shone clear. I doubted a single drop remained. For a moment, I feared someone had tossed it onto the backseat when the ragtop had been down and I'd missed seeing it, lying there in plain view, but that didn't explain how the fire cop knew the brand of a bottle whose label was concealed by the lip of the paper bag. He'd carried it behind his back and coughed to conceal the noise when it dropped onto the seat. I said, "You breath-test me, I'll read zero-point-zero."

He told me to step out of the car. I stared at him. He looked like he meant it. I didn't want to get out of the car because that was the first step toward the back of his car. Maybe he'd search the passenger compartment, find a pack of matches, and call it evidence of arson. "This is harassment. You had no probable cause to pull me over and you have no right to ask me out of the car."

"You want probable cause?"

He stepped back and kicked out my left taillight. The fire cop's partner jumped from the cruiser before the plastic hit the pavement. The speed of her move and the look of confused allegiance on her face convinced me this wasn't being played by the book. I clenched the steering wheel in both fists and stared straight ahead.

Claymore leaned over the door frame. From his breath I understood how he'd known the label on the bottle inside the bag. He whispered, "You think you can show me up and get away with it? You think that piece-of-shit article in that tabloid rag is going to save you? It's nothing. You're nothing. You're an ex-con. You were on the hill when the fire started. You started it. You think that fire was hot? Just wait. I'm gonna roast your ass."

"I told the truth to the reporter. No law against that."

His voice when he ordered me out of the car again struck with a sharp, percussive force. From the opposite side I heard an anxious whine.

I stared straight ahead, said, "Did you wipe your prints from the bottle after you drank it? Or were you too drunk to remember?"

He jammed his left hand inside the door to spring the latch and with his right tried to pull me from my seat by my hair. I screamed at him. The Rott roared and launched across my chest. The struggle and scream were so close to simultaneous that I couldn't tell which of the two set him off. He hit Claymore just beneath the jaw. Had he possessed a set of teeth he would have ripped out the man's throat. My arms wrapped around the dog's chest as Claymore fell back onto the highway. The look on his face was that of a man who thought he was dead. He sat on the asphalt, legs splayed, and grasped at his throat. When he realized he wasn't going to die, he reached beneath his shoulder for his gun.

The Rott's bark was a terrifying thing, the sound of breaking bone and splintering wood. I braced my knee against the frame and held onto his neck. Claymore planted his feet and sighted the gun. I wasn't sure if the barrel pointed at me or the Rott. His partner ordered me to control the dog. I grabbed the animal's ear and yanked it. I didn't yell at him. I kept my voice low and soothing. Had I pulled any harder the Rott's ear would have come off. The pain turned his eyes to me. He'd been completely certain his duty was to tear off the head of the man who'd assaulted me, but when he saw my face a hesitation came into his eyes, and when I saw it I knew I could control him. The fire cop's partner dropped the sights of her automatic and said, "Don't shoot the dog. Shoot a dog and every animal rights nut in the county will be on your back."

Claymore glanced at his partner but mostly his eyes stayed on the dog. "You saw it. The animal bit me. I'm alerting Animal Control. It's a vicious dog. It has to be destroyed."

I laughed.

It infuriated him.

"They're going to gas your dog. You think that's funny?"

"You claim the dog bit you, people will laugh. He has no teeth. Take a look for yourself. Maybe you can claim you were gummed."

I pulled the Rott's upper lip back to reveal the raw gums.

"But the thing's big as a horse!" The disbelief in his voice vied with anger, as though I'd purposely tricked him.

"You make a complaint about getting bit by a toothless dog, jokes will circulate," his partner said.

He told her to take the wheel. I shoved the Rott onto the passenger seat. I didn't see Claymore when I glanced back. I thought he'd already slid into the cruiser until his head popped above the Caddy's right rear fender, as though he'd knelt to tie his shoe.

"Next time I see you, it will be at the Twin Towers," he said.

Claymore's partner didn't wait for the door to close before she geared the transmission and pedaled the gas. I watched the cruiser until it rounded the far curve. The Twin Towers sounded like something out of a fairy tale, but few imprisoned behind its walls enjoyed a happily-ever-after. They'd sent me there the last time I'd been arrested.

"You could have gotten us both shot, you know that?"

In reply, the Rott lifted his left paw and dug his claws into a spot behind his ear. I gave him a scratch. He slobbered on my arm to show his appreciation. I thought about the reasons why a healthy young dog like the Rott would lose his teeth. Before that afternoon I'd thought he'd been in an accident or suffered from a rare gum disease, but it seemed more likely now that he'd attacked someone, and his teeth had been pulled because the owner didn't want more blood on his conscience. I couldn't spit on the sidewalk without risking a parole violation, and I was an easy target for any cop having a bad brain day. The state had pulled my teeth, too, or judged it had. Maybe the Rott and I belonged together.

North of El Matador State Beach a roadside T-shirt and gift shop hung a community notice board on the wall outside the front door. I tacked to the corner a Polaroid snap of the Rott's portrait, my telephone number penned to the bottom. The dog, watching from the car, gave me a recriminating look. "Just because I'm not taking you to the pound doesn't mean we get to live happily ever after," I said, getting behind the wheel. "What if you have an owner looking for you? Sure, we're having a good time. I don't want you to think about this as a rejection, understand? But we have to think about other people who might be involved here." The dog looked like he always did when I spoke, slightly puzzled by the content but happy to hear me talk. "I can't believe it." I put the car into gear. "I'm talking to you like you're my boyfriend."

At a telephone pole across from a corner gas station, I met somebody doing the same thing I was, only he'd lost instead of found. Four days earlier, a forty-two-year-old woman had walked out the front door of a home she shared with her husband and two children and never returned. The woman was smiling in the photograph copied to the notice, and except for her eyes, she looked like a typical suburban housewife: carefully coifed, neatly dressed, and content with life. Her eyes looked sealed beneath a thin sheet of wax.

"My wife," the man said, lowering his staple gun.

"Wish I'd seen her," I said.

His hair was neatly brushed back from his forehead. A Ralph Lauren dress shirt hung sharply from his wide shoulders with nary a wrinkle to mar the crisp look of the fabric. His face looked like he'd died and been left to bloat in the sun. "I put the first notices up two days ago, but people come along and staple their things on top of her."

He eyed the Polaroid snap dangling from my fingers.

"I wouldn't do that, I wouldn't paste over a missing person."

The man tried to smile, like he meant no offense. "The police didn't even start looking until forty-eight hours after she'd disappeared. Then the fire hit, and . . ." He drove the final staple into the telephone pole. His free hand gently brushed the face of the photo posted to the pole. "She's on medication, you know? Prozac. The police think she's having an episode, that she'll walk right back in the front door without even knowing she's been gone."

"They're right ninety-nine percent of the time."

"It's the other one percent I worry about." He crooked his head to look again at the Rott's snapshot. "No teeth, you say?"

"Like a baby."

"Nice-looking dog, though. Good luck to you."

He took his first step toward the next posting place, another telephone pole a hundred yards down the highway.

I said, "I hope you find your wife, sir."

He gave me a little wave with the back of his hand. I tacked the snapshot below the flyer of his missing wife and drove on.

Six

The woman sitting at the window table of Malibu's Surf Coffee Shop watched carefully as I walked past the line of counter stools by the entrance, as though measuring me against her idea of the typical tabloid photographer. I didn't look like a hyena, at least not at first glance, and this confused her, because I was approaching the table as though I expected to talk to her. That meant I was the woman she'd spoken to over the phone, the paparazza from *Scandal Times*, the hyena in human form. Her size surprised me. She looked like an adolescent, and I thought perspective might be playing tricks with me, but she didn't get any bigger the closer I moved. The man who sat across the table from her had been a man of imposing size and strength in his prime, but that prime had peaked thirty years earlier. He still looked strong enough to break my arm in three places, if not fast enough to catch it. He'd known who I was the moment I stepped out of the Cadillac. His hand slid across the table and left a hundred-dollar portrait of Franklin beside the menu.

"Let's make this meeting short and sweet. This bill is yours, right now, you confirm the story you told the newspaper was a lie."

"I don't lie for money," I said.

"That's not what I heard."

"Man your age, I'm surprised you hear much of anything."

Anger flushed a vestige of freckles to his skin. I was accustomed to being insulted. He wasn't. I caught the look of something familiar in his glare, and it didn't take more than a second to place it.

"What were you, LAPD?"

"Interesting you can recognize an officer of the law out of uniform and retired ten years. Only two types of people can do that. Other cops and criminals." He pushed the Franklin closer to the table edge. "You don't look like a cop to me."

"You want to fight, I can give you the names of a couple bars down the highway. I'm here to see if I can be of any help to someone who told me over the phone she was Angela Doubleday's niece. You don't think I'm qualified, ask me to leave."

"Sit down, please." Arlanda Cortes slid to the inside to give me room. Her smile was too brittle to be welcoming, but at least she tried. She probably felt more dread than pleasure in meeting me, considering she sought to discover whether I had told the truth to *Scandal Times* or was just another tabloid scumbag. The old man pulled the portrait of Franklin from the table and stuffed it into the front pocket of his checked shirt. I sat.

"Sorry about your loss," I said.

"We don't know for sure, yet." Her voice had a little crack running through the center of it, caused by grief and exhaustion, I thought at first, but when she spoke again I heard it in the fiber of the voice itself, like an oboe with a split bell. "I mean, it looks bad because they found some remains in her house and she's missing, but they haven't—"

"Told us much of anything," the old cop said. "You want to listen to what this woman has to say, then we should do just that. Listen."

"What he's trying to say is I'm an ex-con, you shouldn't tell me anything the cops say about the investigation." I stared at him head-on. I wasn't ashamed. "Maybe you checked."

"I checked. Charged with first-degree murder, assault with a deadly weapon, unlawful possession of explosives, what else?"

"Double parking. They wanted to execute me for that one."

Nobody laughed.

The old cop said, "All those counts, convicted only on manslaughter, you must've had a good lawyer."

"I should have walked on all charges. I wasn't innocent but after what the so-called victims did to me no jury should have convicted."

The waitress stopped at the table and whipped an order pad from the front pocket of her smock. Nobody ordered food. It wasn't that kind of a meeting. She jotted down two diet Cokes and a coffee. Then I remembered the dog in the car and said, "Can I get a pound of raw hamburger and three eggs to go?"

"Sorry hon, you have to order from the menu." Her answer was rote. She wasn't unsympathetic, just business-like.

"I got a hungry dog in the car, problem with his mouth, only eats raw hamburger and eggs. I'll pay whatever you think's fair."

She said she'd see what she could do.

I didn't wait to be asked. I told my story. The old cop scrutinized my face while I spoke, and I was aware the niece watched me carefully from the side. He asked me to tell the story again. I began to tell it the same way. He said he didn't want to hear that part and moved me forward in the narrative and then back again, claiming every now and then that his memory wasn't so clear, he thought I'd said something different the first time. He tried to take the story apart at the time line and then at the suspect descriptions, but the story was seamless. He couldn't pry loose any part of it. The waitress returned with our drinks and a pie-shaped container used for takeout. People will often do for dogs what they won't for human beings. I asked them to excuse me for a moment and went out to the parking lot to feed the Rott.

The waitress had supplemented the egg and hamburger mix with chunks of white bread, something I hadn't thought of doing. The Rott wasn't much of a gourmet, but the few seconds it took him to bolt the container's contents told me he approved of the waitress's cooking.

"That's a good-looking dog."

I recognized by the crack in the voice it was Arlanda before I turned. Even with four inches of curb at her heels, the top of her head barely reached eye level. I doubt she weighed more than a hundred pounds, and a good part of that was in her eyes and waist-length black hair.

"Hungry, too," I said.

"What's his name?"

"Baby." It was what I called him. I didn't want her to think I wouldn't bother to name the dog I traveled with.

"That's a big baby. How come he eats only hamburger?"

"No teeth."

Her eyes couldn't conceal a stutter of uncertainty. Why would a beautiful animal like the Rott have no teeth? What had I done to him?

"He's a stray," I said. "He followed me to my car the day of the fire. I put up notices this morning. Maybe somebody's looking for him."

The Rott lay on the asphalt, the container between his paws, and chewed on it like a bone. Didn't matter he had no teeth. Instinct.

"Mind if I pet him?"

"It's up to him. But I don't think he's the type to say no."

She knelt on the pavement at the dog's side and quickly found a spot behind his ear he liked scratched. "I bet my two boys would love to meet you. Not many Rottweilers where I live."

"Where's that?"

"Little border town called Douglas."

"In Arizona," I said.

"Been there?"

"Just close enough to see it on the map."

Her hair swayed like a curtain when she shook her head.

"L.A. sure is different."

"Different is what it does best."

"It seems a little overwhelming. I just got in last night."

"Give yourself ten years, you'll get used to it."

"I'll cope a little better after a good sleep." She glanced over to the hotel next door. "Thank goodness all I have to do is crawl up the stairs and I'm in bed."

The motel next to the coffee shop was one of those California structures that slapped together elements of the ranch house and hacienda so haphazardly it succeeded in representing the worst of both styles. The motel wasn't a dive but clung to the wrong side of the Pacific Coast Highway. People with money stayed elsewhere. I expected more glamorous digs for the niece of a movie star. Arlanda's long, burgundy nails scratched the Rott's chest. His leg kicked by reflex. A full stomach and a scratch. Happiness should be so simple.

"I believe you. What you said in there, I mean. About the fire."

"It's what happened."

"The detective we talked to, the arson investigator, he didn't describe it the way you did."

"I know. He wants to think I did it."

"Ben doesn't like him very much."

"That's his name? Ben? He doesn't like me very much either."

The woman laughed and even her laugh had a crack in it, as endearing as a crooked smile. "That's just Ben. He's a tough guy."

"Family?"

"Friend of the family. A good friend."

I opened the passenger door. The Rott jumped into the front seat, expecting to go for another ride. I told him to stay. He looked betrayed when I backed toward the restaurant.

The hand the old cop stretched across the table when I returned was twice the size of mine and spotted with age above the knuckles. "Ben Turner," he said. "Worked out of the Malibu station before they moved everything out to Calabasas. That makes me an old-timer in the LASD. Angela Doubleday was my goddaughter."

I shook his hand, said, "Did Claymore tell you I was a suspect in the arson investigation?"

"Didn't have to. He said you were on the hill when the fire started, trying to get Angela's photograph, and that you lied about what you saw. That alone stamped *suspect* on your forehead."

"Either of the men I described—the shooter or the guy with the gray hair—sound like somebody Ms. Doubleday knew?"

"No, but that doesn't mean anything."

"Why not?"

Arlanda glanced at Ben. His head dipped slightly and he blinked. He wasn't talking, but he wasn't silencing her either, not yet.

"We don't know that much about her life," Arlanda confessed.

I must have looked surprised, hearing that from the woman's niece and godfather. "I heard she was a recluse," I said.

"The last time I saw Aunt Angela was, what, eight years ago? Just after Aurelio was born. He's my oldest. Armando's six. She never even met him. She just seemed to lose interest. Locked herself away in that big old house with a couple of servants and that was it. She wouldn't even return Ben's phone calls."

I expected Ben to contribute to the story but he pulled out his wallet and signaled the waitress. "I want to thank you for your help. You did us a favor coming out here and I want to apologize for being so aggressive with you at the start."

"Most ex-cons don't make reliable witnesses," I said.

"You do. I'd like you to sit with a sketch artist, see if we can't get a likeness on paper of these two men you say you saw."

I told him I'd be willing to do that, even though he wasn't yet willing to concede that I'd seen anybody, only that I claimed to. He said he'd need a day or two to line things up. He'd been retired too long and didn't know who sketched anymore.

"I do," I said. "Walk by a couple every day. Come out to Venice Beach tomorrow, we'll pick one."

SEVEN

The Rott may not have been the brightest animal in the kingdom, but he was sincere in his desire to please, if only because I fed him, and his eagerness improved his performance as a running partner the second morning we ventured onto the boardwalk. He still paused to sniff the spots that called to him with one irresistible scent or another, but he better understood how far he could lag behind without losing me, and I tried not to demand behavior that went contrary to his nature. We didn't encounter any serious obstacles to our morning run until we started up the stairs to my apartment, when the door to the unit just below mine swung open to a young suit knotting a striped yellow tie. His right hand deftly tugged the knot tight and his left tossed up one forefinger to attract my attention, as though the tie alone wasn't enough to stop me.

"Excuse me," he said, "are you allowed to keep that dog under the terms of your lease?"

"None of your business." I wasn't being hostile. I just didn't want to mislead him.

"When that animal wakes me in the middle of the night with his barking, I'd say it is my business."

"He doesn't bark."

"The hell he doesn't."

"He howls. There's a crack in the floor, right above your bed. He puts his eye to that, watches you whacking off at night, and howls with laughter."

"I'll talk to the landlord. Obviously, there's no use talking to you."

I leapt up the stairs to the slamming of his front door. My new neighbor, worked at some ad agency. He'd moved in the month before, replacing the three aging hippie surfers arrested on charges of minor minding a string of West Side burglaries. I'd heard his rent was almost twice as high as mine.

I was stepping into the shower when the front bell sounded. The Rott jumped to his feet, excitement pitching his voice to sharp, warning barks, as though I was hard of hearing, needed him to tell me someone was at the door. I wrapped myself in a towel and put my eye to the peephole. The downstairs neighbor peered at me from the opposite side, his face distorted by the fish-eye lens. I went back to the shower. He gave the buzzer a few more blasts. The Rott continued to remind me someone was at the door. Eventually, either the neighbor gave up or the doorbell gave out. The Rott wound in circles, counterclockwise, then clockwise, and settled onto the bathroom floor. I got through the shower and into my street clothes before the buzzer went off again. I wasn't going to allow myself to be harassed by a legalistic prig of a new neighbor and charged from the bathroom to snap open the door.

"We had an appointment to see a sketch artist, I thought," the old cop said.

Angela Doubleday's niece backed toward the stairs. "If it's inconvenient, we can come back some other time."

The Rott bulled me aside when he heard her voice. She stooped to scratch behind his ear.

"Sorry. I had an argument with a neighbor this morning, expected it was going to be him."

Arlanda's eyes sparkled and the corner of her lip hooked into a smile. "I didn't think you knew us well enough to want to kill us."

"My neighbor doesn't like dogs."

"Never trust anyone who doesn't like dogs," she said.

Ben's sunglasses, dark as the back of a cave, hid his reaction, but he didn't trust me, and the way I'd greeted them at the door confirmed his suspicions. I clipped the Rott's new leash to his collar and led them down the boardwalk.

Hank occupied his usual spot across from the Sidewalk Cafe. Like most caricaturists, he hung a gallery of celebrity portraits on the sides of his drawing easel to attract the tourist trade. Hank had walked out of China a couple of years earlier, ridden the Trans-Siberian Railroad to Moscow, and followed the refugee trail south to Berlin, where he applied at the U.S. embassy for asylum on grounds of religious persecution. Nobody on the boardwalk could pronounce his Chinese name correctly, so everybody called him Hank. He was happy to go by an Americanized name.

His English wasn't as fluent or precise as his pencil, so I spent more time describing the man I'd seen at Doubleday's estate than he took to draw him. He couldn't understand what I meant by prematurely gray, until I remembered a couple of movie stars who grayed early and were confident enough to wave off the hair dye. His pencil rapidly stroked across the sheet of sketch paper, and a portrait of the man emerged very much as I remembered him, even if he looked a little too much like George Clooney.

The gunman was an easier draw. His features weren't so subtle and he wore his hair gelled back the way a lot of guys in L.A. did back when it was the style. Hank liked to put props in the portraits—surfboards and barbells for the boys, Rollerblades and heart-shaped sunglasses for the girls—but I resisted having the gunman's portrait drawn with a .38-caliber automatic. I told him both portraits were not only accurate but beautifully drawn.

Ben paid for the sketches and promised he'd make copies for me. I asked what he planned to do with the originals.

"Look at some mug books," he said. "See if I can match either suspect with any known firebugs. I still know a few guys. I'll ask around."

"You've been a tremendous help," Arlanda said. "You didn't have to volunteer your time like this."

"What I was doing on the hill that day, it's how I make my living. If your aunt had shown her face, I would have taken her photograph. She's a public figure and it's my job. But I don't wish her harm."

"I don't suppose a mosquito means you any harm when it sucks your blood," Ben said. "But that doesn't make the itch go away, does it?"

Arlanda distanced herself by a step. "She's trying to help. Why not be gracious and say thanks?"

"Okay. Thanks."

"I'm not trying out for sainthood," I said. "But I'm not a blood-sucker either. We're talking about public figures here, people who have dedicated their lives to the pursuit of fame and acquired a considerable fortune trading on that fame. What gives them the right to control the media by decree? The public has a right to know, and that's who I serve, the public, all those people standing in lines at the grocery store, looking for a little diversion, a little who's-screwing-who while they wait their turn at the cashier, the same people who stand in lines at the movie theaters, who rent the videos and buy the records. The moment someone becomes a public figure, particularly when they've made a fortune from it, then the public has a right to information, which they aren't going to get from the official star-sanctioned photo ops and interviews set up by publicity flacks."

"And what happens when they want out?" The old cop stabbed a forefinger at my chest, his hardware-store baseball cap shading the flush of anger in his cheeks. "According to you, they're fair game until hounded to the grave."

"Why should they be allowed to opt out? The choices I've made, they follow me everywhere I go. Everybody is bound by the choices they make. You want a public life, you're going to get scrutinized. You can't invent some pretty story about yourself, sell it to the public for ten million a year, and not have somebody like me prowling around, pulling up the corners of your carpet. And the interest in Doubleday was limited to the tenth anniversary of the death of the stalker who drove her into seclusion. I don't think a couple of paparazzi trying to snap your picture once every couple of years qualifies as being hounded to your grave." I glanced at Arlanda. "Sorry. That was an unfortunate choice of words."

"Ben said it first. You've been nothing but helpful. You wouldn't have talked to us if your heart wasn't in the right place."

"If the place isn't in question, maybe the size is," I said. "I'm still an ex-con snooping around celebrity backyards with a camera, not Mother Teresa."

Ben smiled for the first time since I'd met him, a shake-of-the-head, rueful, cracked-lip kind of smile, but a smile nonetheless. "I think we have our differences but I appreciate your candor."

Arlanda gave the Rott a good thump on the ribs, asked, "Is there anything we can do for you?"

"If you're going to make an open offer like that, then yes, there is something you can do for me."

Arlanda nodded lightly, her eyes wide open and trusting. Ben looked like I was going to steal his wallet.

"Take me where the fire was started, the exact spot. Tell me how you think it was done and what the arson guys are saying."

Ben was tensed to say no and did. I asked why not.

"Just can't do it."

"The cops respect you. I understand you don't want to abuse that respect by bringing me into the investigation. If you still suspect I had something to do with the fire then I advise you to thank me for my time and walk away. If you believe I'm innocent then I'd appreciate your help because I have better things to do with my life than spend it in prison on a trumped-up arson-manslaughter charge."

The old cop crossed his arms over his chest in the middle of my plea. I knew his answer before he spoke.

"I still don't think I can do it."

Arlanda nudged the Rott with her knee and stood at my side, the dog between us. "Yesterday you said you thought the investigation was going in the wrong direction."

Ben's arms tightened across his chest and he nodded, once.

"I've said nothing about that so far because you're the one who knows best about these things, but it frustrates the hell out of me that everybody is wasting time while whoever set that fire is getting away with it. You act like you believe her story. You act like you think she didn't do it. If we can prove that for sure, then the investigation will look elsewhere, and that can only help, right?"

Ben had a twelve-inch height advantage and outweighed Arlanda by over a hundred pounds but he was no match for her. "What, you girls trying out as a tag team for World Wrestling Entertainment?" He didn't smile. He was serious.

"We'd kick ass, don't you think?"

Arlanda's language startled me, maybe because she was so small and, up to that point, ladylike. I hadn't expected it.

"You're kicking mine, that's for sure," Ben said.

I took that to mean yes, said, "Something you don't feel comfortable telling me when we get up there, don't tell me."

"Then we might have a pretty short conversation," he said.

We rode up to the estate in separate cars, the old cop leading the way in a battered Chevy Blazer. Arlanda had asked to ride with me, and though her request surprised me, I'd said yes. A few silent miles into the drive I understood that she'd wanted to ride with the Rott. She stared out the window and stroked his back as we rolled from light to light, his massive head in her lap. She mourned her aunt and missed her kids, I guessed, and petting the dog calmed her.

"You have dogs in Douglas?" I asked. It seemed a safe enough thing to talk about.

"Had one. Guapo. Died a couple months ago. He wasn't much to look at but he was the sweetest dog in the world."

"Going to get another one?"

"I should. For the kids if nothing else. But not right away. Kids should learn a little something about death, and I was afraid if I gave 'em another dog too soon they'd think everything was replaceable. I don't care what dog we get, we'll never have another Guapo. I want the kids to realize that. He was my husband's dog originally."

"You're married?"

"Divorcing. He ran off to Houston with some girl about six months ago. Left the kids, the dog, eight years of marriage. Broke the poor dog's heart, if nothing else. Didn't even have the guts to say good-bye to me in person."

I let a mile go by before I said, "Men. Can't live with 'em. Can't shoot 'em."

"You did."

"Got me into some trouble, too."

"I wish I had the guts for a little trouble like that." She pointed her finger out the windshield, said, "Bang!"

"Was that your ex?"

"It was."

"Where'd you hit him?"

"Let's just say he's packing light." Her voice was prim when she said that and we both laughed.

"You'll be all right," I said.

"Me? I'm just a divorcée waiting to happen, a mestiza from an Arizona border town with two years of junior college and a job with a real estate company in a county where the land ain't worth spit. Your life seems a little more exciting than mine."

I was afraid to tell her how boring my life really was. The work was good, but I didn't really care about anybody and that deadened me inside like rotted wood. "You know what I used to do for a living?"

"Rob banks?"

"No, that was later."

She looked at me like she thought I was serious.

"I took pictures of babies, worked in a place called Hansel & Gretel's Baby Portrait Studio, wore a green jumper and little green hat, styled my hair in pigtails, painted big red dots on my cheeks." I held my arm in the sunlight filtering between the seats. "Here, take a look at the hair on my arm."

Though born a blonde, I'd been dying my hair black since my release from prison. Arlanda stared at my arm as though looking for one thing but seeing something else. I knew what she was looking at.

"The color," I said, to redirect her attention.

"It's blond, isn't it?"

I put my hand back to the wheel. "That's right. My name was Mary Alice Baker back then. I changed it. What I'm getting at is I changed my life. You can too, if you want. I'm not saying you should change, understand. And I know from personal experience not all change is for the better. But it is possible."

Beyond Pacific Palisades the coast traffic thinned and the raw beauty of the hills and sea took prominence. I thought she was contemplating what I'd told her, about the possibility of change, but she had something else on her mind. "Those marks on your arm," she said. "They look like cigarette burns."

I didn't want to look at her face, certain the burns repulsed her. The first one scars the inside of my wrist, to the right of the tendon. The second jumps the tendon to the left, higher up the forearm. Eight more crater the inside of my arm like a chain of extinct volcanoes, the tenth and final mark scarring the flesh at my shoulder. "I carry those scars as a reminder of why I was convicted of manslaughter and why I'll never let myself ever be victimized again."

"Who did it to you? The man you killed?"

I didn't want to be mysterious, but I didn't want to talk about it either. I said, "Different guy, but related times."

Arlanda didn't want to see the house—what little remained of it— and stayed behind to watch the Rott chase gulls on the beach. Ben drove me up the mountain. A couple of twisting miles from the coast the road looped above the burn. A tangle of ironwood and sage clung to the mountain above us. Below, the burn cut a swath the shape of an oil spill to the beach. The afternoon Santa Anas had yet to pick up, and the offshore breeze blew cool and clean. To the north the Santa Monica Mountains crashed to sea in a perilous descent, and the informed eye could trace those same mountains breaking free of the ocean depths again in the rounded humps of Anacapa, Santa Cruz, Santa Rosa, and San Miguel Islands before the continental shelf dropped away and plunged the range into the abyss. Out to sea, nothing blocked the line of sight except the earth's curve. Even in devastation, the landscape rivaled any other I'd seen for sheer beauty.

We stepped off the road and down the embankment, where the earth had been scuffed by footprints into a rudimentary path. The investigators had climbed down the hill at the same spot, Ben said, to avoid contaminating the scene. The chaparral near the road was charred, as though the fire had been hot enough to singe but not to incinerate. About ten yards down, the intensity of the burn changed, and nothing but rock jutted from the blackened earth until far below, at the base of the mountain, where a pillar of chimney rose above a cracked swimming pool—the only substantial remains of Angela Doubleday's estate.

Ben stopped where the burn changed and crouched on his heels. He snapped a charred branch from a chaparral and held it up to the blue horizon. "Not burned all the way through, you notice. Why do you think that is?" He stood and sidestepped along the hillside, his gaze pinned to the ground. "I'm not an arson expert but I've lived these hills for thirty-five years and seen my share of fires. I always kept my ears and eyes open, too. Some of the deputies, they shut down after a while, but not me. I always wanted to learn something new. See this here?"

He pointed to a patch where the earth had been cut and peeled away like a square of carpet. To the uphill side the chaparral had not burned completely, but toward the sea only a few sticks poked above the ground. Another dozen yards down the hill the brush had been incinerated. His finger traced the line, shaped like an arrowhead, that marked where the burn changed intensity. I remembered the direction of the wind that day and calculated that had I stood at the tip of the arrow and sighted straight downwind, my spit would have carried to Angela Doubleday's roof.

"Whoever did this figured which way the wind was blowing and how hard and poured gasoline along this line you see. He climbed partway down the embankment so nobody could see him from the road." Ben broke another twig on the high side of the hill. "See, the wind blew the fire downhill. Behind the line, the shrub is no more than singed." He wiped the soot from his hand on his jeans and when he spoke again I heard the anger in his voice. "Maybe he just wanted to start a fire and this looked as good a place as any. That would make Angela's death manslaughter. Maybe the son of a bitch knew exactly what he wanted to burn and put the match to this spot to kill her as sure as a bullet . . ." He pinched the bridge of his nose and every line in his face contracted with a sudden jolt of pain that closed his eyes. "Oh hell, I promised myself I wouldn't do this." His voice tore like old cloth and he wept, trying to hide his face from me.

My first impulse when someone began to cry was to turn and run.

I hadn't cried in years. I still grieved when I lost people. I just didn't cry. When grief came to me it was blank, impenetrable. I didn't eat or talk for days, had hard thoughts, and sometimes, if I could justify it, I hurt the people who had hurt me. But I never cried.

"I don't know what it is, why I get so broken up about this."

"She was your goddaughter."

"Yeah, but I hadn't seen her in almost a decade. I knew her mother, back when. I guess it has something to do with that."

I knew enough about people not to talk. Normal people need to let go every now and then. Sometimes a particular song will do it, or a couple of drinks, and sometimes it takes no more than a memory.

"I knew her father too," he said. "We played football in high school. Defensive tackle was my position. He was the outside linebacker, tough but fast. You know anything about football?"

"Just enough to know when somebody scores."

"On run plays, my job was to plug the hole the running back was trying to run through, tackle him if I could. Force him wide if I couldn't, where Pete could catch him. If I missed a tackle, Pete was always there, covering for me. I don't think he missed but two tackles the whole senior season. Hell, we didn't just play football. We grew up together, best friends since the age of six. Angela's mom was fifteen when she got pregnant. Anabelle. Beautiful girl. Pete, he tried to do the right thing. He married her, got a job pumping gas. But he was too wild. I tried to get him to enlist in the marines with me, figured Uncle Sam would straighten him out, keep him out of trouble. Lots of servicemen have wives and kids at home. But he wouldn't go with me. Took off to Phoenix instead, got involved with some people running drugs over the border. He lasted less than a month. They found his body in the desert outside Douglas. Only parts of his head. He'd been shot in the face with a shotgun."

Ben scooped a handful of scorched earth and let it filter through the crevices between his fingertips. The wind blew the ash downhill, and the dirt fell with a tapping sound onto his black boots. "I enlisted at the end of the summer. Anabelle gave birth a couple of months later. She hooked up with a rancher after that, had another baby, that'd be Arlanda's mom. Anabelle drowned the following year. Drowned in the desert. Isn't that a hell of a way to die? A flash flood got her. She was walking in the dry wash, they said. It wasn't even raining in the desert where she walked. All the rain was in the mountains. But the water sluices down the mountain and into the wash and if you're not paying attention it can sweep you off your feet and drown you. But you know what?"

I met his question with a look, waited for him to tell me.

"I don't think she was walking in the wash at all."

"What then?"

"I think she threw herself in."

He turned his eyes to the sea and didn't say a word after that, except "thanks" when he dropped me at my car.

NINE

Frank was waiting for me on the sidewalk when I pulled into a metered parking spot in front of the building where the two sisters who cleaned for Angela Doubleday lived. I made sure the side windows were cracked open, gave the Rott a reassuring thump on the shoulder, and stepped out of the car counting quarters. Frank lit the cigarette dangling from his lips—his last chance to smoke for at least an hour—and said, "You met Doubleday's niece. Talk to me."

I fed two quarters into the meter, which bought me a mere half-hour respite from the steady patrol of the city's parking police. Frank knew I'd met Arlanda because she had called *Scandal Times* first, asking for my number. "The meeting went fine," I said. "Give me some more quarters."

Frank dug into his front pocket, cigarette smoke curling over his eyebrows. "How did she seem about her aunt's death?"

"Seemed all right about it. Except she didn't admit her aunt was dead. Just missing. Sure, she knows it looks bad, but nobody's identified the remains yet, so she's just, kind of waiting. For the coroner to figure it out."

He salvaged three quarters from a handful of copper and fed them one by one into the meter. "They're doing a dental on her. The heat was so intense it vaporized the flesh from her bones. Nearly vaporized the bones, too. What little was left of the body could be anyone, even that gray-haired guy you saw."

"You think they'll ever be sure who it was?"

"If they've got a couple of teeth, they'll make the identification by the dental records, you know, comparing the teeth found in the skull with Doubleday's dental charts."

"If it was arson, you think Doubleday's estate just happened to be in the way or she was burned out on purpose?"

"You mean an insurance fire or murder?"

"I don't know what I mean. I'm just asking."

"Hard to collect insurance if you're dead."

"What about another stalker, like the one before?"

"She hasn't been in a film for ten years. We're the only ones who cared about her. Even with Garbo, the only people bothering her were paparazzi scum like yourself."

I thanked him for the compliment.

Frank eyed the length of his cigarette, measuring the number of drags that remained. I could generally count on conversations like this lasting no longer than the length of a smoke. He had a few puffs left, asked, "The niece, what did she have to say about all this?"

"I talked, they listened. I finished, they said good night."

"Who's the guy with her?"

"Ex-cop," I said. "Somewhere local. Old guy. Retired."

"You get any photographs?"

"Get a heart, Frank. The woman just lost her aunt."

"I got the Cubs on satellite and a refrigerator full of beer. What do I need a heart for?"

"Mind if I keep mine?"

"A heart in a tabloid photographer is like an appendix," Frank said. "A useless organ." He crushed the butt of his cigarette between heel and sidewalk and jaywalked across the street.

Doubleday's maids rented a one-bedroom unit on the second floor of a two-story stucco box on Santa Monica Boulevard, facing the street. Santa Monica is one of the city's most heavily trafficked boulevards and exhaust fumes tinted the stucco a sooty gray. I followed Frank into the courtyard. The lids to half the mailboxes on the wall

inside the door bent away from their frames or didn't close at all, jim-
mied by mail thieves. The interior courtyard was paved in concrete.
The only public plant was a dead geranium. The railing that led to the
second floor had pulled loose at the top of the stairs, and the paint on
the steps had worn clear through to concrete. Across the courtyard, a
radio played "Besa me, besa me mucho."

The woman who opened the door to Frank's knock didn't stand
much taller than the knob, and the color of her skin matched the door
that framed her. Her face was round as a handmade doll's, and her
body was round, too, with the same lumpy look dolls used to have,
before they were all pumped from a plastics extruder to look like an
anorexic after a boob job. The woman behind her in the hallway
stood even shorter, and she was smiling at us like a long-lost cousin.
The tall one at the door introduced herself as Yolanda and the woman
in the hall as her older sister, Maria.

I offered my hand, said, "Mucho gusto."

The younger sister, Yolanda, looked back at the older one. "Did you
hear that? She speaks Spanish!" She said this as though talking about a
talented dog that had learned to bark the opening bars to "Jingle Bells."

"Solo un poco, y muy mal," I answered. Only a little, and badly.

She invited us into the living room, and before we had the chance
to sit, Maria emerged from the kitchenette with a pitcher of fresh-
squeezed orange juice. Coffee was coming, she said, but they thought
we might be thirsty first. I scanned the apartment like a camera lens,
imagining how I might photograph the sisters. My job was important.
Scandal Times gave equal space to text and photographs. They did so
not from commitment to the art of photography but in consideration
of the paper's many literacy-impaired readers. People don't see your
lips move when you're looking at a photograph.

Vibrant red and green shawls draped the backs of the sofa and
chairs, brightening furniture worn thin by a long history of use. A
framed print of Christ on the cross hung above a shelf braced to the
wall like an altar, surrounded by portraits of Salvadorans from a time
not so long ago. The apartment shook with the roar of a bus passing
on the near side of the boulevard outside.

"How long did you work for Angela Doubleday?" Frank asked
when the bus had passed.

Yolanda looked at Maria while she poured a glass of orange juice. "We started how long ago? Four years?"

"Five," Maria answered. "Five years and three months."

"A little over five years," Yolanda said.

Frank made a scratch mark in his notebook. "Did you work every day?"

"Not every day, no." Yolanda glanced at her sister.

"Every Monday, Wednesday, and Friday."

"Three days a week," Yolanda said.

"You weren't there the day of the fire, then. Say, in the morning?"

The fire had been on Thursday. The sisters looked at each other to confirm what each thought and shook their heads in unison.

"What was Ms. Doubleday like the day before the fire, the last day you saw her?"

"Just like always," Yolanda said. "She never changed. The whole four years we work for her, every day she was the same."

"Crabby," Maria confided.

"We thought she should get out more. Go visit people. We tell her, *Señora, you have to get out more! Is good for you!* But she didn't listen. Told us mind our own business. You know what I think?"

"She didn't have any friends," Maria said.

"Can you imagine that? A big movie star, the way she was? And no friends in the world. She was never mean to us . . ."

"But she didn't like us."

"She didn't like anybody."

"Except . . ." Maria held up a single finger.

"Oh yes, Toy, her chauffeur."

"Toy?" Frank asked.

Yolanda nodded. "Toy. Funny name for a man, yes? She always talked about how handsome he was, how good he take care of her. He drove her around on Fridays."

"And Sundays."

"That's right, Fridays and Sundays. We think . . ." Yolanda's eyes went blank for a moment, as though waiting.

"We don't really know for sure," Maria whispered.

"We don't have any proof but we think . . ."

"They were having an affair." Maria's face brightened at the sound of hot water spitting in the kitchen. "The coffee is ready. You take cream or sugar?"

I pulled the camera from my bag while the older sister stepped into the kitchen. Yolanda looked like she sat in front of a speeding train when I first pointed the lens at her. I ran off a few frames to get a feeling for the light and the planes of her face and asked her about the gardener.

"Lupe," she said and glanced to the spot where her sister had sat on the couch, stymied by her absence.

"Was he good at his job?"

"Lupe?" She frowned as though the question required serious consideration. "The thing about Lupe is, I tell him every week, *Not again, Lupe! It was the same thing with you last week and here you are again. Does he listen? He tries. He agrees with me, he says, You're right, Yolanda, I can't keep doing this, is not good for me.* Next week, is the same thing."

"What thing?"

Yolanda stared at me as though I was deaf. "The thing that's not good for him! Lupe's problem."

I glanced at Frank.

He shrugged.

"The problem," I said. "What exactly is Lupe's problem?"

"Didn't I already say that? I thought I already said that."

Frank and I assured her that she had not.

That she had not already told us took her aback. "The thing with Lupe is—"

"He drinks too much," Maria said, carrying a coffee tray from the kitchen.

"El boracho." Yolanda's curly black hair bounced with the vigorous nod of her head. The drunkard. "Every night he drinks too much. But he's not a bad man. His life, it was hard. His brothers . . . he's very sad, you know? Both of them—"

"Killed in the war, in El Salvador." Maria poured a cup for Frank after I waved away the offer. "His brothers were our husbands." She glanced to the wall behind our heads, which bore a photograph of two couples standing before a Spanish Baroque church, dressed for a wedding. Two studio portraits of serious young men, unsmiling for the camera, flanked the wedding picture.

"The village where we were born, everyone is dead now."

"Not everyone," Maria corrected. "Not Lupe. And not us."

"We're happy." Yolanda's smile was sudden and radiant. "Life is good here. But sometimes I think . . ."

"Death follows us everywhere." Maria's eyes peered at me over the rim of her cup, as black and shimmering as the coffee she sipped. "And last week it found Señora Doubleday."

TEN

I met Arlanda for dinner at a surf-and-turf place off the Pacific Coast Highway, where they served exotic cocktails with little umbrellas and spotlit the surf with klieg lights. The dinner was her idea. Ben was off talking with other cops, and she didn't want to eat alone. The restaurant was my choice. The waiters wore rayon shirts in bright Hawaiian prints, white cotton pants, and easy smiles. They were pleasant and handsome young men whose windblown hair and tanned faces made abundantly clear that waiting tables was just a job; their real ambition was to surf. One whose name tag read "Brad" led us to a table one row back from an ocean view. It had been a couple of months since I'd gone out to dinner with someone, and I'd dressed for the occasion in black toreador pants and an emerald green top. I even applied eyeliner, grudgingly, and lipstick from a tube that promised the color of scarlet mist but looked more like ordinary red by the time it reached my lips. More than one man seemed to be working the kinks from his neck as we passed, and from the looks of the crew at the bar, we could have been the evening's entertainment. The stares I usually encountered were more guarded in their admiration, so I figured it had to be Arlanda. Her hair had been brushed to a high gloss and spilled down the back of a short black dress tapered at the waist. Amid the strands of her jet-black hair, blue highlights skittered like static electricity. The dress showed her well-tooled calves and a scoop of spine and clung in testament to the slim and firm figure beneath. She may have been a petite but what little she had fit in all the right places. I said, "I think the dress is a hit."

"Too inappropriate?" She glanced at me just before she sat, nipping at her lower lip and raising an eyebrow, concerned.

"Inappropriate for what?"

"I'm almost in mourning, for one."

"Sure, but you're not the one that's dead."

"Glad someone noticed."

"I think everyone in the restaurant noticed."

"A town like Douglas, you live there long enough, nobody sees you anymore. Particularly when you have kids." She opened the menu and flipped to the drinks page. "My treat. No arguments."

I didn't have a problem with that. I said, "Talked to your aunt's housekeepers today."

"What'd they say?"

"The gardener is a drunk and your aunt was having an affair with the chauffeur."

"Good for her. About time she had some fun."

Came a little late, I wanted to say.

She glanced up from the drinks menu and tried to catch a waiter's eye. "What are you drinking tonight?"

"Can't drink. I'm driving."

"But you get two drinks don't you? What's the law here?"

"Most people get two drinks, three or four if they space it right. But I'm on parole and the cops sometimes play games with people like me. If I have zero-point-zero-one alcohol in my blood, they can plant an open bottle in the car and claim it's mine. That's a parole violation and technical grounds to ticket me back to the joint."

"They'd do that? Plant evidence?"

"Don't sound so shocked. I'm one of the bad girls, remember?"

"It's not as much fun drinking alone. I'll drive."

"Baby's not drinking. Maybe he can be the designated driver," I said, and we laughed at the image of the dog behind the wheel. Brad dropped by again, with his easy, empty smile. I ordered a Jack Daniel's neat, water back, and figured I'd wing it.

"I love my kids but the life of a single mom in a small town, it gets claustrophobic. Bars are about the only place to go for fun but I can't go in one, because word gets around. Even if I go home after one drink, chaste as a nun, people hear you've been in a bar and think you're a slut, shame about those poor li'l kids left home alone."

We talked about that, and then the drinks came and we clicked glasses. I nearly spilled mine when I pulled it from my lips and saw the red half-moon on the lip of the glass; it had been so long since I'd worn bright lipstick that I'd forgotten how it marked whatever I kissed.

"What's it like living here?" Arlanda asked. "For a single girl, I mean."

"The work is good."

She said that wasn't what she meant.

"I know. You got lots of movies, dance clubs, and more restaurants than people. The only thing that's missing is someone to share it with."

"You're not seeing anyone?"

I finished my drink and shook the fumes from my head.

"Why not? You're a good-looking girl. A little unconventional maybe, but I wouldn't think you'd be hurting for dates. Something wrong with the men here, they don't see it?"

"L.A. is not a true-love kind of town. Like I said, the work is good."

We looked through the menu, and when Brad saw we were ready he ambled by to take our order. Arlanda talked about her kids, how the older one was a desert rat, never could get him to come inside, and the younger one always had his nose in a comic book, she couldn't get him to go out and play. The food, when it arrived, was classic steakhouse by the sea, prepared with a minimum of fuss between kitchen and table.

Midway into a grilled swordfish I said, "Los Angeles is a city where people move to become someone they imagine themselves to be but aren't yet and most likely never will be. Most have great ambitions, but it's not an ambition to do, it's an ambition to be. You meet some-body here, chances are they're doing one thing while wanting to be someone else. Waiters, bartenders, hairdressers, telemarketers, real estate salespeople, even high-priced call girls, they all want to be actors, models, rock stars, film producers. Everybody is in the process of denying what they are now while trying to become somebody else. Tough to have a real life if you aren't who you are. Nobody wants to settle, because who's to say you won't be rich and famous a couple years down the line? Why settle for something or someone you'll just have to dump when you make it big? And the egos we carry aren't sized to who we are now but who we imagine we'll become."

Arlanda waved her knife at me. "C'mon, that's an exaggeration. Not everybody's like that."

"No. But I am. I'm like that. I came here for the same reasons. I wanted to be a fine-arts photographer. Still do. We're all the same. Rootless and shifting, never sure when or where to make our stand. A screwed-up town for dating, that's for sure."

After a shot and half a bottle of wine I felt buzzed but not so drunk I couldn't respect every rule of the road, except the one about drinking and driving. Arlanda had matched me glass for glass and topped it off with a cognac and Irish coffee. She wasn't rolling drunk but she weighed about thirty pounds less than I did and lacked the space for those two extra shots. I wasn't going to let her drive, not in a strange car down an unfamiliar highway, and by the time we greeted the Rott, who waited patiently in the front passenger seat, she had entirely forgotten her offer to drive. I didn't worry much about the cops, not with the bravado of alcohol firing my blood and a witness in the front seat. Midway between the restaurant and the hotel we swung across the highway to let the Rott run on the beach.

A lopsided moon wobbled up the sky, bright enough to cast our shadows across the sand. Unleashed, the Rott streaked in pursuit of gulls, which flapped insolently to sea the moment before he lunged. A ragged line of froth marked the wave edge at low tide, and we walked the hard sheen of sand left in the ebb. Arlanda admired with a word here and there the beauty of the sea and the Rott's tireless energy, her track weaving erratically behind us and her tongue not so nimbly rounding the corners of consonants. "I'm thinking I should move someplace new," she said. "The boys are young enough, not so rooted a move would hurt them. I wouldn't mind living in a place like this, away from the city but close enough to go there when I wanted."

"Living here isn't so easy. If the wildfires, earthquakes, and floods don't scare you off, the real estate prices will."

"I stand to inherit a lot of money from Aunt Angela." The moonlight caught her in a contrite smile when she lifted her head. "Awful, isn't it? We don't even know for sure she's dead yet, and already I'm thinking how I'll spend the money."

"You looked at the will?"

"Nope. Spoke to her accountant over the phone. He's acting as the executor, said I'm mentioned but didn't say exactly how. We're all waiting for the identification. I shouldn't even be thinking about it."

"Can't help it, can you? You inherit money, it changes your life."

"I wish I could grieve a little more, but I just can't. In some ways, Aunt Angela died years ago, when she walled herself away from the world."

The Rott doubled back to check on us, holding still just long enough to allow Arlanda to thump his flanks, then raced up the beach again.

"Family." It was a simple word, heavy with meaning, and she sighed it loudly at the sea, where it sank like a stone. "Is yours as fucked up as mine? Excuse the language."

"I've heard worse."

"I learned to swear from my ex. Don't know why I still do it."

"My dad taught me," I said. "He was a man of few words, most of them four-lettered."

"How long ago did he pass away?"

"What makes you think he's dead?"

"I'm sorry. You said *he was.* You spoke in the past tense."

"He still lives and breathes about fifty miles from here, but he's dead to me." My dad swore like the boxing style of a lead-footed heavyweight, straightforward and predictable combinations that struck with great percussive force. Sometimes I was happy to hear him swear because I could judge from the rage in his voice when words would turn to fists. His silences were worse, because he might be content at that moment or ready to rage from the dark nowhere inside his head.

"I don't have much family left in Douglas. If I move, I want it to be someplace I know somebody. Here I know Ben, and now I know you." She ran after the dog and the Rott was so surprised to see her on his tail he turned sideways and rolled. She tried to leap over him but her skirt was too tight and her foot caught his chest. Her shoulder tucked and when she hit the sand she somersaulted onto her back and lay there for a moment before her laugh cracked over the waves. When I reached her she looked up at me and said she thought she was drunk.

On the drive back to the hotel she fell asleep holding the neck of the Rott, who sat contentedly at her feet. I called her name and when she did not open her eyes or lips I said, "I was meaning to tell you the reason I haven't been seeing anybody, why I'm alone. I was married about six months ago, just after I got out." When I thought about Gabe, my chest tightened and my throat began to swell. I pinched the skin at my forearm and twisted it hard, a trick I'd learned as a little girl to blunt emotional pain, to turn grief to anger. I don't know why I had such a difficult time talking about him. I'd thought about mentioning him to Arlanda during dinner, but I'd held back. I always held back. "My husband's name was Gabriel. He was an Englishman, a paparazzo, maybe the funniest man I've ever met. We got married because I needed some money and he needed a green card. It was supposed to be a straight commercial transaction but then we slept together. Less than a month later, he was beaten to death and dumped in Lake Hollywood. I thought I was in love with him when he died. I don't know what I think now. I just know I'm afraid of getting close to anybody ever again."

Arlanda stirred when the Cadillac rolled to the stairway leading to her room. The Rott rose from beneath her legs and licked her hand. She stretched and blinked, more asleep than awake, and mumbled something that might have been an invitation to sleep in the second bed. I told her I'd be fine driving home and waited until she waved from the open door to her room.

But I wasn't fine driving home. A few miles from the hotel I pulled to the broad dirt shoulder on the ocean side of the highway. The edge of the shoulder sloped to a ragged barricade of boulders tumbling down to the beach. I crawled onto the backseat and cracked the windows facing the sea. To the rumble and hiss of waves sweeping across the sand I thought about my dead husband and about a father who people sometimes say I resemble but whom I've hated most of my adult life, and I thought about my mother, who refused to speak to me anymore, and about my only sister, whom I barely knew, and most of all I thought about the terrible void I felt where family once had lodged, as hurt and hurtful as that family had been, and then a wave larger than the rest washed above the sand and rocks and swept me to a dark sleep.

ELEVEN

Lupe Potrero rented a room in a six-story residence hotel constructed from unreinforced masonry around a central staircase, the type of structure most likely to go down in an earthquake or up in flames, a liability reflected in the room rates. The glass in the windows flanking the entrance hadn't been cleaned in recent years so not much light leaked into the lobby, which was probably a good thing, judging by the patina of grime on the walls and the strands of frayed red carpet that led to the front desk. With great foresight, the management years before had bought vinyl chairs for the lobby, easily repaired by plastic tape that now patched each piece of furniture like a quilt. The residents who sat in the lobby, pretending to stare out the windows, were similarly patched, though with bandages, canes, and pint bottles drunk from paper bags.

"Lupe Potrero? Never heard of him," the desk clerk said. His right eye swam independently of his left, giving him the appearance of a bottom-dwelling sea fish brought too fast to the surface. I couldn't judge his wandering eye but the fixed one looked shrewdly hopeful.

Frank palmed a five-dollar bill on the desk. "You tell me where Lupe Potrero is, and I'll help you find Abe Lincoln."

"Room fifty-four, up the stairs five floors and to the right. He sleeps heavy."

We climbed through floors that reeked of too many people living in too small a space for too long a time, if the alcoholic's slow decay can be called living. A sooty light fell onto the fifth floor from a window above the fire escape at the end of the hall, providing just enough illumination to read the tin numbers. Number 54 hung crookedly on a door midway down the corridor. Frank knocked first. When his knuckles began to hurt, I gave it a try. Down the hall, the head of a young man with swollen eyes and a stitched lip poked into the corridor.

"Algunos de nosotros trabajan por la noche y duermen durante el día, " he said. Some of us work at night, sleep during the day.

I backed away from the door, said, "Lo siento." I'm sorry.

As his eyes cleared he noticed we weren't the usual drunks or druggies banging on doors to disturb his sleep. "¿A quién buscan?" Who are you looking for?

"A Lupe. ¿Le conoce?" Lupe. You know him?

"¿Quiénes son, de la policía?" What are you, cops?

I turned my face away to spit on the floor. Frank, who didn't speak much Spanish, looked at me in horror. He thought I wanted to start a fight.

"Periodistas," I said. Journalists.

Lupe's neighbor ambled across the corridor. His triceps corded from the sleeves of his T-shirt, and beneath his striped boxer shorts his legs bowed. He didn't have an ounce of fat on him and he didn't stand higher than five and a half feet tall. A half-moon bruise purpled the skin below his left eye and I counted four stitches in his lower lip. His arms were longer than usual, not thickly muscled but wiry, and the knuckles jutted ridgelike from his large hands.

"Bantamweight?"

He grinned like a recognized movie star. "El Cangurito. Ventiocho y seis." The Little Kangaroo, twenty-eight wins and six defeats. Not bad, but not good enough for a legitimate shot at a title either. "Le tienen que decir quiénes son, si no, no abre la puerta," he said. We had to tell Lupe who we were or he wouldn't open the door. He knocked and called in a voice loud enough to penetrate the wood, "Lupe! Soy Juan. Dos periodistas quieren hablar contigo."

The door squeezed open to a man with eyes the color of a slain bull and a moustache spraying six directions. He didn't look happy to see us, but then he looked too hungover to be happy about anything. Frank said we were doing a piece on the fire in Malibu and would like to speak to him about his work for Ms. Doubleday.

"No hablo inglés," Lupe mumbled.

I put my foot in the door before he could shut it. "Bueno. Pues, hablamos en español. Ayer hablamos con sus hermanas. Escribimos para el periódico *Scandal Times* sobre la Señora Doubleday y el incendio de Malibu." We spoke with his sisters-in-law yesterday, I said, and wrote for the newspaper about the fire in Malibu.

"I know nothing, no, not about the fire, but okay, sit down." He backed away from the door, forgetting that he didn't speak English and that his room had only one chair. Sun and drink had furrowed his brows, and his cheeks sunk like an old man's. He sat on the mattress and fumbled at a pack of Marlboro Red. I stepped over the beer bottles on the floor to glance out the one window in the room. It overlooked the brick wall of the adjacent building. The bottles, a single bed, chair, and bureau furnished the room. The sink jutting from the wall implied a communal toilet and shower down the hall. Lupe stabbed a cigarette into a mouth missing a third of its teeth. His hands shook with the match so badly he might have lit his moustache save for the last-second influence of his other hand to steady the flame. For once, I was happy for the smell of cigarette smoke, because what it masked was much worse.

Frank asked a few questions, lighting a cigarette of his own. Lupe answered diffidently. He worked on the grounds three days a week, also cleaned the pool and took care of minor repair work around the house. He almost never spoke to the señora. She didn't have much interest in the garden, and he probably could have let everything go to slow ruin except for the close eye his sisters-in-law kept on his work. "I know what they say about me." He spoke to hands clenched tightly on his knee. "They say I drink too much. I'm lucky to have a good job, I lose it if not for them. They yell at me all the time. Son unas brujas." Witches. "I'm not so lucky now, ¿verdad? No money, no job. I ask them, *What gonna happen to me? Just a little money, pay for the room, is that too much to ask? Not for the bottle*, they say, *not one dollar.* They want Lupe to starve. Son unas brujas."

"Sus hermanas son buenas mujeres, intelligentes y simpáticas," I said. "Quesieran solo el mejor á Usted. Es mejor les escuchar." Your sisters are good women, I said, they want only the best for you.

"Las sorpriendo. Yo sé gano el dinero grande." He'd surprise them, he knew how to make big money.

"¿Como?"

He wagged his head, as though unwilling to talk about it or maybe just stung by the injustice of his current situation. "I work hard. I not miss one day of work for six months. Some days, I not feel so good, but I work anyway. I work hard. I'm a good gardener."

I leaned against the wall to steady the camera and took a long exposure of his hunched form on the edge of the bed, his hands clasped like a penitent. I asked, "Then why were the cypress trees in back dying?"

He turned his head to the camera, skin lines fracturing his face into multiple planes. "Is not my fault! I water the trees, my padre was a ranchero, I take care of the land my whole life." He leaned his head forward so his shaking hand didn't have to travel so far to stick his mouth with the cigarette. "Okay, I didn't see right away something is wrong. Maybe I don't look close enough. But why someone poison the trees, you want to tell me that? I don't even think about it until I see they go brown, more and more every day, no matter how much I water."

"What do you mean, poison the trees?"

"Quicklime!" He stared at Frank, then at me, thinking what he said was unbelievable but daring us to contradict him. "I see the water, it looks like milk around the tree, so I taste. Quicklime." He crossed himself rapidly and kissed his fingertips. "I know quicklime. I see it in Salvador. They throw it on the bodies. I think, *Somebody buried under the trees, ¡Madre de Dios!* I dig a little to see, but no, just quicklime, buried one foot deep. Why? I don't understand why."

"How long ago?"

"When I first see?" The concept of time gave him fits, I could see that. Or maybe he was just lying. He lunged for another drag on his cigarette. "After Easter. A month, maybe."

"How long had the quicklime been there, you think, before you noticed?"

"A month?" His answer was more hope than fact.

Frank flicked his ashes into the sink, asked, "You want to show him the sketches?" His notebook dangled between thumb and forefinger at the side of his hip. He hadn't written much down. I'd asked the last few questions. He didn't know what was going on, and he didn't like having the interview taken from him.

I pulled photocopies of the original sketches from my camera bag, careful to keep their blank backs toward Lupe, and passed them across the room. Frank dragged the chair toward the bed and sat, eye level with Lupe.

"Ever seen this man before?"

Lupe was looking at the corner of floor where it ran against the walls when Frank turned over the sketch of the gunman's face. His eyes slid to the sketch and careened away as though hit. The smell of singed hair infused the room and before any of us identified the source, the coal of the cigarette burned through to Lupe's flesh. I was certain he'd recognized the man in the sketch but the moment his eyes shot away he felt the pain of the coal between his fingers and yelped. The cigarette spun to the base of the door. I stepped on it, twisting my foot until I heard the tobacco crackle like a cockroach. Lupe sprang toward the sink and ran water over the burn. He noticed a half finger of tequila in the bottle above the sink and decided that would kill the pain faster than water. He opened his throat to it and set the bottle carefully back on the shelf, even though he'd sucked it dry. Maybe when he looked again a miracle would occur and another swallow would be left.

"You okay?" Frank didn't care about the man at all, but he wanted to finish the interview.

Lupe lit another cigarette and sat back on the bed. "Si, bueno, I'm okay." The focus of his eyes deepened, as though an idea had just stuck him to the hilt. "That man. Who is he?"

"We hoped you knew. You've seen him, then?"

"No. Never."

"Sure, you've seen him. Why else would you ask?"

"He looks like a bandido. He the one started the fire?"

Frank shuffled the sketch of the man gone prematurely gray to the front. "What about him?"

Lupe leaned back as though he didn't focus short distances well and contemplated the sketch through two drags of his new cigarette. Behind the smoke stream of the second drag, he nodded.

"You know him?" Frank asked.

"I think so," Lupe answered, a little uncertainly. "It's George Clooney, verdad?"

Twelve

The air cleared of smog as we climbed the foothills to Sunset Boulevard, and the cars crowding the lanes changed from domestic clunkers to German imports racing from red to red as though the difference between placing third or fifth in the queue really mattered. Frank reviewed his notes as I drove, takeout coffee in a sack at his feet. The Rott stood on the rear passenger seat and hung his head over my shoulder. It was bad enough I had to leave him in the car half the day. Frank didn't care much for dogs so I'd banished him to the rear. I gave him a pat. The Rott propped his front paws on the back of my seat and licked the side of my face. I pushed him away.

"Why you so interested in Doubleday's trees?" Frank lifted the takeout coffee free of the sack and sucked on the drink spout. His eyes bulged and he turned to spray a scalded mouthful into the wind. The first words to follow the coffee were a vulgar and not particularly original riff on the sexual habits of someone he didn't identify by name. After a moment his mouth cooled, and he said, "They have a special technology, these chain coffee places, keeps the liquid temperature two degrees below boiling, then they design this special lid to keep the heat in so you can't drink the stuff until you've driven halfway to San Francisco."

"Take the lid off, let it cool that way," I suggested.

"So you can take a hard corner and spill hot coffee in my lap? Rather burn my tongue, thanks."

"They went up like tiki torches," I said.

"What?" Frank thought I meant his tongue.

"The trees. They were so dry they burst into flame before the fire even got there, just from the heat. They burned so hot and fast they took the house with them. If they'd been healthy, they might have braked the fire."

Frank peeled the lid from the takeout coffee but spread his legs wide to prevent a sudden scalding of his trousers. "You think the trees were deliberately poisoned so they'd burn faster six months later?" He blew across the rim of the cup and took an exploratory sip. Still too hot. "That would make it first-degree murder and one with considerable foresight. Not many murderers think all that far in advance."

"So Doubleday murdered someone and buried the body beneath the trees. You like that idea better?"

"Could be one other thing."

"What's that?"

Frank tried another sip and this time it went down without a face. He capped the cup and said, "The gardener is a lying drunk."

The chauffeur's address matched the brass numbers on a two-story, one-wing apartment building nestled into an oak-strewn hillside off Las Flores Canyon Road, one of a dozen routes that switch through the mountains between Pacific Palisades and the county line just beyond Mulholand. The building had survived the routine threats of earthquake, flood, and fire but had not weathered gracefully the slam-bang shoddiness of its construction—brown stucco sprayed over wire mesh for the exterior walls, gypsum wallboard for the interiors, studs and maybe a little fiberglass insulation in between—the kind of place where a guy slams the door too hard in 1A, half the tenants hug the carpet thinking the big one just hit. The rent was twice that of a similar apartment further inland, but as we climbed the sun-cracked stairway to the second floor the view opened to a striped horizon of sea and sky, and the vast populations in the cities over the hill seemed millions of miles away.

The chauffeur cast a broad-shouldered shadow when he stepped from the doorway of the top corner unit to greet us. My eyes flicked from the shadow to the real thing. His shadow didn't lie. His nose flared too broadly and the lines in his skin etched too deeply to make his face merely pretty, but he had a ruggedly sculptured look, as though nature had cut him like the wind and sea carve rock. Stick a Stetson on his head, he could have been a cigarette cowboy. He asked in a rumbling voice if we were the reporters he expected. Frank assured him we were and produced a business card to verify it. He glanced at the card and then at Frank, as though the face proved the name on the card.

"*Scandal Times*, sure, I see that at the supermarket checkout lines all the time. Can't say I've read it, though." He pocketed the card, led us into the living room of a one-bedroom apartment. Photographs crowded the bone-white walls from the entry to the back hall, where a closed door to the bedroom blocked the rest of the gallery from view. The photographs were nearly all variations of his striking face, taken in close proximity to movie stars, celebrities, and men whose satin windbreakers, beards, and baseball caps identified them as directors or producers. The one thing not a photograph on the walls was a poster of the movie *Independence Day*.

The chauffeur observed me staring at the poster and said, "I was in that picture. Played one of the pilots. That's me and Will in the photograph to the side. Good buddy of mine."

With a gregarious sweep of hand he invited me to take a closer look, and I did. He stood in pilot uniform, arm around the shoulders of the star of the film, who was looking far off camera as though unaware of the man grinning contentedly at his side.

"You're an actor, then." I said it brightly, as though impressed. It's my job to photograph actors in candid situations, and I know how to pitch my voice to a flattering tone while ducking the bodyguards of the famously surly ones.

"Been in six films so far, over a dozen TV shows."

"How'd you get your start?"

"*Miami Vice.* The casting director picked me out of the crowd. I was just a kid. It wasn't a big part, just a couple of lines, but I caught the acting bug and haven't been able to shake it since. I do commercials too, if the product's right. I got to drive a bulldozer in the last one, played a construction worker with aching feet for a foot-cream company that gave me a whole case of the stuff after the shoot."

I said, "Wow."

"Works for women too. I'll give you a tube before you go."

I stepped back and framed his face in the viewfinder. He looked directly into the lens and shifted his head to a rehearsed angle, aware of how he photographed and careful to position himself in a flattering pose. I saw nothing wrong with the pose but no matter how I shifted the lens his eyes refused to catch the light, like the blown-out window frames of a beautiful but gutted building.

"I want to make sure I got your name right. Mind spelling it for me?" Frank didn't know the man's last name at all. The sisters gave us his telephone number, said his name was Toy.

"Troy Davies," the chauffeur said and spelled it out.

"Age?"

"Thirty-two."

"You worked for Angela Doubleday, drove her around, what, Fridays and Sundays?"

"That's right. Other days too, if she requested it."

"Did she?"

"Did she what?"

"Request it?"

"About once a month. Sometimes more, sometimes less."

"Where did you drive her?"

"Around, mostly."

"Around were?"

"We rarely had a destination. We just drove around. *Take me to Beverly Hills*, she'd say, and I'd drive Sunset to Rodeo, cruise past the shops, then drive her around the big estates or maybe over to Bel Air. Sometimes, she'd tell me to take her to one address or another where she knew somebody."

"Then you'd stop?"

"We'd slow down. She'd always make an excuse, bless her heart. Didn't feel like talking to anybody that day, nobody expected her, that sort of thing. Then she'd ask me to take her home."

Frank didn't believe it. His voice jumped an octave. "You never stopped anywhere?"

"Her accountant's. We stopped there. And the drive-through window at McDonald's, though I don't suppose that really counts. She liked the fries there, sometimes ordered a milk shake, too."

Frank glanced around the walls again. He couldn't decide whether the chauffeur was holding back the truth or telling it straight. He knew I'd followed Doubleday's limousine. The chauffeur's account jibed with what I'd seen. But he hoped for a more sensational angle. "Was she the only one you drove for?"

"She was my only private client. Sometimes I drive for a limo service when business is slow, like during the actors' strike. You want tabloid fodder, boy, I can tell you some stories about celebrity sex and drugs in the backseat of a stretch Lincoln."

"You seem to know an impressive number of show people." As Frank spoke his shoulders rounded and he turtled down his head, playing the hapless fat-boy reporter researching a puff piece. "I remember seeing you in that movie too, you played a pilot, right?"

Davies bobbed his head. "That's right. Will's great to work with, real funny, just like you'd expect. We were ad-libbing all over the place, just bombing away."

"What did Ms. Doubleday think about your acting career?"

"You'd think she'd be condescending as hell, wouldn't you? How can you impress someone with four Oscar nominations? But she wasn't. Acting gave us a special bond. She could relate to me. I don't have her talent, that's for sure, but she was real supportive."

"When did you start working for her?"

"A little over a year ago, after her last driver moved on."

"What do you mean, *moved on?*"

"Quit, was fired, whatever."

"Which one was it? Quit or fired?"

"Can't tell you. Angela complained about him, I know that much. Didn't treat her right, she said."

"Didn't treat her right how?"

"Like a star."

"And you did?"

"She was a star. I didn't treat her any different than she deserved."

"What was she like to work with?"

"An angel."

Frank plugged a pinky into his left ear and swirled it around like a Q-Tip. "I heard she was unhappy, could be difficult even."

"Angela was a diva. That was her temperament. Divas are supposed to be difficult. And she was a diva who cut herself off from her fans, her friends, maybe even her family for all I know. Divas are supposed to be center stage. They feed on it. She was like somebody starving but wouldn't eat. So, yeah, she was unhappy. She was the most miserable person I ever met."

"Then why an angel?"

"Because miserable as she was, she still carried herself with dignity and that something special stars have—charisma, great theatrical presence, whatever you want to call it. That woman would've been a star stranded all by herself on a desert island. I mean, the monkeys would line the trees like an audience, watching her."

"When did you start sleeping with her?" Frank said it just bang like that, a fact that needed a simple confirmation of date. The glimmer in Davies' eyes dimmed at the question, and then his face relaxed, as if willing, by an actor's trick, all genuine emotion to sink beneath the surface of his features. He smiled like a salesman who sells his charm more than any product, no matter what he sells, and stepped to a rack of videocassettes beside the television.

"I made a show reel of my performances, you know, scenes from the films and TV shows I've been in. Why don't you make yourselves comfortable on the couch and I'll rack it up for you?"

Frank did not move so much as the tip of his pen. He said, "We know you were having an affair. We just don't know exactly when it began. Was it love at first sight, or did it take time to develop?"

Davies' muscled brows worked to summon the right combination of hurt and indignation, but the emotions weren't genuine, and when he said, "I never slept with Ms. Doubleday," he sounded like not even he believed it.

"That's not what our eyewitnesses say."

"You don't know what it's like to work in a small household." Davies' voice dropped and it forced Frank nearer to catch the words. "The gardener, I forget his name, is a drunk. The housekeepers, Maria and Yolanda, they're nice women and I like them but they're not show people. No way they could understand the relationship between me and Angela. They're village women at heart, bossy and full of gossip. They see the way Angela looked at me or how I looked at Angela, and they think when the door closes we're banging each other's socks off. But that isn't what it was like. We were both artists. I appreciated her because she was a brilliant actress, a theatrical artist of the first order, and she appreciated me because I knew just how good she was."

"Did you love her?" I asked.

"Not in the way you think. She was my teacher." He closed his eyes, struggling with a thought. "No. That doesn't do her justice. She was more than my teacher. She was my master. Not because I was her chauffeur. That's not what I mean. She was my acting master, and I was her disciple."

That was when the first tear emerged. Most people hide their head or wipe their eyes in shame when they cry, but Davies tilted his chin up, so the tears might roll more slowly down his cheeks. That was the image *Scandal Times* would print, real tears to go with the story of blood boiled from Angela Doubleday's body, and though I was suspicious of the staging, I was moved by the sincerity of his feeling for her. I shot out the roll and, knowing I couldn't do any better, packed the camera away.

Frank thanked him for his cooperation and asked if it would be okay to call with follow-up questions, if any should occur to him.

"Sure thing, let me give you my mobile-phone number, in case I'm on the set when you call."

Frank said he appreciated that, because deadlines were strict in the newspaper business and he might have to reach him in a hurry.

"Hold right there a second." Davies trotted down the hall and we lost sight of him for a moment behind the bedroom door. He returned bearing gifts. "These are for you, my compliments," he said and handed each of us an autographed eight-by-ten portrait, what's called a head shot in the business, and a boxed tube of foot cream.

THIRTEEN

I suspected someone had been in my apartment after I keyed the top lock on my door and the key didn't turn to the left. When the door is bolted the key turns twice to the left to disengage the dead bolt from the frame. I wrapped my hand around the untucked tail of my T-shirt and tested the knob. The knob resisted, firmly locked. I keyed open the door and paused at the threshold, listening. My boom box rested on its brick-and-board shelf next to the pair of pewter candlesticks I'd bought for mood lighting, in the unlikely event I slept with somebody. The Rott brushed my leg aside and trotted to the bathroom for a drink from the toilet bowl. Okay, I thought, I'm imagining things. Nothing looked out of place at first sight, but as I moved about the apartment, unpacking groceries and stripping down for a shower, little inconsistencies continued to jab at me: the closet door ajar though I preferred it shut tight, the clothes on shelves in the closet pressed too far back against the wall, the plastic bottle of ibuprofen placed at the rear of the medicine cabinet when I normally kept it in front. Nothing obviously out of place but off register just enough to spook me.

I asked the Rott, "What do you think? Your senses are better than mine. Smell anything different?"

He dug his nose into the doggy bowl and pushed it around the linoleum. I split open a two-pound wrap of hamburger and broke three eggs into the meat. "You want me to add salt and pepper to this? Maybe a little cayenne?"

The Rott stood unwavering at the corner where I'd fed him before, eyes suggesting I stop fooling around. I mixed the egg and hamburger by hand and set it down. "If you stick around much longer," I said, "I'm going to turn into one of those fruitcakes talks to animals all the time."

I washed my hands in the sink, and when I started to unpack my camera bag, I walked backward as though pulled by a string to the closet door. I knelt to the floor and slid out the two cardboard file boxes that hold my prints and negatives. Prints are filed alphabetically by subject matter and negatives by date of exposure, the date and subject of every shot I take recorded in cheap black notebooks. The notebooks look alike and someone not familiar with my system might not return them to the proper order. Someone hadn't. They looked correct, stacked in the corner of the box as before, but the five notebooks had been misordered. The prints were correctly filed, but not the negatives. It's not so easy to read which side is which on a negative and someone had flipped a few of them front to back.

The officer who answered the phone at the Pacific Area burglary desk had little difficulty understanding why I was calling to report that my apartment had been broken into, because the moment I admitted that I'd found no signs of forced entry and that nothing had been stolen, he concluded I was one of the many crazies who call the LAPD to report unprosecutable crimes such as aura theft and harassment from space aliens. "If something is stolen, ma'am, that's burglary. If somebody witnesses an intruder breaking into your place of residence or you find signs of forced entry, that's breaking and entering. But if nobody sees anything and nothing is stolen, it's kind of like a tree falls in the forest and nobody hears it. Hard to prove it made a sound."

He had a sense of humor, this one.

The Rott thought we were going for a walk when I opened the door. I straddled his shoulders to hold him in place while I examined the dead bolt for signs it had been picked. There wasn't anything to see. I thought back to the morning I had left the apartment but could remember nothing that might have distracted me from engaging the dead bolt. Someone had picked the lock clean, then methodically searched the apartment, careful to return everything to its original position. Not wanting me to know he'd been inside, looking for something. Paying special attention to the boxes that held my prints and negatives. Maintaining the presence of mind to lock the doorknob before he left. Thinking I wouldn't notice the dead bolt or would attribute it to my own failure to lock it.

Or I could have been imagining things.

I sat in the corner of the room and stared at the door. The Rott lay on his back, and when I scratched his chest his tongue lolled like a red rag. No matter how long or from what angle I looked at the door the conviction remained that someone had been in my apartment, and I didn't know why. I picked up the landline and called Ben Turner for advice. I felt foolish explaining that, yes, I clearly remembered turning the dead bolt to the locked position before leaving the apartment and, no, nothing was taken, but absolutely yes, someone had rifled through my prints and negatives. He was good about it. Didn't laugh once. Said if I thought somebody had been in my apartment, messed with my things, that was good enough for him.

I said, "I'm thinking it might be connected to the arson fire."

"Sure, that's a possibility." His voice hitched, like he didn't confuse possible for probable. "But it doesn't matter so much who it was. Point is, you believe someone came in without your permission. What kind of hardware you got on the door?"

I described the locks to him. An hour later his Chevy Blazer wheeled into a parking spot up the block. He emerged from the cab carrying a gray toolbox and a thick paper bag with "Ace Hardware" lettered on the side. He shook a new dead-bolt lock and a six-pack of Miller from the sack. The toolbox was a big one, the top trays beveling up and out to configure a portable shop. I've always admired men familiar with the inner workings of everyday items most take for granted and who can fix anything mechanical with the right set of tools. I like to imitate what I admire and could have changed the lock myself with little trouble, but I appreciated his taking the time and effort to do it for me, even though I wasn't sure a new lock was going to solve the problem. I popped the top from a Miller and handed it to him.

"This lock any harder to pick than the old one?"

He eyeballed the back of the dead bolt and selected a Phillips-head screwdriver from the box. "Good locks aren't easy to pick, and the lock on your door now isn't a bad one. Good enough to stop an amateur with a hairpin, at least."

"Somebody picked it, though."

The muscles below his checked shirtsleeve bunched as he worked the screw from the face plate. When the threads loosened and the stem wobbled under the tip of the Phillips head, he twisted the screw free with his fingertips and dropped it into his shirt pocket. Age was slowly withering him but he was still strong and skilled, and the slack skin on his arms tautened with the work. "Lock picking isn't a widely held skill. Less than one percent know how to do it. Less than one percent of one percent. In my experience, it's easier to use a key."

"Easier still if I leave the door wide open, hang a sign above the door says 'Open House.'"

He drew out the second screw and pried the tip of a flathead screwdriver under the face plate until it popped free, exposing anchor screws within. "Previous tenants could've kept a key, given a copy to one of the neighbors," he said. "Who do you know could have a key to the place, other than the landlord?"

I shook my head. Nobody.

"Never had a boyfriend?"

"Just one. A husband. But he didn't have a key."

"He could've made a copy without you knowing it. Maybe he dropped by, wanted a picture for old-time's sake."

"He's dead."

The anchor screws were long and thin and when Ben twisted them out the lock split on opposite sides of the door. He fit the halves together again and dropped the lock into the paper bag. "I'm sorry to hear. You're too young to be a widow."

I didn't know about that. No age requirement for bad luck and trouble. The new lock was a Yale seven-tumbler dead bolt, the best you could buy from a hardware store. We talked about the lock and how long it would take to pick if a professional wanted to break it down. About ninety seconds, I said. I'd once watched an acquaintance from California Institute for Women break down a lock just as good in that time. Then Ben said, "You think the shooter came here, then?"

"Just guessing."

"What would he want with your pictures, you think?"

"He stripped the film from my camera but either he didn't have the time or he didn't think to search my bag. Why should he? I was as good as dead, out cold in the path of the fire. A couple days later, he reads I survived. That had to bother him, maybe scare him enough to act. Who's to say I didn't shoot more than one roll of film?"

Ben's mobile phone chirped. He wore it clipped to his belt, like a detective's badge. The conversation was short, his sentences clipped and to the point. He told the caller he'd be there within the hour and went back to installing the new lock. While he worked I told him I'd talked to Doubleday's gardener, maids, and chauffeur. Nothing I said impressed him much. He grunted when I mentioned the dead cypress trees and the gardener's report of finding quicklime in the soil but neither questioned nor commented on my account. He finished out the lock in silence, tested the throw of the dead bolt into the doorframe's base plate, and satisfied it was properly installed, packed his toolbox. I counted out $42.26 for the lock and started to thank him for his help but he didn't let me get past the first sentence.

"That was Arlanda," he said. "She got a call from the coroner's office. They matched Angela's dental records with the remains from the house."

I said I was sorry and he said it was all right, he'd been pretty sure she was gone since the day of the fire. He picked up his toolbox and walked to the front landing before turning to say, "I'm going to pick up Arlanda at the motel and take her over to my place. She wants you to meet us there. Bring the dog if you can. I'm in a mobile-home park above PCH, Tropical Terrace. You know it?"

I said I'd be there and watched him climb down the stairs, one hand on the railing for support. When he reached the bottom I called out, "You want me there, too?"

"Sure," he answered.

I don't think he meant it.

FOURTEEN

Just west of Temescal Canyon the road to Tropical Terrace Trailer Park peeled away from the Pacific Coast Highway to climb a hillside landscaped in bougainvillea, hibiscus, palm trees, and orange-beaked birds-of-paradise. Signs along the side of the road stated the property was private, and at the top of the hill the road curved around a clubhouse compound more appropriate in a country club than a trailer park. A wrought iron fence extended from the corner of the clubhouse to the management office, and through the bars a swimming pool sparkled green below the fading red band of the fallen sun. The first mobile home beyond the clubhouse flew the American flag from the rim of its peaked roof and parked a vintage Oldsmobile Cutlass in the carport. The trailer's foundation lay concealed behind a facing of grape stake, and the stairs and front porch had been carpentered in matching redwood. The corrugated aluminum siding above the grape stake glistened with a fresh coat of maroon paint. Slanting brass script spelled the family name to the side of the door. It was the best-looking trailer I'd ever seen, until I coasted past its neighbor, a newer model painted sun yellow. The residents strolling and jogging by the side of the road wore the gleaming tennis shoes, crisp sport shirts, and shorts typical of prosperous Californians on the declining side of middle age. Some mobile homes were older and smaller than the others but all looked meticulously maintained, each owner hiding foundations and building patios, porches, and carports to root the trailer in the land.

Ben's trailer was one of the oldest and smallest and lay at the blunt end of the street, just before the land plunged down a steep hillside to Temescal Canyon Road. A bulldozer parked its blade into the earth across the lane, the work of cutting a new lot suspended by nightfall. I parked behind Ben's Chevy Blazer. The Rott jumped the doorframe and patrolled the bushes, his nose low and leg high. The trailer had been installed on the lot like a railroad car, narrow end facing the street. A gated cedar fence extended from the trailer's street-side corner. The fence and lack of a visible front door must have discouraged unexpected visitors. Beyond the gate, stairs mounted to a redwood patio, where a picnic table stood beneath the boughs of a eucalyptus tree. I knocked on the screen door at the head of the stairs and heard Arlanda's cracked voice call for me to come in. The Rott's ears perked. When I opened the screen door he squeezed through the gap between my leg and the doorframe.

Arlanda and Ben sat on a tweed couch to the left of the door, their plans for the evening evident in the half dozen bottles of hard alcohol and mixers scattered on the coffee table. The trailer was long enough for a bedroom to the right, a kitchen directly off the front door, and a living room to the left, but so narrow that if you stood in the center and fell sideways in either direction your head would hit the wall. The room would have seemed claustrophobic if not for the sliding-glass door at the far end, which opened to the last flare of twilight over the Pacific. It may have been a thirty-thousand-dollar trailer but Ben had a million-dollar view. Arlanda and I kissed over the Rott's back. Ben gave me his hand to shake. We should go outside, he said. The night was still warm and the air fresh. It wasn't that he didn't want me in his house, I don't think, but with three people and a dog in that cramped space none of us could have leaned forward without bumping the head of the other.

Ben had a fifth of Canadian Club among the bottles he carried to the patio table, and I started off with that, watered down because it looked to be a long night. Ben and Arlanda talked about whether or

not we should eat something and decided we'd be able to drink more
with something in their stomachs. Ben knew a place that delivered
pizza and called in the order. I complimented him on what he'd done
with the mobile home, on his skills as a carpenter, and on the beauty
of the location. It wasn't much of a place, he said, but he didn't need
much room and preferred living in the area he patrolled as a deputy
to buying a condo across the hill in the San Fernando Valley. He liked
the idea of staying near Angela too, even if they hadn't seen each
other in nearly ten years. He'd always hoped she'd call him, was disappointed that she never had.

Arlanda said, "Don't take it so personally. She didn't call me either.
She didn't call anybody."

"You called her, though."

"On her birthday, and every Christmas, of course."

"She took your calls. She didn't take mine."

They drank and reminisced, alcohol the key to memory as well as
to forgetting. I mostly listened and drank slowly, nothing in the conversation prompting me to remember or to forget. Ben's pronunciation lost its crispness by the time the pizza arrived, consonants and
vowels sliding into each other without respecting where one word
ended and the next began. Still, he maintained a determined drinking
pace, revitalized by the food. The Rott sat at Arlanda's end of the
table. He knew a soft touch when he smelled one. She fed him half
her pizza, bite by bite.

"I'll have to make the arrangements tomorrow," she said. "Not
enough left to bury. Suppose we should go ahead and cremate her."

"Where will you have the ceremony?"

"In Douglas."

"Crap." Ben tilted the bottom of his glass to the stars.

"Has to be there. She had a family crypt built about eight years
ago, when my oldest was born. Only crypt in Calvary Cemetery, rises
above the other graves like a skyscraper. Moved the entire damn family there, including my mom."

"Don't suppose you'll need me at the funeral, then."

"Of course I need you there. If you're too much of a coward to go
back, just say so."

Ben tossed the old ice over the railing and started his next drink with fresh cubes. "No need to insult me. I'll go."

I said, "Little town like Douglas, I imagine the funeral will be a pretty big deal."

Arlanda stroked the Rott's neck, said, "Everybody loves her there."

"That's because nobody has seen her for thirty years," Ben countered.

Mourning the death of a difficult woman is a complex thing, mingling respect and a distant kind of love with resentment and regret. They needed to laugh, not to keep from crying but to stave off anger. They'd missed so much from her when she'd been alive that they weren't sure how to miss her now that she was gone.

"Aunt Angela is about the only claim to fame Douglas has," Arlanda said. "It's a small border town. Drug smugglers and illegal immigrants run the desert outside town and every other vehicle on the road belongs to the Border Patrol."

"Only the ranchers stay from generation to generation," Ben said. "Most everybody else I know left after graduating high school. Sure, a few stayed behind to pump gas or wait tables, particularly if the business was family owned. A couple of the kids I went to school with joined the Border Patrol. But everybody else vanished into the cities. That was the reason Angela was such a big deal. Everybody could point at her, say at least one made it big."

"What happened between you and her?" Arlanda minded her own business when sober but said what was on her heart after a few drinks. Alcohol brings out the intimacy in some people and she was one of them. "I mean, I know what happened because the same thing happened to me, too. She shut herself off. But I never understood why she broke so completely with you. You were always so close."

"I loved her like my own daughter." It was an admission of great emotion but Ben didn't speak with any sentiment in his voice. "She always hid from me, in a way. Here's one for example. I never even knew she was dancing topless in Vegas."

"Oh hell, Ben," Arlanda said, "she was part of the stage show at the Sands, not working in a titty bar."

"She wasn't wearing anything from the waist up, was she?"

"Sure she was. The Eiffel Tower."

"That was on her head, not her chest."

"Don't be such a prude."

"I'm not now, but then, I might've tanned her hide. By the time I heard about it she'd already been cast in that film. Maybe it wasn't much of a part, but it was one of the most famous films of its time and she said it proved she knew better than I did how the world worked."

"She was stubborn." Arlanda said. "Mom told me they got into a fight once when they were kids, and Angela didn't talk to her for three months. Not a word. Just cut her dead. Poor mom. A wallflower with a celebrity sister. She always felt like the forgotten one."

Arlanda caught me staring at her, trying to figure out what happened to her mother. "Drank herself to death." She rattled the ice and drained the last of her rum and cola, winking over the raised glass. "It's a family weakness."

"Hard to be a movie star making a million dollars a picture and take a thirty-thousand-a-year patrol cop seriously." Ben iced Arlanda's glass and eyeballed a jigger of rum over the cubes. His hand moved with deliberate caution, as if completing the task without fumbling or spilling would prove he wasn't yet drunk.

"Of course she took you seriously. She trusted you."

"Not for the last ten years, she didn't."

"What was it about that night outside Spago? I understand it must have been traumatic as hell, I mean, the poor little creep died right on top of her, but why didn't she ever recover? What was it that changed things so much?"

"Hard to say. I think in the end she wasn't happy with her life but couldn't change. Too famous. Too successful. Hard to go back to working at the corner drugstore after they make you a star."

"I don't know if she ever felt like a star, not really," Arlanda said. "Once, when my mom was having trouble coping with things, she put me on a Greyhound bus to California. Aunt Angela was living in Beverly Hills then, a mansion up one of the canyons. Her maid took care of me most of the time, but every night we'd watch a different film in her home theater. I thought that was so cool, to have a little theater in your house. Most of the films were classics, you know, old

ones in black and white. Bette Davis, Joan Crawford, she liked them
a lot, but nobody compared to Garbo. *That's a real star,* she'd say. *The
rest of us are just bright planets.*" Arlanda's voice changed when she
spoke in the voice of her aunt, and the impersonation was close
enough to still Ben.

"She said that?"

"I couldn't make that up, could I? Don't have the imagination."

"She was a remarkable woman. If she was just a bright planet, what
does that make us? Asteroids?"

We thought that was pretty funny, our sense of humor fueled by
alcohol, but then nobody could think of a clever way to extend the
joke and we lapsed into silence.

"Maybe the stalker was just an excuse," Arlanda said.

"Excuse for what?"

"To disappear from public view. To pull a Garbo."

"Bullshit." Ben elbowed his drink and the glass slung ice and vodka
as it tumbled off the edge of the table. My hand flared out to snatch it
midway between table and floor. Ben glared as though I tried to show
him up. Then he blushed.

"'Scuse the language ladies. What was I sayin'?"

I set the glass on the table, thinking he'd had enough but knowing
he wouldn't stop. If he stopped he'd begin the slow descent to sleep
and he wanted to go higher still, until not even more vodka could
propel him further and he fell fast and hard to a thoughtless stupor.
He breathed deeply and reached for the ice.

"We were talking about the stalker." Arlanda said.

"Davis. Andy Davis. Unemployed carpenter from Florida. A poor,
pathetic son of a bitch. I think the whole experience of getting stalked
flipped a switch in Angela's head. We don't know what it's like, having somebody obsess on you like that, hanging around your house,
sending you notes every day. You know he splashed his own blood on
some of 'em? Scared the holy shit out of her. Changed her basic psychology. Like evasion therapy, you know, where you show somebody
a picture of something they want and then give 'em a shock of electricity. Pretty soon the thing they want makes 'em cringe. After crav-
ing fame for so long, she turned to fearing it so much she shut herself
in that big house of hers and didn't let anybody in, not even family."

Ben pushed back from the patio table and when he stood the bench tipped over behind him. The impact startled a bark from the Rott. Ben cursed his own clumsiness and carried his drink to the patio railing. I watched him carefully, afraid he might tumble over to the hillside below. He may have been drunk, but he was still aware that Arlanda and I watched him and straightened his spine, too proud to stoop. The move shifted his center of gravity to his chest, and he swayed noticeably, despite his steadying hand on the rail.

"When something bad happens," he said, "you know how your mind goes back to it, looking at every little event that led up to the moment, trying to find some sign of what was going to happen, thinking, *If I'd only seen this or thought about that or been standing another two feet to the left, it wouldn't have played out the way it did?* Looking for some way to control the situation, if only in hindsight. Trying not to feel so damn powerless. Fooling yourself into believing that if something similar ever goes down again, you'll be ready, you'll know where to look, how to move, you won't let the same thing happen twice." Ben stared at the branches of the eucalyptus overhead. "How was I supposed to know the fool had a doll in his hand? He wrote that he wanted to die with her, wanted to bond himself so damn tight whenever anybody mentioned her name they'd think of him, too. I read his letters. I knew what he said he'd do. I thought he was going to kill her."

"You were the off-duty policeman," I said, remembering the story I'd read in the news clippings. "You were the one who shot him."

"Shot him dead."

"You couldn't have known what was going on in that sick man's mind," Angela said. "Nobody did. Everybody thought he had a knife."

"It's my job to know. I was trained to see the difference between a knife and a doll. A doll!"

"He tricked you," I said.

Ben's eyes caught the glare of the porch light like veined neon. He didn't ask what I meant, except by look, but I suspect he knew where I headed with the remark.

"He wouldn't be the first to commit suicide by cop," I said.

Arlanda placed her hand on my arm to hold the conversation. "You mean he wanted Ben to shoot him?"

"He wanted to be shot. Didn't matter who did it."

"Yeah, I thought about that." Ben cocked his head back and gulped his drink down to the ice. I'd seen him pour three ounces of vodka into the glass. The wall loomed in front of him and he intended to hit it full speed. "It makes sense that's what he was trying to do. But know what? Doesn't matter. I still made the wrong decision. Angela thought so too. Never told me. Didn't have to. The man bled to death right on top of her. Her screaming under him. Out of her mind with fear, screaming." He wiped his face with the broad palm of his hand, said, "Oh, shit." The vodka hit him in waves and he staggered back against the railing, gripping it with both hands behind him like a fighter on the ropes.

Arlanda kicked out from the table to catch him but he wasn't going down, not yet, and he stopped her with an angry swagger of his head. "Sit down. I don't want your comfort now."

"Go ahead and fall on your damn head, then." She wasn't so steady on her feet either and sat down hard.

He tried to smile, liking it that she stood up to him, but rage burned the crescent from his mouth, driven by some pain within that neither love nor vodka could solace. "There's one other thing. Something I never told her. Never told nobody. But she was curious about her father, so maybe she hired somebody, found out. Why she never talked to me again." His chin dipped to his chest, and I thought for a moment he was passing out, but his head jerked up and his eyes when he opened them looked seared blind. "You see, the night her father went on his last drug run? I told the sheriff about it. The local deputy. I didn't want to see Pete running with a drug gang, not with a pregnant wife at home. This deputy, he said he'd arrest the others. Let Pete go free. He was just a kid, right? Scare him good and send him home, the deputy said. I was pretty stupid then. Stupid in the way only a self-righteous eighteen-year-old can be. What I didn't know until a few years later? That pig-fucking son-of-a-bitch deputy was deep in drug money. Pete was running on somebody else's territory. So he got his head blown off."

Ben's knuckles, white from gripping the railing, relaxed, and he took a tentative step forward. On the next step he lost his balance. He braced an arm against the table, and I caught his shoulder, and somehow his legs held.

"I'm okay. I'm fine," he said, though clearly he was not.

I let him go. He passed through the door to his trailer unassisted, and once inside he steadied himself with a hand to the frame. "And you know the pig that pig-fucking deputy fucked the most?"

He stared at us, drunk and defiant.

"You," I said.

"That's right," he said. "Me."

Fifteen

Dawn woke me on the window side of a sagging fold-out sofa bed, Arlanda curled on my left side and the Rott down low between us. I'd experienced worse hangovers before, and knowing this wasn't going to be an epic one gave me some comfort as I swung my legs over the bed. Sitting up was going to take some effort and I didn't think I was quite ready for it so I worked at keeping my eyes open, which was work enough. Arlanda had insisted I join her on the sofa bed rather than go out to sleep in my car, and Baby, who was well behaved enough to sleep on the floor at home, couldn't resist sneaking between us. It hadn't helped that Arlanda encouraged him. She'd been drunk, of course, and alcohol released the wildness in her, just as it unleashed Ben's pain. She asked if what she'd heard about prison was true, that most women became lesbians. I talked about that for a while, and then she asked if I'd done that too, if I'd slept with women there. She snuggled against me when she asked it, and had she not been half asleep I might have thought the question was more than just curiosity. I preferred men, I said.

When I sat up my brain swirled like a goldfish in a plastic bag. I leaned forward, elbows braced against knees and palms cradling forehead—the classic fear-of-nausea position. Did I have any sisters,

Arlanda had wanted to know. Just one, I'd said. Moved away when I was six. Don't remember much about her. Just the fights with my dad. The shouting. The dull thud of her head on the coffee table when he knocked her down one night. The next day she was gone, dead now for all I knew. The nausea subsided and I knew I'd have to sweat the alcohol out of my body. "You need a sister," Arlanda had whispered. "I need a sister, too. I'm all alone now, except for my kids. Maybe that's what we can be for each other. Sisters."

The Rott lifted his head when I stood but the rest of him stayed put. The eye he cast was a reproachful one. What was I doing up so early? I washed my face with cold water in the sink and by the time I emerged from the bathroom he was waiting by the screen door. I gave him a thump on the shoulder and led him to the car. In a rare show of foresight I'd packed running clothes the previous afternoon. I changed behind Ben's fence and attached a leash to the Rott's collar. We followed the main road up the hill, skirted a locked gate marking the far border of the trailer park, and wound through the plush residential streets of neighboring Pacific Palisades. The eastern sky reddened above the rising sun, and a violet ring swung around the horizon line to the west. The air tasted like the sea and as I ran blew cool against my face. Later in the day the land would heat and the desert winds would blow the sea air from the coast. My head throbbed with the first mile's every stride but by the second the blood raced through my veins like a centrifuge, forcing the poisons from the previous night out the pores of my skin. The endorphins kicked in, miracle chemicals that give every runner a sense of joy to counterbalance the pain, and I finished the run feeling almost good.

Arlanda was stepping from the bathroom as I slipped open the screen door. A towel wrapped her freshly washed hair. She smiled and whispered that the shower was free if I wanted it. I did. I found a bottle of aspirin in Ben's medicine chest. That and the shower cleaned up the last of my hangover. When I emerged Arlanda had a breakfast of scrambled eggs, toast, and coffee waiting for me on the patio table, and the Rott was licking a plate clean. She sat on the edge of the bench, head tilted sideways and long wet hair hanging like cloth in the sun. Her face glowed, the early-morning light tinting her light-brown skin in hues of rose and gold.

"Never figured you for an early riser," she said, her voice airy and cheerful.

"Best time to run. Sorry if I woke you."

"Don't worry, I'm used to getting up with the kids."

I was hungry after the run and asked if Ben was joining us. He'd decided to stay in bed for a while, she said. I wasted little time getting to the food. She needed to get up early anyway, she said, to get to a 9:00 A.M. appointment with Angela's accountant.

"Troy Davies mentioned him," I said.

"Who?"

"Sorry. Your aunt's chauffeur. He said she never got out of the car, except when they stopped at the accountant's office."

"He's been taking care of her finances for over twenty years. He's going to read the will this morning."

"I'll drive you out, if Ben isn't up to it."

She matched me bite for bite, looking like she'd spent the evening reading the Bible in her bunny slippers while sipping a mug of warm milk. I said, "You look awfully darn good for someone drank as much as you did last night."

"Was I too drunk?"

"Didn't say that. But you were packing it away."

"I don't get hangovers, not bad ones anyway."

"Lucky you."

"Maybe it's not such a good thing."

"Why not?"

"If I don't suffer much the next morning, what's to stop me from drinking too much the night before?"

"Common sense?"

"Passes out after the third drink."

I always counted my drinks because the final tally told me how I'd feel the next morning. Anything over eight ounces was like jumping out a second-floor window; the ride down would be exhilarating but the pain excruciating when I hit the ground. Without the threat of pain, I wouldn't know where to stop.

I asked, "Your mom, was she the same way?"

The morning glow of her skin dimmed, and she dipped her head once. "To her grave," she said.

&   &   &

Angela Doubleday's accountant was a short, solemn-eyed man who, judging by the parade of golf trophies displayed behind his desk, had dedicated his recreational life to breaking par. He moved with the loose agility of a young athlete as he crossed the office to greet Arlanda, but up close he looked his age, a few years shy of qualifying for the senior tour, his face hatch marked by a life in the sun. He wasn't the suit-and-tie type, not even at 9:00 A.M. on a weekday, dressing in cotton trousers and polo shirt as though he hoped to catch an afternoon tee time with no more than a change of shoes. From an accordion file on the corner of his desk he produced a legal-size white envelope and passed it to Arlanda, asking her to verify that the envelope was sealed. His manner was polite but brisk and left no doubt that even though accounting took second place to golf he was competent at his work. He'd helped Ms. Doubleday in the drafting of the will, he said, so was generally aware of the contents, but the envelope hadn't been opened since he'd sealed it in her presence three months ago.

"She'd changed her will?" I asked. It seemed pertinent.

"She did." He looked at Arlanda as though she had asked the question, subtly letting me know I played no significant role in the proceedings. "I'll fill you in after I've read it. Agreed?"

Arlanda returned the envelope and he broke the seal. The will had been drafted by a local law firm, its language crowded with subclauses, and he read it aloud slowly, repeating key passages for emphasis and clarification. After the liquidation of all investments not including Ms. Doubleday's place of residence, Maria Potrero and Yolanda Potrero, her housekeepers, were to receive five thousand dollars each. A total of forty thousand dollars would be placed in a certificate of deposit to help cover the college-education costs of her nephews, Aurelio Cortes and Armando Cortes. Half that sum would be donated to the retirement home of the Academy of Motion Picture Arts and Sciences. Whatever remained of the value of her cash assets and investment accounts, not including her place of residence or anything within it, and discounting all legal and professional costs associated with settling the estate, was to go to Troy Davies, her chauffeur. Her future income, including residuals and fees from past theatrical, television, and film appearances, would also go to Mr. Davies.

The accountant raised his right hand while he read that provision, as though to stay the distress it might cause Arlanda. "'My private residence, including all furnishings and personal belongings both within that residence and anywhere on its grounds, or the cash proceeds resulting from the sale of aforementioned residence, real estate, furnishings, and personal belongings upon the liquidation of the estate after my death, I will entirely to my niece, Arlanda Cortes.'" He laid the will flat and reached a practiced hand into the accordion file. The envelope he withdrew bore the image of a stag in the upper left corner. "That brings up the question of insurance. Ms. Doubleday carried a full package from Hartford, including theft, liability, and fire. Unfortunately, she only insured the house and contents for two million dollars."

Arlanda fingered the zipper to her purse. The purse was hand-tooled in brown and black leathers. I'd first seen her carry it two nights before, when we went out to dinner. There was nothing wrong with it except that age and wear had frayed the shoulder straps and an uneven stain circled one of the bottom corners. She said, "Two million? Isn't that a little low?"

In some areas of Malibu, two million wouldn't buy a teardown.

"Ten years ago it probably was a fair estimate of value. This year it's not. Estates comparable to hers are currently listing for five million, starting price, and going all the way up to seven or eight. The policy doesn't cover the value of the land, of course, so you might want to add somewhere between one and one-point-five million dollars to the value of the insurance policy, depending on how long you want to wait to sell it. If, that is, you want to sell it."

It wasn't hard to do the math. I said, "She was underinsured by half, then. As her accountant, wasn't it your job to advise her about things like this?"

"Fair question," he said, though the crimson flush beneath his tan contradicted him, and again he refused to look at me. "I urged her to update her insurance policy every two years. She never gave me permission to go ahead and make the arrangements. Didn't want to pay for something she didn't think she'd need, she told me. Particularly when she'd have to economize in order to pay for the increased premiums."

"Look, two million, three million, six million, whatever. It's all more money than I'd probably make in my lifetime." The crack in Arlanda's voice widened under stress, swallowing the occasional word whole. "I know my aunt was having an affair with Mr. Davies, at least, that's the rumor I've heard." She glanced at me, the source of that rumor. "I don't want to seem at all ungrateful to her. If she loved him, then I think that's great. I hope she found some happiness. But to leave him almost everything but the house? It's going to take me a little time to get used to that."

"Your aunt was very nearly broke." He said it bluntly and reached again into the file on the corner of his desk, this time to retrieve a thin sheaf of papers bound within report covers. A preliminary estimate of the value of Angela Doubleday's estate, he said. "Mr. Davies stands to inherit less than fifty thousand dollars, not including future income from residuals, which runs less than twenty thousand a year. Not an insignificant amount, but not a fortune either."

"I thought Aunt Angela was rich." Arlanda glanced over the table of numbers representing her aunt's assets, running a burgundy fingernail down the columns.

"She was rich, ten years ago. Not by the standards of some movie stars, but her asking price then was a million dollars a picture and she made a couple of pictures a year. Remember, your aunt hadn't worked recently, and the cost of running an estate with four part-time employees, it adds up. Still, she should have been able to hang on indefinitely, had she not begun to withdraw significant sums of money above and beyond her normal personal expenses."

"What do you mean? What expenses?"

"I'll explain. As her accountant it was my responsibility to pay all her bills, everything from department-store charges to gas and electricity. Even her groceries were charged and then paid through me at the end of the month. For the last five years, your aunt was withdrawing about twenty thousand a month over and above that."

"It was her money. I feel guilty even asking. But do you know what she was doing with it?"

"Buying art."

"Art? What kind of art?"

"She never said and never showed me any receipts either. She might have spent the money on something else entirely. She might have gambled it away. I don't think we'll ever know. If she was collecting art, it burned with the house. And because it was uninsured, it doesn't exist, not in terms we can deal with here." He spoke indignantly, personally offended that money and assets could not be accounted for.

I said, "Troy Davies told me that you were the only person Angela Doubleday visited. Do you mind telling me why?"

"Are you asking my opinion regarding why she became a recluse or why she deigned to visit me in my office?"

"The second."

"I was her servant. Higher paid than Mr. Davies and the Potreros, but functionally still a servant." He glanced briefly around his office. "As you can see, I run a successful practice. That gave me enough leverage to insist that Ms. Doubleday come here to do business. Don't think for a moment she didn't protest, and strenuously. Our relationship very nearly ended when she demanded that our meetings be conducted at her residence and I refused. But Mr. Davies is being either forgetful or disingenuous when he states I'm the only one Ms. Doubleday visited."

"Why's that?"

"I guarantee her personal physician didn't make house calls, and certainly not her dentist." He placed his hands flat on his desk, signaling he had nothing else to add, and Arlanda and I stood. He escorted us out the door of his office and into the reception lobby.

I said, "You forgot to mention—why did Ms. Doubleday change her will three months ago?"

"Her previous will was ten years old. She had two new nephews and her material circumstances had changed. It was time to update. And she wanted to write one person out of her will. She was quite adamant about that."

"Who?" Arlanda asked, though I think we both knew.

"A man named Ben Turner."

"Did she say why?"

"Your aunt was a mysterious woman," he said with greater grimness than admiration. "She explained very little to me."

SIXTEEN

The two men came at me from the street as I climbed the steps to my apartment, moving so quietly they took even the Rott by surprise. "Mary Baker?" One of them asked. I didn't have to turn and look to know who they were. Mary Baker is my birth name. It's on my Social Security card and driver's license. Nobody calls me Mary Baker except telephone solicitors and cops. These weren't telephone solicitors. Both men wore off-brand sport coats and dress running shoes and, like so many L.A. detectives, sported moustaches like a badge identifying them as cops. So much for the plain clothes. I told them Mary Baker was my legal name and bang like that they advised me I was under arrest.

"But my dog," I said.

The Rott glanced from one to the other, thinking whatever it is that dogs think when they meet strangers who pose no obvious threat. The two detectives swapped glances, then the nearer of the two dropped a cautious hand. The Rott licked it.

"You know somebody can take care of him?" he asked. He looked like a nice enough guy, within the strict parameters of his job.

I said I did but it would take some time for him to get there.

"We should call Animal Control," his partner said.

"No choice really." He scratched the Rott behind the ear, thinking it through. "You have a leash for him?"

I told him he'd find one in my camera bag. I knew enough not to reach into my bag. Women in Los Angeles have been shot for less than that. He lifted the bag from my shoulder and zipped it open. The Rott didn't have a clue what was going on. The detective snapped the leash to his collar, said, "Don't worry about your dog. We'll stay until Animal Control arrives, then I'll call your friend, say where he can pick him up. Imagine you'll want to save your one phone call for a lawyer."

I thanked him. His partner nudged me down the stairs with a hand between my shoulder blades. I knew the routine. I placed my hands on the cruiser's roof and widened my stance. He ran a practiced hand under my arms and along my torso down to my feet, twisted one arm and then the other into plastic cuffs behind my back, all while reciting my Miranda rights in a monotone. The Rott, tied to a street sign, barked once, confused. The partner guided my head under the doorframe, sat me in the prisoner compartment, and shut the door. Baby howled. They tried to quiet him but he howled until they opened the door again. I leaned forward in the seat because it's not comfortable to sit back when your hands are cuffed. I told the Rott I was going to jail and he was going to the pound. It wasn't fair. He hadn't done anything wrong. It was guilt by association. He'd be out in a couple of hours. Ben and Arlanda would take good care of him. It might be some time before I saw him again. But he'd be okay. I promised him that.

Then the Animal Control wagon rolled up the street and the detective behind the wheel started his engine. The Rott jumped and strained against the leash. I pressed my face against the glass as the car accelerated from the curb, trying to let him know things would work out for him, not to worry. The cruiser turned the corner and I leaned back in the seat, ignoring the bite of the cuffs at my wrists.

"Don't worry, he'll be fine," the detective said, the one who'd leashed the Rott.

I thanked him for waiting until Animal Control arrived. We rode in silence for some miles, then he turned to look at me through the Plex-iglas divider. "I got a question for you. Not a legal one. A personal one."

I told him to go ahead.

"You always talk to your dog like that?"

"Like what?"

"Like he's human, I guess."

"If my dog was human," I said, "I probably wouldn't talk to him."

Those unfortunate or deserving enough to be arrested in Los Angeles County are eventually delivered to the Twin Towers, the eight-story high-security pillboxes that hold accused felons awaiting trial or bail and prisoners serving out their sentences on misdemeanor charges. Fresh arrests are brought by squad car and police van to the Inmate Reception Center, located in a low rectangular building between the towers. A sheriff deputy confiscates the prisoner's civilian identification, wallet, purse, address book, jewelry, keys, and all other personal items. Another deputy instructs the prisoner to extend her left arm and clips a plastic identity bracelet to her wrist. A bar code is printed across the bracelet face. The bar code contains information that, when scanned, tracks the prisoner's movements within the towers. For the practical purposes of daily life, this bracelet is the prisoner's new identity.

The attending deputy instructs the prisoner to disrobe completely. If you're lucky, the audience is limited to this deputy and one other, both female. If not, the door will be left open to anyone walking by, or overcrowding will force you to disrobe in the corridor. The business of running a jail the size of the Twin Towers is a bustling one, and regulations on privacy and basic human dignity are often sacrificed to expediency. The deputy instructs you to raise your arms over your head. If you have large breasts, you're told to lift them to reveal the underside. You raise your bare feet to expose the soles, and if your hair is long you pull it up to show the roots at the nape of the neck and then you shake it out. The deputy tells you to turn 180 degrees, bend, and grab your ankles. This instruction is delivered in a voice no different from the one that told you to raise your arms and feet. You wonder what could possibly be going through the deputy's mind while she examines you, then she tells you to stand, and you look at her. Her face is flat of expression. She's bored. You realize you're just another piece of meat to her. You feel good about that. If she treated you like a human being, the indignity would be worse. It's nothing personal this way. You wait, the cold concrete floor numbing your ankles, while she inspects your street clothes, feeling each seam and investigating the pockets. Her hands are gloved. It can't be a pleasant job. Your street clothes go into a blue plastic bag tagged with your prison identification number. You'll be allowed to wear them again when you go to court. If your underwear is clean of contraband, the deputy will return it to you. In prison they issue every inmate one size fits all. Not in jail. In jail you get to keep your underwear. The deputy hands you a pair of orange overalls, bright as a traffic cone. You zip it over your body. It fits like a traffic cone, too. All that's left of you then is your face and hands.

Those accused of a violent felony or whom the processing deputies deem to be a risk to other inmates are diverted to cells designed to hold one prisoner but that, due to overcrowding, usually contain three. All others are channeled to the chicken house, a dormitory with two hundred beds and what seems like twice that many inmates. I was diverted to a cell. The two inmates who occupied the cell were Chicana gang girls, one not older than nineteen going on forty, the other with a homemade tattoo of a tear dripping from the corner of her eye, marking her as an ex-con on her way to becoming a con again. They sat on the lower bunks, backs against the wall and feet kicked out. I vaulted onto the top bunk.

The older one spoke up, the one with the teardrop tattoo. "¿De dónde eres, nena?" Where you from, girl?

"Instituto para mujeres en California, CIW. ¿Y tú, guapa?" California Institute for Women. And you?

"También." The same.

Most inmates don't mix with those of different races but some Anglos and Hispanics crossed race lines, so we knew some of the same people. We talked about our experiences at CIW not much differently than graduates of the same university, comparing cellblocks instead of classrooms and prison guards rather than professors. The time passed that way and then the bolt holding the cell door sprang back and a deputy called my name.

I followed the deputy down the corridor. Each floor in the Twin

Towers is designed to be self-sufficient. Prisoners eat, sleep, and exercise on the same floor. This restricts the movement of prisoners to a minimum. The strict control of the flow of prisoners reduces the risk that something unforeseen happens. In life, the soul delights in the unpredictable. In jail, the unpredictable is the enemy of authority and exterminated. At each security door we waited for a control-booth deputy to spring the electronic locks and let us pass from secure area to secure area. The last door buzzed open to a small room with table and chairs and a shatterproof Plexiglas observation window. The deputy instructed me to step inside. I did, and the door clacked shut behind me. A few minutes later the glance of my parole officer burned through the Plexiglas. I waved. She didn't wave back. The electronic bolts threw and the door opened to a muscular blonde my age plus six with eyes the color of steel. By the look of her charcoal-gray pantsuit she'd appeared before the judge that afternoon, testifying on behalf or against one of her charges, something she'd soon be called upon to do for me.

"You want your attorney present?" My parole officer set a file folder on the corner of the table and pulled out a chair.

"Not to talk to you, I don't."

"Six months between arrests, that's quite an achievement." She didn't look at me. She sat in her chair and brusquely pointed to the chair opposite. I sat down, too.

"Just lucky," I said.

"You call arson-murder lucky?"

"I'm a walking target for every incompetent cop with a crime and nobody to pin it on. I'm lucky I lasted six months."

"It's not your fault, right? You tried, right? But everybody is against you, right?" Each time, she pronounced *right* like a rifle shot. "Tell me something I haven't heard before. Something I don't hear every day in this stupid, thankless, piece-of-crap job."

"I thank you."

"Why should you?"

"You've done great by me. I think you're a great parole officer. Given of course that it's a thankless piece-of-crap job."

She almost smiled but suspicion cut the smile dead. "Your personal evaluation of my job performance doesn't carry much weight with

me or my superiors." Anger clipped her pronunciation to hard consonants and she gripped her pen in her fist, better prepared to stab than
write. My parole officer is full of rage, just like me. "I'm thirty-six
years old and my hair is turning gray. You know why?"

"No, ma'am."

"Most of the parolees assigned to me, they're cons to the core.
Nothing I can do except the paperwork until the courts ticket them
back to prison. And I'm happy to see them go, because they're dangerous people, dangerous to themselves and others. But a few in my
caseload, they're not worthless. I can talk to them. They listen. They
want to improve their lives. So I work with them. Get them training,
counseling, a decent place to live. I start to think they have a chance.
I even start to hope a little bit. I'm rooting for them, you see, because
I like them. For all their sins and crimes of stupidity, I like them." She
reached across the table and gripped my wrist. She worked out regularly with free weights and trained in judo. Her grip was fierce to the
threshold of pain. "You know what I found last night?"

"No, ma'am."

"This girl, this twenty-year-old girl fresh out on parole. Not violent
at all, served eighteen months on soliciting and crack possession. Naturally smart, a good-hearted girl in a bad neighborhood. I thought I
could do something for her. I got her into a computer training course.
I really thought she had a brain in her head. I really thought she'd
make it. Do you know where she made it?"

Her grip tightened yet again and I might have buckled under the
pain but I didn't. I said, "No, ma'am."

"The morgue. That's where she made it. Stuck in her womb by a
knife-happy street trick. She crawled behind a car and bled to death
waiting for her pimp to show up."

"I'm sorry."

She heard the strain in my voice and released her hold. She hadn't
been trying to hurt me. "Don't ask me to care about what happens to
you. You can't care in this job. You care, it kills you."

"I don't need you to care. I need you to be fair."

"That I can do." She pulled a visitation form from her file folder
and began to fill it out. The tension in her shoulders released at the
same time. The great joy of bureaucracy is it dulls the mind. "As your

parole agent, I advise you to fully cooperate with the investigative officers on all charges. The more cooperative and truthful you are, the more likely they'll be convinced of your innocence, and if you've transgressed, the more lenient the court will be in sentencing you." She filled out my name and the date and place where the visit took place, signed the form, and returned it to the folder. "Claymore drinks." She used her bureaucratic voice, her low and bored tone a warning. "He used to be a top-rate arson investigator. Now he drinks too much and it's affecting his performance. Some of his superiors are looking for a way to get him into a program or wash him out. He needs a high-profile conviction right now to save his career."

"And I'm it," I said.

"If you misuse this information in any way you'll never have my support on anything ever again." By that I knew that she felt like a traitor to law enforcement by warning me. She knocked on the Plexi-glas observation window and she didn't say good-bye or look back when the door buzzed her out.

I waited by the door for the attending deputy to escort me back to my cell and when she didn't show I sat down and kicked my feet up on the table. If they'd forgotten about me, they wouldn't come look-ing until the next head count raised the alarm. I closed my eyes, hop-ing for a moment of sleep. The security door snapped open and the deputy ordered my feet off the table. The man standing behind her in the corridor wore jeans and a jeans jacket over a western-cut white dress shirt affixed at the top with a turquoise bolo tie. The scarred leather bag slung over his shoulder looked more appropriate for the classroom than the courtroom. Even with the heel boost of ostrich-skin Nicona cowboy boots he stood a full six inches shorter than the deputy, but the size of his mouth more than made up the difference. He gave me a professional kiss on the cheek, said, "Darling! We have to stop meeting like this!"

"Is your fifth wife getting suspicious?"

"Please, sixth. My fifth was a nightmare."

"And the sixth is a dream come true?"

He laughed. "Hardly, but she's not so jealous you have to get your-self arrested every time you want to see me."

The man was my lawyer, Charles H. Belinsky, and my only advantage over the thousands of inmates doomed for prison, other than my innocence. He asked for a plain and unadorned recitation of what happened on the day Angela Doubleday's estate burned. Where I'd been. What time I'd arrived. Why I was there. Who I'd seen and when.

I gave it to him.

"What I don't understand is what I'm doing here," I said. "I've admitted I was on the hill the time the fire started. That's never been any secret. I mean, I shouldn't be surprised that I'm here. Claymore told me he was going to take me down when he first interrogated me. But he didn't have enough to arrest me three days ago, so why now?"

"They found a witness."

"A witness to what?"

"To you walking away from your car on Encinal Canyon Road, carrying a five-gallon can of gasoline."

I said, "Oh."

Belinsky waited for me to protest. I don't think he was terribly concerned with the truth, but he expected his client to believe in her own innocence, even if no one else did, and if she wasn't innocent to at least pretend to be so. But the mention of a witness stunned me speechless.

"The witness describes himself as a fitness enthusiast hiking above Encinal Canyon Road. His description of you and your car is appallingly accurate. According to his statement, he struggled with his conscience for a few days, then decided to report what he'd seen to the police."

"I get it. A concerned citizen. Doesn't want to get involved at first. Thinks it over, decides it's his duty."

"Not an unassailable witness. A judge and jury can get suspicious when a witness takes too much time to come forward."

"The detective heading the investigation. Claymore. I've heard he drinks too much, needs the arrest to stick to save his career."

"Allegations that Detective Claymore is an alcoholic have been circulating for some time. The problem, friend, lies in proving first that he is an alcoholic and second that his drinking led to specific and significant acts of incompetence during the investigation."

"And if you talk to the cops about his drinking, they'll stonewall you."

"A cynical observation about the blue wall of silence and all the more sad for being true. The DA plans to file arson-manslaughter. Your arraignment will be tomorrow morning. I'll request bail but I doubt his honor will award it in consideration of your past record of transgressions against the law. You understand what I'm telling you?"

"I can go ahead with plans to redecorate my cell, because I'll be here for some time."

"That's what I like about you," he said. "You're always quick to grasp the implications."

SEVENTEEN

Sleep is one of the great constants in life, and little difference exists between the darkness of one sleep and the next. When the lights of my cell went out, with all the lights in all the other cells, the silence was forced, the smells foreign, and the bed hostile, but I closed my eyes to the same familiar darkness behind my eyelids that greeted me wherever I closed my eyes, and uncounted minutes later I drifted into the same suspended state of being where the same dreams and nightmares flashed amid fields of blankness. Sleep is the one escape the authorities can't prevent, and in dreams resides the sole opportunity to experience the unpredictable. In sleep, the inmate is just as free as anyone else.

The 5:00 A.M. wake-up call is a brutal reminder that sleep is a temporary refuge. They give you fifteen minutes to shake reality into your head, slip into your overalls, and stand by the door. The door bolts open and you step into the corridor, where you turn and move in single file to bathroom and breakfast. Breakfast consists of toast and scrambled eggs. Both are tasteless but edible. If you have a court date, a deputy collects you after you eat. You change into the clothes you wore when arrested. If your lawyer brought a fresh change of clothing, something less likely to scare the hell out of a judge or jury than the togs you were arrested in, you put on those. You pull the overalls over your court clothes. The bright orange marks you as a prisoner every moment except the few you'll spend standing before the judge.

Other deputies take control of you in the subbasement. If you're one of the dangerous ones, they shackle you. I was one of the dangerous ones. The steps I took were short and careful. They measure the chains at your ankles by the height of the steps to the transportation van. You can take one step at a time. No more. They loaded me into the van first. I sat at the end of the bench running along the side of the van. Seven prisoners were loaded in after me. All were shackled. All were dangerous. The deputies slammed and bolted the rear doors. The prisoner compartment contained no windows. I felt the van lurch into gear and move forward. The trip offered no escape, no stimulus different from that of my cell. Nobody said anything. We had been there before. We knew there was nothing to say until the events of the day determined our fates.

After uncounted minutes, a change in angle shifted us toward the front of the van, and by that I knew we ramped down the garage below the Los Angeles County Courthouse. I felt the centrifugal force of a sweeping turn, the change of gears to reverse, a pump of brake to freeze the wheels. The rear doors cracked open. A new set of deputies flanked the corridor, indistinguishable from the previous set. They loaded and unloaded prisoners eight hours a day. We looked indistinguishable to them, too. We shuffled down a concrete corridor to a holding tank in the courthouse basement. We waited. One by one, we were called from the tank. The deputies removed our shackles and we stepped out of our overalls. We rode a secure elevator from the basement, passed through a back corridor, and walked, upright and in our own clothes, into a courtroom. We could see friends and family then, watching us from the gallery. We might smile at each other, if feeling hopeful. It was as close to freedom as many of us would come for a long time.

Belinsky stood and greeted me like a friend when the deputy escorted me into the courtroom. The gesture was a theatrical one, meant to humanize me in the eyes of the judge. More eloquently than words, the gesture said I was not a killer, a thief, or a thug. He led me to the table for defense counsel, arm wrapped protectively over my shoulder. "Somebody pulled the tablecloth from beneath the prosecutor's neatly laid table," he said. His chin pointed at a navy-blue-suited woman who stood at the back of the courtroom going face-to-face with a burly and balding sheriff deputy. "Right now I suspect she's counting the china, trying to decide if she has enough dishes left to host the party."

He squeezed my hand. The prosecutor was striding down the aisle. When Belinsky greeted her by name she flashed her teeth in what looked to be a compromise between a smile and snarl. She wanted to talk to him for a moment, she said. Did he mind stepping over to the prosecutor's table while she checked her case file? It looked like business as usual to me. Belinsky liked to hide his intentions behind the folksy manner of a cracker-barrel philosopher, one of those country-porch sitters who can talk anybody into thinking left is right and right is upside-down. It was an act. He had degrees from UC Berkeley and Bolt, the requisite Mercedes, and a mansion in Hancock Park. Juries adored him. Sometimes, he just plain confused me.

I glanced at the gallery. The four rows behind the railing were packed shoulder to shoulder with friends and relatives of the inmates to be arraigned that morning. Arraignments do not run by precise schedule, and those attending in support of an inmate arrive early and stay until the case is called. The process is brisk, with no more than fifteen minutes spent on each case. None of the relatives or friends in the gallery was mine. I gave a nod to a reporter from the *Times*. A consummate professional, he stared through me. Frank sat in the second row with a green-haired man I recognized as a rival freelance photographer at *Scandal Times*. It had taken Frank less than twenty-four hours to replace me. They took alternate turns making notations on a sheet of paper between them. Frank noticed that I watched and hoisted the paper above his head. They were playing hangman, the word game where failed guesses draw gallows and victim. The victim was a stick figure with a camera around her neck. Frank smiled at me. She was fully hung.

The bailiff called out the case number above the background clatter of shifting chairs and conversation, and the judge whacked her gavel, once, not bothering to lift her eyes from the surface of the bench, where she marked something with flicks of a gold-plated pen.

Belinsky slid behind the table for defense counsel and shook his head, annoyed by something. The judge lifted her gaze from the notes on her desk and asked the prosecutor to proceed. She didn't look at me. I was one of fifteen inmates to be marched before her bench that morning. She needed to glance through the evidence documenting the charge against me, ask how I planned to plead, and listen to the prosecutor and defense counsel bicker the question of bail. As bail was out of the question in my case, her job was straightforward. She didn't need to look at me. She asked the attorney for the prosecution to begin.

The prosecutor asked to approach the bench. Belinsky made a big show of tightening his bolo tie and slicking down his hair as he skirted the defense table to join her before the bench. The prosecutor straightened the back of her skirt with a practiced hand, the type of person concerned that her panty line might show from behind as she spoke to the judge. Belinsky listened, delivered a succinctly angry point, listened again, then said something that made the judge laugh. Even the prosecutor smiled a little. In the gallery behind me, other inmates' relatives and friends whispered among themselves and shuffled back and forth from the bathrooms. Unless you're directly concerned with the outcome, arraignments are a bore.

The prosecutor stuffed a file into an accordion briefcase and announced, "The state of California declines to bring charges against the defendant based on the evidence presented."

The judge whacked her gavel and ordered that the defendant be released. The defendant. Me. I grabbed Belinsky's arm, asked, "What's going on here?"

"That's the last magic trick your Detective Claymore will try for some time to come. The rabbit he pulled out of the hat turned into a skunk."

"The witness?"

"He's done what skunks do when pulled out of a hat."

"What happened?"

"Three months ago your fitness-enthusiast witness was busted for selling ecstasy at a rave in Calabasas, that's what happened."

"Criminals give eyewitness testimony all the time," I said. "That's never stopped the prosecution before."

"It's difficult to build a case around the eyewitness testimony of someone who sells mind-altering drugs for a living, but something else stayed the prosecution's hand, something related to your Detective Claymore."

"He was the arresting officer," I guessed.

He shook his head, eyebrows furrowed in a look of comic disappointment. "Someone at the rave thought it would be fun to turn a parked convertible into a bonfire. The explosion sent three kids to the emergency room."

"Claymore took the arson call."

"Not only took the call, interrogated the kid about the fire. The kid was carrying his stash, stoned out of his mind. You know the type, buys ten hits of this, ten hits of that, sells enough to make his money back, swallows the rest. He wasn't a bad kid. A nineteen-year-old philosophy student at CSU Northridge. The kid's lawyer got him a suspended sentence."

"Meaning if he got busted again he'd catch not only the new charge but the full weight of the suspended sentence."

"And the courts are much tougher on repeat offenders, don't forget. You can fill in the dots from here, can't you?"

"Claymore rousts the kid. The kid is carrying again, and if he's not, a bag of something mysteriously finds its way into his pocket. Claymore gives him a choice. Two pops on possession with intent to sell, that's a ten-year fall. Or say you were hiking up Encinal Canyon last Thursday, saw a woman who matched my description carrying a gas can away from a Cadillac convertible."

"Is that really the way you think it happened?"

I said I did.

"All you ex-cons are the same. Cynical. No faith in the law."

"Why should we have faith in the law? Everybody I knew in prison was innocent, and yet every single one of us had been convicted."

I have no doubt that more than half of Belinsky's clients were guilty not only as charged but of a hundred other crimes at which they hadn't been caught. He appreciated the humor. I said, "What I don't understand is why he thought he could get away with it."

"Nine times out of ten he would have. If you'll pardon me for pointing this out, you look like the kind of person who might need a court-appointed lawyer. Detective Claymore had every expectation that you would be represented by an overworked, underresourced, and underpaid public defender who would plea-bargain you back to prison or sleep through half the proceedings. The system runs on money, pure and simple. You can't necessarily buy yourself a verdict of not guilty, but without dedicated legal representation, you're standing in the way of a steamroller with nothing more formidable in your hands than your own sweet ass, which you can kiss good-bye."

I began to thank him. He told me I wasn't as quick as he'd given me credit for, I'd missed the point. "I'm answering your question regarding why Detective Claymore thought he could get away with it, not why, in fact, he did not. Those are two entirely different things. I didn't do a doggone thing to help you this morning except show up for work. Sure, I bent the ear of the prosecutor and gave the judge a giggle, but I'm not the one who tracked down the witness's arrest record. I'm not the one you should thank."

"Then who?"

"Your friend Frank Adams. As a tabloid journalist he may be lower than the teats on a snake but when he puts his mind to it he's one hell of an investigative reporter."

Eighteen

You don't go home after court, no matter what the verdict. Guilty, innocent, or uncharged, you're returned to the courthouse holding pen. You step back into the overalls. You wait until the morning session is finished. The deputies come for you after the last case has been heard. They don't come to release you. If you were transported to the courthouse in shackles, you leave in shackles. The deputies treat you no differently than when you arrived, even if the judge has thrown all charges out of court, even if you're innocent. You're meat on the hoof, to be moved from one point to another. The inmates who came with you follow you into the van. Some have been arraigned and others tried and sentenced. The return trip to the Twin Towers is not silent. "Fifteen years!" An inmate shouts. "Can you fucking believe that? Fifteen fucking years!" The caged dome light in the prisoner compartment flickers. You can't see anybody's face. "That fucking bastard," another moans again and again. She never says who.

No link exists between the computer systems in the Los Angeles County Courthouse and the Twin Towers. The process depends on slips of paper carried by transportation deputies. The slips of paper document which prisoners have been released from the jurisdiction of the court and which have been ordered to serve time in the peni-

tentiary, the only two ways out of the Twin Towers, other than escape
and death. When the transportation van returns you to the Twin Towers, the deputies log you back into the system by scanning your identity bracelet. A deputy escorts you to your cell. You wait. If you're
lucky, record of the verdict will be entered into the central database
of the L.A. County Jail, and within twenty-four hours a deputy will
bolt back the cell door and escort you to the Inmate Reception Center, where your keys, purse, wallet, clothes, and all other personal possessions will be returned to you, and you will be processed out. If not,
the slip of paper recording your release from the jurisdiction of the
courts will be misplaced or lost, and days later, sometimes weeks, the
administrative error will be corrected, and they'll release you then.
Nothing you say will make a difference. It is given that every prisoner
is a liar. Only time, patience, and a good lawyer can help you. I was
one of the lucky ones. I had a good lawyer.

The plastic bracelet that identified me as an inmate of the Twin Towers was clipped from my wrist eight hours after all charges were
dropped. One final security door bolted open and I walked free into the
night. The citizens loitering on the sidewalk beyond the release point
didn't look much different from the inmates I'd just left. That they
looked alike made sense. Some were family. Others were friends into the
same things that got those inside arrested. Some were predators: pimps
and dealers ready to welcome the released back onto the ride to
nowhere. Some had been inside minutes before, newly released inmates
with no one to greet them and nowhere to go. These stood uncertainly
by the curb, afraid that the entire course of their lives hinged on whether
they veered left or right and knowing that choice was most likely between a bad end and a worse one. One of those waiting by the curb was
big and black. His happiness distinguished him from the others. He
pranced on the sidewalk, tongue rolling from a broad, toothless smile. I
called to him and he charged forward, standing on his hind legs at the
last to see me better. I let the Rott lick my face and though I haven't
shed tears in sorrow for five long years I nearly cried then for joy.

Ben nodded once, his sunglassed expression inscrutable. I said,
"Thanks for coming to pick me up."

"I'm retired. Got nothing else to do. They feed you well enough in
there?"

"They fed me. If I didn't eat, it's my own fault."

"Get in the car, you'll find a little something."

I opened the sack on the front seat to a hamburger from In-N-Out. The Rott nestled against my legs, eyes expectant.

"Don't give him much. He already ate plenty." Ben cased his sunglasses and started the car. Wearing sunglasses on the street at night was one thing, while driving another. "Arlanda flew back to Arizona late this afternoon. Otherwise, she'd have been here."

"Time to get back to her kids?" I bit into the hamburger to conceal my disappointment. I'd wanted to see her. The Rott nudged my arm. I tore off a chunk of meat and fed it to him.

"Angela's funeral is tomorrow afternoon. Sorry. Didn't get that right. Her memorial service. People don't have funerals these days. Arlanda wants you to come."

"I'm not sure I belong there."

"Arlanda is. She offered to pay your ticket, you want to fly."

"What do you think?"

"I think she wouldn't offer if she didn't mean it. I don't think she understands how complicated it is for you to travel, though."

"I wouldn't want to go without the dog. Maybe I can drive out. But I need to talk to my parole officer first, get permission. It's one of the conditions of my parole. I can't cross the state line."

"I know where she is right now, you want to drop by."

"You mean Terry Graves?"

"That's the name, all right."

"How come you know where my parole officer is?"

"I know how the system works."

I guessed that meant he wanted me to go to the funeral. His opinion shouldn't have meant anything. He was an ex-cop. I was an ex-con. Cats and dogs. But it did.

A mid-rise around the corner from Inglewood City Hall housed the Region III parole office. It was an ugly building, smoked-glass windows winking from a concrete-and-stucco facade, but it didn't stick out because the neighboring buildings were just as ugly. The intersection of two avenues a few numbers down hummed with the last of rush-hour traffic. I stepped out of the Blazer and looked up. A passenger jet sliced across the sky ahead of the sound of its engines, descending to Los Angeles International Airport five miles to the west. The parole office had been the first stop after my release from prison. That's one of the conditions of parole. You have to see your parole officer within three days of release. After the first visit, she comes to your place of residence or work. I hadn't been back since my first visit. The building hadn't looked so ugly to me then, but on that first day an abandoned lot festooned with bits of torn paper and plastic had looked like a field of wildflowers.

Terry Graves appeared behind the swinging glass at the entrance. She carried a leather satchel the size of a Pony Express bag strapped over her shoulder. Ben had called from his mobile phone to warn her we were coming.

"You're working late. I hope it's not just because of me," I said.

She let the door swing shut behind her and stepped toward the street, heels clicking on concrete. "I work late every night." She flapped an envelope between thumb and forefinger, stopped at the curb, and pivoted. "Every time one of my charges gets punched back to prison they send me two more in her place."

I took the envelope, peeked at the seal of the state of California on the release form inside, said, "You don't like your job, get a different one."

"Tough to go back to a regular job after the excitement of working with junkies, whores, and killers."

"Hey, I represent that remark."

She smiled. "That's an old joke."

"Sure, but you laughed anyway."

"My job, it's a little short on humor. I'm a cheap laugh."

"Did you think I did it?"

"You mean set the fire?"

I nodded.

Her eyes flitted away. "It doesn't matter what I think."

"It does to me."

"No, I didn't think you did it. Claymore was an incompetent investigator. The charge was bullshit." Her eyes turned on me, hard and unforgiving. "But do I think you're capable of violating the terms of your parole? Yes. Are you still capable of committing a criminal act as bad or worse than the ones that got you imprisoned in the first place? In my judgment, yes. Yes and yes. Most of my charges, they're whores and drug addicts. They're victims. Some people call prostitution and drug abuse victimless crimes. Bullshit. The victims of prostitution are the whores themselves, just as junkies are the true victims of drug abuse. But not you. You're not a victim. Maybe once you were. But not now. Most of my charges, they're not violent to anyone except themselves. Give them a gun, they'll blow their own brains out. But not you. Put you in the wrong situation and give you a gun, you'll shoot somebody."

Nothing much I could say to that. She was right. The problem was, I wouldn't want to be any other way. "You've been fair to me, Ms. Graves. I owe you for that."

"I'm doing my job. You don't owe me anything. The person you owe is yourself. And if you screw up, don't blame the law. Blame yourself."

"Thanks for the advice."

"Anytime," she said.

I walked back to the Blazer, cursing myself for considering her opinions important, for even listening to someone appointed by the law to chain my stride. My curses rang false, because Terry Graves was the only person I'd listened to consistently since I'd been released from prison.

Ben eyed the envelope when I stepped into the car.

"Get your pass?"

"Got my pass."

"She give you a hard time to go with it?"

"Do I look like she gave me a hard time?"

Ben started the engine and pulled into traffic.

"My parole officer is worse than God. She doesn't let me get away with anything. At least God turns a blind eye every now and then."

"It's her job to sit on you, don't forget," he said. "If you don't feel her weight on your back, she's not doing her job."

"If I felt any more weight, I wouldn't be able to stand straight."

I held on to the Rott's neck and squeezed, let his animal warmth

and the hum of tires on asphalt calm me. Ben talked about arrangements for the funeral, how long it would take me to drive out to Douglas, and where I'd stay. I didn't do much to hold up my end of the
conversation, and he must have tired of talking at me, because after a
while he tuned the radio to a country-and-western station.

"You like this music?" he asked.

"Not particularly," I said.

Ben flicked off the radio, and an angry look crossed his face, at least
I thought then it was angry. He said, "You're wrong about God, about
turning a blind eye. I know something about crime, something more
about guilt, and most of all, I know about punishment. God never
turns a blind eye. Everything you do and that's done to you is seared
into your soul. Some people, you don't even have to be God to see
the marks burned into them."

He reached out unexpectedly and touched the lowest scar on the
skin of my forearm, where a man had once methodically stubbed out
a half pack of cigarettes into my skin.

"Sometimes we feel invisible, thinking no one can see who we are
or what we've done. That's wrong. People we don't know by name,
they see us walking down the street, they recognize us, see what kind
of person we are by the way we move, the way we dress. Think about
all the people you know without saying hello to. You get an idea what
most of 'em are about, don't you? We forget that people see us a lot
more often than we see ourselves. We're not invisible, not to somebody who has the time and inclination to look. You don't even have
to look that hard to tell about some people. Some marks, everybody
can see." He moved his hand from my arm and wrapped it around the
steering wheel. "But maybe only God can read what those marks say,
understand what they mean."

He tugged the wheel to the right and pulled the Blazer to the red
zone across from my building, tires squeaking against the curb. I
thanked him for the ride and stepped out of the car. He was right. I
did think myself invisible, at least those hard and dark parts of myself
that shamed and scared me the most. I didn't mind his being right,
because he spoke about himself, too. We were both scarred individuals, and more stoic than might be good for us. As his headlights
washed across my back and down the street, I remembered his con-

fession from two nights before. I had told him very little about myself, nothing that he couldn't have learned from researching the news archives, and just as I approached the steps to my building the car door ahead of me winged into the sidewalk and out stepped Detective Claymore.

"You must feel pretty good about yourself tonight," he said.

The edge of the car door gouged into the concrete on opening, and when he tried to kick the door closed nonchalantly, with the back of his foot, the resistance knocked him off balance. He swore furiously, whirled, and flung it shut with both hands, the violence of his effort throwing him again off balance. When he righted himself a second time, he glowered at me as though I was somehow responsible.

"You think it's funny?"

The Rott growled, his body tensing against my knee. I grabbed his collar and moved toward the steps. Claymore leapt onto the third stair to cut me off. The Rott lunged forward. I clamped his sides between my knees and hitched the leash to his collar.

"Get out of my way," I said.

"Or what? You'll call the police? Or maybe you're planning to loose that toothless dog on me?"

I backed the dog down, away from the stairs. Claymore planted his feet broadly, fists on his hips in a Superman stance, but still he swayed, his head inscribing subtle arcs, like a bumped lightbulb hung from the ceiling on a cord.

"You don't know anything about me or what I'm thinking," I said. "Every time you make a guess about me, it's wrong. No, I don't feel particularly good about myself tonight. No, I don't think anything about you is funny. No, I'm not going to call the police. And no, I'm not going to let my dog anywhere near you. What I am going to do is wait here until you decide to leave."

His unbuttoned sport coat fell open to the butt of an automatic in a holster beneath his left shoulder. "You want to know why I came?"

I let what passes for silence at night in Venice answer for me.

"I came to apologize," he said.

"For what?"

"For misjudging you."

That didn't sound right. I figured he hated me. I never gave him good reason to hate me. His reasons for hating me lay in his head and nowhere else. Those reasons could disappear as capriciously as they appeared. "I understand the way the system works. I was the most logical suspect," I said.

He nodded, as though contrite about it. "You're much more clever than I gave you credit for. I thought you'd set the fire to photograph Ms. Doubleday running to escape and nearly got caught in your own trap, which would be a stupid thing to do. I was wrong about that, and I apologize."

"Apology accepted," I said. I wanted to let him off the hook, if that was what it took to get him out of my life. Give him the dignity of an apology and the illusion that I harbored no resentments.

He wagged his head; I misunderstood. "I was wrong to think you were stupid. It wasn't until this afternoon that I understood how clever you were. Your job gave you a perfect reason to be on the hill, but that wasn't why you were really there, was it?"

"Why else?"

"You set the fire. I'm right about that. But you didn't set the fire to photograph Ms. Doubleday. I was wrong there. You set the fire to kill her."

I backed the dog again, afraid this time I'd be the one to lunge.

"Bingo," he said, then threw his hands into the air as though signaling defeat. "Knew I was right, but I can't prove it now. You're too smart for me. Maybe I'm not as sharp as I used to be. Maybe that's part of the reason you got away with it. Who's in it with you? I know you didn't act alone. It's Doubleday's niece, isn't it?" He glanced up to the sky as though trying to snatch a suspect from the stars. "Arlanda Cortes. Sure, it's her. She's going to be a rich woman now, and you two got so close so fast. Why is that? You can tell me. I've already shot my bolt. Nothing will happen to you."

"You're drunk," I said.

"Tell me the truth!" He stumbled down the stairs, no fear of the dog, no fear of me, but the sound of footsteps brought one steadying hand to the rail while the other discreetly closed the top button to his sport coat.

"She is telling you the truth, Detective."

I took my eyes off Claymore long enough to glance over my shoulder.

The voice was Ben's, and I welcomed the sight of his slow, angry stride with a nod.

"Maybe if you sobered up, you'd see it."

Claymore extended his forefinger and stabbed at the air. "You're the one used to be a patrol deputy, aren't you?"

"And you're the arson investigator who's been dodging my calls since the day of the fire."

Claymore reached a slow hand into the side pocket of his sport coat to withdraw a stick of spearmint gum. He unwrapped the stick carefully, first pulling the green covering apart at the seam and then lifting the corners of the tinfoil, nodding all the while. "You spent how long as a patrol deputy?"

"Twenty-five years."

He folded the stick of gum in half, wedged it between his teeth, and bit down hard. "All those years, and you never made it out of a patrol car. Must have been frustrating, not to mention humbling as hell."

Ben folded his arms across his chest. The comment had been meant to wound him, and maybe it had, but with his arms across his chest and his eyes cloaked in sunglasses, I couldn't tell. "You've already made yourself into an ass, Detective. Don't add a hole to the end of it. Go home. Let the lady do the same."

Claymore's gum popped rapid fire, jaws pounding it to pulp. "My mind's just going now, flat out fast as it can, trying to connect the dots. What's an ex-cop doing with an ex-con? What's the attraction here? Wait a minute." His jaw stalled, the gum a slight bulge in his cheek. Then his teeth flashed white in the streetlight. "I get it now. You're Doubleday's godfather. Any chance you're mentioned in the will?"

"He was written out three months ago," I said, as though that proved something.

"Angry that she wrote you out, aren't you?" He smiled again. He'd already known.

"Don't give a damn," Ben said.

"Wouldn't expect you to admit you did. But it makes a nice motive for murder, doesn't it? Particularly if the niece cuts you into the will on the back end."

"After today, they'll give you just enough time to clean out your desk, so I'm not gonna worry about your wild-ass theories."

"I'm not going anywhere, Deputy, except up the chain of command." Claymore backed a step toward his car. "Twenty-five years and never made it out of a patrol car. That has to be some kind of record, doesn't it? Most cops, they get stuck behind a wheel all those years, they're smart enough to take their twenty years and get out. But you went nowhere for twenty plus five." He opened the door to his cruiser, the gum snapping in his mouth, and pointed at his head. "At least I know who's not the brains of the outfit."

He gunned the engine and jetted from the curb, tires squealing and back end fishtailing down the street, not too drunk to drive but too drunk to drive well.

"Word is, he's going to be placed on administrative review," Ben said. "He won't last out the month."

"Let's hope we live that long," I said.

NINETEEN

The deputy behind the desk of the Cochise County sheriff station took a long look at me when I walked through the door. For a moment, I regretted that I hadn't washed my face and run a brush through my hair to make myself seem more respectable. I'd crossed the border into Arizona at sunrise, the Colorado River flowing blood-red below me, and the couple hours of road sleep I'd managed on a highway spur outside of Yuma hadn't much refreshed me. Then I noticed the decor. On the wall at the far end of the lobby hung the portraits of county sheriffs past, twelve of them dating back to the early twentieth century, all hard men who looked like the only smile they enjoyed was a rictus one. Little wonder the deputy stared at me. He didn't have much else to look at. Pinned to the border between Arizona and Sonora, Mexico, he probably didn't see many women walk into the station, let alone ones with a nose stud and six hundred miles of road dust. He was young and beefy, about two hundred pounds and not an ounce of it hair. He didn't look at me the same way L.A. cops did either. His glance was less wary and a lot more curious. I flashed my press pass.

"You here to cover the memorial service?"

"Yes, sir, I am." I slipped the parolee release form from its envelope and laid it flat on the desk. "My parole officer told me I should check in with you first thing."

He twisted his head sideways to read the print, and when he finished, he read it a second time. When he felt sure he had it, he looked at me again, still curious. "Okay," he said. "Good thing you stopped by." He carefully copied my name on a pad of paper. "What did they put you away for?"

"Manslaughter."

He thought that over. Manslaughter covered a wide range of crimes. I could have killed my husband with a thrown flowerpot, missed the apple low when playing William Tell, or chased a car going sixty miles per hour into a gas pump.

"Voluntary or involuntary?"

"Voluntary."

He thought that over, too. "Drug related?"

"The only drugs I have any use for are ibuprofen and hard alcohol."

"Okay, then." That was apparently what he wanted to know. Not too many felons come to Douglas to rob the bank. "Where you going to be staying?"

"The Gadsden Hotel."

"It's full up, I hear. You have a reservation?"

"A friend made one for me."

"Okay, then." He wrote the hotel down next to my name. "Keep yourself out of trouble."

As though I'd come to town looking for it.

I found Ben sitting on a stool at the Saddle and Spur, the Gadsden Hotel's house bar, his back straight and a bottle of Corona standing slope shouldered next to an empty glass. I'd come into the bar through the lobby, startled to find a magnificent turn-of-the-century hotel with a white marble staircase and stained glass ceiling in a town that looked like it would have trouble supporting a Motel 6. The Gadsden seemed far too grand for Douglas, except for the few telling details that pinned it in place, such as the row of cowboy codgers sitting on the lobby furniture and the mountain lion stuffed at the top of the stairs, which had been shot, a brass plaque read, by the hotel proprietress.

"The old Gadsden, she's got quite a history," Ben said, dipping his head at the bartender to order another beer. "She was first built during the days of Pancho Villa, before Arizona became a state. You see the marble staircase?"

I nodded.

"Imported all the way from Italy. Douglas was an important town when the copper mines were booming. The original hotel, she burned down in the '20s. The owners rebuilt, bigger and better, and some time after the mines failed they discovered not all their guests were strictly living."

I said, "Huh?"

"This place is haunted. You didn't know that?"

I said I didn't.

"One night, when I was a kid, I spent the night beneath one of the tables in the restaurant. A buddy of mine, he dared me, so I said, *Fine, I'll do it*. The only ghosts I saw were a couple of drunken guests with sheets over their heads, trying to scare the hell out of each other. Maybe that's the secret. If I drink enough tonight, maybe I'll finally see one. You believe in ghosts?"

"I have a hard enough time believing in the living, let alone the dead."

"Maybe we'll both get smashed tonight, see some ghosts. What you drinking?"

The bartender cracked a bottle of Corona, set it on the bar, looked at me like I was just another thirsty cowgirl. That's one of the things I like most about bartenders; as a breed, they're nonjudgmental.

"Just coffee," I told him.

Ben said, "Since when did you join the sisters of sobriety?"

"I didn't get more than two hours' road sleep. If I start drinking now, I won't make it through the memorial service."

He hid a bitter grin behind the lip of the bottle and just before he sipped said, "I should be so lucky."

I pulled the Nikon from my camera bag, thinking about Ben and why he dreaded the service. When I focused on his face the expression wasn't friendly.

"Don't point that thing at me."

"You nervous?"

"Just camera shy."

"I mean about being here. About the memorial service."

"I hate this town. Just hate it."

Pain fused with anger in the glance he turned to me. I took his photograph, the parabolic lens bending the bar away from him like a reflection in a mirrored globe.

"What's to hate? A few streets, the desert, an old hotel? It's not like L.A., where it's hard to pick out what you hate the most, because there's so much to choose from. There's not much here to react against."

"Other than a good hotel, that's about all this town has. Nothing. Plenty of that to go around. You like nothing? This town's for you."

"At least it's quiet."

"So's the grave."

"You got out, didn't you?"

"I'm back now."

His bitterness surprised me. He was sixty-something. I thought people were supposed to mellow with age. It didn't leave me hopeful about my own future. I said, "People know what happened between you and Pete?"

"It's a small town," he said. "I'd be surprised if people didn't."

"You still know anybody here?"

He raised his glass to his own reflection in the bar, said, "Just ghosts." He took a long swallow, but his thirst must have abandoned him, because he asked for the bill and left the beer half finished on the bar. I followed him out to his car, parked on the town's main drive. Black ribbons festooned the lampposts and swaths of black crepe paper hung from the balconies. Many of the windows bore messages of condolence to Doubleday's family and appreciation for her contributions to the town. In a few places, residents confused by tradition had tied yellow ribbons instead of black ones, but even that error seemed heartfelt.

"How long before Halloween?" Ben asked.

"Less than a week," I said.

"In a couple of days, they'll string up some orange to go with the black, won't have to change decorations hardly at all."

He drove briskly, looking neither left nor right except when safety required it, as though willing himself to see as little of the town as possible. He turned once off G Avenue, once again onto a street of aging tract homes, took that about a half mile, and pulled to the side. A half dozen cars clustered near the end of the block, where the street ended and the desert began. We stepped out of the car. That time of the year the afternoon sun still burned hot, and the air smelled of baked earth and rock. I let the Rott patrol ahead of us and followed Ben toward a house with cars parked in front. Like her neighbors, Arlanda lived in a single-story cinder-block ranch house with an attached garage and a white-rock on tar-paper roof. Prickly pear and cholla cacti ranged across the dirt front yard, with rocks carried from the desert scattered among the cacti in an arrangement that might have been intentional. Cinder block marked the boundary between her property and the street. Sidewalks didn't exist in the neighborhood because, presumably, nobody was fool enough to walk in weather hot enough to fry a lizard more than six months out of the year.

A little boy answered Ben's knock. His black hair was short and he'd gelled it straight up, like exclamation points. The moment he saw Ben he twisted around and yelled to his mom. Ben grabbed the door-knob and lowered himself onto his heels, and when the boy turned around again he gave him a punch on the arm and a candy bar. "Don't tell your mom I gave it to you, all right?"

The boy's smile revealed a couple of teeth missing. It was a real Norman Rockwell moment. Ben pulled himself straight, knees creaking all the way up, and that was when the boy saw the dog. At first, the size of the Rott scared him. He stepped back and half hid behind the door. Then he looked up at me, asked, "You the dog lady?"

I'd been called a lot of things before and not all of them complimentary, but never that. "You want to say hello to my dog? His name's Baby."

The name offended the boy. "He's no baby. He's bigger'n I am."

"You're smart. You play with him awhile, you'll figure out why I call him Baby." I grabbed the Rott by the collar and followed Ben inside. Anybody who grew up around tract housing could have followed the floor plan blindfolded. Bedrooms off the hall to the left of the entry, living room to the right, kitchen straight ahead. Arlanda met us at the entrance to the kitchen. As Doubleday's closest relative, the town gathered around her for the memorial service, and since late morning friends and neighbors had been dropping by the house with food, drink, and the quiet companionship that marks a funeral crowd. Arlanda had dressed her muted best, in a flowing black midcalf skirt, long-sleeved silk blouse, and loosely woven cotton shawl that matched the skirt. It wasn't until the introductions were nearly complete that I noticed another boy hiding behind the skirt—her youngest. I knelt to his level and introduced him to the dog. The older boy dared closer then, overcoming his fear if only to impress his younger brother. After a few minutes of careful approach and retreat, they understood the dog wouldn't intentionally hurt them, and following Arlanda's suggestion, I let them out in the backyard to play. Like most dogs, the Rott responded to the boys' frenetic energy with equal enthusiasm.

Ben disengaged himself soon after the introductions and stood in front of the television set, pretending to be interested in the blank screen. Arlanda's friends and neighbors perked up when they learned what I did for a living, wanted to know about this celebrity or that. I didn't tell them that almost everyone I photographed hated my guts. After a while I looked for Ben again and saw him out back, playing with the kids and dog.

The memorial service was held before the altar where Angela Doubleday had been baptized, in a brick church glowing red against the blue Arizona sky. The church had been built when copper made the town prosperous and thankful, and to a size that seemed optimistically large on most Sundays but was welcome that afternoon, with mourners and the curious packing the benches and spilling into the aisles. Most of the people attending hadn't seen Doubleday in thirty years, if at all, Ben said. I stood at the back and watched him file into the front pew next to Arlanda and the boys, the spot her husband would have taken had he stuck around. I wondered briefly whether he would return now that she was soon to become the richest woman in Cochise County and whether she would take him back if he did. I doubted she would. Few things expand the horizons like a fat bank account.

Maria and Yolanda sat in the second row, wearing black as though born to it, trapping a scrubbed and sober Lupe between them. Arlanda reached over the back of the pew and shook the hand of each one, beginning with Maria. In the car Ben had told me that she had flown them in for the service, paying for it out of her expected share of the estate. Troy Davies left his seat at the end of a row across the aisle and solemnly greeted the two boys, then clasped Arlanda's hand in both of his and whispered his condolences. Her eyes never left his face while he spoke, forgetting, for the moment, her resentment over his share of the inheritance. I couldn't blame her for staring. Troy would be the best-looking man in any crowd, even though he had all the substance of a film set. He snubbed Ben, who stared the other way and pretended not to notice.

The mourners took their seats and the organ music faded. The previous week I'd been invading Angela Doubleday's privacy with a five-hundred-millimeter lens. I didn't belong at her memorial service. I hadn't been to church in twenty years, and even back then, we weren't a church-going family. I believed in God or, more accurately, had a notion of something people have called God over the millennia, but still I felt a fraud being there. When the pastor began to read Scripture, I slipped out the door and took the Rott for a walk.

The cemetery where Angela Doubleday's ashes were to be interred rested at the edge of town, open to the winds sweeping from the desert and to whatever creatures followed the wind. Beyond the cypress trees that lined the entrance, the graveyard spread barren of any living thing, the earth too hard and dry to support a single twig of green. The crypt Doubleday had built for her family towered above the humble population of graves like a temple, its columns and pediment carved from a rose-colored granite that glowed when struck by the rays of the setting sun. The crypt straddled the Protestant and

Catholic sections of the cemetery, which otherwise were as strictly segregated as any living people divided by race and religion. Gray granite tombstones studded the Protestant section to one side of the crypt, the names chiseled into the prosperous stone testifying to English, Irish, and German heritage. The Catholics were mostly Mexican-Americans, their graves marked by simple crosses, often constructed from metal pipe and decorated by riotous displays of plastic flowers, ribbons, and balloons. Along the border with Mexico, to be a dead Catholic was a more festive affair than to be a dead Protestant.

The interment was meant to be a private ceremony but it proved impossible to control admittance to a cemetery open on three sides to anyone who wished to walk in, and as the location and time of the ceremony were open secrets known to everyone in Cochise County, the number of unofficial mourners easily tripled the invited. The ceremony was short. The pastor read Scripture and led the crowd in prayer. The fire that killed Angela Doubleday reduced her to splinters of bone and teeth, and so what little remained of her had been formally cremated and placed in a copper-and-cloisonné urn. The urn was engraved with red and yellow flowers that might have been orchids. It seemed too handsome to be shut inside a crypt but I'm sure Arlanda, who had made most of the arrangements, wanted each detail to honor her aunt. Arlanda's mother and father were interred there too, and as she lifted the urn to the vault reserved for it, I'm sure she was thinking that her own remains would one day rest beside them.

I stood amid the sun-bleached plastic flowers of the Catholic graves, away from the crowd yet near enough to hear the reading of Scripture. When everyone bowed their heads and closed their eyes in prayer I figured I could pray just as well with my eyes open. I framed a group shot of the mourners huddled before the mausoleum and clicked the shutter. Troy Davies kept his eyes open too. He hadn't noticed me until then, or at least hadn't made a show of it. Tears streamed from his eyes, and though I've heard actors often use glycerin drops to simulate emotion, his seemed real enough. The pastor led the crowd in a final amen, told us to go in peace and to go with God. Ben and Arlanda embraced. Other mourners in the crowd turned to each other and shook hands in condolence and good fellowship.

Not Troy Davies. He broke from the crowd, zigzagging through the tombstones to get to me. He tried to keep his voice to a low hiss but he'd trained as an actor and spoke as loud as a stage whisper. "You have incredible nerve to show up here!"

I put my eye to the lens again and snapped his picture. That may not have been the wisest thing to do but it's what I do for a living and I do it naturally. He must have thought he was Sean Penn because that was when he tried to hit me. Sean Penn can punch; Davies couldn't. I took a step back and watched his fist do a flyby. Ben charged from the blind side and wrapped Davies' arms but not his mouth.

"You were arrested for Angela's murder, and you have the gall to show up at her service?"

His voice wasn't a whisper then.

Ben told him to control himself.

"You were on the hill that day, weren't you? You work for that cheap tabloid, the one that wouldn't let her live in peace. And to think I let you interview me! Have you no shame? The lady is dead! You can't take her picture now!"

"She's invited," Ben said. "She's a friend of the family."

"What are you talking about?"

Ben explained it to him again.

"But the police arrested her!"

"They made a mistake," Ben said.

The muscles at the base of Davies' throat relaxed and as the fight left him his shoulders sagged. Ben asked if he could control himself, and when Davies nodded, he let him go, warning me with a look to back off. I held my hands up, palms forward, the camera dangling innocently from my neck. Davies shuffled his feet on the packed earth, brushing the wrinkles from the coat of his suit. He didn't look me in the eye, focusing instead on my camera, as though it represented all the evil in the world. "I don't know how you got yourself invited, but I respect the wishes of the family." He turned his shoulder, about to leave, but he was too angry to let it go. "You're still a cheap camera snoop. Angela would have hated you."

I might have answered him, but he was right. She would have despised me, and I probably shouldn't have attended either service. He didn't want to hear what I had to say anyway. He hurried off alone, probably believing he was the only one there who really mourned her death. He might have been right in thinking that, too. I caught Arlanda's eye and shrugged. She gathered her sons to her side and moved away.

I felt a gentle punch on my arm and turned to the first smile I'd seen on Ben's face all day. He said, "Looks like you're even less popular in this town than I am."

"You like that, don't you?"

"I sure do." He wrapped my shoulder with his arm, said, "What do you say we go scare up some ghosts."

Douglas was a drinker's town, with a half dozen bars on its main street, and so the doors to the Saddle and Spur creaked open and shut like a metronome, with people coming in from the street for a quick one and others stepping out to try the next bar down. A funeral crowd claimed most of the tables, though it was hardly a solemn or quiet one; the locals, many still in their church clothes, had turned garrulous with drink. They had lost a living icon and gained a dead one and so had much to talk about but little to mourn.

Ben and I grabbed a couple of barstools near the taps. The bartender was a good one; busy as he was, he didn't make us wait more than two minutes before asking what we were drinking. I'd left the Rott with Arlanda or, rather, with her kids. He seemed to take naturally to the boys and served as playmate and babysitter while Arlanda greeted those who dropped by her house after the service.

"You don't get angry when you drink, do you?" Ben asked.

"You mean lose my temper, get into fights?"

"It happens with some people."

"Not me. Now my dad, he's a mean drunk. In fact, he's just plain mean."

"I notice you have a mean streak, too."

I looked at him, shocked. "You really think so?"

"You were ready to clock that guy in the cemetery."

"I never took a swing."

"You wanted to."

"I wanted to kick his testicles over the moon, too. But I didn't." When I turned to my drink I glimpsed my reflection in the mirror behind the bar. Even then, six months out of prison, the sight of my reflection startled me as something foreign and defaced. Access to mirrors is strictly controlled in the penitentiary. Sometimes, I forgot what I looked like and expected to see the innocent young blonde I'd been, rather than the raven-haired and pierced virago I'd become, staring back at me.

"Nothing wrong with having a little mean streak," Ben said. "I've got one. Every sheriff deputy who ever put on a badge has one. Got to have a mean streak if you're going to survive on the job. The difference is, you're putting that meanness into serving the law."

"And I'm dedicated to breaking it?"

"Don't get me wrong. You're the nicest, most decent felon I've ever met. But you're more of a law-unto-yourself type."

I signaled the bartender for another round. "I prefer to call it self-reliance."

He thought about that long enough for the drinks to be delivered. "You'll forgive me for giving you a little fatherly advice?"

"All my life I've been waiting for that."

"For what?"

"A little fatherly advice."

"Okay then, here it is." He gripped his drink before him like a shield and stared me straight in the eye. "Don't change. I like you just the way you are."

The remark caught me by surprise. Nobody had said that to me since the days I wore pink lipstick and painted my nails to match, back in the days when I worked at Hansel & Gretel's Baby Portrait Studio and people liked me because I wasn't who I was but who they wanted me to be. I found myself blushing, and I felt an odd swelling in my throat, as though I was about to cry, something I hadn't done in years. I lifted my glass from the bar, clicked it against his, and swallowed the emotion with my drink.

Three drinks into the evening a man strode into the bar from the street, glanced around just long enough to spot Ben at the bar, walked up to him, and said, "I heard this was where you were hiding out, thought somebody should come over and tell you what a low, stinking son of a bitch you are." Black crescent moons cut beneath his nails and dark lines creased the skin between his thumb and forefinger. I'd seen a lot of car mechanics with hands like that. No reason a car mechanic can't be a belligerent drunk looking to pick a fight with a stranger, but the man's anger seemed more particular than that.

Ben sat straight-backed on his stool, watching the man's reflection between the bottles in the mirror behind the bar. "Glad to hear your opinion, son. Now you've stated it, your business is done."

A lock of hair spilled down the man's brow when he shook his head. "If you weren't so fucking old I'd kick your ass."

There was a brief, violent time in my life when I might have broken my whiskey glass on his face, but I've matured since then. I pulled the Nikon from my bag and slid off the stool. He glanced at me when I moved. Only natural. But he wasn't afraid of me. I was a girl, right? I was supposed to get out of the way. The pupils of his eyes were big as eclipsed moons, and thick blood vessels veined the whites. He'd probably had a few to bolster his courage. I powered up the flash attachment with a flick of my thumb and fired it into his eyes. A good paparazza bobs and weaves like a middleweight because movement attracts the eye of the subject and makes you harder to hit if the subject objects. The first shot flashed into his brain like a fireball and the second blinded him.

"Beautiful, baby, just fabulous," I said, giving him the full routine, patter and all. "You're just what we're looking for, a little local color. We're doing a piece in next Sunday's issue of *Scandal Times* comparing people to animals. Would you mind if we put your portrait next to a picture of a jackass? That's right, look this way—beautiful!"

He flung his arm up to his eyes after the third flash, stumbled back, and nearly toppled over a chair. That made him mad at me, too. "You do that one more time and I'm gonna take that camera away from you."

"You're welcome to try," I said, and when he lowered his arm I fired the flash again. "Then my publication can sue you, your boss, your boss's boss, and run so many lawyers down your throat you'll be gagging on court dates for the rest of your life."

I was smart enough to be standing at the opposite end of a table then, because he was big enough to do serious damage if he caught me. But he wasn't going to catch me. He'd come to pick a fight with a man and instead faced a weird-looking girl with a flash camera. It wasn't going the way he'd planned it in his head while he was drinking a few to get his courage up. Had he really wanted to fight me, he could have come over the table and the backs of those around it, but I wasn't the one he wanted. I could see how he'd find the situation confusing. It took him some time, shielding his eyes with his palm as he tried to process the information, but soon enough he figured out what to do.

"You're not wanted here." He pointed his finger at Ben, who remained seated at the bar, and then at me. "And you aren't either. Get the hell out, the both of you, while you can still walk." He showed us how to do that by walking out the door himself.

The bartender got a fresh drink to me by the time I reached the bar. When I reached for it I saw my hands were shaking. I drank it down like the sedative it was and nodded for another. Ben stared straight ahead, watching the room in the mirror behind the bar. I packed the camera in my bag. Neither of us spoke for some time, though everyone else in the bar did, conversations booming loud and fast. A little threatened violence always excites a crowd.

"Nothing worse than a lippy, pushy broad," Ben finally said. "You scared the hell out of him."

"Any idea who he was?"

"Pete had some brothers. Probably one of their brood."

"A nephew? But Pete died over forty years ago. The guy who came in here, he wasn't even born yet."

"People around here hold grudges a long time. Forty years is nothing to a small town. People don't have much else to do. Hating fills the time."

I said, "It seemed a little undignified, a man your age in a bar fight."

"Ten years ago I could have taken a guy like that down, no problem. Now, I don't know. I still know the moves. I'm just too old to do them anymore. Your courage starts to waver when you get old, too.

I'm not as flexible. My balance isn't as good. Speed? Forget it. And my bones feel brittle. It's a different thing, going into a fight knowing you'll break something even if you take your opponent down. I got to admit, though, it took guts to take his picture like that. He could have hit you."

We drank to that and a dozen other things, Ben's ramrod spine softening by the fifth drink and wilting completely by his tenth. When the bar emptied out, just past 2:00 A.M., he sat hunched over the dregs of his last drink, ready to call it a night, his ghosts forgotten. He'd outdrunk me two to one toward the end. I slid off the stool to walk him into the hotel lobby. I felt high more than drunk, my mind clear and thoughts lucid, even if my tongue thickened trying to express them and my feet moved less nimbly than my tongue. We shook hands solemnly at the steps, and I waited until he'd climbed halfway to the first floor before I decided he'd be okay. Nothing I could say or do would prevent the rigors of the following morning's hangover, but I thought fresh air might do me some good, and so I pushed out the front doors of the Gadsden Hotel to work on walking a straight line.

It had been some time since I'd been under an open desert sky at night. The marine air obscures the stars at the beach like a thick glass bowl, dulling the edges of the bright ones and blotting out the distant, dim ones entirely. The dry desert air puts nothing between the eye and the stars except space, and even that is black and lustrous and more alive than not. Every sector of the desert sky swarms with stars, bright clusters of flickering light small and large, distant and near, as though space was a ragged curtain thrown between this world and the vibrant, pulsating energy of another. I never believed in the image of God the Father, a fable allowed to those whose lives have been blessed by a decent and caring father who, no matter how demanding or stern, would protect good children who honored and obeyed. If I believed in any God at all, it was a God of light, and I wondered, as I roamed the streets of Douglas, my head tilted toward the stars, how differently I might believe if I had a less violent and capricious father, if my father had instead been someone like Ben. I did not idealize Ben. He was chased by demons, and I'd seen him blasted by guilt and self-doubt. But he believed in a code of right and wrong, of justice and injustice, of good people and bad, and the power of redemption to bridge the two. Like most decent beings he could love others as much as himself because he didn't hold himself or his sufferings in such high regard. No matter how hard the world hit him or he hit himself, he got back to his feet, because he believed that strength of character was a prime virtue in the world, and though it might be wise and just at times to yield, the honorable never gave up. I never asked for a perfect father, but a tough and caring one might have made all the difference. Then I began to laugh, because that was like wanting to be six foot tall and pretty as a beauty queen; no amount of wanting would make it so. Wanting what I couldn't have was the surest route to misery I knew.

I made sure to drink three glasses of water from the bathroom sink before collapsing onto the covers. Alcohol dehydrates the body, making a bad hangover worse, and unless I'm too drunk to care, I make a point of downing several glasses after a night of drinking. What goes in must come out, and about two hours later it flushes through my system with enough force to lift me from the ruins of sleep. I was neither awake nor asleep when a scratching sound lured me toward consciousness. I thought at first that a rodent rustled in the hollow space within the walls, and not being the type to be afraid of rats, not even the two-legged kind, this didn't much disturb me. The tick-tick-tick of something being picked at didn't move about the room as a rodent might, and as I woke I pinpointed the sound not in the walls, but at the door. It was Ben, of course. We'd made fun of the ghosts rumored to roam the hotel at night, and he'd joked that the only way to see a ghost was to get drunk enough to believe that your best pal draped in a bedsheet was an apparition from the spirit world. He stood on the opposite side of the door, scratching the wood, in a drunken attempt to scare a laugh out of me.

I knew I'd have to be quiet if I wanted to surprise him, and it took me a few moments, perched on the side of the bed and feeling the floor with my toes, to find my jeans. I slipped into them, buttoning just the top, and crept across the room, suppressing a laugh, because it was going to be funny when I snapped open the door and said, "Boo!" The doorknob turned as I approached. That wasn't supposed to happen. My feet stilled as I leaned forward, listening. The door swung a wedge of light into the room when it opened. The figure slipping through the jamb preferred a black hood to a white sheet and carried a knife big enough to gut me at a stroke.

The only weapon I had was my voice. I used it.

I bolted forward as I screamed and rammed my shoulder into the wood above the lock. The door gave a foot and held, braced by the intruder's body trapped against the frame. Something stung my upper arm and a violent shove from the other side of the door pushed me off balance. My legs skipped back, set, and fired forward again. The door shot closed against the jamb, my head whacked the wall, and I found myself a moment later on my knees, staring at the slice of hall light on the carpet. I pulled myself up and jerked open the door. Ben pounded down the hall, his red-checked boxer shorts flapping with each stride. Somebody tried to break into my room, I said. He pulled my hand away from my head to see how badly I was injured and asked whether I'd seen which direction he'd run. I answered with my feet.

Adrenaline and momentum carried me down the first leg of stairs, but the knock I'd taken wobbled my legs. I slowed and grabbed the rail at the turns. Nothing stirred in the lobby, lights turned low in the hours between midnight and dawn. I jogged to the entrance. The desert air splashed cool against my face, bracing my senses. Nothing moved on the street or sidewalk either, the only sound that of car metal clicking as it contracted in the chill night air. I backed into the lobby, saw a hallway leading to the rear of the hotel, followed it past the kitchen entrance to a door that opened onto the parking lot. In the distance I heard a car accelerating at speed. I peered across the blacktop. He could still be out there, hiding behind one of the parked cars, but I wasn't going to search for him, not in the dark and not in bare feet.

The night clerk greeted me when I turned back into the lobby. He was a little man in a rumpled white shirt and slept-on-wrong hair. His smile was forced and his eyes groggy. "Did you see the ghost?" he asked.

"Somebody tried to break into my room," I said.

The clerk chuckled. He was accustomed to drunken, terrified guests tearing through his hotel at three in the morning. "Did you hear strange noises, scratching at your door?" His eyes brightened, as though everything would be explained in just a moment.

I turned to see Ben crossing the lobby. I must have moved faster than I'd thought. He was still in his boxers. "Get a towel, damn it!"

The clerk blinked. He was expecting the usual explanation, the we-were-just-fooling, did-we-scare-you? of nights past. "What? Why a towel?"

Ben gripped my arm like a tourniquet just below the shoulder. "Because the lady is bleeding on your floor," he said.

Twenty One

The cut took six stitches, administered by a sleepy-eyed ER doc who worked the needle through the wound with the speed and care of someone lacing up a pair of shoes. The pain was a welcome respite from my head. Ben wasn't feeling much better. He kept me company while the doc stitched my arm. We didn't talk much. We felt too hungover, tired, and awful to talk.

A sheriff deputy came into the emergency room while I worked out payment, Stetson in hand and cowboy boots clacking against the linoleum floor. The duty nurse greeted him by name, asked if he wanted a cup of coffee. He settled into the lobby furniture, balanced his pen and clipboard on the armrest to his right, and looking as comfortable as a man in his own living room, asked us what happened. The name on his badge read "Acuña."

I told him.

"Did you remember to lock your door, ma'am? The doors at the Gadsden, it's an old hotel, they don't lock automatically. You forget to throw the bolt, anybody can just turn the knob, walk in."

"I turned the bolt," I said.

"Did you secure the chain?"

I admitted that I hadn't.

"The Gadsden's full up tonight, what I hear. Lots of folks in town for the funeral. Were you drinking much?" Acuña didn't make it sound like an accusation. He was an easygoing guy. Likable. The graveyard shift had taught him that at four in the morning the simplest explanations worked the best. If he knew I was a paroled felon, he didn't mention it.

"Some," I said.

"If it was just some, you were one of the sober ones. I heard the bartender was kept hopping till closing time. Full hotel, lots of drinking, somebody might get confused which room is which, stumble into yours by mistake, don't you think?"

"He was wearing something black over his head."

"Get that a lot at the ghost hotel. You'd be surprised what people put over their heads, pretending to be a ghost."

"This ghost carried a knife."

"How much did you have to drink?"

"Not so much I hallucinated this." I lifted my arm.

"That cut's real enough, all right. But the hardware on those doors, it's pretty old, some of the base plates have sharp edges."

"I don't expect you to make an arrest. I'm the only one saw the guy, and I wouldn't recognize him if he walked up to me on the street tomorrow morning. But I'd appreciate it if you'd take my statement without trying to make me admit to being a drunken fool."

Disappointment moved Acuña's glance toward Ben and back to me. I don't think my rejection of his version of events bothered him so much as the sharpness of my tone.

"It's been a tough night, Officer," Ben said. "You want my two cents, I'd say somebody tried to break into her room, and she scared him away. But can't prove that, so you'll have to make your own call how to write it up."

Acuña said he'd do that. We all knew nothing could be done about what happened; we couldn't even agree on the facts of what had happened. I thanked him for his trouble and wished him a safe night.

Dawn was a welcome sight after two hours of fluorescent lights, the trailing edge of night flaring red over the distant Chiricahua Mountains.

Ben drove cautiously, aware that the level of alcohol still circulating in his blood was not strictly legal. The taxi ranks in a town like Douglas were pretty thin at that hour, and neither of us wanted to walk. Cops break the law like everyone else, I've observed, but are less likely to be stupid about how they break it. When he pulled off the highway, he asked, "Think it was the same one broke into your apartment?"

"Hope so. Hate to think I've got more than one person trying to break into the places I sleep."

"Doesn't make sense though, does it?"

"Why not?"

"Why chase you all the way out here? Easier to kill you in L.A."

"Good point. Reassuring too."

I watched the corner of his mouth flicker, his way of smiling at gallows humor. He put his hand on my knee and squeezed it. "You get your dog back, you'll be okay. He'll protect you."

"Right. Somebody breaks in, he'll gum them to death."

He parked in front of the hotel, stepped onto the street, and stretched. Morning slowly stirred in the bracing air, the town so quiet at that hour I could hear the booted clicks of a man walking to work on the sidewalk across the street. Ben was flying back to Los Angeles that morning, wouldn't be able to sleep again until he boarded the plane in Tucson. "Something else." He came around the hood of the car, stood with his hands in his hip pockets. "Don't know if it's important, but I'm the one reserved your room for you."

I opened my bag, pulled out my wallet. "I'll go in and pay for it right now."

"I'm not afraid you're going to stiff me. The point I'm making is that I reserved two rooms in my name, secured the reservation with my credit card."

I couldn't reserve a room with a credit card because I didn't have one. Ex-cons are bad credit risks. "Thanks for making the reservation, but I'll pay for my own room."

He shook his head and rocked back on his heels, amused. "You still don't get it."

"It's been a long day, so forgive me if I'm a little slow."

"What makes you think he was after you?"

"I see what you're saying." I closed my eyes, remembered how quickly the guy had backed out the door at the sound of my voice. "You think he was trying to break into your room, made a mistake?"

"I'm the one with enemies in this town, not you," he said.

I looked forward to a sounder sleep, thinking Ben had been the target of the attack and not me. He'd be safe enough back in Los Angeles, and if he was right, I could enjoy the kind of sleep that lets you wake up at the end. I bolted and chained the door and wedged the back of a chair against the knob just to make sure. I banked six hours' sleep before a firm and persistent knock woke me. I thought it was the maid and told her to go away. The knocking settled into a consistent rhythm. I stumbled to the door. Arlanda's voice called my name. I pulled the chair from beneath the knob, turned the dead bolt, and unlatched the chain.

"You just knocked me up," I said.

Arlanda laughed. "That must have been some dream. Sorry I woke you."

I let her into the room.

"It's an expression I learned from my English husband. It means when somebody wakes you by knocking."

"I get it. Knocked up, out of bed. Must have been interesting, being married to somebody from a foreign country. The only expression my husband taught me was *Gimme another beer, bitch*."

"Have you heard from him? Since your aunt died?"

I left the bathroom door open so we could talk while I washed.

"He called a couple times, talked to the boys. Wanted to talk to me, too, but I told him to go sit on a rattlesnake."

"You think he wants to come back to you?"

"What makes you say that?"

"Because you're now one of the richest women in town."

Arlanda thought that was funny. "That's like being called best looking in an ugly-dog contest. The woman who owns this hotel, she's got some money, but that's about it for Douglas. And me? Maybe I'll see something in six months or so, but I haven't quit the day job. I'm on lunch break right now. The kids are in school and Baby's in the car. So put a little more speed on your toothbrush."

We ate in the hotel restaurant, El Conquistador, where the Spanish colonial decor was almost as heavy as the food. Word of the altercation in the Saddle and Spur had come to Arlanda from the friend of a friend, who'd been there drinking with somebody else's boyfriend and seen it happen. That's how news traveled in Douglas.

"There are no secrets in a small town," Arlanda said. "But what happened between Ben and Aunt Angela's biological father, Pete, that's as close to a secret as this town has ever had. I started hearing rumors about it in high school, about how Aunt Angela's 'real' dad died. But nobody seemed to know for sure, and then I didn't hear anything else until about five years ago, after my youngest was born. That's when a stranger showed up in town, asking questions of the old-timers."

"Who was he?"

"Said he was a journalist at the time, or so I heard, but now I think he was somebody hired by Aunt Angela. People started to talk again."

"Why? What happened, it was a long time ago."

"What else do people have to talk about here? The weather? When it's either hot or boiling hot and dry or bone-dry, you soon run out of conversation. Angela Doubleday was about the only thing people had to talk about. And Ben, he was the victim of that."

"People know what happened, then."

"Some do, some don't, everybody gossips. But I think he has a point when he says the person who attacked you last night was looking for him. He has enemies here. You don't."

"Troy Davies doesn't like me much."

"Troy Davies doesn't have a reason to attack you, not like that. He's already going to inherit what's left of my aunt's money, the bastard. Wish I could hate him." She laughed, her voice cracking on the high notes. "But he's too damn cute."

"Your aunt seemed to think so, too."

"Good taste in men doesn't run in the family. The fact that I think he's cute doesn't mean I trust him. If anything, makes me trust him less.

If I stop to think about it, I mean, what a sleazebag. He drives for my aunt for a year? And he gets all her residuals? He'll have money coming in for the rest of his life. The way he talks, they were artistic soul mates. You heard him talk about their so-called special relationship?"

I nodded.

"You know what I say?"

I shook my head.

"I say bullshit. He took advantage of a vulnerable older woman, made love to her a couple of times, and it turned her head. I can't say whether or not he intended to worm his way into her will, but I'm sure he was using her to advance himself, one way or another."

"But he is cute," I said.

She laughed again, said, "Why is it all the really attractive men are either gay or worthless shits?"

A trim gentleman in a blue suit and pencil moustache stopped by the table to offer Arlanda his condolences. Snowbirds crowded the tables at El Conquistador, in town for the warm weather and cheap room rates, but the restaurant also functioned as a meeting place for the town's elite, such as it was. The gentleman's offer of condolences included an invitation to dinner when her grief allowed.

"Sells car insurance," Arlanda said after he left.

"Might be a good catch for you, then."

"Biggest catch in town. Car insurance is a big business here, Americans need it to drive in Mexico. He sells insurance to half the cars crossing the border."

I said, "Wow."

"It passes for glamour around town. In my age range, there are about three available men, and he's at the top of the list. Everybody else is married. I could always date one of the widowers, I suppose, but I'd like a man I don't have to push down the sidewalk in a wheelchair." The way she was talking, I didn't think she'd date the insurance salesman for long, if at all. The minute her inheritance cleared, she'd be on her way to Los Angeles. Then she said, "I need you to do me a favor, when you get back to L.A."

"Sure, whatever you want."

"That thing about what the accountant said, about Aunt Angela buying art? It's been bothering me. So I called around when I was in L.A., galleries listed in the Yellow Pages. I didn't have any luck until some-body suggested I try a place I didn't see in the Yellow Pages at all. And I found a salesman there who said she'd been what he called a patron. But he wouldn't say anything over the phone, and before I could get to see him, I had to come back here to make arrangements for the memo-rial service."

"You want me to go see him for you?"

"Would you?"

"Sure. What do you want to know?"

"What she bought. How big it is, how much it cost. You see what I'm saying? Maybe she didn't keep her purchases at the house. I'm trying to find out if she kept a storage vault somewhere her accountant didn't know."

"If she did, would you inherit it? Whatever was inside."

"Why wouldn't I?"

"Because the will gives Troy Davies whatever's not in the house, if I remember right."

"She was my aunt. I won't let him have it. Not the storage vault, not if there's anything in it. That's part of the house." Her voice rose at the end to a firm and strident tone that turned heads.

"How is a storage vault part of the house?"

"The key." She said it like "checkmate," as though the logic was in-escapable. "And that's another thing. What if they were stealing from her?"

"Who?"

"Davies. Her housekeepers, too. Who knows? They all had access. They could have stolen her blind. If I know what she bought and it shows up for sale somewhere, then I'll be able to do something about it. Now, they could sell what they stole from her and I'd never even know."

"Do you really think Yolanda and Maria would steal from your aunt?"

"We're talking about two, three million dollars. For that kind of money, most people would be willing to do more than just steal."

She was right. Money does things to people, always has. Arlanda didn't seem so immune either. "What's this gallery you want me to check out?"

"You'll find it in Beverly Hills," she said. "It's called Harry Winston. Like the cigarette."

Twenty Two

Harry Winston is not just anywhere in Beverly Hills, it's on Rodeo Drive, and though it doesn't define itself as an art gallery, its customers are convinced the work on display is every bit as much art as any canvas by Jasper Johns or sculpture by Henry Moore, even if the colors are limited to basic colors such as diamond white, ruby red, emerald green, and those of the world's precious metals, above all platinum. The manager stared at me like I'd come to rob the place when I walked through the entrance and bent over the glass of the central display case, which contained a diamond necklace that may have weighed more than my head. "Umm, may I help you?" He said it doubtfully, polite by training but painfully aware I was beyond help.

"Got anything with genuine zircon?" I pointed to my left nostril. "Preferably in a nose stud."

"Perhaps you could try Wal-Mart. I understand they carry, ah, zircon products."

He pronounced *zircon* as though allergic to the word. I handed him the notarized letter of instructions Arlanda had given me, with an explanatory note from Doubleday's accounting firm. He warned a sales associate with a glance that I needed watching and excused himself, passing through a door behind the counter. When he returned a dozen minutes later, his smile was a well-practiced welcome, and he invited me to join him privately, in his office.

It didn't hurt to be nice. I said, "Come Oscar time, I see Winston jewels on half the stars of Hollywood."

"Yes," he said. "The well-dressed half."

I heard another language buried within his vowels, and I wondered whether it was genuine or an act to impress clients who thought being from Europe prestigious. The walls of the office were soft green and if I knew what a Persian carpet looked like I would have bet my chair rested on one. The manager sat behind a gilded desk, the surface as neatly manicured as his nails. One of the many ironies of Beverly Hills is that ninety-nine percent of the sales staff have better taste and manners than their customers.

"May I ask what your role is in this?"

"Friend of the family," I said.

"Certainly not of Ms. Doubleday's."

Like he knew her well enough to know I wouldn't.

"Her niece and principal heir."

"The fire, such a tragic catastrophe."

"Yes. The world mourns. And her niece looks for assets."

His eyes shot to the ceiling and he shook his head, sighing at the responsibility to carry on despite the burden of grief. "Ms. Doubleday came to us twenty years ago, when she was nominated for her first Oscar. She hadn't been a Harry Winston star before then, but the moment we dressed her in jewels, she became the embodiment of Harry Winston." He closed his eyes to better remember, and when he spoke again, his voice glowed with pride, or perhaps just good sales-manship. "That first night she wore a necklace of perfect white emer-ald-cut diamonds and two-tier diamond-drop earrings. Simple but classic. She loved our jewelry, and we loved her."

"The necklace and earrings, did she buy them?"

"Not those. Harry Winston loans many of its jewels to the Oscar nominees, and we bejeweled Angela Doubleday for each of her Oscar appearances, free of charge."

"Must be good advertising."

"The most beautiful jewels for the brightest stars. We're pleased to do our part to support the Academy."

"Did she buy any of the later jewels?"

"The items on loan for her Oscar appearances?" He pursed his lips, an expression I took to mean he disapproved of breaking the confidence of a customer, even a dead one. "Just one item. An exquisite articulated brooch depicting an American Beauty rose, crafted in rubies and diamonds. She bought very few of our signature pieces. After what happened, I'm not sorry she didn't. Many of our pieces are unique. I shudder to think what happened to them in the fire, poor things."

"The diamonds, would they have survived?"

"Oh yes, beyond doubt. But perhaps not the platinum. If stored in a fireproof safe, then yes." He fingered the diamond clip pinned to his tie, a gesture of alarm, like the sign of the cross. "Are they missing? The insurance company usually contacts me in cases like this."

"Her policy hadn't been updated in several years."

"That is tragic."

"Could you provide a list of what she bought from you?"

"It would take a few days."

"The list is extensive?"

His fingers slid up the tie and tugged at the lapel of his suit coat. "Oh, very. As I said previously, she bought very few signature pieces, but she loved diamonds, and over the past five or six years, she couldn't visit without buying something."

"She visited often?"

"Every month."

"I thought she didn't visit anybody."

"Harry Winston isn't just anybody. We felt honored, of course. Everybody knows how terribly she suffered, how she recoiled from public life. Diamonds were one of her joys, particularly toward the end, and we were happy to bring her joy."

"She came by limo?"

"Always."

Troy Davies hadn't mentioned visits to the jeweler. Perhaps he lied to protect Angela Doubleday's privacy. That seemed a reasonable explanation. He might have thought it none of our business. But where money is concerned, seemingly reasonable explanations do not always hold true, and I wondered if he was playing games with the estate, aware of the stipulation in her will that awarded him her investments and cash assets. Arlanda couldn't claim what she didn't know existed. If he knew about a safe-deposit box, he wouldn't warn her before claiming the contents. Somebody needed to talk to him, and I knew it couldn't be me. Davies would just tell me to go to hell. I said, "I heard her chauffeur brought her joy, too."

His glance changed, and I thought the remark offended him. Then he said, "He was very attentive to her *every* need," and I realized he was speculating, curious to see if I'd elaborate. If the sex life of Hollywood stars didn't enjoy broad appeal, the tabloids wouldn't sell millions of copies every week.

"Did he come into the store with her?"

"Always. They'd pull to the front five minutes after closing time. We'd open for her, of course; we're always open by appointment to special customers. If there was space at the curb, he'd come right in with her. He never said much, but if she so much as sniffled, he'd have a handkerchief ready for her."

"He saw what she bought?"

"The British say the queen has no secrets before her servants, and that saying is no less true among a certain class of people in America. He looked at nothing and saw everything."

"And she bought?"

"Oh, yes. Bought and bought. Most often, I served her right here, in this office." He showed his palms to the walls, as though they shimmered in reflected glory. "She liked to have the jewelry brought to her, you see, rather than picking through the display cases. *You know my tastes*, she'd say. *Choose something I'll like.* She'd enthuse over the finer pieces, but then, after threatening to buy something really grand, she always selected a smaller piece, a bracelet or earrings, some of our more anonymous pieces, actually. Poor dear, she was on a budget, I'm almost certain of it."

"So in the end, what she bought didn't amount to much."

"By the standards of the house of al-Saud, no, but very few of our customers meet that high standard. Over the years I personally sold more than a million dollars in jewelry to Ms. Doubleday. Well over a million. Closer to two."

TWENTY THREE

Maria Potrero opened the door to Lupe's room just wide enough to allow me to slip through the crack, shutting it quickly and quietly as though afraid someone—or something—might follow me in. Yolanda tended a votive flame on the dresser, the wick spiraling smoke before a framed print of the Virgin of Guadalupe. Lupe's down-the-hall neighbor, El Cangurito, stood by the window, big-knuckled hands respectfully folded at his belt. The sisters had phoned my mobile a half hour earlier, their voices so despondent that I'd rushed over from Beverly Hills despite their inability to say what precisely was wrong. They both wore loose-fitting black cotton dresses hemmed at the knee, the same dresses they had worn at Angela Doubleday's memorial service. The smell of candle wax and vanilla masked the alcoholic's reek of smoke and sweat.

"¿Qué pasa?" I asked. What's going on?

A string of rosary beads wound through Yolanda's fingers and she crossed herself before the Virgin. El Cangurito, watching closely from the corner, matched the Father–Son–and–Holy Ghost movements of her fingers and clenched his hands again at his belt.

"We hear Lupe's voice, crying to us," Yolanda said.

"We think something bad happens to him," Maria added.

"You heard his voice?" I asked. "He called you on the phone?"

Yolanda's eyes glimmered in the candlelight. "He calls my heart. He is lost somewhere, in terrible pain."

"She started to hear his voice last night," Maria said.

Yolanda stared at the ceiling, head tilted as though listening. "His cries are weaker now. He's still here, but he's leaving us."

I edged to the far corner of the room, near El Cangurito, who followed the conversation with one eyebrow flexed in concentration, the other eyebrow arched in the confusion of one who understands no more than half of everything said. I asked, "He didn't come back to his room last night, you don't know where he is, that's the problem?"

Maria's fingers worried at the seam of her dress as obsessively as Yolanda worked her rosary beads, and when she nodded she meant far more than a simple yes. "He's in trouble. We know."

"Lupe drinks," I said. "He probably went drinking last night, found a best friend, closed the bars, and fell asleep on somebody's couch." I didn't want to say what I really thought, that there was no best friend, only the bottle, and his couch was the lot or alley where he'd passed out.

Maria clasped my arm to her side and turned to El Cangurito. "Tú hablaste con Lupe ayer. Dinos, ¿qué te dijo?" You talked to Lupe yesterday. What did he tell you?

He unclenched his hands, let them hang at his side, big and agile things in movement but awkward when they had nothing to do. He dressed carefully, for the sisters or perhaps in respect for the occasion, his slacks neatly creased, his cotton shirt crisp, and his hair freshly slicked back. His eyes drifted up at the mention of his name, and though he may have been fierce and graceful in the ring, he stood stiffly in Lupe's room, his glance failing to project beyond the surface of his eyes. "Lupe se vino a mi habitación ayer tarde en la mañana. Le había prestado algo de dinero la semana pasada." Lupe came to his room yesterday, he said. He'd loaned him some money the week before.

"Nunca deberías haberle dejado ese dinero," Yolanda said. He never should have given Lupe money.

The boxer's hands fluttered at his sides as though wishing to fly up to his face in defense. "No fue mucho, sólo veinte dólares, pero me tenía que pagar ayer." It was only twenty dollars, he said, but Lupe was supposed to pay him back.

"¿Y no lo tenía?" I asked. He didn't have it?

"No, no lo tenía, pero me dijo que si le podía esperar un día más, me daba cien dólares." No, he didn't have it, but he promised to pay him a hundred dollars the day after, if he'd wait.

"¿Cien dólares?" I asked, not sure if I'd heard right.

The swelling from the blows he had taken in his last match had receded to a dull yellow, and his lip had healed enough to allow an embarrassed smile. El Cangurito didn't understand either. He didn't want a hundred, he'd said to Lupe. He'd loaned out twenty. He wanted twenty back. Lupe could pay him when he had the money, but he had to pay him, because neither of them were rich men. Lupe laughed and said he'd be rich that night, because he knew the secret of the trees. That sounded a little crazy to El Cangurito and so he asked, "Lupe, have you been drinking?" But no, he said he hadn't, maybe just a little, for courage. He was just excited, and maybe he was afraid, too.

"¿De qué tenía miedo?" I asked. Afraid of what?

"Se iba a encontrar con alguien, con un hombre." He was going to meet someone, a man. "Parecía tener miedo de ese hombre, pero lo tenía que ver para coseguir el dinero." He seemed afraid. But he had to see the man to get the money.

"¿Dijo cómo se llamaba el hombre?" Did he say the man's name?

El Cangurito slowly shook his head.

"¿Te dijo algo sobre el hombre?" Did he say anything about him?

"Sólo que era peligroso." Just that he was dangerous.

"¿Dijo dónde se iban a encontrar?" I asked. Did he say where they were going to meet?

"Yo sé donde," Yolanda said. She knew where. "When he speaks to me, I hear the sea."

¢   ¢   ¢

We found Lupe's pickup truck parked on the shoulder of the Pacific Coast Highway a half mile from El Matador State Beach and less than a mile from the ruins of Angela Doubleday's estate. He'd parked legally, but the beach is difficult to access until the park entrance, and his truck stood alone, buffeted by the wind and the slipstream of vehicles racing east, toward the city. I told Yolanda and Maria to stay in my car with the Rott and approached the truck alone. The accuracy of Yolanda's prediction didn't surprise me; the area around Doubleday's estate would have been one of the first places to look, based either on premonition or logic. Rust fringed the truck's wheel wells, and the back bed was heavily scarred, the factory white scraped and burnished orange from the oxidizing steel below. The truck was old and battered and because it looked like what it was, a gardener's truck, it did not seem out of place parked between the gated and heavily landscaped estates on both sides of the highway.

I examined the ground for footprints before I approached the cab, not wanting to scuff existing ones or to leave my own should the truck become a crime scene, but the ground near the highway was packed hard as sandstone and took no marks. I slipped my hands into a pair of cotton gloves taken from my camera bag and tried the door. Locked. I peered into the interior of the cab, careful not to get too close to the glass—forensic science had made great strides in the past decade, and I didn't know whether or not nose prints were admissible evidence in a court of law. Fast-food wrappers and crumpled cigarette packs littered the floor on the passenger side, and a clipboard rested on the bench-style seat. Nothing had been written on the clipboard. The clipboard didn't even have any paper.

I backed away from the truck and scouted the shoulder of the highway toward the state beach, looking for bloody footprints, cigarette butts with Lupe's brand stamped near the filter, or bread crumbs leading into the brush; I found more fast-food wrappers, plastic bags, and a condom. Based on the evidence, Lupe could have walked either up the highway or down it, crossed to the other side, or become the latest victim of an alien abduction. I skirted the truck and returned to Yolanda's and Maria's anxious expressions. They sat together in the front seat, Yolanda's worrying her rosary beads and Maria's fingers interlaced so tightly on her lap the tips had whitened to the color of bone. Even the Rott seemed disturbed, whining and panting on the rear passenger floor.

"Nothing," I said. "He probably parked and walked down to the beach."

I pulled onto the highway, wheels hewing close to the shoulder, and watched the side of the road, driving as slowly as I dared. "Lupe mentioned money to me, too, when I went to visit him," I said. "He was angry, said he was going to make big money, prove to you he wasn't a bum."

Maria's hands flew apart as though uncaged, her simple gold marriage band glinting when struck by the late-afternoon sunlight. "We give him food, we pay his rent, what more could we do?" Her hands fluttered above the dash, clashed, and settled again on her lap, tightly clenched.

"Lupe's a grown man. He makes his own decisions," I said. "You can't stop people from hurting themselves, if that's what they're determined to do."

Fewer than a half dozen cars parked in the dirt lot above El Matador State Beach, about average for a weekday afternoon in autumn. I angled the Cadillac into a corner spot and walked to the vending machine planted at the trailhead. The machine spat out a parking voucher good for the rest of the afternoon. Maybe that was the reason Lupe had parked on Pacific Coast Highway; he hadn't wanted to spend the money for parking.

"One thing we don't understand," Maria said.

I slipped the ticket underneath the windshield wiper and gave the Rott an apologetic pat before locking him in the car. Further down the trailhead a graffiti-scrawled state-park sign read "No Dogs."

Maria glanced at her sister, who nodded.

"El secreto de lo árboles," Yolanda said, repeating what El Cangurito had told us in Lupe's room. The secret of the trees.

"The cypress trees at the back of the estate were dying," I said. "Lupe told me he found quicklime in the soil."

"¡Madre de Dios!" Yolanda crossed herself. "Quicklime is for the dead."

"What could he have seen that you didn't?"

Yolanda looked at Maria, whose gaze dropped to the ground.

"There is something," Yolanda said.

Maria nodded, once. "Sometimes, when the weather was warm . . ."

"Or when he drank too much . . ."

"He slept in his truck."

"The señora didn't notice."

"He parked his truck around the side of the garage," Maria said. "Where no one could see him."

I asked, "He'd stay the night at the estate, asleep in his truck?"

The sisters nodded.

"You think he saw something one night? Something that might be worth money if he threatened to expose it?"

The sisters glanced at each other, reading each other's thoughts as though a lifted eyebrow here and a tightening of the lip there conveyed the meaning of sentences. Yolanda looked at me. Her shoulders lifted and dropped.

"We don't know for sure," Maria said. "But we think, yes."

Beyond the headlands of Malibu's Point Dume, the coast angles north to confront the relentless energy of the Pacific. The beaches have a fierce, carved look to them, the sandstone bluffs spilling into the ocean in great clumps of rock beaten by the waves and polished by the wind. A person lying on the flat, featureless beaches of Santa Monica Bay is visible for miles; El Matador State Beach is a warren of coves, rocks, and isolated stretches of beach accessible only during low tide. The Potrero sisters searched to the south, I hunted to the north, and even then, broken into teams, we didn't cover the territory until sunset, when I returned to the meeting point to find Yolanda sitting in the sand, weeping, and Maria standing above her, staring out to sea.

"I don't hear his voice anymore," Yolanda said. "He's gone."

"He could be anywhere," I said. "Maybe his truck broke down. Maybe he didn't have bus fare. Maybe he met somebody. Maybe he got drunk and needs a day to sleep it off. The point is, we don't know what happened, and when he turns up at his room tonight, you'll feel pretty foolish at having suffered so much for no reason."

"When our husbands were killed, all we could do was wait," Maria said. "We couldn't go to the police, because the police were friends of the ones who took our husbands. We don't want to wait anymore. Nothing is worse than waiting."

"You want to go to the police?" I asked.

She nodded, once and slowly.

"We'll go to my apartment, then, make some calls." I led them up the bluff to the trailhead. It's not easy going to the police in a county as big as Los Angeles, not when you want to report a person missing less than forty-eight hours. Unless the person is a child or evidence points to a forced abduction, the law will tell you to take a number and wait. Hundreds of people go missing every day, from runaway teenagers to senior citizens who decide from one day to the next to walk out of their lives and aren't heard from until a week later, a thin voice calling from Florida, New York, Las Vegas, wherever. Ninety-nine point nine percent of all missing persons turn up alive some-where, sometime, and the law can't be expected to roll out the squad cars every time someone gets too drunk to make it home or decides home isn't home anymore. Still, a person can call the county and ask if a name has been booked into the Twin Towers or the morgue, and I was planning the calls I'd make when I saw the park ranger scuttling from windshield to windshield in the parking lot, checking for expired parking vouchers. I hailed him with a raised arm and a shout. He waited for me to approach, pen on his ticket pad. He thought I'd come to beg him not to ticket my car, and from his expression, he wasn't going to listen.

"We're looking for somebody, left his car parked on the road a half mile back," I said, waving toward the highway. "He's been missing since last night, a gardener, Hispanic, about forty years old, likes to drink every now and then. You seen him?"

The information sparked his eyes.

"Hispanic, you say?"

"About forty." I pointed at my lip. "Wears a moustache."

The park ranger nodded. "I didn't see him here, no."

I thought that might be the end of it, but he looked over my shoulder at the Potrero sisters, who waited respectfully at a distance, and then back at me, as though he might have something else to say. "Are you relatives?"

"Two of us are," I said.

He swallowed. "I don't want to alarm you, but they pulled some-one from the water ten miles up the coast this morning who fits that description. Didn't have any identification, so they tagged him Juan Doe."

Twenty Four

Since I'd first visited Ben's trailer a backhoe had joined the bull-dozer in cutting the new lot from the adjacent hillside, and by the look of the trench dug into the ground, preparations were being made to lay the water and gas pipes. The Rott jumped from the open ragtop the moment we stopped, put his nose to the backhoe's steel tread, and then changed ends to mark it as his territory. I keyed the trunk, pulled out a sack of groceries, locked my camera bag with the spare tire. The Rott charged toward Ben's gate and pranced as though expecting something or someone on the other side.

"You think Arlanda's here, don't you?"

He responded to her name by wagging his truncated tail so hard he turned two circles trying to catch up to it. I opened the gate. He nosed through ahead of me. I liked Arlanda too, and I knew it was petty to be jealous of my dog's obvious affection for her, but that didn't stop me from feeling jealous anyway. The front-porch door swung open and Ben peered into the dark.

"Took your time getting here," he said.

He'd called four hours before, impatient to show me something.

"Long drive from the morgue," I said.

"What were you doing there?"

Ben stooped to thump the Rott's flank and stepped aside to let him in the trailer. The dog checked one room and the next, then doubled back to the first one again.

I said, "We better feed him something or he won't get over his disappointment at not seeing Arlanda here." I pulled the package of hamburger from the grocery bag and broke the plastic skin. The Rott laid his head against my side and sniffed. "You my best friend now? That the way it works?"

"A dog's loyalty is as deep as his stomach," Ben said.

"They say that about men, too, don't they?"

"Sometimes."

Ben stooped to pick a bottle of beer from the refrigerator.

"Were you on assignment?"

"When?"

"The morgue."

I mixed a couple of eggs and some bread into the meat and set it down on the floor. The Rott promptly forgot about me and dug his nose into the bowl. The morgue is a dreadful place, even if you aren't required to identify a body, even if you do nothing more than wait in the lobby, imagining the smell of formaldehyde leaking from beneath the door that leads to the meat, even if those you've accompanied do the dirty work of confirming that the cold husk slabbed out on a steel plate is someone they once loved. I told Ben about it.

"I'm sorry to hear it," he said. "Can't say I knew him, but the three of them were nice enough to me at Angela's funeral. Will you give my condolences to the sisters next time you see them?"

I said I would.

"Any determination of cause of death?"

"Too early," I said. "He checked in as Juan Doe."

"No rush on the autopsy, then."

"They'll get to it faster now they know who he is, particularly considering he was murdered."

"How do you know he was murdered?"

"The body had no teeth."

"No teeth?" Ben twisted the top from the bottle of beer and dropped it into the trash beneath the sink. "Was the man in possession of his natural teeth? Did he wear dentures?"

"He didn't have all his teeth, no, but he didn't wear dentures."

"You mean somebody knocked all his teeth out?"

"Or pulled them."

Maria Potrero had mourned too many people to seek pity or even solace, but the sight of Lupe, face sunken like an old man's, had shaken even her to tears.

Ben said, "Maybe he was supposed to drift a little more than he did. Enough time in the water, not even his sisters-in-law would have recognized him."

"No teeth," I said, "no way to identify the corpse."

"C'mon. I want to show you something."

The something Ben wanted to show me lay inside a three-ring binder set on the coffee table. He gestured at the couch and took the end chair for himself.

"I want you to relax a moment. Clear your mind. Forget the morgue, forget the stress of the road, forget the dog, just relax."

"You going to hypnotize me or something?"

"Forget the wise-ass jokes, too. Can I get you something to drink?"

I asked for a Coke and while he went to get it I craned low to look at the edges of the binder. Paper of some kind, probably photocopies.

When he came back with the Coke he said, "I'm going to show you some pictures. We're going to take our time with them, but no more than ten seconds on each to start. I don't want you to fall in love with any particular one, understand?"

"It's a mug book," I said.

"Homemade. I've been collecting mug shots for a while now, known firebugs mixed in with just plain bad guys. And those sketches we had done, I've been faxing those around too, worked on little else since I got back from the funeral."

He squared the book to my eyes and turned back the cover. The face that squinted from page 1 was pulled from the landscape of nightmare.

"Not only don't I know him, I don't want to know him."

"No comments. Just observe."

Ben's voice was gentle, and he watched my expression while I viewed the paper lineup of faces. Though unkempt and weary, most of the men in the book looked surprisingly ordinary, as though photographed after a hard night of partying, and no more dangerous than any other man waylaid at four in the morning. Evil does not show clearly in most faces, and when it does, it's nearly always an impoverished, low-forehead kind of evil; the clever ones learn how to look benign at an early age, no matter how deadly their thoughts. My guy was midway through the book, staring from a mug shot taken somewhere in Florida. I obeyed Ben's instructions, said nothing, and watched carefully for the second one to flash by. He didn't. Outside the trailer, a big engine fired and revved.

"Did you recognize anyone?"

"George Clooney, a little more than halfway in."

Even retired, Ben took his work too seriously to smile.

"Mr. Clooney is not a suspect as far as I'm aware."

"I recognized the man I saw at Angela Doubleday's estate, the one with prematurely gray hair."

"Could you go through the book, page by page, and show him to me? Again, take your time."

I didn't need the caution, but still I directed my attention toward each face as I turned its page. I'd flipped through a quarter of the book when the earth rumbled and a jolt shook the trailer so hard I thought the big one was hitting. The Rott barked once, confused. I leaned back against the couch and held on. Ben shot to his feet, shouting. As loudly as Ben yelled I barely heard him, the outrage in his voice overwhelmed by the grinding roar of what I thought to be the earth. The trailer lurched backward in a shriek of cracking pipes and shredding aluminum. The kitchen-cabinet doors bolted open, the Rott yelping amid plates and glasses shattering to the floor. Cables snapped and the lights crashed out. Beyond the sliding-glass door the hill sloped ominously down to the Pacific Coast Highway. The walls shuddered and the tin foundations crumbled, pitching the trailer toward the lip of the hill. Since childhood I'd been told never to run outside during an earthquake, instead to seek shelter in doorframes, but the roar accelerated in pitch to an anxious mechanical whine, like the complaint of overcranked pistons, and when I stood to surf the floor I glimpsed out the street-side window the bright yellow of a bulldozer.

I shouted to get out as the trailer slid from under my feet. While falling I stretched to slap the Rott on his flank. The dog yelped in surprise and shot out the front-porch door. The trailer canted sharply toward the sea and planed over the lip of the hill. Everything not bolted down—from pots and pans to chairs and tables—flew toward the low end. I went fetal, shielding my head with my arms. A stool knocked Ben to his knees, and the collapsing bookcase laid him flat. I braced my feet to stand and failed. Beyond the front door the hillside careened past, chaparral raking the trailer but not impeding its velocity. The walls shook so violently I feared the frame would burst and strew us, dead and doll-like, among the wreckage.

I shouted at Ben, kicked his arm. He didn't move. I twisted to latch on to the back collar of his shirt and pulled, but he was too heavy so I wrapped my arms beneath his shoulders. My heels dug into the carpet and I thrust backward, hugging him to my chest. The trailer's leading edge bumped something that felt like a boulder and the sickening lurch in my stomach informed me the trailer was whirling around. I dug in my heels and pushed again. The walls split with a deafening crack and the trailer rolled. I kicked out a final time and for a moment touched nothing but air. Ben came loose from my arms and I was soaring, the trailer spinning from my feet. The roll broke its back. Glass, wood, and metal sprayed the hillside. The earth crashed onto my shoulders and I broke too, all breath and fear speeding away on impact.

Consciousness and awareness are not the same thing and though I retained the former the landing was a hard one and stunned all thoughts of time and self. I didn't feel pain. I didn't think I'd been gravely hurt. I didn't think or feel at all. A worried shadow hovered over me and something wet flicked my face. I didn't think about that either, merely noticed it, as one might an image on a muted television set in the far corner of the room. The shadow seemed anxious, and the flicking wet covered my mouth and nose. I couldn't breathe, hadn't breathed since impact. I gasped and awareness returned with the air. I must have moaned because the shadow backed off and barked. After a moment, I sat up.

The trailer lay scattered down the hillside, parts strewn like the wreckage of an airplane. The Rott barked again and advanced to lick my face. I held on to his neck and breathed. It hurt my bones to shout

Ben's name, and when I didn't hear him respond it hurt again, and deeper. "Find Ben," I told the Rott. He backed away and whined, confused. "Where's Ben? Find Ben." I waved him down the hill and he put his nose to the ground, understanding what I'd asked him to do.

The hillside skidded beneath my boots, the desert earth hard beneath a slick layer of sand. I searched for a foothold of chaparral to help me stand. The pocket of my leather jacket vibrated. A good leather jacket won't make you immortal, but as every motorcyclist knows it helps to have one on when sliding along the asphalt after laying down a bike, and it had saved me from more serious injury on landing. My pocket moved again, as though it held something alive. My mobile phone. I'd set it to vibrate. I looked at the number lighting up the display. I didn't know the caller.

I said, "Hello?" like not even I knew if I was in or not.

The connection severed after a one-word reply, and that word was not polite. The voice had been male, and angry. I stored the call in memory. Funny time to get a wrong number.

The Rott barked a dozen yards down the hill, and from the anxious edge to the bark I knew he'd found something. The night was lit by the glimmer of a low moon, just bright enough to see a man's shape crumpled in the shadow beneath the dog's chest. A dim circle of light skittered, birdlike, along the scrub brush beside the dog. A voice called out for survivors. I traced the circle of light to a flashlight near the crest of the hill.

I stood and waved.

TWENTY FIVE

The medevac arrived like an angel in blinding light and fierce winds. Ben was unconscious when the Rott found him, his left arm splayed at an unnatural angle. I felt lucky that the landing had done little more than knock the wits from me, but other reasons than luck figured into the difference between our injuries. I was young·and flexible. Ben was thirty-some years older and sixty pounds heavier. He hit the hill with considerably more force than I. His bones, brittled by age, had snapped on impact. The paramedics who prepared him for the flight had wrapped an inflatable cervical collar around his neck before sliding the stretcher under his body. In the portable work light they'd brought down the hill I could see the jagged edge of bone sticking from the bloody sleeve of his upper arm.

I cowered beneath the blades, eyes squinted against the wind and dust, and watched the paramedics secure the cables to the stretcher. The hoist cranked Ben's body off the ground, and the cockpit glowed in the reflected arc lights as the copter hovered, waiting for the stretcher to clear. Then it banked gently and soared to sea, where it banked again on a course that would take it to the roof of Saint John's Hospital in Santa Monica. The injured man was a cop, I'd told the paramedics. I have no doubt they do their best for everyone, but the best

they can do for an injured cop is considerably better than the best they
can do for most anyone else.

"Never seen anything like it in my life," one of the paramedics said,
surveying the ruins of the trailer below. His hair was red as blood and
danced in the wind. "I'll say one thing, if you were in that thing when
it went down, you're both lucky to be alive."

"If we stayed inside the trailer, we wouldn't be."

He pointed at my jacket. His large and freckled hand circled the
air. "Guess I'd better give you a quick look before we go up. Hurt anywhere particular?" He smiled. "Or just all over?"

"I'm all right," I said.

"Won't hurt to take a look."

I stood there, watching him, thinking, I could go for a guy like this,
somebody who likes patching people up more than taking them
apart.

"You want to remove your jacket?"

I shrugged the leather from my shoulders. My skin cracked, the
shirt wet on my back. I glanced over my shoulder. His eyes were cat
green. Freckles swarmed across his cheeks, too, like a constellation of
stars. A look came into his eyes, of seeing something that shouldn't be.
He circled to my downhill side, asked me to put first one hand out,
then the other, gently feeling the bones for breaks and asking if I felt
any pain.

"Why don't you come in the wagon with us?" He said. "How are
your legs? Think you can walk up the hill?"

I rolled my shoulders and hurt down to my tailbone. But everything moved, more or less in the same order it always had. "I think I
broke some scabs," I said. "I slid down a mountainside last week. Am I
bleeding bad?"

"You're bleeding. You'll need to have the wounds cleaned and
bandaged. A full exam wouldn't hurt either."

"Look," I said. "I don't have health insurance and my bank account
is a little low this month. Can you examine me here?"

I liked the look in his eyes. He didn't feel sorry for me because I
was poor. He wanted to solve the problem. "Let's do it this way," he
said. "We'll do a quick prelim in the back of the van, and unless I

find something serious you won't have to go anywhere but home. Agreed?"

"Agreed," I said. "As long as we define serious the same way."

"How do you define it?"

"I don't have a fifty-fifty chance of surviving the night."

"Pretty tough, aren't you?" He smiled when he said it, as though he liked that.

"Not tough, just broke," I said.

I didn't feel so tough after a couple of steps up the hill. My body has always been slow to respond to pain. My father trained me well in that respect. If I cried or flinched when he hit me, he hit me again, and harder. I learned to isolate pain. If my ankle hurt, the pain stayed in my ankle and didn't show in my face or voice. This pain was a little harder to isolate because it affected just about every bone, joint, and muscle in my body. Halfway up the hill the paramedic extended his arm. I took it.

Emergency lights strobed ambulance blue and police cruiser red at the top of the hill. A few trailer park residents huddled behind the flashing lights, but the helicopter had been the high point of the show, and now that it had flown away, most of the spectators were wandering away as well. The paramedic guided me into the back of the van and shut the door. He asked, "Are you the modest type?"

"As modest as I need to be," I said and bit my teeth against the pain while I peeled the shirt to expose my back.

He positioned me to take advantage of the light. "Looks clean enough. I'm going to abrade, disinfect, and bandage in that order." He dipped into his med kit for a squeeze bottle. Liquid stung the stretched skin between my shoulders and trickled down my back. He asked, "What's your name?"

"Nina. What's yours?"

"Michael."

"Like the angel."

"That's not what my ex-wife says."

"You look like an angel to me."

He sprayed the wounds with disinfectant and they stung so much I almost swore. Almost.

"You hurt like the devil, though," I said.

"Two sides to every person, isn't there?"

He pulled a roll of gauze from his med kit and played it out across my upper back, his hands gentle but firm. "You're a gutsy lady. Maybe too gutsy for your own good. I'm gonna give you my phone number, okay? You should be fine, but if you feel any pain, more or different than you feel now, call me."

Pain covered a lot more territory than just nerve endings. His job was to patch broken bodies, but lives often break before bodies and he'd seen his share of that kind of pain, too. In his line of work, he had to. As I pulled down my shirt it occurred to me he might be flirting.

"How about if I'm just lonely?" I asked.

He laughed, said, "Even better."

The busiest hours in an emergency room begin with rush hour and end after the bars close. These are the peak times of sickness and accident, when those who have suffered feverishly through the workday seek medical respite, when cars crash into things, when people bicker and fight, and above all it's the time when people fall off ladders, scald themselves with boiling water, stick their fingers in light sockets, and fall victim to multiple other domestic mishaps. Most accidents occur in the home, they say, though I don't believe having your home pushed off a cliff by a bulldozer figures high in the statistics.

I waited until Ben made it out of surgery before I called Arlanda. He'd broken two ribs, his collarbone, and humerus, the long bone in the upper arm. He hadn't yet regained consciousness. Most comas don't last more than twenty-four hours, the doctor said, two or three days at the most. I didn't tell her that as a precaution he was breathing by respirator.

"What's his condition?"

"Critical but stable. He's resting peacefully right now. He might awaken during the night, but the doc said we shouldn't expect any change until tomorrow morning at the earliest."

"How about you?"

"Fine."

"And Baby?"

"Not a scratch."

The operator asked for more money. I fed another ten quarters into the slot and told her about what happened to Lupe. She asked how Maria and Yolanda were taking his death.

"With courage," I said.

"Do you think I should fly out?" she asked.

I didn't know what to tell her. Whether she flew out or not was her business, not mine.

"Did you check out the gallery, the one I asked you to?"

"Harry Winston isn't an art gallery," I said. "They sell some of the most expensive jewelry in the world. Your aunt bought up to two million dollars of their merchandise over the past five years."

"Two million?" Her voice thinned and on the second syllable of the sum it nearly cracked in half. "She didn't declare any of it to the insurance company, just two pieces she'd bought years ago."

"Your aunt barely insured the house, so why should she insure her jewelry?"

"I'll put the kids with the neighbors again, try to catch a flight tomorrow afternoon."

"You need me to pick you up?"

"The accountant released some funds from the estate. You know, to take care of expenses. I'll use that to rent a car. When I get to the hospital, I'll give you a call."

We both hung up, and as I walked to the hospital parking lot I badly wanted to believe that she was flying out to take care of Ben but suspected her aunt's diamonds provided the greater motivation. Just as Ben didn't believe that someone had chased me to Arizona with the intent of assaulting me in a hotel room, I thought it improbable that someone had followed Ben from Douglas to push his trailer off a cliff. The attack had been launched in darkness, but I hoped with some reason that a neighbor had witnessed who operated the controls of the bulldozer. I hoped again that the description would match one of the two men I'd seen at Angela Doubleday's estate the day it burned. Hope may spring eternal, but the higher it springs, the harder it falls. Eyewitness accounts are rarely detailed enough to identify a suspect. I'd done some things myself that people should have seen and didn't. Even the most specific forms of evidence—fingerprints and DNA—require a suspect to match against, and the only suspect I'd been able to identify went down with the mug book in Ben's trailer. But I knew a mug shot existed, and I also knew a tabloid journalist who might be able to reconstruct how Ben had found it.

TWENTY SIX

Frank answered the door to his apartment tented in a red and black Chicago Blackhawks sweatshirt worn extralarge over baggy jeans. I carried a sack of takeout coffee in one hand and my duffel bag in the other. He didn't step aside to let me in. He asked, "You get any photographs when the trailer went down the hill?"

"No," I said, "I didn't."

He grinned. It was a joke.

Then he saw the dog.

"Can't he stay in the car?"

The request so deflated me I couldn't even come up with a smart reply. I turned back down the steps, didn't stop until he called my name.

"I'm sorry," he said. "You look like shit. I shouldn't be giving you a hard time." He swung the door open and ushered both of us in. "But if we order pizza, he takes his share out of your end, understood?"

I tried to be amused. He meant well, in his own cynical, smart-ass way, but nobody likes to hear they look terrible, not when they feel worse than they look. "I could use some bathroom time and a washing machine. And maybe something to wear while my clothes dry." I looked at the size of his jeans. I could have fit my entire body into one of the legs. "A fresh shirt, anyway."

"Sure, but maybe you want to sit down a minute, tell me a little more about what happened."

While I briefed Frank at the kitchen table, the Rott checked out the furniture, intent on mapping the terrain and cataloging the smells. Frank's attention strayed, as though he feared the dog would either eat the sofa or lift his leg to it. The Rott found momentary distraction in a pair of dirty socks left beneath the coffee table, but the apartment had never seen another dog or cat, and he soon lost interest, settling at my feet. Frank relaxed. "Tell me about the mug shot," he said.

"It was the guy in the house, I'm sure of it. Early thirties, prematurely gray hair."

"What else? What did the tag say?"

"The tag?"

"City, date, arrest number?" He looked at me like I was an idiot. "The stuff tagged to the bottom of the mug shot."

I tried to remember, couldn't. "Florida. Any more than that, I'd be inventing."

"Go take your bath," he said. "Maybe that's all I'll need."

Baby followed me into the bathroom. He dipped his nose into the toilet and backed away, drinking instead from the spigot while the bath filled. Frank wasn't much of a housekeeper, and I couldn't blame the Rott for seeking a fresher source of water. I filled the tub to six inches and sponged carefully around the bandages. Fear leaves an acrid scent on the body, and I washed it gladly from my skin. Frank tossed an extralarge Chicago Bulls T-shirt through a crack in the door, asked if the clothes I needed washed were in the duffel. I pulled the shirt over my head. It fit me like a granny dress.

"Nothing sexier than a girl in a Bulls T-shirt," Frank said when I walked from the bathroom. "Except maybe a girl in a Cubs uniform. I've got one in the closet, if you'd feel more comfortable."

I peeled back the lip of a cup of takeout coffee and blew the liquid cool enough to drink. In my youth, a calendar of women half dressed in men's sporting apparel hung from a wall in my dad's garage, the same calendar, year after year. The photographs confused me, as photographs of naked women confuse most children, and I wondered then why the models dressed like men yet looked so much like women. My dad always preferred the company of men to women. Maybe the calendar allowed him to pretend women were men, without doubting his heterosexuality. My own style of dress was distinctly masculine. The thought that my sexuality was linked to my dad was not one I wished to consider, not then and maybe not ever. I asked, "Why do you live in L.A. if you think Chicago is so great?"

"What would I write about in Chicago? How wonderful the people are? How deep and profound the culture? I'm an anarchist, a bomb thrower by nature. I love Chicago. No way I can write about it."

"And L.A.?"

"It's much more interesting to write about something you despise and love in equal measure. Take celebrities, for example. There probably isn't a single one I wouldn't want to fuck or befriend, given the chance. But I'm not given the chance and never will. They're the golden gods and goddesses of show biz, and I'm a creep. They could care less about me and I hate them for it, in the same way I hated the most popular kids in junior high school, the ones who passed through adolescence without a blemish or doubt about their superiority."

"Sounds like you've got it pretty well worked out. How many years you been in therapy?"

Frank held up his ballpoint pen like a middle finger. "See this? It's all the therapy I've ever needed." He turned his PowerBook so I could see the screen. "Is this the guy?"

The screen displayed the Web page of the West Palm Beach Police Department. "Wanted by WPBPD," it read. The man I'd seen at Angela Doubleday's estate on the day of the fire was pictured in the upper right half of the screen. Even reduced to a photo on a police website he was a handsome man. Biographical data ran in a column to the left of the photograph. His name was Ray Belgard. He was born on September 22, 1967. He was a Caucasian male six feet in height and weighing 180 pounds, possessing gray hair and brown eyes, a medium build, and no known tattoos or scars. The state of Florida wanted him for fraud and abduction.

"Same guy Ben showed me, the one I saw at Doubleday's." I ran my finger below his photograph. "No tag, as you call it. This looks like one of the pictures they take for your driver's license."

"Probably is. He's never been arrested."

Frank swung the PowerBook around again and stroked the keys. I pulled my chair behind his and held the coffee under my nose like smelling salts. I knew he was on the Internet but that was about it.

"You've heard of LexisNexis?" he asked.

"It's a brand of car, right?"

His fingers paused above the keyboard, a gesture meant to convey incredulousness, and his glance slunk sideways to judge whether or not I was teasing. I wasn't.

"It's an on-line information archive. Most major newspapers and magazines feed into its database."

"Including *Scandal Times?*"

"I never claimed it was encyclopedic. But if you're not looking for information about two-headed babies, it's a good place to start. I should alert you that I'm cheating a bit here; I looked up Ray Belgard while you were in the bath."

Pages flashed across the screen like a slow-moving slide show and stilled on a headline, "Wine-Cooler Heiress Missing," from *The Palm Beach Post*. The story was common enough. A woman had gone for a stroll on the beach one sunset and never returned. The doorman of her apartment building had seen her leave. Sunset walks were part of her routine. His shift changed an hour later, so he wasn't around to notice that she never returned. Her bridge club reported her missing two days later. Ray Belgard's name wasn't mentioned until the next to the last paragraph. The police thought he might have information about her last known whereabouts.

Frank hit a couple of keys. The screen flashed and morphed to a piece of investigative journalism entitled "The Gigolo and the Heiress: Strange Bedfellows End in Tragedy." Frank read the opening in a terse baritone: "'You see them all over Palm Beach during the high season, handsome young men with no visible means of support other than brand-name clothing and a ready smile . . .' Hey, that's not bad, maybe I can get her to write for us."

"I don't know, Frank, more competition for the Pulitzer."

"You noticed the heiress was forty-eight years old?"

"So what?"

"Almost twenty years older than Belgard."

"You think there's something wrong with a woman using her wealth and prestige to hook a younger man?"

"Not at all. Personally, I go for any woman below the age of dead."

"Forty-eight," I said. "She was about the same age as Angela Doubleday."

"Didn't think I had a point to make, did you?"

Frank tilted the screen so we both could read the rest of the article. Wine-cooler heiress Peg Olson had met Ray Belgard at a charity auction two months before she disappeared. He'd claimed to be a Wall Street investment adviser setting up a practice in Palm Beach. Peg Olson was attracted to his good looks and eager charm and wise enough not to trust any more than a token sum to his care. It was a downpayment, she'd told one of her friends, on some of the best sex she'd ever had. She knew he was interested in her money, and like a gambler who enters a casino willing to lose a predetermined amount of money and no more, she enjoyed herself while resisting his attempts to increase her stake. Who knew? If his investments earned a fair return, she might trust him with a larger amount and emerge from the affair with sex life and profit intact.

Peg Olson proved easier to fool for a few nights than a few months. Though superficially fluent, Belgard's knowledge of how markets worked seemed thinner at times than Olson's and certainly wasn't equal to the rigors of Wall Street. Not that it disappointed her terribly, but still, they quarreled. She hadn't admitted to wanting to end the affair when she disappeared, according to friends. She may not have held his financial acumen in high regard, but she trusted him, it seemed, to her death. When the police later searched her apartment, they noted over a million dollars in jewels were missing, among other items of significant value.

I gasped when I read that.

Frank's eyes broke from his notepad, where he'd been preparing facts for the story he'd write that night. "What?"

I didn't want the million-plus readers of *Scandal Times* to know about Angela Doubleday's missing jewelry, not until I'd given Arlanda a fair chance to find it. I cast my eyes to the end of the article, which mentioned that Ray Belgard's brother attended the University of Miami.

"It says he's got a brother, Jack Belgard." I said.

"So?"

"Maybe the brother can tell us where he is."

The sound that came from Frank was too derisive to be a laugh.

"Why don't I just call him up and ask?"

"Put his name in your hyperdrive, see if you catch anything."

Frank set his notepad on the kitchen table, glanced back at me, straightened in his chair. "You mean 'search engine.' And a search engine doesn't catch things, it gives you hits."

Like there was an engine out there in cyberspace, spewing oil and smoke to power Internet searches. My request took his focus from the jewels, but he was a methodical journalist, and I had no doubt he'd conclude that Doubleday had been bilked out of something of value before she'd been killed. Given Doubleday's hermetic existence, I wondered how Ray Belgard had managed the introduction. Maybe Doubleday hadn't been as isolated as I'd been led to believe. Davies had lied about her monthly visits to Harry Winston. He might have lied about other trips. But I'd characterized Davies as the Romeo. The Potrero sisters suspected they were lovers, and though he'd denied it, his protestations sounded more coy than genuine, and he certainly grieved convincingly. Could Doubleday have been enjoying affairs with both of them? Celebrities are rarely known for their circumspect sex lives. After six months of pursuing the famous I'd learned not to discount any possibility. The notion posed a greater practical than moral problem. As her chauffeur, Davies would have known about other dalliances. Maybe they were enjoying a torrid ménage à trois.

"I can't get anything recent on him," Frank said. "The last page hit I get was six months ago."

I wasn't paying close attention, said, "What was it?"

"A Yahoo chat group."

I had a vague idea what that was. I leaned close to the screen, read an archived message Jack Belgard had sent to the group, a question about something called bitewing X rays.

"What was he chatting about?"

"Dentistry."

"Oh," I said.

Frank cracked the top of his second cup of takeout coffee and put it in the microwave to warm. "I'd think about alternative housing, if I were you," he said.

"Don't worry, we'll sleep in the car, leave you to your work."

"That's not the point I'm making. You're welcome to my couch. You'd be foolish to sleep at home the next few days. This is hitting the front page day after tomorrow. You need to stay somewhere safe. If they've been fooling around so far trying to kill you, they might get serious when the story comes out and they realize you're the sole witness."

"I can't just run."

"Sure you can," he said. "It's just like walking, only faster."

Twenty Seven

I awoke the next morning to the Rott's tongue on my hand. When I pushed him away he returned with greater determination, anxious to make his morning patrol. I sat up, glanced at the kitchen table. Frank's PowerBook was gone. I'd fallen asleep on the couch sometime after dawn. Frank possessed undiscovered domestic talents; my clothes, washed and dried, lay folded on the breakfast table next to keys to the apartment and a short, handwritten note. The note read, "Be careful, okay? . . . Breakfast in the fridge." I opened the refrigerator door, found a half-empty package of Ball Park franks, a jar of mustard, three six-packs of beer, and the dregs of the last cup of takeout coffee.

"Be careful of what?" I said. "Food poisoning?"

The Rott nosed against my side. He wasn't the type to complain about raw hot dogs for breakfast, though he passed on the mustard. I warmed the dregs in the microwave, shrugged into my freshly laundered clothes, and checked my mobile phone for voice mail. Arlanda had already called from the hospital.

After walking the Rott I took unfair advantage of Frank's hospitality, using his phone to make long-distance calls for information that I didn't plan on sharing with him, at least not immediately. A call to

directory assistance in Florida yielded the phone number at the reg-
istrar's office of the University of Miami, where I misrepresented myself as a dental assistant, pitching my voice to rise uncertainly at the
end of every sentence. "I have an employment application? From a
former student of yours? At least he claims to be a former student?"
Whenever somebody speaks like that to me I want to stop whatever
I'm doing, help them out in the same way I want to help lost children, stranded cats, and other helpless creatures. "Name's Jack? Jack
Belgard?"

The woman on the other end of the line must have felt the same
way I did, because she promised to retrieve the information with a
calming, "Don't worry hon." Through the telephone lines I heard the
distinctive clicking of fingernails on a computer keyboard, then, "Is he
a recent graduate?"

Good question.

"His application form? Just says he was enrolled last year?"

"Got it," she said. "Will you want a copy of his transcript?"

"Could you confirm his telephone number and address for me?
Make sure we're talking about the same Mr. Belgard?"

She read them off for me, added, "I'm not supposed to give out any
information over the phone, other than to confirm enrollment, but
you'll want to look at this transcript before hiring. I mean, ninety-nine
point nine percent of our students make great employees, but . . ."

When she failed to complete her sentence I asked, "His grades?
There was a problem?"

"His grades were fine. Students begin to practice on patients in the
second year of the program, and, well, Mr. Belgard was expelled for
behavioral reasons. If you need to know more than that, you have to
look at the transcripts."

I gave her my address, changing my apartment number to a suite.
Students get expelled for a number of reasons, some relatively harm-
less. Maybe Belgard was caught with his nose in the nitrous oxide.
Maybe he'd gone berserk, assaulted one of his professors with a dental pick. I dialed the telephone number she'd given me. Discon-
nected, no forwarding. I doubted he'd left a forwarding home address
either.

Frank would ask me who I'd called if I left a twenty for the calls. I'd buy him lunch later, not mention why I was picking up the tab. I turned his note to me over to the blank side and drew a dog's paw. I wrote, "Thanks fer da barkfast," and signed it in the Rott's name. Frank hated cute stuff like that. Maybe he'd get the point, buy breakfast foods edible by species other than dogs and bachelors.

The woman at the patient-information desk at Saint John's Hospital checked Ben's name against her computer screen and gave me a room number in intermediate care. He'd been transferred from critical care that morning, she said. I took the elevator up, found Ben sleeping against the far wall, one of four patients in a six-bed room. I walked softly, looked at him from the foot of his bed. The bed tray held the picked-over remains of lunch. He'd barely touched his food. Considering what he'd gone through, he didn't look too bad. I lifted the flap of my camera bag, groped for a pad of paper and pen to write him a message.

"They sure have some weird-looking nurses in this hospital."

I glanced up, startled. He peeked at me from behind a sliver of raised eyelid. I reached down, gave his good hand a squeeze.

"You should see the patients," I said.

Ben's lips trembled out a smile. It wasn't funny, what I said, but it warmed him to joke with someone.

"I got a message from Arlanda this morning, said she'd be here."

His hand fluttered in the air, fell heavily.

"Already come and gone. Saw her this morning. Talked to the police, too. The detective, good guy, he told me about the trailer."

"It's totaled. I'm sorry for that."

"It's insured."

"You still have the lot, that's the valuable thing."

He swallowed heavily, as though parched. His water bottle came with a built-in straw. I guided it to his lips. He drank, nodded when he'd had enough. "I don't remember a damn thing," he said.

"You got your bell rung pretty good. If you can remember your name, where you keep your money, you'll be okay."

He tried to widen his eyes, but the effort cost him, and he let them fall half closed. "The last thing I can remember? Getting off the plane."

"Do you remember Ray Belgard?"

He didn't answer.

"The mug shot you showed me?"

He answered after a long silence. "There's just nothing there."

I squeezed his hand again. "Don't worry about it."

"The detective, he told me what you did, pulling me out of the trailer. Saving a man's life, can't do much more for somebody than that. I've been thinking this morning about my life, what it's worth, and after going back and forth on it, I've come up with an appropriate reward." He caught my attention with a flickering glance. "Next time we go out drinking, the first round is on me." He laughed at his own joke and winced in pain. "Damn, I've got to stop being so funny, it hurts too much when I laugh."

The laughter and pain took the last of his energy. His face smoothed of thought, his breath deepened, and soon, he slept.

I asked the nurse for the nearest place someone could make a call and followed her directions to a bank of pay phones on the ground floor. I checked the pay phones against the number that Arlanda had called from that morning. No match. I thought she'd called from the hospital. Maybe I'd misunderstood. I gave the number a try. She answered on the third ring. I asked, "Where are you?"

Her breath came heavily, as though she'd picked up the phone at the end of a flight of stairs. "At the estate."

"Angela Doubleday's estate?"

"Right. Where are you?"

"The hospital." It came out more reproachful than I intended and did not invite a response. She had rented a mobile phone with a car at the airport. I felt stupid not to have figured it out earlier. "What are you doing at your aunt's place?"

"Digging," she said.

"What?"

"I'm looking for a safe."

"You don't even know she had a safe."

"That's why I'm sifting, too. If the diamonds weren't in a safe, maybe I can sift them out. You want to come up and help?"

I drove up the coast thinking Frank was right, a few days out of town would do me good. I could drive up the coast, find a cheap motel room in Morro Bay, take long walks on the beach with the Rott. As I passed Temescal Canyon Road I spotted the ruins of Ben's trailer on the hillside above Pacific Coast Highway. I slowed and, ignoring the bleat of a tailgater's horn, turned left across the highway into a beach parking lot. The ruins were too distant for a good photograph, but I didn't care about that. I parked across from a cube of pay phones on the beach side of the lot, opened the trunk to get my camera. Baby took the stop as an excuse to patrol. I attached the five-hundred-millimeter lens and put the viewfinder to my eye. Shards of aluminum glinted in the early afternoon sun, ribboned by yellow police tape flapping in the wind. It was an ugly photograph, the perspective flat and the light hot, but I took it anyway. I wanted documentation.

Baby was lifting his leg to the cube of pay phones when I turned back to the car. I called his name, said, "Bad dog." He looked up, his expression bewildered. The smell of urine at pay phones didn't disturb him at all. The sight of the pay phones jogged a memory. I pulled the mobile phone from my pocket, scrolled through the numbers until I found the one that had called the night before, when I stood across the highway amid the ruins of Ben's trailer. I returned the call. Above the dull crash of surf a bright ring sounded, echoed by a buzz in my mobile phone. I strode toward the pay phones, lifted the one that faced the hill, heard my own voice speak back to me when I said hello.

Whoever pushed the trailer off the cliff made his way down to the pay phones. He knew my cell-phone number. He'd called to hear whether or not I was alive to answer. He wasn't after Ben. He was after me. That was all the motivation I needed. I combed the ruins on the hill for an hour, collecting Ben's few possessions that hadn't shattered beyond recognition, and packed them into the trunk of the car. I hoped to do the few things that needed doing and be on the road to Morro Bay by nightfall.

The Santa Ana winds picked up that afternoon, and as I climbed the drive to Angela Doubleday's estate, ashes swirled above the ruins

like a swarm of insects. Charred foundation walls outlined the shape
of the house, the former location of the rooms hinted by the upright
pillar of chimney and patterns in the debris. Arlanda knelt in the ash
toward what had been the rear of the house, overlooking a swimming
pool emptied of all but a couple feet of water at the deep end, now
scummed in refuse. A memory of her aunt's bedroom might have led
her to that spot to scrounge for the diamonds. She gripped a kitchen
colander in both hands and shook it, like a prospector panning for
gold, fine ash sifting into the wind and swarming up to sting at her
eyes. Soot blackened her hands and smudged her face. She picked
through what remained in the colander and, finding nothing but cinder, tossed it onto a growing pile to one side. To the other side, where
she might have placed objects saved from the fire, there was nothing.

"Look at you," I said.

She jerked back on her heels, so intent on her work she hadn't
heard me approach. A gust of wind blew ash into her eyes and she
dipped her head to shield herself.

"I know. I look like a mess."

"It's not how you look. It's what you're doing."

She tried to clean her eyes with the sleeve of her blouse but that
was as dirty as the rest of her. She threw her hands up in frustration. I
knelt next to her, moistened the tip of my finger with my tongue, and
gently rubbed the corners of her eyes.

"You plan to sift the entire remains of a six-thousand-square-foot
house through that little colander of yours?"

"If I have to."

"You want my opinion, you're losing perspective."

"It's not your two million in jewelry missing."

"That's right. And nobody's trying to kill you."

She clenched her eyes, tearing up from the pain or frustration or
both, and when her eyelids fluttered open again a black speck floated
free. "Tell me what to do, then," she said. "I live in a dump, my husband has run away from me, I've got two boys to raise, and a crappy
job in a dead-end town. I've lived my entire life clinging to pennies.
Should I not be trying to find the diamonds?"

"You should be trying to find the people who burned your aunt,
put Ben in the hospital."

She got the point then, and it stung.

"I'm being a fool."

"We're all fools. I'm just asking you to fight against the natural impulse a little harder."

Arlanda stood and tried to dust the ash from her clothing, but her hands were so caked in soot she smeared black into the legs of her jeans. "The last time I talked to the police, they didn't seem that interested in what I had to say."

"Maybe they'll be more interested if you give them something specific, like a suspect."

"You think I'm hiding one in my back pocket?"

"Ben identified the man I saw in your aunt's house the day of the fire. I was going through the mug shot book he'd prepared when we were hit."

"Who is he?"

"Name's Ray Belgard. Wanted by the police in Florida. They think he murdered a local heiress. Stole her jewelry, too."

She grabbed my forearm. "Her jewelry? You told the police?"

"Can't."

"Why not?"

"They won't believe a word I say."

"Then Ben?"

"Doesn't remember a thing."

She released her grip on my arm. "Looks like I branded you." She smiled, pointed at the print of her fingers on my flesh. "I didn't tell you this, but Ben called me that night too, before you visited. He told me about Ray Belgard, that he'd identified him from a mug shot."

"He did?"

"No." She laughed, happy to have fooled me. "But that's what I'm going to tell the police when I call them. Will you coach me?"

I didn't until then realize her talent for scheming. We walked toward her car, parked at the bottom of the drive.

"If we find Ray Belgard," she said, "maybe we'll find out what happened to the diamonds, too."

Twenty Eight

The Malibu Beach Inn perched across the point from Malibu Colony, the exclusive gated enclave of celebrity homes that was to paparazzi like me the Holy Grail: eternally pursued and never captured. The inn had been built on the beach side of Pacific Coast Highway, a two-story hacienda-style structure with an arched entry flanked by palm trees. The rooms came standard with ocean-view balconies and fireplaces and rented for two hundred fifty bucks a night. Arlanda was rapidly becoming accustomed to the prospect of having money, even if the money was not yet hers. Judging by the shopping bags next to the bed, she'd found time to stop at Beverly Hills before visiting Ben that morning.

I called Doubleday's accountant while Arlanda showered off the soot and ash. To keep the mirror from steaming up she left the bathroom door open, and I could hear her singing, tunelessly, amid the splashing water. The accountant gave me the name and number of Doubleday's dentist, his voice brusque in the habit of men who bill by the quarter hour. I called the dentist's office and explained to the receptionist that I needed to make an emergency appointment for the niece of Angela Doubleday. My gaze drifted while I waited for her to check the appointment calendar. The receptionist asked if we could be there within the hour. I cupped the phone to my breast. "Can you be ready in thirty minutes?"

Arlanda looked at me over her shoulder and nodded. I noticed that two children hadn't distorted the curves of her body. She'd had the children young. She was two years younger than I.

I told the receptionist to expect us and hung up the phone.

Arlanda lifted a towel from the rack and turned to me, rubbing her hair. "Why are we seeing Aunt Angela's dentist?"

"I want to talk about your aunt's file."

"What about it?"

I wanted to think she was as unconscious of her nudity as a sister accustomed to sharing a bathroom, but the eyes that riveted mine were less than completely ignorant of the power of her body. I wondered if she was attempting, consciously or not, to manipulate me. "Ray Belgard's brother studied dentistry at the University of Miami."

She nodded, as though understanding what that might mean, then said, "Why's that so important?"

"That's what I want to ask your aunt's dentist."

"What will she tell us?"

I knew what she wanted to hear, so I said it. "Maybe something that will lead us to the diamonds."

Though intimately familiar with some of the most famous mouths in film and television, Elaine Scarpers, DDS, looked nothing like a movie star herself. A tall and thin woman with an angular face, her eyes were abnormally magnified by thick, black-framed glasses, so that when she rested her elbows on the desk in her Beverly Hills office and gently pressed the tips of her fingers together directly under her chin, she resembled a giant praying mantis. "I was terribly shocked and saddened to hear of the death of your aunt," she said to Arlanda. "She had been my patient for twenty years. Sending her file to the coroner's office was one of the most difficult things I've ever done."

Arlanda nodded her thanks, said, "It's very kind of you to see us on such short notice."

"No problem. What can I do for you?"

"We have some questions?" Arlanda turned to me, oddly nervous, her fingers twisting the straps to the purse on her lap.

"What kind of stuff goes into a patient's file?" I asked.

"Stuff?" Dr. Scarpers' smile patronized me. "It's all pretty standard, no matter who the patient."

I was too ignorant to articulate the dread I felt in my gut, which had as much to do with the smell of disinfectant and the imagined screams of patients being prepared for root-canal surgery as it did my suspicions. I'm a coward in dental offices, the kind of person who, before any dental work can be done, needs something stronger than Novocain or nitrous oxide, like general anaesthesia and a big hammer. I said, "Educate me."

Few people can resist the opportunity to demonstrate their expertise, and Dr. Scarpers was not one of the few. "The most important items in any patient file are the X rays. We follow the American Dental Association standard of care, which requires one full set of X rays be taken every three years, supplemented in off years by bitewing X rays."

"What are those?"

"The little ones you have to bite down on," Arlanda said.

I looked at her, surprised.

"I thought everybody knew that."

"Not everybody, obviously," Dr. Scarpers said with a deferential nod to Arlanda. "Bitewing X rays provide a view of several consecutive teeth, such as the molars on one side of the jaw. We use a panoramic X ray for the full set, where all thirty-two teeth appear on one set of film. I did a panoramic on Ms. Doubleday this past summer, so that would be her most recent X ray. Then each file includes a dental chart."

She lifted a photocopied chart from the drawer to her left and spread it flat on the desk. The photocopy depicted top views of the upper and lower teeth. From the holder beside her computer monitor she selected a red pencil. "When we examine a patient, we mark any problems that need to be corrected in red." She drew a solid red circle on one of the molars and replaced the red pencil in favor of a blue one. "Then when we've finished the work, we mark blue over the red, to indicate the problem has been corrected. This lets us see at a glance what work we've done on any particular patient."

"Only your work? Not other dental work?"

"Just what we've done. If we want to see her entire dental history, we consult the X rays. The file contains a few other items, such as the patient's preferred method of payment, their health history—allergies, known problems, and so on—and we ask them to fill out a short form that asks certain questions which might be of importance to us, such as whether the patient has ever had an unpleasant dental experience."

"Hasn't everybody?"

She didn't smile. "Some people love the dentist, and those who see their dentist regularly have fewer problems and thus little pain. If you don't see the dentist for five years, I guarantee you will not have a fun time when you finally go. Imagine a person who doesn't exercise. When she finally tries to work into shape, it's going to hurt, isn't it?"

Whenever something hurt, it almost always turned out to be my fault. I asked, "Angela Doubleday's file, did you send the whole thing or just part of it?"

"The entire file."

"And the coroner looks at everything in the file?"

"I wasn't there during the autopsy, so I can't tell you definitively what parts of the file he consulted and what he ignored, but I can tell you that he would have no reason to look at anything other than the most recent X ray."

"Why not?"

"For the very reason that teeth are so accurate in identifying human remains. The first eight or so teeth examined are usually enough to eliminate everybody except the patient. Say a person has an MOD silver filling in tooth number two, number four has a crown, and another filling is in number five. The odds are greater than a hundred thousand to one that the same combination repeats in another patient in the same locations. All the coroner really needs is the most recent record of the patient's teeth to make his identification, and he'll find that in the X ray."

"Did you examine the file before you sent it off?"

Dr. Scarpers leaned back and stared at me down the length of her nose. She had a long nose, and it was a long stare, as though she considered my question one of the oddest she'd heard in an odd lifetime. "I never even considered examining the file. Why should I do that?"

"To make sure everything was there."

"My filing system is very precise. Of course everything was there. Where else would it be?"

"I just thought, when your office was broken into, you would have opened it up, verified the contents."

Arlanda glanced at me, startled. It was the first she'd heard of it. First I'd heard of it, too.

"No, that's not true." Dr. Scarpers shook her head to emphasize the denial. "We haven't had any burglaries. Not this year and not last year. We've never been robbed. We have an alarm system, because of the drugs and equipment."

"I didn't say you were robbed. I said someone broke in."

"Are you talking about the false alarm?"

"I don't know what I'm talking about, not really, but that's never stopped me before." I waited for a smile from Dr. Scarpers. I didn't get one. "Of course I'm talking about the false alarm."

"One night the alarm went off. The security company responded, like they always do, to check the premises. Everything was locked tight. I checked my supplies the next morning. Nothing was stolen. They said it was a false alarm, happens every now and then."

"How long ago?"

Dr. Scarpers flipped through a leather-bound appointment calendar on her desk. "Two weeks ago yesterday."

"Three days before the fire," I said, counting the days in my head.

"Are you suggesting there's a problem with the identification?"

"Let's assume that the teeth identified as Angela Doubleday's aren't hers at all, but those of somebody else. How could the coroner have possibly misidentified them as her teeth?"

"Wait a minute," Arlanda's voice cracked. "Aunt Angela is dead, right? I mean, the police say she's dead, the coroner says she's dead, the newspapers say she's dead, the entire town of Douglas showed up at Calvary Cemetery to bury her, minister, mayor, and all, and you're trying to tell me that you don't think it was her we buried?"

"I'm not trying to tell you anything yet, okay?" In fact I was trying to tell her something and dreaded it, because if Angela Doubleday wasn't buried in the crypt bearing her name, she might still be alive. "The man I saw inside Doubleday's house the day of the fire, his brother studied dentistry. The brother, they expelled him before the end of his second year, but he took enough courses to know his way around a set of teeth. Maybe he's the guy who shot me, the dark-haired one in the sketches we had made. Maybe he's not. But I want to look again at what happened, this time with a different set of assumptions, only I'm too ignorant about dentistry to figure things out myself."

Dr. Scarpers leaned back in her chair. She was not a woman given to smiles, and when she did, it nearly unhinged her jaw. "When I first began in practice my partner and I had an idea about that. We plotted and schemed like a couple of real criminals. If you give me the right person and a long day of work, I can make two people's teeth match on X ray exactly."

"Any two people?"

"You'd want two people of similar age and dental condition, to save yourself a lot of work. What you need to do is examine each set of teeth and match the work tooth by tooth. If the first person has a crown on tooth number four, you put a crown in number four on the second person. If the second person has a filling in number fifteen, then you drill number fifteen in the first person, too. Understand? You cross-reference and duplicate the work found in both sets of teeth, so they line up exactly. On the X ray, nobody would be able to tell the two apart. My partner and I fantasized about staging a fake murder and running away to South America on the insurance money."

"Sounds like you have a fun partner."

"I did, once. She committed suicide."

"I'm sorry."

She shrugged, the gesture of a survivor past caring why she was the one who survived. "You'd need a corpse, of course, or someone you plan to make the corpse. That was the major sticking point in our plan, the need to kill someone, though I suppose we could have stolen a cadaver from somewhere."

"It sounds a little complicated. If I understand you right, the killer would need not only to match somebody's teeth to Angela Double-day's but drill and X ray Doubleday too, to match the work done in the cadaver's mouth. Then he'd have to break into the office and replace the latest X ray in Doubleday's file with the new X ray."

"This conversation is making me nauseous," Arlanda said.

Dr. Scarpers searched a drawer to her left, pulled out a white paper sack, and offered it across the desk.

Arlanda stared at it, confused.

"In the event you can't make it to the bathroom in time."

She took the bag and clutched it against her lap.

I said, "Wouldn't it be easier to bypass all that work and just switch files?"

The magnified eyes behind the big black-framed glasses stilled, and after a moment, Dr. Scarpers pursed her mouth, as though sucking on a pleasantly sour lozenge. "The date and patient's name are hand-labeled on the X rays, so you're right, those could be easily switched, because there's nothing in the X ray itself that would identify the pa-tient, except for the teeth. The chart could be forged, too. All dentists use a similar system for marking work done, so any perpetrator with basic knowledge of dentistry and practice could forge one." She smiled at the word *perpetrator* as though, having waited for years to use it in conversation, she was proud to have used it appropriately. "The chart and labeling are done by my assistants, and I've had several over the years, so it's not easy to identify whose handwriting is whose, either. And nobody would have to break in, though they'd need to break out."

"Break out?"

"I don't employ a full-time receptionist. Someone could stroll into the office near closing time and hide in one of the rooms until we've left. Once inside and alone, they could switch items in any file they chose. That might explain the so-called false alarm, too."

"They're already inside the office, they open the door to leave . . ."

"And the alarm goes off."

"Your rent-a-cops investigate, but no broken glass, no obvious sign of entry, so everybody assumes the system malfunctioned."

"This is all terribly clever. Someone could very well have switched the files, and I wouldn't have noticed."

Arlanda stood so rapidly her chair squealed on the linoleum. "This is too much. I need some air." The white bag fluttered to the floor and she was gone, brand new heels tapping down the corridor.

Dr. Scarpers allowed a moment of polite silence to pass before she asked, "She's Ms. Doubleday's sole surviving relative?"

I confirmed that she was.

"Then she must be very upset right now."

"Very. But her feelings are secondary."

Dr. Scarpers didn't need much encouragement to continue. The puzzle intrigued her. "You'd still need a cadaver to work with, and a single X ray probably wouldn't be enough," she said. "What if the coroner picks up the wrong X ray to start? If you're going to the trouble of making the switch, you might as well take several sets of X rays. Each one requires no more than a few minutes. Ms. Doubleday was my patient for twenty years, so she'd have seven full sets of X rays in her file. A couple of hours of work."

"That way, the coroner picks up any of the other X rays, at least he's looking at the same set of teeth."

"Correct. I guarantee you he will not check each X ray, but he might glance through them, and if they're not the same mouth, he'd notice."

"Then how do we prove a switch has been made?"

"By the time line."

"You mean the time line in the X rays, from the first to last?"

She nodded, waited for me to figure it out.

"But each X ray is the same," I said. "So there is no time line."

"And that's how you prove the file has been tampered with. If every X ray is the same, that means she hasn't had any dental work done in the twenty years she has been in my care. I know I've worked on Ms. Doubleday's teeth in the last twenty years, and my billing records will prove it. The coroner can also compare the X rays against the dental chart."

"Because the dental chart might show work that the X rays wouldn't confirm?"

"Exactly. And let's say whoever may have done this—" She raised a cautionary finger. "And I stress *may have*, because this is speculation, not fact—let's say he went to the trouble to drill and fill randomly between sets of X rays, to show a progression of work. I'd still be able to nail him with the billing records, which document precisely when I performed each procedure."

"So no matter how it was done, you'd know."

"He'd need to be working from an exact copy of Doubleday's mouth to fool me."

"That's not likely," I said.

"Not likely at all. But proving something could have happened isn't the same as proving it did. Have you voiced your suspicions to the coroner?"

"Why would the coroner listen to me?"

"You're right." Her eyebrows arched and dipped above her glasses. "He wouldn't. But he'll listen to me. If there's even a remote chance that he incorrectly identified the remains, it means Angela Doubleday could still be alive. I imagine the coroner would like to be the one to break that news, rather than have the news break him."

TWENTY NINE

On the western edge of Beverly Hills, Sunset Boulevard turns serpentine, dipping and rolling through Bel Air on its way to the sea. It's a beautiful drive in a convertible, the verdant landscapes of multi-million-dollar estates fringing the boulevard north and south, and the closest to wealth I'd ever get. Behind the wind-flicked tendrils of her hair Arlanda's eyes were veined from the effort of crying. "You must think I'm horrible!" she shouted above the wind and engine. The Rott sat on the floor at her feet, his head cradled mournfully in her lap.

"I know some people who'd kill to be in your situation. On one hand, you have a sizable inheritance, and on the other . . ." I straightened the Caddy out of a curve and looked at her for as long as I dared in traffic. Her eyes were huge with anticipation. "On the other hand you have an aunt you've seen a dozen times in your life. I don't think you're horrible. Not at all. I do think you're confused. I'll admit to that. But anybody would be confused. And I think most of us would admit in the darkest corner of our heart we'd take the money, no question."

"I feel terrible even thinking that way." Again, shouting over the wind. "It's her money, not mine. She was incredibly generous to give me anything at all. And now, when you suggest she might not be dead, I . . ."

"Resent me for it?"

"Don't support you as much as I could."

I caught a red light at Hilgard, and her voice quieted to a whisper.

"Do you really think she's alive?"

"I think it's possible she was alive the day after the fire, less possible she's alive now."

"But why would they want her alive at all?"

"For the same reason they might want to kill her."

"For the diamonds?"

"We know she collected them, we know Ray Belgard was at her house the day of the fire, and we know he's wanted in the disappearance of another woman whose jewels went missing when she did. We don't know where your aunt kept the diamonds, and if Belgard and his brother don't yet know where they are either, then there's a chance she's still alive."

"They'd torture her, wouldn't they?"

"We don't know what they'd do."

The light changed and the Caddy accelerated with the flow of traffic past the 405 Freeway and down the long slope of Sunset to the sea. Arlanda brooded in the passenger seat, the Rott staring up at her, sad eyed, knowing in the way of animals that something troubled her. He probably thought she was like him, hungry and needing to run. The wide blue Pacific opened above the road, and we coasted down to the Pacific Coast Highway.

"We have to find her," Arlanda shouted, not above the wind this time, but from intensity of feeling. "I'll put full page advertisements in the newspapers if I have to."

"Talk to the police first. They may not want you to do that."

"They might not want to do anything, and I swear to God, I'll kick their butts in the press if they don't cooperate. I'll offer a reward, a hundred thousand dollars. And I'll make sure you get part of it, no matter what. I wouldn't even know about the diamonds without you."

"Thanks for the offer, but I'm not doing this for money."

"And I am? Doesn't that make you superior."

"Doesn't make me any better. Just makes me who I am."

"And what does that make me? A money-grubbing opportunist?"

It wasn't up to me to accuse or console her, not when she was blaming me for her current troubles, and so I remained silent until she said, again, "I'm horrible, I know."

"Like I said, you're confused. Tell the police what you know. If your aunt's dentist talks to the coroner like she promised and the coroner sees that the file has been forged, they'll want to cooperate with you, unless you start out to make them look like fools."

"You'll come with me when I talk to them?"

"Can't. I'm going away for a couple of days, up the coast."

"Strange time to take a holiday, isn't it?"

"I've got health problems."

"You look fine to me."

I shrugged, not wanting to spell it out.

"Can't you stay? I need you."

"Somebody has tried twice to kill me. Ever heard of the expression 'third time's a charm'?"

A poster on a telephone pole flitted past to spark a memory of someone else gone missing. My foot kicked the brake. The Cadillac swerved to the shoulder and I leapt from behind the wheel before the dust from the wheels settled. The missing woman whose photograph had been stapled to the telephone pole had been caught in the act of turning toward the camera as she held a cake, perhaps in celebration of a child's birthday. Her smile was generous, as though genuinely delighted to be there, but couldn't conceal the pain in her eyes. I'd captured the same pain in photographs of my mother. It was the expression of a woman who coped and pretended it was happiness. The woman had gone missing a few days before the fire. I'd met her husband further up the coast, across from a gas station, while posting found-dog notices. She'd been on medication at the time of her disappearance. Prozac, he'd said. I carefully tore the poster free of the staples and ran back to the car.

"This is the woman whose remains might be in your aunt's crypt." I tossed the poster onto the dash in front of her. "I'm not sure, and I don't know whether anybody can ever be sure because the remains are cremated, but look at the dates. They line up perfectly."

The Rott raised his head at my obvious excitement, his rump of a tail wagging. Arlanda blinked, twice, and each blink fell like a door slamming behind her as she retreated deep inside herself, to a place where she couldn't be touched. Then she leaned forward, her jaw trembling, and cried, in grief or disappointment, I didn't know.

THIRTY

I found an envelope taped to my front door when the Rott and I climbed the steps to my apartment. One floor below, the door of my downstairs neighbor slammed shut with vindictive force. The envelope was addressed to me in my landlord's distinctive, blunt-lettered hand. I peeled away the tape and slit the lip with the nail on my right thumb, the only nail I haven't bitten down to the nub, and keyed open the door. The form I shook from the envelope was an eviction notice, dated the day after I'd left for Arizona. I set the camera case and duffel bag on the floor just inside the doorway. The Rott trotted into the bathroom to drink from the toilet. The apartment smelled stuffy and ripe, as though something small had curled up and died. I followed my nose to the sink, where a half week of unwashed dishes rotted. I'd neglected to take out the trash, too. Home sweet home.

My initial reaction to bad news is to ignore it. The red light of the answering machine steadily blinked in the corner of the room. I tapped the play-messages button and prepared to repack. Envelope? What envelope? There wasn't any envelope taped to my door. I haven't been home the last four nights. Somebody must have ripped it off, thinking there was money inside. Ostriches might not rule the world, but they haven't gone extinct yet, so there must be something to the head-in-the-sand strategy. I opened the closet door and rummaged around the bottom shelf for a change of socks and underwear. Frank's digitized voice played through the answering machine, reminding me that his Pulitzer Prize–worthy article on the Belgards would hit the newsstands the next day; I should take a vacation because he didn't have the time to write my obituary. Sweet guy. I kept the boots on my feet, tossed my sandals into the closet, and repacked the sneakers, looking forward to running the beach in Morro Bay. I packed two bottles of water and a copy of Dickens' *Bleak House* and took my overnight kit into the bathroom for restocking. Three calls were from a Detective Alvarez. He wanted to talk to me about Lupe Potrero. The third time he called he said he found it interesting that I was on parole for manslaughter and didn't return his phone calls. Just what I needed—another cop on my tail. The Rott stuck his nose into everything I opened, probably thinking he'd find food in there. When I finished packing I sat on the toilet and unfolded the notice.

In the judgment of the landlord, I had violated the terms of the lease by changing the locks without his permission and by keeping a dog on the premises, the keeping of any pets strictly forbidden by clause such and such of the lease agreement without prior permission of the landlord. As a result of these violations, he was terminating our lease agreement and serving notice that I had until the end of the month to quit the premises or face legal action to evict. I tore the notice into strips, tore the strips into wedges, and flushed the lot down the toilet.

Problem solved.

The doorbell rang as the last scrap glugged down the hole. The bell startled the Rott, who went into a barking fit deep and loud enough to rattle the fixtures. I glanced into the peephole and came eye to parabolic eye with my landlord, the fish-eye lens sharpening his nose and bending his face like a cartoon character. My downstairs neighbor had probably called him the moment his front door slammed. I grabbed the Rott by the collar and pulled him into the bathroom. He whined in protest. I shushed and locked him in. The bell rang a third time just as I opened the front door, chain attached. The effort of pressing the bell had flushed my landlord's skin red and beaded his forehead with perspiration. His gaze traveled the short length of chain, offended that I wasn't opening the door wide to let him in.

"Did you receive the envelope I left for you?"

I said nothing.

"Did you read the notice?"

Again, I said nothing.

"I heard the dog as I was ringing the bell. I know you've got one in there."

"You might have talked to me before acting," I said.

"You changed the locks without permission, without notifying me. That alone is grounds for eviction." His lips pursed as he fingered the front-door knob, a gesture of deep moral indignity.

"Someone picked the last lock, broke into the apartment. I filed a report with the police. Now that I think about it, maybe the lock wasn't picked. Maybe it was you. You let yourself in while I was gone, snoop around my underwear drawer?"

"I own this apartment. I have the legal right to a key and to let myself in to check on the condition of the premises."

"This isn't about keys or dogs. It's about money."

"You violated the terms of your lease."

"You moved to evict without even talking to me."

"I'm talking to you right now."

"You already find somebody to rent the apartment at double what I'm paying, maybe a friend of the geek downstairs?"

"What I do with this apartment is none of your business."

The phone in my apartment rang.

I said, "If you intend to grub after money like a pig, at least have the guts to admit it."

"Conversation over. You're out of here!"

He shouted at me like it was a game of baseball we were playing.

"You refund my deposit, with three months' rent as a penalty for the inconvenience, then I'll willingly leave. I know a lawyer who'd love to work pro bono on a case involving illegal eviction. Even if he loses, it's six months of court costs for you, minimum, before I'm out. Your choice. Excuse me, I have to take this call."

I shut the door gently, proud of my self-restraint. I could have slammed it in his face. I could have snaked a left through the gap and tagged him in the jaw, too. I was maturing as a human being. The answering machine picked up before I made it to the phone. I should have guessed the caller: Detective Alvarez, clearly identifying himself as a homicide investigator with LASD. He needed to talk to me about Lupe Potrero, he said. It was important. My hand was reaching for the phone when he said I was not a suspect *at this time*. I pulled back, angered. That he didn't consider me a suspect at this time meant he already suspected me but didn't have the evidence, and if I refused to cooperate promptly that would be evidence enough. He recited his phone number twice, told me again to call him, and hung up. The last thing I wanted to do just then was to talk to another bullying cop. I let the Rott out of the bathroom, snatched the duffel bag from the floor, and sped down the stairs, flipping off my astonished landlord and downstairs neighbor on my way to the open road.

Thirty One

My parole officer let me run sixty miles, the Cadillac's headlights flashing through the tunnel of night north of Ventura, before my mobile phone lit with an incoming call and I felt the jerk of her chain at my neck. I let it ring, arguing the consequences of waiting for voice mail to pick up. I wanted to be free for a few days, free of the person trying to hurt me, free of the cops, free of her. The argument was a short one. Trying to withhold information from my parole officer was like getting an arm stuck in a tree shredder; the longer I waited the more I lost. I opened the connection, said, "You shouldn't be working this late, Ms. Graves."

"I wouldn't be working this late if you weren't such a pain in the ass. You want to tell me what's going on?" My parole officer liked to make open accusations and wait for the confession.

"Not much. Just a beautiful night and the open road."

"You sound too cheerful."

"Is that a crime?"

"Are you running from something?"

"A lot of things. I'm running from a lot of things. But I'm not fast enough. Things are catching up. You want to save the state a big phone bill, tell me what I'm being accused of now?"

"You'd help your own cause if you tried to be in the least bit help-ful. I just got off the phone with a homicide detective from LASD."

"Alvarez?"

"So you know he's been trying to reach you."

I glanced at the dashboard clock.

"I've known for a little over an hour."

"He's been trying to reach you since yesterday afternoon. When you didn't return his calls, he called me, wondering why you were avoiding him."

"I didn't get home last night."

"Where were you?"

"You sound like my mother."

"Your mother doesn't have the power to recommend the court revoke your parole. Answer the question."

I answered the question. I spent the night at the apartment of a colleague, working on a story that was going to break the next morn-ing, a story that the reporter thought might make me even more of a target than I already was. I considered telling her about the attack on Ben's trailer, decided she sounded angry enough. I'd mention it later.

"That remark about the open road—you're leaving town?"

"Just for a couple of days."

"You're involved in two murder investigations, Ms. Zero. I have no reason to believe you're guilty of anything more than wrong place, wrong time, but you are definitely walking the edge of the precipice. You're putting yourself into situations where you're bound to violate the terms of your parole, sooner or later, you understand me?"

I said, "Yes, ma'am."

"Normally, I'd demand some serious face time, but under the cir-cumstances, I think you're doing the right thing—for once—in getting out of town. Two things you have to do to square things with me. You ready to hear them?"

I said, "Yes, ma'am."

"Call Detective Alvarez. Now. Cooperate fully."

I said, "Yes, ma'am."

"Where you going?"

"I thought Morro Bay."

"You call and leave a message, the phone number and motel where you're staying, then you check in with me every twenty-four hours. Is that clear?"

I said, "Yes, ma'am."

"One other thing. Detective Claymore was placed on administrative leave. He's supposed to check into a detox program."

"Good for him," I said.

"Maybe not so good for you, though. Right now, he can't touch you. But just because he crossed the line doesn't mean he doesn't have friends. I can think of a half dozen officers who consider it their personal duty to put you behind bars again."

"So I should get me to a nunnery?"

"I'm not sure even a nunnery would be safe," she said.

Morro Bay is too far north for even the most fanatical of Los Angeles commuters, and the once pristine sweep of bay, anchored on the north by a bullet-nosed rock 575 feet high, is raked to the south by three toweringly obscene power-station smokestacks, sticking like fingers into the eye of any south-facing view. The ugliness of the electrical station was a brilliant stroke, saving the town from the kind of tourist gentrification that results in hundred-dollar-a-night-minimum hotel rooms and downtown streets that look like they were constructed from a dollhouse kit. People fish in Morro Bay, elbow to fin with plentiful seals and otters, the kids surf the other side of the rock, birds flock to the local wetlands and wildlife sanctuaries, and the tourists mostly stay away.

I searched the streets for a pets-welcome sign and checked into the Log Cabin Inn, one of those 1960s California structures designed to look like its name. The rooms weren't deluxe but neither were the prices. My rapidly thinning sheaf of twenties would cover three or four nights; after that, I'd need to find paying work or start kiting checks. I used the phone in the room to call Detective Alvarez. It was past 10:00 P.M. Funny enough, he wasn't in. I left a message saying sorry I'd missed his call, I'd try again later. My parole officer didn't answer the phone either. I told her where I was staying and took the Rott for a walk.

Morro Bay is a safe town at any hour, and I pride myself at being tough and savvy enough to walk alone down most streets without fear, but still I felt, if not exactly afraid, oddly alert while I followed the streets down to the fishing harbor. I didn't see or hear anyone but imagined that someone followed me, and that alone was enough to spook the walk short. When we got back to the room, I chained the door, wedged a chair beneath the knob, and let the Rott sleep next to me on the bed.

The feeling had dissipated by the time the Rott woke me the next morning, anxious to start his morning patrol. I took him for a long run on the beach, past Morro Rock, moated by high tide, and back to the motel on a trail that passed along the estuary. We didn't encounter any trouble on the run, aside from a silky terrier who took exception to the Rott, barking and charging on the end of his leash as though, if the owner had been foolish enough to let him go, he'd launch all seven and one-quarter pounds of his ferocious self straight for the Rott's throat. I'd never seen the Rott afraid of anything like he was afraid of that little dog. When I keyed the door to the room we'd been gone a little more than an hour.

"Mary Alice Baker?"

Conditioned by experience, I crossed my wrists behind my back at the mention of my birth name.

"Or would you prefer I call you, what's your alias, the one your photographs run under?"

I glanced back over my shoulder, said, "Nina Zero."

"I'd like to talk to you, if you could spare a few minutes."

The man was a mid-forties Chicano, his skin pebbled by old acne scars. A silver horseshoe belt buckle supported a paunch just big enough to make his Levi's fit awkwardly. The bulge was beneath the right side of his beige windbreaker, making him a left-handed shooter.

"Detective?" I asked.

He slapped his forehead, as though embarrassed to have forgotten to introduce himself, and produced his badge wallet from the left side pocket of the windbreaker. "Alvarez. I called and left a bunch of messages on your answering machine."

I nodded. "You got the name of the motel from my parole officer."

He pocketed his badge wallet, said, "I wouldn't mind getting a little something to eat, if you want to get yourself cleaned up and join me."

"Long way to drive to interview a witness," I said.

He pointed to a white Chevy Caprice in the far corner of the motel parking lot. "I'll wait for you in my car. I'd appreciate it if you'd make the shower a fast one. Like you said, it's a long drive."

The restaurant he chose for breakfast was a flapjack-and-bacon place a block from the motel. My parole officer had said a number of cops wanted me behind bars again, and as I hastily showered and pulled on my clothes, I wondered if Alvarez was one of them. We sat at a window booth. I'd tied the Rott to the end of a row of newspaper vending machines, where I could keep an eye on him. He was a big, friendly dog but still, most people bought their news from the opposite end of the row.

"I hear you've had a few problems with the law," Alvarez said. He'd reached the age where he needed glasses to read the fine print on the menu, and he jabbed a glance above the top rims to test my reaction.

"A few," I said.

He nodded, flipped the page. "When I got up this morning, I thought, this is a great opportunity to get out of the city, take a little drive up the coast on the county's tab, breathe in some sea air, make a good half day of it while acquiring some information from a key witness." He snapped the menu shut and signaled the waitress. "But I didn't drive all the way up here to listen to one- or two-word replies to my questions, particularly not when I'm buying."

The waitress kept her distance from the table when she came to take the order, sensing rightly that Detective Alvarez and I had been thrust into the same booth by some unpleasant circumstance, or maybe she was just wary of those who weren't local. She warmed a little when I asked for a plate of steak tartar for the dog, said she had a dog herself, a Lab, and turned on the rubber heels of her orthopedic shoes to place our order.

"I'm not stonewalling you. You need to make your question a little more specific," I said. "For example, are you talking about my past problems with the law, which I've fully bought and paid for, or are you talking about the fact that I'm neck deep in law-enforcement officials because I was unlucky enough to be on the hill above Angela Doubleday's place the day it burned? I hope you're talking about the latter because every time somebody tries to use my so-called criminal record as a club I just turn stubborn."

We stared each other down over the ketchup and syrup bottles.

"You're a real pistola, aren't you?"

"Only in self-defense."

He slowly reached for his coffee cup and took a sip. "Relax, I came for a friendly interview."

I smiled, trying to look friendly.

"You may have heard that Detective Claymore has been placed on administrative leave."

"I heard."

He waited for me to amplify my remark. I didn't.

"When the charges against you fell apart, the department decided to step back, take another look at the evidence . . ."

"With someone new in charge, thank God," I said.

"I don't know if you have God to thank, unless you consider the chief to be divine. I do know he's pretty damn close to considering himself divine, so maybe you got a point after all. It's pretty obvious, when you look at things, that you're in the center of what's going on. Now, the previous investigator took that to mean you were guilty of lighting the match that killed Angela Doubleday. If you're not guilty of that . . ."

"I'm not," I said.

"Good to hear it. No disrespect intended, but if we relied solely on confessions of innocence, we'd never get anywhere with ninety-five percent of our cases. But with you specifically, I see no reason to doubt your word. Just to keep things official, tell me where you were Sunday night, between, say, eight P.M. and two A.M."

Sunday night, the night Lupe Potrero had been murdered.

"The slow lane on Interstate 10, between Phoenix and Indio. After midnight I pulled off the road to sleep out the sunrise."

"Anybody with you?"

"The dog," I said, pointing out the window with my chin.

"I don't think his word counts. Anybody see you on the road?"

"A couple of gas jockeys."

"Would they remember you?"

I shrugged.

He didn't look happy. He needed a firm alibi to clear me as a suspect, and that I didn't have one meant one more loose end to tie.

I said, "Arlanda Cortes will verify that I was in Douglas at one-thirty in the afternoon. The fastest anyone can drive the stretch of road between Douglas and Malibu is twelve hours."

"Why Malibu?" His tone was as sharply suspicious as his glance.

"What, you think that's a detail only Potrero's killer knows, like the coroner found saltwater in his lungs? Potrero's body was found in the ocean off Malibu, and I saw his truck parked by the side of the road, that's why Malibu. You want to know if I could have been in Malibu during those hours to kill him, right? If I drove like a maniac, sure, I could have leapt out of my car and hit him over the head with a sack of takeout burgers bought on the way and still had a good five seconds to spare. Unfortunately I don't have a motive, unless you believe I have a cop fetish and did the whole thing just so one would finally ask me out to breakfast."

He took another sip of coffee. "When you get wound up you really let go, don't you?"

"You're the one said he didn't want any one-word answers."

He set the coffee cup down, watched me with worn but patient eyes. "As I was saying, when you look at this, it's pretty obvious that you're at the center of things. Claymore thought it was because you'd set the fire. But let's try another angle. Maybe you're at the center because you told the truth, because you saw the people who set the fire. Follow me so far?"

I nodded.

"So what I need from you is a complete statement. I want you to walk me through everything you can remember that might be important, starting from that day on the hill above Angela Doubleday's place, and ending"—he glanced at his watch—"about a half hour ago."

"You want me to talk about both Doubleday and Potrero?"

Alvarez slipped a pad and pencil from the inside breast pocket of his windbreaker and started to jot down a few details of the conversation we'd already had. "As much as you can remember."

"That means you see their deaths as linked."

"That's one of the possibilities we're checking."

"Are you heading both investigations?"

"Me personally? No. We work in teams at LASD."

"But you're one of the lead investigators."

He shrugged as though it didn't matter, meaning yes.

I told him everything, talking through a breakfast of pancakes, eggs, bacon, sausage, and bottomless cups of coffee. He took detailed notes in a slashing hand, left elbow angled sharply out and his writing hand curved above the line in the backward style of most lefties. He asked pointed, intelligent questions that switched rapidly back and forth along the time line of incidents, making sure I told the story straight and that he understood it. When finished we walked out to the row of newspaper vending machines, where I untied the Rott, asked, "You didn't by any chance get into town last night, did you?"

"This morning," he said.

"I had a strange feeling last night, somebody was behind me, hoped maybe it was you."

"I didn't leave L.A. until six this morning."

"I'm sure I'm just being paranoid."

"Considering the story you just told me, I'd say a little paranoia is justified." Alvarez knelt to get up close and personal with the Rott, dropping his voice an octave and calling the dog a good boy. "You take this dog with you everywhere?" He scratched behind the dog's ear and adjusted his collar.

"I'm not sure if I take him or he takes me."

"He's big enough, that's for sure."

Alvarez stood and offered his hand. I took it. He told me to be careful and to call if I thought of anything else. I promised I would. When he drove away I gave the Rott a pat, thought Alvarez was a pretty decent guy, for a homicide detective.

The Rott and I took a long walk that day around the wetlands to the north, the Rott tightly leashed because of the herons, sandpipers, and other coastal birds. For the first time in what seemed like years, I felt vaguely hopeful that things might turn out well for me. Most of the prisoners who greet the outside world with certainty on parole plan to return to the same ways and habits that imprisoned them. They fall back into the life of drugs and thievery because that's what they know, and there is great comfort in the familiar. I'd never been a criminal. I'm allergic to drugs and I can't steal things. I wasn't afraid of returning to the criminal life because I'd never lived it. The life I'd lived before had vaporized. I had nothing to go back to. No friends, no job, no family. A deep and abiding rage took their place, combined with an interest in photography and a little hope. I wasn't angry at everyone, and I wasn't angry all the time, but my rage was never distant, and it was the closest thing I had to a best friend. When I needed my rage, it was there, and it saved me from harm on more than one occasion. It also came to me when I hadn't called it, and when it did, I always regretted the wake it left behind.

My rage nearly burned itself out after my husband died, like a star that goes supernova and all at once collapses. For a while, I felt nothing—not grief, not pain, not regret. My emotions spun down to a hard, black core from which no light escaped. Only my love of photography remained, and for a while, that sustained me. I have suffered through emotional changes often enough to know that I was passing through another one, that this too would end, but I didn't know whether it would end someplace better or far worse. An odd thing happened then. A toothless dog walked out of a brushfire and into my life. The Rott had suffered too, but he was a happy animal. His happiness was infectious. I couldn't fairly say I'd caught it completely, but the dark and oppressive pull of my heart lightened. I began to feel again. Those feelings were awkward, sometimes stumbling things and maybe not always appropriate, but I was beginning to think that I might make it, that my life wouldn't turn out as badly as I'd feared.

Arlanda's call came while I was eating dinner at an outdoor fish-and-chips place on the waterfront. The Rott was a good companion, though having him by my side limited the choice of restaurants, and our dinner conversation was a little short of stimulating. I welcomed a call from Arlanda, even if she didn't sound particularly happy.

"We need to talk," she said.

"Normally, it's rude to talk on the phone in front of your dinner companion, but I don't think Baby will mind." I was trying to be funny, cheer her up a bit.

"I don't want to talk about this over the phone."

"Why don't you come up tomorrow, relax a bit?"

"I'm not free to just pick up and leave," she said, a stab at me and forgetting that she had done just that in flying to California. "When do you think you'll come back to L.A.?"

"How's Ben? I didn't call him today."

She didn't answer.

"You didn't talk to him either," I said.

"I don't need you to guilt-trip me about Ben."

"Fine," I said, meaning the opposite. "I was thinking about going to see him anyway. Should get there about noon tomorrow, if you want to meet me there."

My anger didn't last more than a few minutes after I hung up the phone. All friendships have their awkward moments, particularly at the start, when one doesn't know the other's blind spots and insecurities.

Every now and then I resented something about her—her easy command of the Rott's affection, her tendency to cling to me one moment and cast me aside the next—but the resentment passed the moment I saw her again or heard the crack in her voice when she laughed. I went to bed that night looking forward to seeing her again.

Ben was sitting in a cranked-up bed when I got to the hospital, carefully spooning rice pudding while he read a copy of *Sports Illustrated* propped against his water container. "Hey, I thought you were up north somewhere," he said, setting the spoon aside.

"Still am," I said, taking his hand between both of mine. "Just came down for the day."

"Not on my account, I hope."

His grip was stronger than the last time I'd seen him, but his skin looked like parchment, thin and dry, and I felt the bones in his hand click together when we shook. "Thought I'd check how long it's going to take you to recuperate," I said. "I don't have anybody to drink with anymore. The darn dog quits after one beer."

He laughed, waved me to sit down. "Your Rottweilers don't strike me as a drinking breed. You want a dog that drinks, try a poodle. I had a girlfriend once, her dog was a toy poodle, little thing not much bigger than a cat, but he could really pack it away. We'd have these backyard barbecues, set up a keg with a bowl beneath the spigot to catch the spill, and he'd keep that bowl dry as a bone."

"You had a girlfriend?"

"Don't sound so surprised. I haven't been celibate my whole life. Just for the past—" He glanced at the ceiling and made a show of counting. "Twenty years."

Arlanda poked her head around the door, her face framed by a bouquet of flowers from the hospital florist. "You want to keep it down in here? This isn't a bar, it's a hospital. I could hear you halfway down the hall." Her smile contradicted the attempt to admonish us. She kissed Ben on both cheeks, gave me a nod, and arranged the flowers on the bedside table.

"Ben was just telling me about his ex-girlfriend," I said.

"I wasn't talking about her at all," he protested. "I was talking about her dog."

"Who was she?" Arlanda stood at the end of the bed, shifting her weight from one foot to another.

"Name was Barbara. Worked as a dispatcher."

I asked, "You ever marry?"

"Her?" He grunted. "No."

"I meant anybody."

He looked at me like, back off.

"Just curious," I said.

"Only time I wanted to, didn't work out."

"You didn't miss much, if my experience is any guide," Arlanda said and took a step toward the door. "Nina? You have a moment? We need to talk." She nodded to Ben. "You'll excuse us?"

I stood, irritated and confused in equal measure, and followed her down the hall. She walked quickly, veering toward the elevators past the nursing station. "You leave Baby in the car?" she said.

The elevator doors slid open. I followed her inside.

"You leave him in the car a lot, don't you?"

"Is that what you want to talk about?"

She waited, watching the floor numbers light as we descended toward the ground floor. "No. I talked to Dr. Scarpers yesterday. The coroner is sticking with his identification of my aunt's remains."

She bolted from the elevator the moment the doors opened. I chased her heels through the lobby. "Did you expect him to admit he was wrong?"

She glanced once over her shoulder, eyes like bullets, and pushed through the doors into the central courtyard. "Dr. Scarpers examined the file herself. She agrees with the coroner. Nothing contradicts the original identification."

"And nothing disproves the switch either, I bet."

When she finally stopped, at the corner of the terrarium, she crossed her arms over her chest and stood with the toe of her right pump kicked out. "You just have to be right, don't you? Well, here's another one. Remember the missing person poster you tore off the telephone pole? I called the number listed on it, spoke to the man who put them up. His wife called him last week, from Seattle. She'd left him for another man, her high-school sweetheart, it turns out. He thought he'd taken all the posters down, but I guess he missed one."

"Just because a few of the details are off doesn't mean the whole theory is wrong. They could have used a cadaver. In fact, it makes more sense that—"

"Let it go!"

It had been a while since someone had shouted at me and the shock of it snapped my head back.

"I've felt so crappy the past couple of days, ever since I got here, really, and it's taken me a little while to figure out it's because of you."

"Me?"

"What is it with you? My aunt's death is none of your damn business, but suddenly, you seem to think you're the only one who knows the truth. Ever since I asked you to call a few art dealers for me, you've been treating me like I'm a money-grubbing bitch interested only in my aunt's money, and I don't need the guilt, particularly not when it's false guilt. My aunt is dead, do you understand? The coroner has declared her dead, the state has declared her dead, the entire town of Douglas turned out for her memorial service and the church buried her. I don't need to feel guilty that I'm not mourning her properly just because you're the only one who thinks she's alive."

"I'm not telling you to feel anything."

"Yes you are! It's not just that you've wasted my time and played hell with my emotions. Nothing you've done has helped, and nothing you've said has turned out to be true. Let's just cut the bullshit and look at what's happened. You've been arrested for arson, wild rumors are being printed in the tabloids about my aunt's death, Ben's in the hospital, and his home's in ruins."

"That's all my fault?"

"It all comes back to you, to the lies you've told."

"Lies? When have I—"

"The two guys on the hill the day of the fire? Everything Ben and I thought and did came from the belief that you were telling the truth, that there were two guys on that hill who might have murdered my aunt. Well, guess what? You're the only one who saw them. Nobody else saw them and nothing proves they exist."

"But Ben found one of them, put him in his mug—"

"Ben doesn't remember, does he? And it doesn't matter anyway, because you just point to a guy who looks like the fantasy arsonist you described and say, That's him. Who's to know the difference? And the guy who supposedly attacked you in Douglas? Funny, but you're the only one who saw him, too."

"I'm not telling lies, and I'm not inventing things. Lupe was just murdered, remember?"

"And who's to say you didn't kill him?"

"What?"

"Maybe he saw you that day. Maybe Detective Claymore was right. Maybe you lit the match that killed my aunt after all."

I walked back to my car, opened the door, stuck the key into the ignition, stared out the windshield. I thought about going back to say good-bye to Ben but couldn't work up the will to do it. After a while, I strapped on my seat belt and started the engine. The Rott must have sensed my depression, because he dropped his head onto my lap and didn't move it, except for the occasional attempt to lick my face during the ride to Beverly Hills. "That's one of the things I like about dogs," I said. He looked up at me. I gave him a pat. "You get to know one, you can depend on him. He'll get up the same time most mornings, want to do the same things he does every morning. You feed him, he'll eat. You take him outside, he'll want to run. You call him, he'll come to you." I looked down at the Rott. His big eyes looked back at me. "Well, maybe he won't always come to you, but he won't turn around and bite you for no good reason either. Not like people. Not like people at all."

At a stoplight I lifted the mobile phone from my jacket pocket. A business card dropped onto the seat beside me, pulled out with the phone. I didn't recognize the name at first, just the title. Paramedic. The red-haired paramedic had given me his home phone number the night Ben's trailer went down, said to give him a call if I was feeling any pain. As though I'd actually give him a call. I tore the card in half, then in half again. The pieces fluttered to the floor.

I dialed Dr. Scarpers.

THIRTY THREE

I waited thirty minutes in the lobby of Dr. Scarper's Beverly Hills office, sandwiched between patients who looked cut from the pages of the glamour magazines and entertainment trades they thumbed, before the hygienist popped over the reception counter to call my name. She led me down the hall and into the dentist's office. Before I had a chance to sit Dr. Scarpers brushed past the door, pulling a pair of latex gloves from her hands. "Let's make it fast. I'm working from a full appointment calendar today." She bumped the door shut with her hip and hovered at the corner of the desk.

"Was I completely wrong?"

She must have heard some anguish in my voice because she stilled long enough to appraise me with a glance, her eyes enormous behind her heavy black glasses and, for a moment at least, compassionate. "Honestly, I can't say one way or the other," she said and waved me into a chair before sitting behind her desk. "The coroner is satisfied he made the right decision, and I couldn't prove otherwise."

"You examined the file yourself?"

"The coroner was not interested in raising questions about the identification. He gave me five minutes to verify whether or not the contents of the file came from my office. That gave me time to check the X rays and the chart but nothing else." She lifted a gilt dental probe from the penholder beside her computer monitor and, bracing the base of her palm against the desk, scraped beneath the nail of her left index finger, the task giving her a moment to think and, perhaps, to decide whether or not to level with me. "As I told you before, there's nothing particularly individual about an X ray, except the teeth themselves. The film isn't stamped with the date or patient's name. That information is affixed by printed or handwritten labels. The X ray from one office is going to look the same as one from any other office. A forgery can be discovered only by checking the contents of the X rays, and even then, someone who knows what they're doing can duplicate the work from one mouth to another, if he has a model to work from."

"Creating the time line you were talking about before," I said when her pause extended long enough for me to show I understood.

"The X rays I examined showed a reasonable progression of care. Somebody hadn't simply taken seven panoramics of the same mouth on the same day and slapped different dates on them. The records of the teeth themselves changed. Starting from the first panoramic, dated 1980, each subsequent X ray showed some work had been done during the intervening years, except a few that showed no new work, which is reasonable. People don't always develop cavities between X rays."

"And the hand chart, the one with the red and blue pencil marks?"

"Matched the work seen on the X rays perfectly."

"Then the identification was correct," I said, feeling stupid. "The teeth in the X ray are Doubleday's, and the X rays matched the teeth found in the ruins of her estate."

Dr. Scarpers lurched forward and returned her dental probe to the penholder. "You can come to that conclusion if you wish. The coroner certainly did."

"And you?"

She stood with an abruptness that brought me to my feet, too. "And me? I'm late for my next appointment," she said.

I put my hand on the knob, as though I intended to swing open the door and leave, but instead turned and leaned against the jamb. "Something didn't fit," I said. "What was it?"

"You're persistent," she said.

I nodded. Nothing if not that.

"I didn't have time to check whether the work I'd billed matched the time line of the X rays."

Her glance pinned mine, her enormous eyes charmingly ghoulish, curious whether or not I'd figure it out.

"So the only thing you verified was that there was no obvious forgery, that they could have been Doubleday's records. You didn't prove that they in fact were her records."

"Correct. I did observe one discrepancy in the file, specifically in the first panoramic, dated 1980. Ms. Doubleday was twenty-nine years old then, but that first X ray showed a mouth with more than twice the usual amount of dental work."

"Meaning?"

"Meaning nothing, because I can't swear that Doubleday didn't come to me in that condition. Meaning if you want the coroner to agree to a more thorough examination, you'll have to come up with proof that Doubleday is either alive or buried elsewhere."

She reached for the door then, and I allowed myself to be ushered into the hall. She walked me as far as the reception counter, and when I turned to thank her one last time, she asked, "Now why would somebody have twice as much dental work as the average person of the same age?"

My tongue ran along the back of my teeth, remembering the many cavities I'd suffered through. "She didn't remember to brush and floss regularly?"

She shook her head as though I'd disappointed her. "And?"

I didn't think it through so much as wait for it to occur to me. "Because you were looking at the combined dental work from two mouths," I said, "or the mouth of someone much older than twenty-nine."

She pursed her lips and pulled her head back, as though the idea had never occurred to her. "Really?" She smiled mischievously. She'd been baiting me. "That would be clever, wouldn't it? But how do you prove it? How do you convince the coroner to let me prove it?" She flapped her hand at me once, a mixed gesture of dismissal and good-bye, and slipped through a doorway off the hall.

As I walked toward my car in the lot the mobile phone vibrated in my jacket pocket. I didn't recognize the number flashing on the display and picked up to a tentative voice, unsure he'd reached the right number. "Hello? I'm calling about the dog? The Rottweiler?"

I said, "What about it?"

"Well . . ." The voice hesitated, surprised, perhaps, by the sharpness of my tone. "I think it's mine. You put the poster up, right? That's how I got your number. Black Rottweiler, male, two years old, brown markings on the chest? Oh, and no teeth, of course that's the most obvious characteristic."

I said, "Oh."

"You have him, then? The children will be so happy."

The dog ran away from me, I wanted to say. I took him for a walk on the beach and he bolted. I'm so sorry. I said, "Children?"

"Two. Five and seven years old. They've been heartbroken."

"Describe the collar."

"I understand, you need to be sure." The voice spoke with the confidence of a good memory. "Brown leather collar, silver tag engraved with the name, Dog."

"Why Dog? What kind of name is that?"

His laugh had a smug sound, as though he'd answered the same question many times. "It was the only name our five-year-old could pronounce at the time. His full name is Dogbert, after the comic-strip character in Dilbert, but the kids just call him Dog."

I could tell him things had changed, I wasn't interested in giving up the dog, tough luck for him and his kids. All he had was the number of my cell. Easy enough to change numbers.

"I'd be happy to offer a reward," the voice said.

"The only reward I need is to be sure he's going to a good home. You mind telling me what happened with his teeth?"

"The vet said it was a rare gum disease, even suggested we put him down. But that would have broken the kids' hearts, so we spent what had to be spent and nursed him back to health. He's been eating well with you?"

"A couple pounds of hamburger every day."

"I'm so glad you found him. We've all been terribly worried. Could you bring him by my office early this evening? We're working late. Anytime between now and eight P.M."

I said, "Okay."

"My name is Dr. Trip Payne. That's P-A-Y-N-E."

He gave me his address, Santa Monica Boulevard near Saint John's Hospital. I told him I'd be there before eight and hung up the phone, thinking I didn't have to show up, I could drop my phone down the nearest storm drain and never hear from him again. The Rott barked once as I approached, a short protest that he'd been locked too long in the car. I drove south and then west, skirting Santa Monica Boulevard in a wide circle, to Venice Beach. The Rott didn't know anything was wrong, and I was careful to keep the worry from my voice. I walked him toward the pier, through the clusters of Rollerbladers, bicyclists, surfers, Tai Chi practitioners, lovers, and meditative strollers who congregate at the beach each day at sunset. When we reached the sand I unclipped his leash, and he got a five-mile run chasing seagulls, who flapped from his leaping jaws at the last moment, lazily circled the waves, then landed another few hundred yards up the beach, again out of reach. He would have chased them until he dropped dead, the dumb animal.

I settled into the sand and called him to my side. He trotted up to me willingly enough, tongue hanging loose from his mouth like a red rag. "I should have known you had family somewhere when I saw you with Arlanda's kids," I told him. I gripped the mobile phone in one hand, scratched his ear with the other. "I'm happy you got family. You're a good dog. You deserve people who love you." I watched the sun burn, enormous and oblong, to shimmering extinction at the ocean's end. "We've had a good time together, haven't we? We made a good pair. You understand this has nothing to do with how I feel about you. Part of me wants to throw this stupid phone into the waves, right now. A big part. But I can't do that. Even though I'd take care of you and love you like my own dog if I could. I know that would be the best thing for me. To keep you. But it wouldn't be the best thing I could do for you. I live in a tiny apartment, and when the landlord throws me out, I'll move to another tiny apartment, because it's all I can afford. I work out of my car, and when I'm not in my car,

I'm on the street or working assignments where I can't take you. You spend most of your time in the car, waiting for me to get back, and what kind of a life is that? No life for a big dog like yourself. The guy who called, he's a doctor with a family, probably owns a big house with a yard you can run around whenever you want. You'll be happier with them. Sure, you might miss me, but you'll be happy to see them, too. In a couple of days, you'll forget about me. It's the right thing to do. It sucks, but it's the right thing to do."

My throat constricted and my vision blurred as I drove east on Santa Monica Boulevard toward Saint John's Hospital. My chest convulsed too, and it had been so long since I'd felt anything like it, I didn't realize at first what was happening. I'd been convicted of manslaughter and sentenced to seven years, abandoned by friends and family, and within one month of my release I'd married, fallen into a warped kind of love, and witnessed my husband stretched out dead on the shores of Lake Hollywood. I had not cried, not once, not on the witness stand when called upon to testify in my defense, not alone in the privacy of my prison cell, not while I knelt above the body of my husband, and not when the cop who interrogated me afterward said my obvious lack of emotion implicated me in his murder. I had not cried in terror, pain, grief, or indignation. And now I was choking up in my car because I had to return a stray dog to his rightful owner.

Even stone cracks when the right seam is struck.

My mobile phone vibrated in my jacket pocket and I answered, hoping it might be the doctor calling to tell me he had changed his mind, I could keep the dog if I wanted him.

"Why didn't you tell me you got into trouble out of state?" It was my parole officer, outraged. "I just got a call from a sheriff in Cochise County, asking all kinds of questions about you."

"I followed the rules. I checked in."

"What are you getting yourself involved in?"

"Nothing."

"Nothing? You call someone breaking into your hotel room with a knife nothing?"

"The local law seemed to think the guy was a lost drunk."

"The local law didn't know you were a paroled felon with a record of violence when he interviewed you."

"Like I said, I checked in."

"I got another call this morning, from an LASD detective working assaults, said you and another man were the victims of vehicular assault in Pacific Palisades, involving—and I had a hard time believing this one—a house trailer and a bulldozer?"

"That's right," I said.

"The other victim was hospitalized, and you didn't even bother to report this to me?"

"I forgot."

"Spare me the crap. Where are you, right now?"

I didn't see a reason to lie to her.

"Santa Monica."

"You are the subject of four separate police investigations. Four. I've been around enough to know what you're doing here. What are the odds that you'll duck charges on all four? Do you want to COP?"

COP was parole-speak for "continue on parole."

"I haven't done anything."

"You will. You're heading for a parole violation, and not a small one either. When that happens I won't stand up for you, not again. I won't COP you. You need to take a long, hard look at your life. If you don't, you'll go straight to jail, do you understand me? It's just a matter of time."

"I'm not asking you to do me any special favors. I'm not asking you to COP me. You want to call the police, have them come and get me now, before I hurt somebody? Maybe that's what you should do. You can threaten me with prison all you want. It doesn't scare me. I've already been there. I survived it. Maybe I belong in prison, you know? Maybe that's the best place for scum like me." I didn't realize I was shouting until I pulled up at a red light, heard my voice above the still traffic.

"We need face time, right now. Be at your apartment in one hour."

"I have an appointment."

"Break it."

"I have to give Baby back. I can't break it."

"Wait a minute, that's your dog, the Rottweiler?"

"The owner's expecting me."

"You have to give your dog away?"

"Yes!"

I was shouting again.

"Where are you meeting the owner?"

I recited the address.

"This is what we'll do. First, I want you to get a hold of yourself. Maybe I don't give you enough credit sometimes. You're a smart girl. You know people can do bad things when under stress. So I want you to pull off the side of the road if you have to, take deep breaths until you feel you can control yourself. If you get to the address before I do, go ahead, meet the owner. I'll be waiting for you in the parking lot when you get out. If I'm not there, wait for me. Is that clear?"

I said it was.

"Okay then. Do it. You'll be fine."

Thirty Four

I parked in the lot behind the courtyard building where Dr. Payne held his practice and leashed the Rott. I didn't give him one last hug and I didn't think about what I was going to do. It felt like I was jumping off a cliff, and if I thought about it, I wouldn't do it. The knob to Payne's door turned in my hand, the office open late as promised. I tugged the leash to let the Rott in first. The overheads in the waiting room had been dimmed but a bright light spilled into the hallway from an area behind the reception desk. I called hello repeatedly, my voice bouncing back louder each time from the empty hallway. A shadow jutted into the hall and its voice said, "Just a minute."

I reached down to give the Rott a reassuring pat. He trembled violently, and his throat squeezed out a thin, anxious whine. I looked down to see what was wrong. He was pissing the rug.

"I'm so happy you brought Dog back to us," the voice said.

I glanced up to the face of the man who had shot me on the hill behind Angela Doubleday's estate, his gelled hair and constant two-day stubble dark contrast to his medical whites. I pulled the Rott's leash and stepped back. The front door jerked open behind me and before I could turn to confront whoever came through it something hard streaked against the side of my head. I stumbled over an end chair and struck the carpet awkwardly, head to shoulder, bringing the chair down with me. The two men moved as a team, like coyotes bringing down prey. I rolled to my stomach and kicked forward, but the weight of the man behind hit my back, knocking the air from my lungs. Cotton padding flashed before my eyes to clamp my mouth and it was then that I thought, too late, to scream. The air tasted of alcohol and ether. I tried to shake free my mouth. A forearm pinned my head to the floor. I willed myself not to breathe, knowing that when I did, I'd get a lung full of chloroform. In the very corner of the room, the Rott watched, trembling with terror. I blinked at him, trying to convey that it was all right, I didn't blame him for failing to protect me, and then everything else was all right, too; the weight on my back lightened, the forearm pinning my head to the floor turned to a caress, and I was floating down the hall, the ceiling a tunnel of gray fog. A chair rose from the floor to enfold me, the straps that bound my wrists to the armrests of no greater concern than gentle hands holding mine. Voices fluttered past like rustling leaves, and then the pain began, a dull throb at the back of my head and sharper stabs, behind the eyes, from the dissipating chloroform. I snatched at the words as they rippled by and caught and held two of them, "nitrous" and "oxide." The reply was incomprehensible, something about talk. And then I heard a sentence quite clearly, "We can take them out in the desert."

"We have the tools here," another voice said. "We have time."

Take what out, I wondered, and time for what?

The face of the gray-haired one stared down at me, his eyes warm with concern but no less predatory. "Hi there," he said. "Sorry about all this. It's not my style to be so, I dunno, brutal? Right. Brutal. Do you feel okay? We didn't hurt you?"

I stared at him.

He smiled, the roguish curve of his lips confident of their power to charm. "I'm happy that you're okay. We didn't expect you to fight so hard. But I want to assure you, regardless of the surroundings, we're not interested in pain. We don't want to hurt you. We're going to ask you some questions. After you answer them, we'll give you a little gas, to help you sleep, and we'll go away."

I tried to rub my eyes and couldn't, something catching my wrists.

I lay in a dental chair, my wrists bound to the armrests. I stretched my legs. My ankles were bound, too. I struggled to animate my tongue, and when it failed to respond, I nodded.

"We'll start with an easy one," he said, gently stroking my forehead. "The day you were on the hill behind Angela Doubleday's house, did you see anyone?"

I glanced beside his shoulder, where his brother examined probes, mirrors, and curettes, one by one. The grip of a .38 revolver jutted obscenely from the drawstring of his trousers.

"You saw my brother. Good. And?"

I stared at him.

"And me?"

I nodded.

"How many rolls of film did you take?"

I moved my lips, and the word "one" came out.

"Was that roll in the camera when my brother found you?"

I nodded.

"That roll contained all the pictures you took of us?"

I nodded again.

"You didn't, for example, shoot two rolls and put one in your pocket or camera bag?"

I shook my head.

He gave me a friendly pat on my shoulder, said, "Good, we really appreciate your honesty. Can we assume that you're the source behind the recent articles in the tabloid press?"

"My job," I said.

"How did you discover our names?"

"Computer. Mug shot on a website."

"Clever. That was really clever."

"Really fucking inconvenient," his brother said, and the probe he'd been holding clattered onto the tray like an exclamation point.

"We have to take the bad with the good, and think how much good she did for us," the gray-haired one said. Ray, that was his name, Ray Belgard. He stroked my brow again, and this time, my reactions returned to normal; I flinched. "When you were arrested for setting the fire, that was good for us. We owe you a big favor for that one. I mean, wow, we really appreciate it. But this new story, it's not good for us, not good for us at all. Have you talked to the police about it?"

I nodded.

Ray winced, said, "Not good. Not good at all."

"They know you killed Potrero."

"Portray-who? Who's that?"

His confusion seemed sincere.

"Doubleday's gardener."

"We didn't kill him." He got a little twinkle into his eyes when he smiled. "He committed suicide."

"He tried to extort you?"

"Goodness, no. We hardly knew the man." Ray looked back at his brother, said, "You know, when you stop to think about it, this has turned into a complete fiasco."

"He's your friend." Jack positioned an examination light over my head, the bulb unlit. "*We can trust him*, you said. Sonny fucking Crockett, my ass!"

"The dog," I said. "You'll let him go?"

Again, the hand stroked my brow. "Dog? We'll take good care of him, don't you worry about that."

"He was your dog?"

"Again, thanks for finding him. It worked out really well for us."

"His teeth. He didn't have any gum disease, did he?"

Ray propped his hand against the headrest beside my mouth and turned to his brother.

"Why did you pull them?" I asked.

Jack Belgard loomed over me, a surgical mask covering the lower half of his face, his eyes shielded by plastic goggles. In his right hand he held a pair of stainless-steel forceps. Behind the plastic his eyes glistened, moist with excitement. His latex-gloved thumb clicked a switch and the examination light stabbed my eyes. He didn't have to answer my questions. I knew the answers already, just as I had known since regaining my wits that they were going to pull my teeth and bury me in one of the many deserts surrounding Los Angeles; after a few weeks in the ground, robbed of my documents and teeth, not even God would be able to identify me. I glanced at Ray Belgard's hand.

"You want my teeth?" I said. "Go ahead, take them."

I snapped my head to the side and bit him just above the wrist. As I bit down I screamed from animal rage and a little human guile. Mine wouldn't be the only blood evidence left at the scene. He tried to pull his arm away but I'd bitten so deeply into the flesh that my teeth locked onto bone. His screams, openmouthed, were louder than mine. He clubbed at my face with his fist. The black-haired one lunged across my chest, his latex gloves clawing at my mouth. We were all yelling in the violence of the moment. Blood gushed from my mouth when they ripped the arm away. Ray howled, turned his back to the room, and clutched the wound to his chest. I screamed and thrashed. His brother backed toward the door, panicking, and jerked the pistol from his drawstring. A low roar sounded from the hallway and a muscular black shape hurtled into the room. Jack turned to the Rott leaping for his throat. The gun went off, a hard sound like cracking metal, brutal to the ears. Ray jerked forward near the far wall, and I thought for a moment he might have been hit, but he moved too frantically for a gunshot man, and I realized he was trying to get away from the pistol. His back had been turned. He couldn't see it. He didn't know where it pointed.

The Rott's paws skittered on the slick linoleum floor as he tried to get his legs beneath him for another lunge. Jack backed against the doorway, shouting to get out of the way, the dog scrambling to its feet at his brother's heels. The strap binding my right wrist loosened and I wrenched one hand free. The Rott sprang forward. A second shot splintered the air. Ray stumbled in his panic and brought the instrument tray down with him in a spray of probes and picks. The Rott hit the gunman chest high and knocked him back into the hallway. I twisted to the side, ripped the strap from my left hand, and sat up to free my legs. The Rott rolled once and tried to get up for another attack, but something in his front legs failed him, and he yelped. Jack Belgard's hand trembled when he raised the gun again, nerves strung taut between adrenaline and fear. I opened my mouth to scream but another voice sounded first, from the hall, ordering him to freeze. Belgard couldn't freeze. He was shaking too hard.

The voice was a woman's, and it brooked no nonsense.

The gun slipped from his hand like ice.

"Nina! You okay in there?"

It was my parole officer's voice.

I scrambled out of the chair and kicked Ray Belgard in the face before he could even think about going for the gun. "I think my dog's been shot," I said.

Graves ordered Jack to the floor, and the first I saw of her was her automatic, pointed at his head, as she pulled first one hand, then the other behind his back to cuff him. I tore the restraints from the dental chair. Ray was lying on his belly, hands clutching his face. I jerked his wrists behind his back and tied them tight enough to pop the fingers from his fist.

One of the bullets had sheared through the window looking onto the courtyard, and through the hole pulsed the wail of distant sirens. Graves looked at me and winced. "Your mouth," she said.

I wiped my face and my arm came away red with Belgard's blood. She thought they'd been pulling my teeth. I edged around the dental chair. The Rott lay against the far wall, trying to lick the ragged star of flesh the bullet had left between his chest and shoulder. He looked at me, his brown eyes brave with pain, as though apologizing for his condition.

Graves said, "Hang tight, assistance is on the way."

I squatted between the Rott's front and back legs and slid my forearms beneath his body. The Rott weighed eighty pounds. I braced my back against the wall and pushed up from my heels, clutching the Rott against my chest. My legs trembled and held. I could have lifted a small car just then. The Rott yelped but he didn't struggle. He was a good dog. He knew he needed help, and he trusted me to do the right thing for him, even if it hurt doing it.

"What are you doing?" Graves said.

"Taking my dog to the vet."

"You can't just walk out of here."

"You'll have to shoot me to prove I can't."

"Put him down. We'll get somebody to come."

"You can't get an ambulance to come for a dog."

I staggered around Jack Belgard and down the hall.

"You can't leave a crime scene like this!"

I walked down the hall.

"Do you want to go to prison again?"

The front door hadn't latched. I pried a crack with my foot, turned, and used my hip to nudge it open.

"Wait! Who are these guys?"

I told her to call Detective Alvarez.

"Last warning. If you walk out now, I won't COP you."

"I already made my choice," I said and backed out the door.

Thirty Five

The animal hospital lay less than a mile distant, through streets showing stretches of open asphalt—space to run the Caddy fast and hard. I gunned out of the lot, the Rott's shoulders in my lap, head in the crook of my arm, his eyes rolling back as the blood seeped into my jeans. The alarm company's patrol car swung wide across my windshield, nearly clipping my front fender as it lunged across the sidewalk and into the lot. In my rearview mirror I caught the flash of lights as he braked to catch the color, make, and model of my car. I kissed the brake and yanked the wheel right onto Santa Monica Boulevard, sliding through the stop sign without appreciable loss of speed. Three SMPD cruisers sped in tight, bumper-to-bumper formation through the opposing lanes, the red strobe of emergency lights cleaving traffic to the curb on both sides. They clipped past and spun left onto the street I'd just left, heading for the medical center. I took full advantage of the good citizens who pulled to the side of the road, palmed my horn to keep the lane clear, cut left across accelerating traffic, then right onto Wilshire Boulevard and right again into the parking lot of Wilshire Animal Hospital, slinging the Caddy to a stop beneath a sign marked "Emergency Entrance." I was out the door while the smoke was still rising from the tires. With the Rott braced against my chest I elbowed the emergency-service buzzer, didn't release the pressure until the door opened to an angry countenance that pulled sharply back to alarm at the sight of the dog and my trembling arms. She led me down a hallway smelling of fur and antiseptic and into the operating room, centered by a waist-high stainless-steel table.

"Put him down," she said and was gone.

I tottered forward and eased the Rott onto the table. His limbs had begun to loosen in my arms, and I understood this meant he'd gone into shock. I took his head in my hands, trying to comfort him, but the animal I knew wasn't there any more, not yet dead, but wandering the void that divides the living from the dead.

"A gunshot wound, you said?"

The veterinarian moved quickly to the site of the wound and called for an intravenous line to the assistant who had met me at the entrance.

"Thirty-eight-caliber handgun." My legs trembled from the strain of carrying the Rott. My voice shook from nerves. I didn't think it made much difference what caliber of bullet hit him. I just wanted to help.

"You did well to get him here so quickly," the vet said. "Now I'm going to ask you to wait in the lobby, let us do our work."

She glanced up from her inspection of the wound when I didn't move right away. Her blond hair was going gray, and she wore it tied behind her neck. The lines in her face spoke eloquently of long days stretching into nights, nights stretching into mornings, and she moved with the practiced precision of someone who knew what needed to be done when.

"Just save him," I said. "Please." And backed out the door.

I paced the lobby while they operated, seven strides forward and seven back, willing myself to trust in whatever God might be. I knew my life's course had veered in the past hour, and I wanted to be smart enough to calculate where that change in direction might take me before the only choice left was the sharp edge of a cliff and a hard fall. I needed money, and a lot of it. The Rott's medical bill would be considerable if he lived, and I wasn't willing to consider any other possibility. Terry Graves had threatened to ticket me back to prison for

leaving the scene of a crime. The police wouldn't place my arrest very
high on their list of priorities, but that wouldn't make me any less
arrested once they got around to knocking on my lumber. I still hadn't
paid my lawyer for his previous services in my defense, and if I was
going to have any chance of slipping by without prison time, his fees
would be considerable. That was the way the system worked: if you
could buy a good lawyer you were assumed to be a productive mem-
ber of society and given every possible break; if you had state-
appointed counsel, you were a bum, and you did time. I didn't want
to do time again.

The quickest route to money was to find Angela Doubleday or
what remained of her. Even a photograph of the room in which she'd
been murdered or a shot of her makeshift grave would bring something from the tabloids. Maybe I could get close enough to photograph her before calling the police, if she was held captive and alive. I
had no idea where the Belgards might have taken her, but I thought I
knew how they'd met. "He's your friend," Jack Belgard had said. Then
something about Sonny Crockett, followed by an expletive. My brain
had been as poisoned as everyone else's by the television shows of the
1980s. Sonny Crockett was a character in *Miami Vice*, played by Don
Johnson, the man I wanted to marry when I was fifteen years old. The
man was the personification of '80s style, all sunglasses, swept-back
hair, and blue jeans, a sports car of a man as hot as his Ferrari. The Belgards didn't have the class to know Don Johnson, but I knew someone with *Miami Vice* on his résumé and who would claim not only to
know him but to be a close personal friend. I called Frank at *Scandal
Times*. He answered with a stressed shout, wondering where I was.

I didn't answer him, not then.

"Troy Davies," I said.

"What about him?"

"You're going to do a major story on him."

"Why should I?"

"Because I think he kidnapped Angela Doubleday."

"What makes you think that?"

"I found the Belgards or, rather, they found me."

Frank was a quick thinker, but that took him a few seconds to
process. "You're still talking, so you must be okay."

"They shot my dog, Frank. I'm not okay."

"Where are you?"

"At a vet on Wilshire."

"Where are the Belgards?"

Frank knew how to get to the point quickly.

"Cuffed to the floor of a dental office, surrounded by cops." I gave him the address, heard the clatter of his chair falling back and the wheezing of his lungs as he hurried out the door. "I need you to do a background check tonight on Davies, no matter what."

"I'll get to it," he promised. "One last thing?"

"What?"

"Did you get any photographs?"

I almost smiled at his audacity. Then I hung up on him. I hoped a background check would tell me whether Davies had ever lived in Florida. The older Belgard looked about the same age as Troy. Maybe they had worked or gone to school together. I switched the mobile phone from vibrate to chirp. I didn't know where the next eight hours would take me, and I didn't want to miss Frank's call.

"Are you the owner of that dog?"

The vet stood in the doorway behind me. Her voice was harsher than I expected. I'd put the dog in harm's way. Maybe she blamed me. Maybe she thought I'd shot him.

"I don't exactly own him," I said. "I found him a little over a week ago, after the fire out in Malibu. But he's my dog now, no question."

Her stare was inquisitional, the kind of stare cops give me when they learn I have a record.

"I didn't shoot him, if that's what you're getting at," I said.

"Somebody pulled his teeth, and I don't see the reason for it."

"That's the way I found him."

"Does he exhibit signs of aggressive behavior?"

"No, ma'am. He's the kindest, gentlest dog you could ask for."

"If I could see some evidence of gum disease, I'd understand."

"Will he be okay?" I asked, meaning, will he live?

She shrugged, said, "I can't say for certain. He's young and otherwise a healthy animal, but he lost a lot of blood. The bullet passed beneath his shoulder and deflected off his rib cage. Another inch to the inside and he would have died instantly. He won't walk for a while, and his gait will probably be affected by the ligament damage, but mostly, I'm concerned about the loss of blood. We should know in eight hours or so. If he doesn't run well or limps, will you still want to keep him?"

"I want you to do what's best for the dog."

Her glance probed mine a little deeper, dropped to take in my black leather jacket and bloodstained jeans. "I'm required by law to report all gunshot wounds," she said. "The police might want to talk to you about what happened."

As though that might make me turn and run, abandon the dog. My screams had broken through his terror of the Belgards to trip an ancient instinct to protect. He'd saved my life.

"You'll take my check?"

She said a check would be fine, her assistant would be out in a moment to prepare a preliminary bill.

"I'll pay whatever you ask, but I'm a little short right now," I said, stripping off my leather jacket. "I've got about two hundred dollars in my account. I'll have more in the next few days. If the bill is more than two hundred, take my coat as collateral."

She looked at the coat as though it might jump up and bite her. "A hundred dollars will be fine for now. You can keep the coat. I can't tell you what the full cost will be until we see how the dog does over the next twenty-four hours."

I thanked her, asked again that she do everything she could to save him. She said she would, added, "If you locate the original owner of the animal, I'd like to talk to him. It's possible there's an innocent explanation for what happened to his teeth. But I suspect something different, and if my suspicions are correct, the police should be notified."

"They already know," I said.

Troy Davies bolted from his Las Flores Canyon apartment before midnight, a duffel bag slung over one shoulder and a suitcase in his opposite hand. He tossed the bags into the back of a green Isuzu Rodeo, the cabin light clicking on to a tight, pale face, and sped down-canyon, toward the sea. He turned north on the coast highway and drove it with a controlled fury, taking the corners past advisable speed and stitching between lanes when passing slower cars. Still, it wasn't difficult to keep pace. The coast highway is heavily patrolled, and the lights are timed to slow Porsches. I hung back, accelerated when I saw he was going to make a traffic light and I might not, just enough cover traffic to keep my lights out of his rearview mirror.

South of Ventura he cut east on Highway 126, four lanes through rolling oak hills, and I thought then his destination might be the Mojave Desert, where the topography of mountains, arroyos, and salt flats serve as a twenty-five-thousand-square-mile body dump for every professional killer in Southern California. If Angela Doubleday was buried in the desert, Davies would want to move her to a fresh grave before the Belgards confessed the location. He had to fear one of them would make a deal for a lighter sentence. If he was the only one who knew where the body was buried, he might never be con-

victed of her murder. But then Davies veered course again, swinging
north on Interstate 5, toward the vast agricultural flats of the San
Joaquin Valley, and I knew we were in for a long drive.

I'd staked out his apartment equipped for a long watch, jumbo cup
of coffee and sandwiches on the seat beside me. Though I'd topped
off the tank earlier that night, I was concerned that I'd run out of gas
before he did. But his run had been a spontaneous one, and he pulled
off the freeway at the base of Tejon Pass into a cloverleaf road stop
with two fast-food restaurants, a sit-down café, and four gas stations. I
wheeled behind the pumps of the next station down from the Exxon
station chosen by Davies. While the tank filled I snapped open the
glove box, and fumbling through the discarded film canisters and
candy wrappers for a highway map of California, my fingers stumbled
over an eight-by-ten glossy head shot of Troy Davies and a boxed tube
of foot cream. Davies had given both to me on the day Frank and I
had interviewed him for *Scandal Times*. He'd played a construction
worker with aching feet, he'd said, even got to drive a bulldozer. Playing a construction worker didn't make him one, no more than an
actor in medical whites makes a doctor, but he'd probably learned
enough about operating a bulldozer to push Ben's trailer off a cliff. He
was in Douglas the night I was attacked, too. When Davies emerged
from the cashier's office he carried a bottle of water, nothing more.
He didn't need coffee. He was running on adrenaline.

The speed limit on Interstate 5 increases to 70 mph between the
base of the Tejon Pass and Stockton, 250 miles north, but excluding
major holidays the route is thinly traveled by private traffic, and those
obeying the speed limit are likely to get rear-ended by the stream of
trucks doing 75. The freeway is straight and lightly patrolled on the
southern end of the San Joaquin Valley. Davies risked 90 mph and
even then we weren't the fastest ones. The white lines streaked to a
continuous blur, the thin fog common to the valley blotted out the
stars, and the road stretched on and on like a tunnel through the night
and fog. The hum of tires on the road provided a meditative rhythm,
like the bass line in a jazz trio. My thoughts spun in wide loops over
the Rott struggling to live through his loss of blood and Ben asleep in
his hospital bed, around Arlanda dreaming of inheritance in a $250-a-
night hotel room, and Frank, huddled over the keyboard as he hacked

out another story about blood and scandal, as though writing about such things had the power to change a society that gave them pride of place.

But most of all, my thoughts wound in tightening spirals around what Troy Davies had done and why. His outrage during Angela Doubleday's funeral had seemed so legitimate that I'd discounted him as a suspect, but then, I hadn't appreciated his acting talent, and this was quite obviously the role of his lifetime. He knew the terms of Doubleday's will. If he was her confidant—and I didn't seriously doubt that he was—he would also be aware that she was nearly broke on paper but rich in one unknown asset: diamonds. The police would take one look at Doubleday's finances and conclude that Davies wouldn't inherit enough from the estate to make murder worth his while. But if the diamonds were to appear later, in a safe-deposit box or some other location, he could, according to the will, legitimately claim them. The diamonds were motive enough for murder, but I suspected his real ambition was something even diamonds can't buy: fame. He could exploit his newfound notoriety in Hollywood—as Doubleday's last intimate he was rapidly becoming a celebrity in his own right, if Kato Kaelin types are considered celebrities—and live high on a seemingly legitimate source of wealth. He must have considered himself one lucky man.

Just north of Sacramento Troy Davies struck a new course, jumping east on Interstate 80 toward the foothills of the Sierra Nevadas. The fog dispersed as we climbed toward the suddenly clear sky, rolling oak falling away and pine forests marching down steepening mountain sides, our headlights spraying across huddled pines at each curve in the road. We drove with the turn of the earth, east into a bluing sky, leaving the night behind as we climbed ever higher. As the sun broke over the trees Davies turned south toward Lake Tahoe. The road descended, through slants of golden light, toward a giant blue pearl of water set against the mountains.

Midway around the western rim of the lake Davies slowed and turned across traffic onto a lane winding toward the water. I braked well behind him, not wanting the Caddy's distinctive grill to show in his rearview mirror when I made my turn. The lane split in three directions, each hidden by dense pines. I powered down the windows, cut the engine, and listened. A faint rumble moved through the pines straight ahead. I started the engine again and followed at a cautious distance. A couple of hundred yards down the lane a private road tracked to the left. I switched off the ignition again and listened. The carpet of pine needles and dense drapery of trees muffled the thump of a car door shutting, the only urban sound in that quiet place. I drove on, to where the gap in the trees widened, and parked the Caddy.

My first breath outside the car cooled and cleared my lungs. I hadn't been to the mountains in years and had forgotten how a single breath could be like a sip of spring water. I slung the Nikon around my neck and set out for the lane. The trees grew densely together near the lake, and little thrived in the dim light at their base. I skirted the lane and slipped past the first rank of pines. The needles gave softly beneath my boots. I moved quickly from trunk to trunk, making little noise with each step. The house was set a hundred yards back from the access road, peaked roof showing against the blue of the lake. The pines sectioned my view into narrow, geometric shafts, like an abstract painting, but even at a distance, I didn't mistake it for a humble cabin. I approached it head-on, flitting quickly and quietly between trees, waiting, and moving again. Somewhere in the forest behind me a car door thudded shut. I leaned against a tree trunk, forehead pressed against the bark as I listened, and heard nothing above the thumping footsteps of my own heart. I crept forward again. The house contained one sprawling story studded with gun-slit windows nearly as tall at the peaked center as the surrounding pines. At first, when I didn't see the Isuzu, I feared that my ears had misled me, that Davies had taken some other road to some other place, but the house was anchored on the far end by a three-car garage, and he'd want to park out of sight.

I uncapped the lens and put my eye to the Nikon's viewfinder. The sun was rising above the lake, casting the front of the house in deep shade. If anyone stood behind one of those windows, I couldn't see them. If I couldn't see them, I couldn't shoot them. They could see and shoot me easily enough, which discouraged too direct an approach. I kept my distance, slid around the near side of the house. The forest floor sloped as I neared the lake. When I couldn't take another step without swimming, I stopped.

The color of Lake Tahoe is a sparkling blue created by the clarity and depth of the water, the thin mountain air, and pure-blue skies. I'd been told that a few hundred feet below the surface the temperature remains so perfectly cold throughout the year that the drowned never decompose and so never swell to the surface. Not just the drowned drift in the lake's chilled depths. The authorities aren't capable of dragging a lake a thousand feet deep, not one with over seventy miles of shoreline, a fact that didn't escape those looking for a place to dump what they wanted to stay dumped. If Angela Doubleday had been murdered, I suspected her body would be drifting somewhere below the surface, skin as blue as her grave.

The plate-glass windows at the rear of the house stretched from floor to ceiling to take advantage of the lake view. A redwood patio extended from the house on stilts, the steps descending from the sides of the deck onto well-worn paths to the lakefront. I crawled the stairs on the near side and peered over the top. Sunlight raked through the windows at the low angle of morning, casting long shadows into the rooms beyond. I lifted the viewfinder to my eye and peered through the telephoto lens. The furniture clustered around the chiseled-granite fireplace had the casual leather look of a decor meant to be woodsy but probably cost over a thousand dollars per piece. I panned from the fireplace to a seating group near the window, where some-one might sit and watch the lake. Every chair in the room was empty.

The room directly before me, ten yards across the redwood deck, was faced in roughly hewn timber. Gold draped the window above it. The drapes were slightly parted at the center, but from the angle of the bottom step I lensed nothing but ceiling. I stood and climbed, one step at a time, until the top of a painting of trees on the far wall came into view, then the arch of a bed frame, and then something distract-ingly white, half hidden behind the edge of the drape. I nudged the focus ring and the object sharpened into hair, drawn tightly back above white gauze.

The edge of the drape concealed the rest of the figure and room, like a curtain parted midway on a mysterious tableau. I ran off a few frames of film but knew if I wanted to see what lay behind the drape I would need to change my angle. I couldn't move to my right without falling off the patio, and if I moved left, I'd expose myself to every window in the house. I bellied down and crawled forward. The timber facade extended waist high below the window. I pushed myself into a crouch and put the viewfinder to my eye again, knowing that the black of a camera peeping into a window is not as startlingly visible as white skin. I rose up like a telescope, fragments of the room sharding into my eye—a blurred doorframe, a chest of drawers, a nightstand with a water glass, half full. I pulled back from telephoto to a wider angle. A body lay on the bed, half covered in sheets, arms folded neatly across the stomach. The face was so heavily bandaged it took a moment of focus and concentration to recognize it as Angela Double-day's, and even then, I wasn't sure. Gauze bandaging wove a white tapestry from her hairline to her chin and wrapped her neck to the collarbone. Behind the shroud of gauze her eyes were heavily pur-pled, as though she had been badly beaten. I admired her then, even as I clicked the shutter again and again, for the courage of her resist-ance. They had beaten her nearly to death, it looked, and yet still she lived, which meant she hadn't yet yielded the secret of her diamonds. I shifted my feet on the deck and took another photograph, from a different angle, and as I moved to bracket exposures a shrill chirping pierced the air, like the song of a deranged, electronic bird.

My mobile phone.

I gripped the camera with one hand and fumbled through the side pocket of my leather jacket, the phone chirruping twice before I pulled it out. I recognized the calling number as Frank's before I thumbed open the line.

"Can't talk," I whispered, ready to thumb the line closed again.

"Then just listen for once," Frank said. "Troy Davies changed his name. I know, I know, that's what actors do, they change their names. Only our Troy Davies changed his from Tom Davis."

Frank paused, waiting for me to get it.

I didn't.

"The brother!" He shouted, as though that made it obvious.

"Gotta go."

"Where are you?"

"Outside a cabin in Lake Tahoe, looking at Angela Doubleday."

"Look, get out of there. It's—"

"Hey, Frank, I got the pictures," I said and thumbed the connection closed.

I put my eye to the viewfinder again and raised the lens to finish bracketing exposures before I fled, unsure how much light the tinting in the windows would cut. At first I confused the white of pillow for gauze and pulled back to a wider angle. The pillow where Doubleday's head had lain was bare, and the covers twisted across the bed as though thrown back in a hurry. I panned the lens around the room. She was gone. I needed to be gone too, and fast. I pulled into a crouch and scurried across the deck, preparing to vault the railing and run. I accelerated near the corner of the house, counting steps for the jump. Something came from my left so fast I barely had time to turn my head away from the blow and I went down hard, rolled, and came up eye to barrel with a pump-action shotgun three feet from my head. Troy Davies stood behind it. My ear stung and the side of my head ached where the barrel had struck a glancing blow, but I felt momentarily fortunate that he'd used the shotgun as a baseball bat and not blown my head off.

"Mobile phone," he said.

I dipped two fingers into my side pocket, pulled it out by the stubby antenna, laid it on the deck beside my knee.

"Camera," he said.

I unstrapped the Nikon from my neck and set it next to the mobile phone.

"Hands behind your head, lay flat on the deck."

That wasn't as easy to do as it sounded, but I accomplished it, dropping to elbows and knees and then going flat. Davies stepped around me. I flinched when his boot lifted above my face, but the sole came down on the mobile phone. The little things are more rugged than they look. When the casing held after two stomps, he took the heel of the shotgun to it.

"Keep your hands behind your head, get up."

"I gotta roll onto my back to do that," I said.

He kicked me then, for talking or just from spite.

I rolled onto my back, sat up, got my knees under me, and stood from there.

"Walk," he said.

I walked toward the wall of glass at the back of the house.

"You see the door. Open it."

A sliding-glass door leading to the living room had been left cracked open. I stopped a few feet short of it.

"I'm not going inside," I said.

"You have to open the door!"

The discordant note in his voice sounded like anguish, and that surprised me. I didn't expect anguish from a killer. I kept my hands behind my head and turned to face him, knowing it's harder to shoot somebody in the chest than in the back. "I'm not going inside. I'm going to lower my hands, take the car keys out of my jacket pocket, leave them here for you. Then I'm going to walk into that forest. You know, I don't really care if you get caught or not. I'm not a cop. I didn't come here to arrest you. I came to take photographs. You were right. I'm a cheap camera snoop. I'm also a real slow walker, and I don't like knocking on the doors of strangers. You'll have all the time you need to get into your car, get far away before anybody knows what I've found here."

"And what have you found here?"

The voice was a woman's and it came from behind me. I looked over my shoulder. The woman I took for Angela Doubleday stood at the crack in the sliding glass door. She slid the door fully open, as though inviting me inside the house, and pointed a little black Beretta at my gut.

THIRTY SEVEN

I stepped through the gap in the sliding-glass door, lowering my hands because the idea of escape had become impossible now that the woman I'd come to help rescue seemed to be pointing a gun at me. A ruby-and-diamond brooch shaped like a rose sparkled from her pale-blue sweater. Gauze so completely covered her face that I couldn't be sure who stared from behind the mask. Who else but Angela Doubleday would wear that brooch? Her hair, pulled back in a taut ponytail, was a shade of black as false as my own. I called her name, uncertain I called her or some impostor. The woman neither confirmed nor denied the name. The eyes matched in color, shape, and expression Doubleday's eyes, and the voice sounded like hers, a voice that one film critic described as an iron fist in a velvet glove, but I knew her solely from her films, and film can lie.

She glanced at Davies, who kicked the sliding-glass door closed with his heel. I wondered if I'd entered a scenario in which the kidnap victim so completely bonds with her kidnappers she becomes complicit in the crime.

"I already talked to the newspaper," I said. "They know you're here. I told them I found you." I stepped away from Davies, toward a row of suitcases, packed by the door. "Killing me will just add to your problems, not solve them."

"And who am I?" The woman pointed the gun not just at me but everywhere, as though she held not a deadly weapon but a glass, a cigarette, a rolled-up script—any prop that didn't inhibit the articulate gestures of her hands.

I said, "Angela Doubleday."

"But my face is covered in bandages. Really, anybody could be behind this mask."

"I know your voice."

The gauze around her mouth crinkled, and by that I knew she was smiling. The voice that projected from the mask changed to the distinctive cracks and staccato rhythm of Katharine Hepburn. "You can't believe everything you hear, now can you?" The voice shifted rhythms, dropping and deepening to a breathy tone that made every syllable sound like sex. "But what's a girl to believe? She has only her senses. If she can't believe her ears, what can she believe?"

"My mistake," I said. "You're really Marilyn Monroe."

"I can do Elvis too, but I'll spare you." Her free hand, unadorned by rings or bracelets, played out to a beam of sunlight streaming from the wall of windows. The iron returned first to her voice and then the velvet, and when she spoke again, she was unmistakably Angela Doubleday. "Impersonations are a cheap trick of the trade, but identity, that is an act of true creation. There are two great philosophical questions: What is God? and Who am I? There is no answer to the first. The actor realizes the answer to the second is multiple-choice. Whatever is invented can be reinvented."

I looked again at the bruising of her eyes and the gauze covering her face and said, "You haven't been beaten."

She shook her head, said, "No."

"You've been to a plastic surgeon."

"Yes."

"You're pulling a Garbo. You never want to be seen again, not as Angela Doubleday."

She dipped her head like bowing before an audience. "How much will it cost for you to go away?"

I didn't understand, said, "I'm sorry?"

"Money," she said, speaking the word with malice. "How much is this going to cost me?"

I'm not much of an actor. I needed money, but the last thing I expected with two guns pointing at my chest was a payoff.

"Come on, don't play stupid," she said. "I don't have the time or patience. How much would the tabloids pay you for a photograph of me?"

"It would be safer to kill her," Davies said.

"Our safety isn't the only issue." Doubleday spoke sharply, confident of her command. "We're not killers."

"But she fucked up everything!"

"How was I to know you hadn't kidnapped or killed her?" I asked him, trying to sound reasonable.

"If you knew anything at all, you'd know I could never harm her. But you don't know anything, do you? And so you stumble around like a blind cow, breaking things you're too stupid to understand."

"Her niece is worried sick. I'm here for the newspaper, yes, but I'm also here because she asked me to help save her aunt."

"Arlanda? Is she worried, really?" Doubt laced Doubleday's voice, but wonder too, as though such an idea astonished her.

"Yes," I lied.

"Does she know I'm alive?"

"She suspects it."

"And that's why you're here? For her?"

"Yes," I lied again.

"She's playing a game with you, Angie. She's not a friend of the family. She works for the tabloids. She's your enemy."

Doubleday lowered her little black Beretta, said, "I know who my friends and enemies are, and I know my conscience." She turned her back to me, and I was afraid that she might tell Troy to shoot me, but instead she circled slowly behind him and, laying her head on his shoulder, pushed the barrel of his shotgun until it pointed to the floor. "We're almost home, Troy," she whispered. "No one must be hurt, remember? It's the only way we can live in peace, you and I."

Davies tilted his head as though her words caressed him, and when he looked at her, his eyes gleamed with a weird light, brighter than admiration and fiercer than worship. She stepped around him, walked up to me, and took my hand in hers. Her eyes were marvelously complex instruments, brimming with no single emotion and not a mixture of emotions either; fear and hope resided in the same glance, simultaneous and separate, and the flint in her eyes yielded at closer look to someone not just vulnerable but in pain. "If you're a friend of my niece, you will not want to see her aunt jailed and disgraced and the small fortune I left for her canceled to pay for my defense fund." She spoke to me simply, like a woman with an open heart. "So I ask you the same question, this time not as my enemy but as the friend of my niece, how much do you want to go away, pretend you saw none of this?"

I didn't believe she was lying, but I didn't think she told the truth either. She couldn't tell the truth because she didn't know it. "Nothing," I said.

"But I must give you something. It's not fair that you get nothing. You followed Troy all the way up here. You found me. It's not your fault I wasn't the same Angela Doubleday you sought."

"I don't want any of your money or your diamonds," I said.

"We can't just let her walk away!" Davies' voice was anguished, something tearing him apart that I was too blind to see. He sidestepped toward the front door, and when Doubleday's back was clear of the line of fire, he raised his shotgun again.

"Troy?"

The note of surprise in Doubleday's voice frightened me. Not even she knew what was going on. Every appearance deceived. Her disappearance. Her murder. Her voice. Her face. And Troy Davies, who wasn't even Troy Davies by birth but someone else named Tom Davis. Then I got it, what Frank had been trying to tell me.

"Does she know who you are?" I asked. "Have you told her your real name is Tom Davis?"

Doubleday turned to me and didn't notice how the question paled him. "Davies or Davis, what's the difference?" She said. "Natalie Wood was born Natasha Gurdin. Almost every actor changes her name."

"The name Davis means nothing to you?"

Her eyes trembled behind their white mask, as though from some terrible inner shift of recognition. I slid a step to the side to bring her into the line of fire. I knew what it was like to be accused, how emotions long choked down could suddenly burst free. I spoke to Davies gently. "Did you abandon Tom Davis ten years ago, when you changed your name and moved to L.A.? Or was he always lurking beneath the surface, urging you closer to the woman who must have caused you considerable pain?"

In color and expression his face turned cadaverous, so pale and still I wasn't sure he heard anything at all. The barrel of the shotgun dipped to the floor.

"I'm not an actor," I said. "So I don't understand these things, not the way you do. Where does Tom Davis end and Troy Davies begin? Do they stand side by side, front to back, or does one sit inside the other, pulling strings? Troy Davies may be innocent, but what about Tom Davis? He's been preparing for Angela Doubleday since the day his brother was shot to death for stalking her. What other possible motive could he have—could you have—except revenge? But you haven't harmed her, not that I can see, and so I wonder, who are you right now? Tom Davis or Troy Davies?"

He wiped at his face with his left hand and backed toward the stone fireplace. Braced under his right shoulder, the shotgun threatened nothing for the moment but the hardwood floor. I contemplated flight, five steps back and a quick cut down the hallway that branched away from the main room, but I didn't know the layout of the house and wasn't certain of my escape. He could too easily shoot me in the back before I found a way out.

"I don't know." His admission fell softly into the room. Those three words were all he said for a minute, and with his head lowered, I couldn't tell whether he gathered himself together or pried himself apart. "I wanted to hurt you, Angie. That's a good place to start. For years, before we ever met, I wanted to hurt you. In my darker moments, I considered murdering you. It didn't seem like it would be that difficult from a distance. You had abandoned the world. You lived alone in a big house. You saw no one. I decided instead to make love to you. And when you loved me to the point of dependency, like my brother loved you, I would abandon you. Either that, or I'd kill you."

Doubleday didn't shrink back on hearing his confession, but stepped nearer. She said just one word, "Yes?" and it conveyed more emotion than a speech.

"I thought I'd have the strength to pull it off, but I'd never met anyone like you before." A smile whispered across his lips like the punch line to a grim joke. "When I'm not around you, it's hard to explain, it's like I'm not there. I'm a hollow shell, waiting to be filled. Funny thing is I think I was always that way. I just didn't realize it until we met."

"That's why we act," she said. "To fill that sense of hollowness at the center of our being. Did you really wish to kill me?"

"Yes," he said. "When you first confessed to me that you wanted to disappear, six months ago, I was still thinking I'd do it. It was as though you were asking me to kill you. I had the perfect opportunity. But I no longer had the will."

"Then do it now. Kill me now."

He raised the shotgun, the tears in his eyes desperate to escape, but he didn't point it at her. "I can't," he said, pointing the shotgun at me instead.

She moved, calmly and deliberately, between the barrel of the shotgun and my chest. "But I want to die," she said.

When Davies shook his head the tears leapt free, and again, he dropped his shotgun as though incapable of harming her even if she commanded him to. He stumbled backward, until his heels struck the front ledge of the fireplace, and then he sat down hard, cradling the shotgun against his chest, and wept.

I said, "Lady, you don't want to die. If you're that unhappy with humanity, go buy yourself a shack on a deserted island someplace. You can afford it."

"I'm not unhappy with humanity. Not at all." She stepped toward the suitcases packed at the door, wrapping her arms around her chest as though suddenly chilled, the Beretta still in her grip but forgotten. "I'm unhappy with myself. And I've already lived on an island. What was my estate in Malibu, if not an island? No matter where I went, you'd still find me, and I'd still be me."

I tried to protest but she silenced me with a pinpoint glance.

"If not you, someone else. I'd always be hunted. To be a celebrity, it's the life of a criminal, not a human being. Do you know what it's like, to be hunted every moment of your life? To not be able to make a simple trip to the grocery store for fear that some poor deluded soul has fallen in love with that glimmering image on the screen and thinks that image is you? To be accosted everywhere you go by strangers who protest they know and love you, so that no public place offers any refuge, not even a stall in the ladies' room? And those are the ones who wish you well, not the ones who have appointed you to star in their own private psychodrama, who claim to everyone they're engaged to you or married to you, that they sleep with you regularly and ecstatically, the ones who stalk you on the street, send you letter after letter of abject longing and utter delusion, who protest their love one moment and threaten you with the most horrible insults the next, who are so desperate for any kind of attention they will assault or kill you just for that moment of frisson when you recognize them? Can you blame me if, in the words of dear Garbo, all I want is to be alone? I can't be alone!"

While she spoke she held the little black Beretta more like a prop than a deadly weapon, slapping it against her thigh in frustration one moment, pointing it like a finger the next. Not until she mentioned Garbo did she look at it for what it was, but even then, her glance was absent of understanding its mortal power.

"Not in this life," she said. "Not as Angela Doubleday. I'm so terribly tired of playing Angela Doubleday."

"So tired that you killed for the privilege of leaving her behind?" The question came out more angrily than I had intended.

"I killed no one. Troy? Tell her."

"We used a corpse to double for Angela's body, I mean, Ray and his brother did." Davies' face glistened from the wet work of crying. The fierceness in his eyes had dulled, the indignant anger in him extinguished. "That was always the plan, to steal a cadaver from UCLA Medical School. I gave the Belgards plaster casts of Angela's teeth, so they could match the dentals."

"I never would have countenanced harming anyone," Doubleday said. "I thought about this carefully, and that was always a precondition. No one must be harmed."

"What about Lupe Potrero?"

"Who?"

She didn't know his name.

"Your gardener."

She nodded as though recognizing the function he filled, if not the man or why I had mentioned him.

"Lupe saw one of the Belgards at the estate some days before they burned it, talking to Troy." I glanced at Davies. He didn't contradict me. "Lupe tried to blackmail you. Five days ago, the Belgards murdered him. They not only murdered him, they pulled out all his teeth and threw him into the sea."

"Troy?" Doubleday's eyes flashed, wild and stunned as those of a bird after it smacks into a plate-glass window, wrenched from the trance of flight by something unforeseen. "Is it true? Are we murderers?"

"You aren't responsible. It's my fault. I brought them in. But I couldn't control them."

I asked, "Were you there when they murdered him?"

"No." He stared at a spot on the floor as though it held a secret to himself he was just understanding. "But I let them do it."

"Do they know Doubleday is still alive?"

"I told them I killed her. They know about my brother, you see. They thought it was personal."

Her voice brightened. "So it's all over?"

Troy didn't answer, his glance immobilized.

"I wanted my anonymity back," she said to me. "Everyone has the right to make a new life for themselves. Isn't that what being American is all about? To be able to move on after having failed miserably at being who you are? Not having to settle, but to move somewhere else, to a new neighborhood, new friends, new job, a new sense of self? To find your true self or to shed your self completely, like the skin of a snake? The only way I can reinvent myself now is to die. Death is the last, great reinvention of the self. And complete anonymity."

Her glance traced the contours of the grip and barrel of her little black Beretta, and such was the brilliance of her transparency I could see her imagine the trajectory of the bullet, watch her contemplate her own suicide.

Whatever Davies had sought in staring so long at one spot on the floor changed him when at last he looked up. "We can still escape. We just have to do one more thing." He stood, his left hand gripping the ridged walnut pump below the barrel of his shotgun. "I warned you once," he said to me. "In Douglas. But you didn't listen. I knew I'd have to kill you, after that. You should have died when the trailer went down, you and the son of a bitch who killed my brother. And still, you keep coming around, fucking things up." When he pointed the shotgun at me this time it was clear he intended to fire.

Doubleday shouted his name and leapt between us. I backpedaled for the sliding-glass door that led to the patio, to the lake, to safety. His first shot jerked high and to the side, shattering a floor-to-ceiling pane of glass. She lunged for his gun. He tipped the barrel toward the ceiling and snapped the butt forward. The blow struck her full in the face, the sound of it like a ripe melon hitting the floor. I half turned to work the latch as the gunstock wedged into his shoulder and felt rather than saw that I wasn't going to have enough time to make it. I dove parallel to the wall of plate-glass windows the moment before the violent hurl of buckshot punched out the glass door at the level of my head. I landed on my back and slid on the polished hardwood floor, kicked with my heels, and took cover in the coffin-size space between the back of the couch and the window.

The rafters echoed with the metallic sling and clack of the pump action bolting another load down the hole. A flash of movement turned my head. The window wall above me, tinted against the sun, reflected the room like a bleached-out movie screen. The butt of the shotgun had dropped Doubleday to her knees between Davies and the blown-out door. He laid his hand gently below the crown of her head, where the strands of her ponytail pulled together.

"Trust me," he said.

A dark stain spread from the center of her face. Her nose, broken by the plastic surgeon, had been smashed by the blow. "No . . ." she whispered, her voice thick with blood, ". . . violence."

"Too late for that," he said and stepped around her. "Too late for that at the start."

I don't think he bothered to look for my reflection in the window. He knew where I hid. He could hear my feet bracing against the jamb where the window met the floor. When I leapt from behind the couch he'd shoot me like skeet. At that range, the question wasn't whether he'd hit me but where. He closed the gap to the couch with the shotgun at his shoulder, his feet crossing toe to heel to improve the firing angle. My only chance was to take him head-on, low enough to duck the blast. I concentrated on the movement of his feet in the glass, timing my leap for the moment they crossed, the one moment he might be unbalanced enough to jerk his shot high.

The brain does funny things to time in moments of physical stress. It works at furious speed, deconstructing each moment into separate facets of sound, movement, color, and shape, some fading into an irrelevant background, others pulled forward into sharp focus. The perception of time compresses and stretches, objects moving as though weighted in a hundred feet of water. My glance met the reflected eyes of Angela Doubleday, burning blue behind her gauze mask, and locked onto her steady gaze for what seemed like seconds but was probably less than the time it took Davies to shift his weight from one foot to the other. She stood up behind him, her limbs loose and graceful as a fairy rising from the lake, and when he raised on his toes to angle the shotgun over the top of the couch, she lifted her hand, the little black Beretta at the end of it, and shot him.

He fell sideways and back, the tension in his limbs releasing with the sudden awkward splay of a dropped marionette. His head bounced off the hardwood floor, and when it landed the second time, eyes shocked open, the rest of him already lay still, arms thrown wide, the ankle of one leg pinned beneath the knee of the other. A bright gob of red stained the side of his blue shirt, just below the shoulder joint. The blood seeped from him slowly, and the stain never spread far from where it began. The bullet had lanced between his ribs and ripped his heart.

The shock of seeing him die settled into an awareness that my own heart beat fast and strong. I pushed myself from behind the couch. Doubleday had not moved since shooting him, her face a mask of blood, the gun still pointing at where Davies had been the moment she shot him. I stepped over the barrel of the shotgun, past his blank eyes, and placed my hand on her wrist. She glanced at me as though startled from a trance, her fingers springing away from the gun. I caught the Beretta by the barrel before it fell, slid my opposite hand beneath the hem of my T-shirt and used it as a mitten to hold the gun. I said, "You have to answer one question, that's all."

I waited for her head to turn to mine.

"Do you want to go to prison?"

"I am in prison," she said. "I can't escape."

"I spent four years in prison." I looked at the stone fireplace, the cathedral ceiling, the wall of windows framing a million-dollar lake view. "This is not prison. You saved my life, and like I told you before, I know your niece, so I'm willing to take a risk. But I won't help you unless you snap out of your self-pity."

"No," she said.

"I'll call the police then, wait outside."

A slant of sunlight reflected off ceramic tiles in a room off the hall-way to the right, below kitchen cabinets painted pale yellow. I moved toward it, the gun cradled in my T-shirt. Big houses usually have kitchen phones.

"No, I don't want to go to prison," she said.

Her voice shook but her eyes held mine steadily enough. I walked the gun to the body and stepped over the legs, watching the floor for drops of blood that, if stepped on, would betray what I was about to do. I knelt by his right hand and pressed the butt into the palm, again and again, to make overlapping impressions. Angela Doubleday had put in motion a scheme that, even though she insisted no one was to be hurt, had sent Ben to the hospital and Lupe to the grave. Even at her most benign imagining, she had been willing to torch twenty acres of Malibu hillside and bilk an insurance company out of two million dollars. But she also had saved my life, and that act had conse-quences as well, consequences that—for that moment, if not in retro-spect—overruled the others. "I have some experience in breaking the law," I said. "This is the way we'll play it."

THIRTY EIGHT

Twenty-four hours later I prepared to turn myself in to Terry Graves at the Region III parole office in Inglewood, leaving the Cadillac on a residential street with no parking restrictions and walking a half mile to wait on the sidewalk by the building entrance. I'd showered, carried enough change in my pocket to call my lawyer, and wore clean underwear. Someone could swing by and pick up the car later if needed. Experience counts for something in life, in knowing how to maintain the small comforts in difficult circumstances if nothing else.

Graves strode around the corner a few minutes before 8:00 A.M., Pony Express bag slung across her shoulder, office keys in one hand and a cup of takeout coffee in the other. Her key hand slid toward a gap in her bag when she noticed someone waiting by the door, then fell back to her side when she saw it was me. Wariness, if not fear, was constant in her life. Paroled felons are not the most stable individuals, and many remain capable of great violence. Who knew which of them might decide she should no longer be allowed to live? Angela Doubleday had railed against paparazzi and obsessive fans, but my parole officer dealt daily with persons far more dangerous, and at $50k a year she didn't ask people to treat her like a star.

"Good morning, Ms. Graves," I said.

She looked at me, her mouth a sour curl beneath impenetrable sunglasses. "Put your hands down. I'm not going to cuff you."

"You're not?"

"Of course not. If I want you arrested, I'll call LAPD. I won't do it myself. You should know that by now."

"Sorry, ma'am."

She opened the door, gestured me inside with a curt nod.

"Are you?"

"Am I what?"

"Sorry."

"For what?"

"For leaving the scene of a crime when I ordered you to stay."

I thought about it, but not long.

"No," I said.

"How about for chasing Troy Davies up to Tahoe and putting not only yourself but Angela Doubleday in danger?"

"No," I said again.

"Then cut the bullshit. What I don't understand is why he didn't shoot you on sight. You're going to tell me all about it, aren't you?"

She sipped her coffee and tapped the eraser end of a pencil on the surface of her desk while she listened to my story. Her desk, like her office, was stripped of personal ornaments. It could have been any-one's desk. No visible paperwork, no mementos, and above all no photographs. Not once during the six months I'd known her had she mentioned a family. I didn't know whether or not she even had one. The story I told was identical to the one I'd related to the Placer County Sheriff Department and then, six hours later, to Detective Alvarez of the LASD. I'd followed Troy Davies to Tahoe in hopes of photographing Angela Doubleday, because I thought with good rea-son he'd kidnapped her. He'd ordered me at gunpoint into the house, where I found Doubleday in a state of mental confusion. She com-plained about being a prisoner, I said, and begged Davies not to hurt me. I tried not to make statements I knew not to be true, except the one about the little black Beretta. He'd carried it tucked under his belt, I said. When he first raised the shotgun to shoot me, the motion pulled on his shirt, and the Beretta tumbled to the floor. Doubleday picked it up. Davies was too intent on chasing me to notice. She shot him as he came around the couch to kill me. I mentioned nothing about her confessed role in her own disappearance. I didn't say that she seemed drugged and terrified by Davies, but I implied it. By omission, my statement to the police was a complete fiction.

When I finished she said, "It's hard to believe, isn't it?"

My parole officer was unforgiving of any lapse or inconsistency of truth, and even though I'd coasted through my interviews with the Placer County Sheriffs, and Detective Alvarez never seriously questioned my account, her mere glance made me sweat.

"What," I said.

"What made him think he could get away with it?"

"With shooting me, you mean."

The back of her hand arced across the desk, as though swatting away my misunderstanding. "Not that. He blows a hole in your chest, fills it with rocks, and sinks you in the lake. Killing you was the least of his problems."

"That's reassuring," I said.

"And I understand why he hesitated. He wasn't a stone-cold killer. He needed to work himself up to it, to justify killing you in his own mind. What I don't understand is how he thought he'd get away with kidnapping Angela Doubleday. He didn't seem completely delusional. He couldn't have planned to keep her locked up in the Lake Tahoe place forever."

"The police know more about that than I do," I lied.

"But I'm asking you."

I repeated the story Doubleday had told me, the story we had both told the police, a story verifiable in fact if not truth, based on the ruins of their plan. "He planned to move her to a house in Wisconsin, outside Green Lake, is the way I understand it. He'd already taken her to a plastic surgeon in Tijuana, arranged a complete set of documents for her in the name of Angie Budd. He rented the house in Lake Tahoe because he needed someplace quiet to keep her while her face healed. He was going to pass her off as his wife."

"And he thought she'd just go along with him?"

"He was obsessed with her. Maybe the plastic surgery, the false documents, were just a fantasy. Maybe he had another plan, if she resisted."

"Murder-suicide?"

I didn't want to seem too informed. If I knew too much, the story would smell cooked. I said, "Who knows? I'm a photographer, not a psychiatrist."

Her smile turned predatory, and I knew then I was in trouble. "He was gone from the Lake Tahoe place for days at a time, wasn't he?"

I nodded, wary of the question and all it implied.

"And she was, what, tied up all that time?"

"He kept her in a storage room when he was gone. I didn't see it, but I understand the conditions were pretty primitive."

"A secured room, no windows, steel-reinforced door, triple locks?"

"No windows. I think the door was braced on the other side by a chair or something."

"All that time, a chair between her and freedom, between life and death for all she knew, and she didn't find a way to escape?"

And that was the single obvious flaw in the story I'd devised, with Doubleday's help, after she'd saved my life. Nobody knew about the diamonds except Harry Winston, Arlanda, and me. The Belgards had worked from plaster casts of Doubleday's teeth; they thought she was a murder victim. Evidence that she had been complicit in her own disappearance existed, but it would take a combination of suspicion and determined detective work to root it out. The story of her kidnapping seemed incredible, but far more believable than the truth. All this clicked through my mind as I tried to figure out what Graves wanted to hear, and she read my calculation for what it was.

"You're hiding something," she said.

I tried to hold firm. I've lied enough in stressful situations to be good at it, particularly if the lie is made in self-defense to a stranger. But I respected my parole officer, and though her opinion of me wasn't the same as my opinion of myself, I held myself accountable to her. She didn't have to stare at me for long before I felt the ground shift beneath the careful facade I'd constructed.

"Angela Doubleday wasn't always an unwilling captive," I said.

"She bonded with Davies?"

I nodded.

"The Patty Hearst syndrome," she said. "The kidnap victim grows so dependent on the kidnapper she begins to identify with his goals, to the point of becoming complicit in the crime. It's not uncommon for a kidnap victim to want to sleep with her kidnapper. It's a way of trying to survive. Do you think that's what happened?"

"I think they slept together, yes."

"It also makes his actions more understandable. If, like you said, he was obsessed with her."

"Why's that?"

"He already had what he wanted. He wanted her. Once she'd bonded with him, he'd achieved his goal. He would have been just as happy to die with her. People like this, they're sick individuals. They're losers who want to become celebrities the easy way. They know they're losers, and the only way they can redeem themselves, in their twisted little minds, is by leeching onto a celebrity."

I shrugged, as though such complex questions of criminal psychology were beyond me, relieved that a partial truth held firm in place of the whole one. I knew then that Angela Doubleday would get away with the crime of attempting to murder her self, and not just because of her fame and the brilliance of her acting. She would claim under interrogation—gentle and respectful interrogation—that she had been kidnapped and drugged, that she had awakened with her face heavily bandaged from a trip to a plastic surgeon somewhere south of the border, that Davies had this mad idea of passing her off as his wife in the Midwest. Even those who suspected that she concealed something would not imagine the truth. They would sense a dark secret, perhaps, and logically suppose that she had turned during her captivity into Davies' willing lover. Love breeds quickly in moments of dependency. My father beat my mother, brutally and regularly. She loved and feared him, believing her love would keep him from going too far, from finally killing her. Who could blame Angela Doubleday for bending to the needs of survival? They would never imagine that the secret was darker still.

"Did you tell Detective Alvarez about this?"

"He didn't ask," I said.

Graves leaned far back in her chair and stared at something other than me for a while. "I always thought Patty Hearst got shafted," she said. "Bonding with your kidnapper isn't a crime, so your silence isn't the same as withholding evidence. It would be conjecture on your part anyway. As you said, you're a photographer, not a psychiatrist. Just don't think you can hide things from me and get away with it."

I said, "No, ma'am."

"How's the dog?"

"He's going to live, the vet says."

"Good to hear. Do you plan to keep him?"

"Yes," I said.

"What about your apartment?"

I looked at her like, what about it?

"You'll be violating the terms of your lease if you keep the dog."

"The landlord is going to evict me anyway."

"I know," she said.

"You already talked to him?"

"Like I said, don't think you can hide things from me."

"Nothing in the parole agreement says I can't have a dog."

"Calm down, Nina."

Her voice was stern, and only on hearing it did I realize my own voice had lashed out with considerable anger. I said, "Yes, ma'am."

"I'm not against you keeping the dog."

"You're not?"

A smile jarred the stern set of her jaw. "I think the dog is good for you. Gives you something to care about other than yourself. A lot of my charges straighten themselves out after they have a baby, so why not a dog?"

Thirty Nine

The Rott lay on his side in a pen not much bigger than his body, one of a couple dozen stacked along the walls of the canine ward. The terrier in the neighboring pen yipped anxiously at my approach, quieting only when I crouched to let him sniff my hand. The Rott was twice the size of the next biggest animal. Bandages swathed his chest, slung around the forelegs, and wrapped his ribs. A conical collar of translucent plastic extended like the bell of a gramophone over his head. I knelt in front of his pen, reached through the door, and gently stroked his neck. His eyes fluttered once, as though my touch sparked a dream in the far-off land he roamed.

"The collar is to prevent him from worrying the wound," the vet said. She watched me from the door, the concern in her expression no less genuine for being professional. "Almost all animals lick their wounds in the wild, which is the best they can do to heal themselves. If he didn't wear the collar, he might try to bite through the bandaging."

"Thanks for taking such good care of him," I said.

"He's heavily sedated, so don't expect him to wake. I'll keep him tranquilized for the next several days to give him a chance to rest and heal."

I pulled a dirty T-shirt from my bag, the one I'd worn up to Lake Tahoe. "Is it okay to leave this with him? I figure when he wakes up, he might smell me on it, feel better knowing I'm still around."

She said she thought that was a good idea. I wadded up the shirt, left it at the edge of the pen. His breath came heavily but so evenly I could have set a watch by it. I laid my hand on his neck, said a wordless good-bye, and stood. The vet led me from the pens, and as she turned down the hall toward reception, she tossed a question over her shoulder. "I read about you in the morning paper, didn't I? You're the one who found Angela Doubleday."

I didn't say yes or no. She cut behind the reception counter, leaned over a computer terminal, and gave the mouse a few clicks. By the satisfied nod of her head, what she saw on-screen confirmed something for her. "You're Nina Zero, aren't you?"

I couldn't deny it.

"That Rottweiler, he's a special animal. Most animals would have died from shock with that kind of wound. I've handled animals all my life, and I still don't know how you managed to carry him in here all by yourself. I'm pleased to know he has a special owner." She paused, but not long enough to allow my escape, and the lines in her forehead deeply creased to underscore her sincerity. "If you see Angela Doubleday again, tell her there are a lot of people who considered her a role model, back when we were young women. Tell her we're with her in spirit, will you? There isn't much we can do for her except watch her films and admire the women she played, but maybe it will help if she knows people still care about her."

As I drove north to Malibu I wondered what a strange world it had become, where the outsize personality required for celebrity could be so easily confused for substance and where people who performed work that really mattered to the welfare of the world looked for meaning to those whose most significant efforts produced nothing more than a few hours of flickering light, and who couldn't guide their own lives without guile and tempest. What was it about movie stars that so touched the imagination of even the most dedicated and intelligent? Troy Davies wasn't the only one who sought to fill a personal void with the shimmering persona of a star. Hundreds of millions around the globe sought daily refuge in the cinema to watch beams of light play upon lives that seemed to matter much more than our own. We could be ugly and unloved, broke, boring, and unhappy, unlucky not just in love but in every choice we ever made, but when the houselights dimmed we became, like everyone else in the audience, the same characters living the same story. For a few brief hours we might experience lives more coherent than our own, shaped not by raw chance but by the rules of drama, lived not in obscurity but glorified in shifting light, personified by actors gifted with beauty, charm, and soulfulness we wished for ourselves. What right did I or any other tabloid journalist have to throw on the lights in that dark place and reveal that we filled ourselves with a blank, white screen?

Arlanda was standing at the checkout counter, signing charge slips, when I walked into the lobby of the Malibu Beach Inn. She looked good, long hair jet-black against an ivory suit that had been worn the day before by a Rodeo Drive mannequin. The bag at her side was new, too, a beige and gold model initialed LV.

"I have to get to the airport earlier than I thought to pick up Aunt Angela," she said and gave me the side of her cheek to kiss to avoid smudging her lipstick. "I'm sorry I won't have much time to talk."

I shrugged, as though any time was better than none, and when she had signed her last slip, we wandered to the patio at the back of the hotel, overlooking the ocean. I felt rough and dowdy next to her. She kept her distance at the rail, said, "My aunt told me you saved her life."

"Your aunt is a confused woman right now. The way I remember it, she saved mine."

"She never would have escaped from that monster without your help. She thinks I was the reason you were there, that I sent you to find her. She thinks I saved her life, too. Did you tell her that?"

"I said a lot of things in the heat of the moment."

The sun hung midmorning low behind us and cast the sky above the sea into hues of deep, silky blue. Pelicans skimmed the rolling surface just beyond the wave break, their heavy-beaked flights awkward until they soared skyward with sudden, improbable grace and dove at shadows below the surface.

"I know I behaved badly," Arlanda said. "I said some really ugly things to you the last time we met."

She didn't elaborate, and I didn't answer.

"And still, after what I said, you lied to protect me. You made me look better to my aunt than I really am."

"When somebody points a shotgun at you, you say whatever you think will keep the trigger from pulling. I didn't lie to save you. I said what I said to save me. I thought Davies would be less likely to shoot if he thought you sent me."

"When I think about how much she must have suffered . . ." She stained her teeth with lipstick, worrying her bottom lip. "Everybody was telling me she was dead except you, and nothing else you said proved true. Do you blame me for not believing you? How was I to know?"

We both stared at the sea.

"Troy Davies was a monster," she said. "I'm glad he's dead."

Arlanda had no truer idea of what happened in Lake Tahoe than my parole officer or the Rott's vet or the newspaper accounts trumpeting Doubleday's daring rescue. The reports were accurate in an unintentional way. I had saved Angela Doubleday—her identity if not her life—though my meddling had resulted in Troy Davies' death. I wasn't sure I wanted sole responsibility for the way things turned out.

"You believed me at first," I said. "And you sent me to Harry Winston, which led directly to Troy Davies. The only reason I did some of the things I did was because I wanted to help you. Maybe your intentions weren't always crystal clear, but you were just as important as anyone else in finding your aunt, and maybe the most important one of all."

Her enormous eyes hung on mine, wondering if I believed what I said or merely wished not to speak ill of the dead, my kind words a eulogy of sorts for our personal relationship, which seemed about to be buried. I don't know what conclusion she reached, but she offered a tentative smile. "My aunt has asked me to help her get through the next few weeks."

"Good idea. I suspect she needs someone she can trust right now."

"Longer than the next few weeks, actually. She wants me to move in with her, put the kids into private school. I'll be something like her secretary. She said she wants to act again, she'll need someone to help organize her personal life."

"They call it a personal assistant in the business."

She laughed, said, "You can see how much I know."

"Does the offer appeal to you?"

"Compared to selling real estate in a town where the only thing more worthless than the land is my sex life? In a word, yes."

I picked up her bag, walked her out to her rental car.

"We'll be staying at the Beverly Wilshire," she said.

The most luxurious hotel in Beverly Hills.

"You'll fit right in."

"Think so? I'm a little nervous, seeing my aunt again." She opened the door, keys in hand, ready to go. "How's Baby? I've been so worried about him."

"The vet thinks he might limp a bit, but other than that he'll make a full recovery," I said.

"I'm so happy to hear he's okay." She offered me her cheek to kiss again, shut the door, and wasted no time accelerating onto the coast road. Some people aren't good at good-byes. Maybe she was one of them. Maybe Arlanda and I had learned too much about each other too quickly. Not all friendships are for life, and the ones that fail to endure are no less genuine during their brief moments than those that thrive. I should have expected to see more of her, now that she was moving to Los Angeles, but I feared I'd never see her again, except in passing, at a premiere or awards function, where she'd be escorting her aunt down the red carpet and I'd be one of the jostling horde behind the gilded ropes, popping flashes and shouting blandishments.

_____ FORTY _____

B en looked every one of his years on the day the hospital released
him, shuffling unsteadily down the corridor with his neck braced
and left arm in a shoulder cast. I'd bought him a pair of chinos a size
too big, a button-up flannel shirt, and baseball cap, and he wore those
for his release, one arm of the shirt cut away to accommodate the
cast. The cap covered a twelve-stitch wound at the crown of his
head. He refused my arm, intent on walking out the front door unassisted. Past the entrance, the walkway ramped toward the sidewalk to
allow wheelchair access. He leaned back in anticipation of pitching
forward, as though the angle in front of him was as sharp as the descent of a roller-coaster ride. The brace on his neck kept him from
looking down, he said. When the ground sloped away, he couldn't see
his feet.

I extended my arm a second time. He took it.

"They offered me a wheelchair, the sons of bitches."

"Who?"

"The doctors."

"Why's that?"

"They didn't think I should walk out."

"You're showing them, aren't you?

"Damn right. Bastards would be happier seeing me go out in a box than on my two good legs."

"They probably thought walking wouldn't get you out the door fast enough. With your attitude, you're lucky they didn't send you out by cannon."

He grunted at me, annoyed that I wasn't taking his side. I popped the Caddy's trunk and tossed his kit bag into one of the boxes that contained the possessions I'd scavenged from the ruins of his trailer. The sight of his things surprised him, and he picked out a framed publicity still of a costumed Angela Doubleday from *Desire Under the Elms*, immersed in the role of Anna. The glass in the frame had broken, and shards obscured the inscription she'd penned at the bottom.

"I wasn't able to save much," I said.

"You saved more than I expected. I thank you." He started to tear up, and that embarrassed him. He turned away and shuffled to the passenger side. "I miss seeing that funny old toothless dog of yours. I trust he's mending a bit faster than I am?"

We ate at a café a few blocks from the beach, one of those places with waitresses old enough to be your mother and a nine-page book of a menu, three pages for breakfast alone. We talked about Arlanda's new life as Doubleday's personal assistant, neither of us mentioning that we would be unlikely to see much of her in that new role. Ben waited for the food to arrive before he said, "What I don't understand is how the coroner misread the X rays to begin with. A lot of grief could have been avoided if he'd said it wasn't her from the get go."

"He didn't misread the X rays, not really."

He salted his eggs vigorously, glanced up at me with a dubious look, and shook the pepper so forcefully I thought he might pop the head off. "He said the body was Angela's while the lady was being held prisoner up in Lake Tahoe. If that isn't misidentifying a body, I don't know what is."

"I didn't say he didn't misidentify the body."

"Didn't you? I thought you did."

"I said he didn't misread the X rays."

"Same difference." He picked up a piece of toast, glanced at the sealed minicontainers of butter and jam, tried to figure out how he was going to get his toast buttered with only one arm.

"I'm not trying to cover up for the guy." I peeled open the butter and jam containers, picked up his other piece of toast, dipped my knife into the butter. "But the forgery was clever, and he had no reason to suspect it, not at first."

His face reddened, and he slapped his knife to the table. "I'm not helpless. I can butter my own damn toast, thank you."

I slathered on the jam and took a bite. "I'm not buttering your toast, I'm stealing it," I said.

"Go on, eat my whole damn breakfast if you want. Guess I've been spoiling for a fight ever since the morning." He wiped his eyes dry with his napkin, said, "Forgive me if I'm such a dumb old man, but what the hell are you talking about? What forgery?"

"The X rays."

"Can you do that? Forge them?"

"Takes time and equipment, but the Belgards proved it could be done."

"Okay, you got me hooked now." He took a big bite of egg, part of the yolk dripping down his chin. "How'd they do it?"

"Davies provided them with plaster casts of Doubleday's teeth, one that showed all her dental work. They'd smuggled a cadaver out of UCLA Medical School and drilled and filled her mouth, taking X rays in between, so every one of Doubleday's fillings showed up on the final X ray."

While I was talking, Ben snatched one of the strips of bacon from my plate and popped it into his mouth. "Then they broke into her dentist's office and switched out the X rays from her file?"

"Didn't even have to break in. Walked in when nobody was working the reception desk, hid in an unused room until closing, then walked out. The chart matched the X rays, the X rays looked like they'd been taken over a period of twenty years, and most importantly, the last X ray taken matched the teeth found in the ruins of Doubleday's estate. The coroner had no way of telling it was a forgery, except for one thing, and there was no way he was going to look for it. No reason to suspect anything, right?"

"What was the thing? The one thing he missed?"

"Two mouths, twice the number of fillings. The first X ray, supposedly taken when Doubleday was under thirty, already had the dental work of a woman of fifty—the age of the cadaver—plus all of Doubleday's original cavities."

"You figured all this out?"

"Doubleday's dentist did."

That satisfied him through half of an egg and a couple sips of coffee. "So you figured it had to be Davies because he was the only one who could have known the Belgards?"

"Pretty much."

"You followed him to Lake Tahoe and he caught you sneaking around the cabin. That the gist of what happened?"

"My mobile phone rang—can you believe it?"

"That was a stupid thing to do. You want to know why?"

"I'll remember to turn off my phone next time, don't worry."

"The phone isn't the issue. Going to the cabin was a stupid thing to do, period."

"Stupid?" Nobody had said that to me before. "Why so?"

"One of the most important lessons you learn as a cop is you don't cowboy around. You do something the least bit dangerous, you have backup. You went in there without backup. That's why it was a stupid thing to do. Understand?"

I put my fork down, folded my hands in front of me, said, "Yes, Dad."

"You're lucky he didn't kill you."

"He's dead. I'm not. End of story."

We stared each other down for a while, then he reached out with his good hand, gave me a gentle punch on the jaw.

"You're such a hard-ass," he said. "Too bad you can't be a cop."

I smiled then, because maybe I was a thirty-year-old ex-con without much of a future, incorrigibly stubborn and prone to trouble, but I had a good dog and a few good friends, and that was so much more than I expected from life I considered myself blessed.

Acknowledgments

The novelist's ability to convincingly render the most arcane subjects is often due to the guidance given by persons truly knowledgeable about things novelists only pretend to know. The experts whose advice guided me in the preparation of this manuscript included dentists, veterinarians, parole agents, lawyers, filmmakers, and photographers. Special thanks are owed to Terrence J. Moriarty, DDS, who patiently informed me about the mysterious workings of dental offices one afternoon in Tucson; to Allen Plone, who seems able to answer every question I ask of him; and to Sandi Erba, who tracked down information for me when I was too far from the field of action to do so personally. Geri Orthmeyer, RVT, and Richard Bruga, DVM, kindly reviewed and answered my questions about veterinary medicine. To those who generously shared their knowledge with me but were too modest to want mention or were prohibited by their jobs from sharing information they shared anyway, my silent and anonymous thanks.

This manuscript was edited by Amanda Murray at Simon & Schuster, who proved an ideal reader.

I owe a debt of hospitality to the inhabitants of the city of Prague and the Catalan village of Sant Pol de Mar, Spain, where this book was written. Děkuji Vám, přátelé. Moltes gràcies, amics.

A graduate of the University of California at Santa Cruz and a UCLA film school dropout, Robert Eversz lives, at various times, in Los Angeles, Prague, and Sant Pol de Mar, on the coast of Catalonia. His Nina Zero novels have been translated into ten languages. More information about him can be found on the website www.ninazero.com.